God save the King . . .

Dahut cast herself against him. Her tresses swirled tangled, her cheeks were flushed and radiance was in her eyes. "Father, father," she caroled, "I am she! I could wait no longer, you had to know it from me, father, beloved!"

For a moment he could not feel the horror. It was like being sworded through the guts.

"Behold!" Dahut took wide-legged stance and tugged at her dress under the throat. The lacing was not fastened. The cloth parted. For the first time he saw her breasts bared, firm, rosy-tipped, a delicate tracery of blue in the whiteness. They were just as he remembered her mother's breasts. The same red crescent smoldered between them.

Whatever was on his countenance sobered Dahut a trifle. She closed the garment and said, carefully if shakily, "Oh, 'tis sorrow that Fennalis is gone, but not sorrow either, she suffered so and now she is free. The Gods have chosen. Blessed be Their names."

Again joy overwhelmed her. She snatched both his hands. "'Tis *you* will be my King, you, you! Together we'll make the new Age!"

The ice congealed within him, or the molten metal, it did not matter which. "Dahut," he heard himself say, word by dull word, "daughter of Dahilis, I love you. But as any father loves his child. This thing cannot be."

THE KING OF YS, BOOK III

DAHUT

POUL AND KAREN ANDERSON

DAHUT: THE KING OF YS, BOOK III

Copyright © 1988 by Poul and Karen Anderson

A Baen Books Original

Baen Publishing Enterprises
260 Fifth Avenue
New York, N.Y. 10001

First printing, January 1988

ISBN: 0-671-65371-7

Cover art by David Mattingly

Printed in the United States of America

Distributed by
SIMON & SCHUSTER
1230 Avenue of the Americas
New York, N.Y. 10020

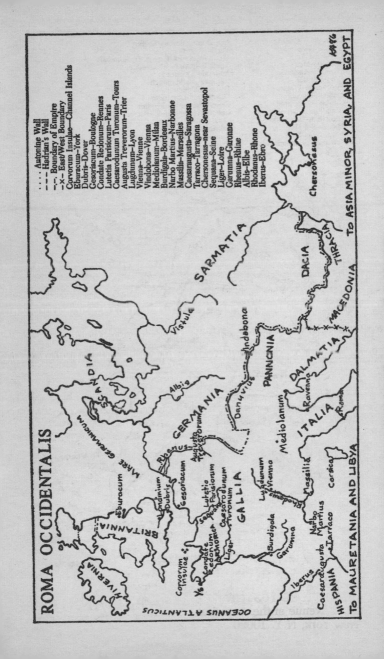

ROMA OCCIDENTALIS

..... Antonine Wall
--- Hadrian's Wall
-..- Boundary of Empire
-x- East/West Boundary
Corvorum Insulae—Channel Islands
Eburacum—York
Dubris—Dover
Gesoriacum—Boulogne
Condate Redomum—Rennes
Lutetia Parisiorum—Paris
Caesarodunum Turonum—Tours
Augusta Treverorum—Trier
Lugdunum—Lyon
Vienne—Vienne
Vindobona—Vienna
Mediolanum—Milan
Burdigala—Bordeaux
Narbo Martius—Narbonne
Massilia—Marseilles
Caesaraugusta—Saragossa
Tarraco—Tarragona
Chersonesus—near Sevastopol
Sequana—Seine
Liger—Loire
Garunna—Garonne
Rhenus—Rhine
Albis—Elbe
Rhodanus—Rhone
Iberus—Ebro

Luguvalium–Carlisle
Isurium–Aldborough
Eburacum–York
Mona (1)–Man
Mona (2)–Anglesey
Deva–Chester
Viroconium–Wroxeter
Lindum–Lincoln
Glevum–Gloucester
Isca Silurum–Caerleon
Segontium–Carnarvon
Abonae–Sea Mills
Aquae Sulis–Bath
Borcovicum–Housesteads

Isca Dumnoniorum–Exeter
Vectis–Wight
Venta Icenorum–Caister St. Edmunds
Venta Belgarum–Winchester
Anderida–Pevensey
Rutupiae–Richborough
Dubris–Dover
Durnovaria–Dorchester
Camulodunum–Colchester
Calleva Atrebatum–Silchester
Corstopitum–Corbridge
Sabrina–Severn
Tamesis–Thames

BRITANNIA

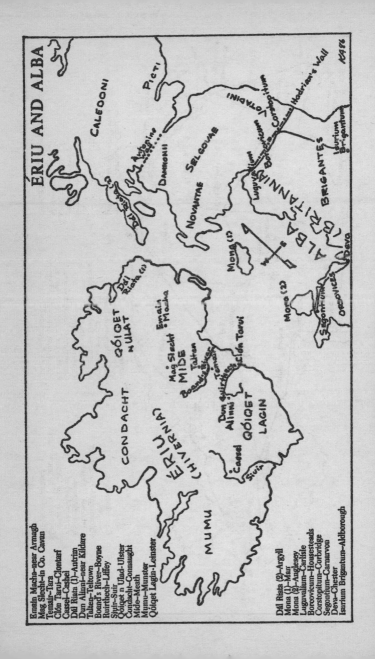

ÉRIU AND ALBA

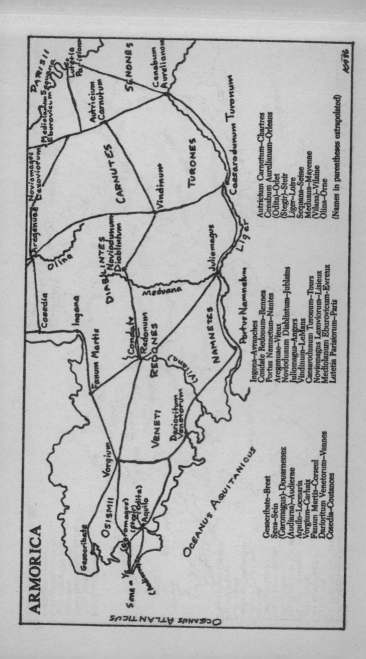

ARMORICA

Ingena–Avranches
Condate Redonum–Rennes
Portus Namnetum–Nantes
Aregenuae–Vieux
Noviodunum Diablintum–Jublains
Vindinum–LeMans
Juliomagus–Angers
Caesarodunum Turonum–Tours
Noviomagus Lexoviorum–Lisieux
Mediolanum Eburovicum–Evreux
Lutetia Parisiorum–Paris

Autricium Carnutium–Chartres
Cenabum Aurelianum–Orleans
(Odita)–Odet
(Stegir)–Steir
Liger–Loire
Sequana–Seine
Meduana–Mayenne
(Vilana)–Vilaine
Olina–Orne

(Names in parentheses extrapolated)

Gesocribate–Brest
Sena–Sein
(Garomagus)–Douarnenez
(Audierna)–Audierne
Aquilo–Locmaria
Vorgium–Carhaix
Fanum Martis–Corseul
Dariortium Venetorum–Vannes
Cosedia–Coutances

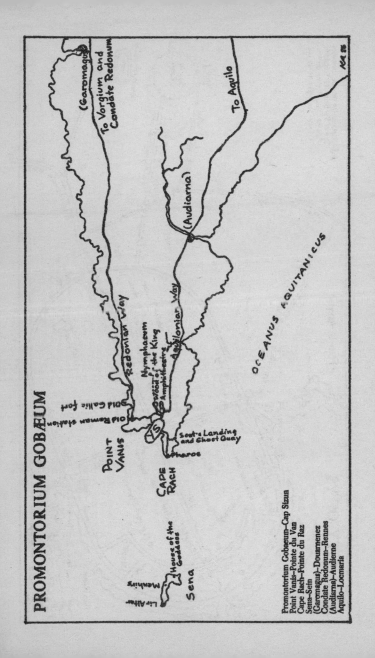

PROMONTORIUM GOBÆUM

Point Vanis

Old Roman station · Old Gallic fort

Redonian Way

Nymphaeum
Sword of the King
Amphitheatre

Sextr's Landing
and Ghost Quay

S

Pharos

CAPE RACH

Sena
Menhirs
House of the Goddess
Lir-Altar

(Garomagus)

To Vorgium and
Condate Redonum

(Audiarna)

To Aquilo

Redonian Way

OCEANUS AEQUITANICUS

MA 76

Promontorium Gobænum—Cap Sizun
Point Vanis—Pointe du Van
Cape Rach—Pointe du Raz
Sena—Sein
(Garomagus)—Douarmenez
Condate Redonum—Rennes
(Audiarna—Audierne
Aquilo—Locmaria

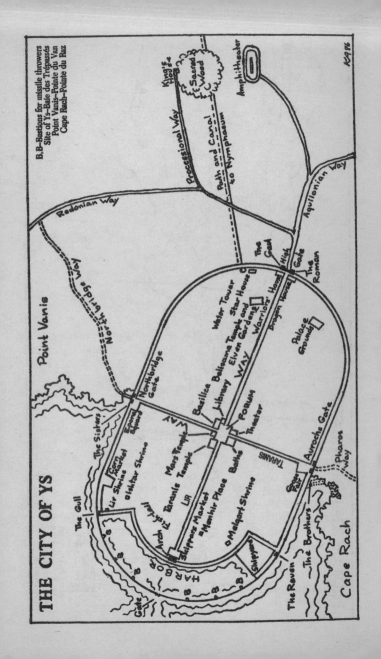

THE CITY OF YS

B.B.-Bastions for missile throwers
Site of Ys-Baie des Trépassés
Point Vanis-Pointe du Van
Cape Rach-Pointe du Raz

Point Vanis

The Gull

The Sisters

Northbridge Way

Redonian Way

Processional Way

Path and Canal to Nymphaeum

King's

Sacred Wood

Amphitheater

Aquilonian Way

The Gaol

High Gate

The Roman

Northbridge Gate

Water Tower

Balisama Temple

Star House

Warriors' House

Dragon House

Palace Grounds

ELVEN WAY

Epona Square

Corn Market

Ishtar Shrine

Ur Shrine

Mons Temple

Basilica

Library

Elven Gardens

Baths

FORUM

Theater

HAROR

Arch Jail

Gate

Skippers' Market

Menhir Place

Melqart Shrine

Brannis Temple

LIR

TARANIS

Aurochs Gate

Shipyard

Raven Tower

Pharos Way

The Raven

The Brothers

Cape Rach

KG 96

WHAT HAS GONE BEFORE

Gaius Valerius Gratillonius, born in Britannia, joined the Roman army at an early age and rose to be a centurion in the Second Legion Augusta. Distinguishing himself in a campaign to stop a barbarian onslaught from overrunning Hadrian's Wall, he was chosen by Magnus Clemens Maximus, military commandant in the island, for a special mission. With a small detachment of soldiers he was to go to Ys, at the western end of the Armorican peninsula.

That city-state, originally a Phoenician colony, had always been mysterious. Since the days of Julius Caesar it had been technically a foederate, a subordinate ally, of Rome. However, he never mentioned it in his writings, and such other notices of Ys as chroniclers made had a way of becoming lost in the course of time. Gradually it withdrew entirely from the affairs of the troubled Empire. Gratillonius was now supposed to fill the long vacant position of Roman prefect, an "advisor" whose advice had better be followed. With this power, he was to keep as much of Armorica peaceful as he could in a difficult period soon to come.

Unspokenly but clearly, the difficulties would result from an effort by Maximus to overthrow the co-Emperors of the West and make himself supreme. Gratillonius hoped such a strong man could put an end to the corruption, civil strife, and general weakness that were making Roman lands the prey of barbarians. His assignment was given him despite his being of the dying

1

Mithraic faith, in an age when Christianity had become the state religion.

Having marched across Gallia to Ys, he was stunned by its beauty. Then suddenly he found himself in single combat.

Battles of this kind, held in a sacred grove, determined who would be King of Ys. That man was required to answer all challenges and to spend the three days and nights around full moon in the Red Lodge at the Wood of the King. A new winner was immediately married to the Gallicenae, the nine Queens. These were recruited from among children and grandchildren of their Sisterhood. Such a girl must serve as a vestal virgin until age eighteen—unless first, at the death of a regnant Queen, the Sign, a tiny red crescent, appeared between her breasts. If it did, she was consecrated and married to the King. Otherwise she had to remain a maiden until her term was ended, at which time she became free and received a generous payment. A Queen conceived only when she chose; to avoid it, she need but eat a few flowers of the Herb ladygift, blue borage. She bore only daughters. Most Gallicenae in the past had possessed strong magical powers, but in later generations these had been fading away.

All this had been ordained by the three Gods of Ys, Taranis of the heavens, triune female Belisama, and inhuman Lir of the sea. Other deities could be honored if so desired, and under Roman pressure Ys maintained a Christian church serving a minuscule congregation. Aside from the ritual combat, the city was highly civilized. For the past five years the King had been brutal Colconor. When the Nine could endure him no longer, they cast a curse on him and a spell to bring yet another challenger. This they did on the island Sena, out among the rocks and reefs beyond the headlands, reserved to them alone. Except on special occasions and in emergencies, one of them must always be there, holding Vigil.

They conspired to get Colconor drunk and pique

him, so that when Gratillonius arrived he gave the Roman a deadly insult. Nevertheless Gratillonius should not have lost his temper and gotten into a fight. Afterward the centurion wondered what had possessed him. By that time, to his astonishment, he was victorious, proclaimed King and wedded to the Nine.

They were aged Quinipilis; aging Fennalis; stateswoman Lanarvilis; stern Vindilis; gentle Innilis; lazy Maldunilis; scholarly Bodilis; Forsquilis, young and passionate and owner of more witchy powers than the rest; and youthful Dahilis. The last of these came first to his bed, and he and she fell deeply in love. He must consummate his marriages to the others, and eventually did, except for Quinipilis and Fennalis. They being past childbearing age, he was excused. This was fortunate, since his Mithraic principles would not have allowed him to sleep with Fennalis, she being the mother of Lanarvilis. He found that a King was always potent with any of the Nine, and impotent with all other women.

Gratillonius's faith caused more conflicts, but did not prohibit his carrying out his duties as high priest and avatar of Taranis. He was also head of state, presiding at meetings of the Council of Suffetes, the magnates. And his was the ceremonial task of locking and unlocking the sea gate.

In the time of Julius Caesar, Brennilis, foremost among the Gallicenae, had had prophetic visions. She foresaw that rising sea level would drown the city unless it was protected, and got Roman engineers to build a rampart around it. The Gods demanded that this be of dry-laid stone, so that Ys would always lie at Their mercy. Floats operated to open the seaward gate as tide ebbed; it closed of itself when waters rose. In times of storm, when waves might swing the doors wide and come raging in, a heavy bar kept the portal shut. Counterweighted, it could be raised or lowered by a single man. The King did this, locking it in place or releasing it, unless he was elsewhere. The Key that he must carry while in Ysan territory was his highest emblem of rank.

Ys believed that Brennilis had inaugurated a new

Age, and that the city's often helpful obscurity, despite its brilliance, was due to the Gods—the Veil of Brennilis. Its manufactories, trade, and ships had made it the queen of the Northern seas; but the troubles of Rome inevitably affected it too.

Unlike many past Kings, Gratillonius took vigorous leadership. Besides influencing the Roman authorities in Armorica to stay neutral in the civil war, thus safeguarding Maximus's back, he sought to cope with the Saxon and Scotic pirates whose seaborne raids had devastated the coasts. There was much objection to his proposals. Among frequent opponents were Hannon Baltisi, Lir Captain, and, to a lesser degree, Soren Cartagi, Speaker for Taranis as well as being a wealthy merchant. Soren and Lanarvilis had when young intended to marry; but before her vestalhood ended, she was Chosen. While adultery on the part of a Queen was virtually unthinkable, they remained secretly in love and publicly often worked together for the good of Ys as they conceived it.

In Hivernia, which they called Ériu, the Scoti were divided into tuaths, not quite the same thing as tribes or clans, each with its king. Such a king was usually subordinate, together with others like himself, to a stronger lord. The island as a whole held five Fifths, not truly kingdoms though as a rule one man dominated each. They were Mumu in the south, Condacht in the west, Qóiqet Lagini in the east, Qóiqet nUlat in the north—and Mide, which an upstart dynasty had carved out of Condacht and Qóiqet Lagini. The high Kings in Mide centered their reigns, if not their residences, on the holy hill Temir. Niall maqq Echach now held that position, a mighty warlord and the mastermind behind the assault on Britannia that Maximus had turned back. Smarting from this, he plotted fresh ventures against the Romans, beginning with an attack on Gallia while they lay at war with each other. He would steer wide of Ys, whose Queens had magical powers. His son Breccan, young but his eldest and most beloved, persuaded the King of Mide to take him along.

Fearing that sort of event, Gratillonius made preparations. At his urging the Nine conjured up a storm which blew the Scotic fleet onto the rocks outside Ys. Survivors who made it ashore were mostly killed by Roman soldiers, Ysan marines, and the mobilized seamen of the city. Niall escaped but Breccan perished. Grief-stricken and furious, Niall vowed revenge on this folk who had done him such harm when he intended them none.

Among the Romans lost was Eppillus, Gratillonius's deputy and fellow Mithraist. Fulfilling a promise, the King buried him on Point Vanis, the headland he had defended, though the Gods of Ys had long commanded burials be at sea unless well inland and the necropolis on Cape Rach now crumbled unused. Further religious conflict arose when Gratillonius unwittingly initiated another legionary, Cynan, into the woman-banning Mithraic faith, in a stream sacred to Bellsama.

·This happened at the Nymphaeum, which the vestals tended up in the hills. Gratillonius and Dahilis had gone there to get a blessing on her unborn child. She came upon the ritual and was appalled, but continued to love him. Later she discovered that Vindilis and Innilis were lovers. Ys banned such doings. Dahilis did not think it was terribly wrong, and persuaded the other two to reveal their secret to the whole Sisterhood, who accepted it and kept it to themselves. Indeed, as an act of reconciliation, Innilis let herself become pregnant too.

Forsquilis's arts seemed to show that the Gods would grow peaceful toward unrepentant Gratillonius if, among other things, a Queen with child took Vigil on Sena at midwinter, when normally all Nine would be ashore. Innilis was the logical choice, but suffered a miscarriage. This left only Dahut, very near her term.

Gratillonius returned from a political journey around Armorica, learned how matters stood, and tried to stop the dangerous plan. The Queens, including Dahilis, refused. He did insist on accompanying her. Men were not allowed on the island (except when repair work was necessary, and then certain conditions were set) but he could wait at the dock. She went off on her religious duties. When she had not returned by nightfall and a storm had arisen, he violated the commandment and went in search. He found her crippled by an accident, unconscious, dying, and yet in labor. He cut the child out of her.

Numbed by sorrow, he broke with custom and named the girl Dahut as a memorial. He must then marry the newly Chosen Queen, Guilvilis, a homely and dull-witted young woman. The Gallicenae, Soren Cartagi, and others felt that Dahilis's sacrifice had appeased the Gods, and were ready again to work with the King.

On a later night, the knock of an invisible hand summoned the fishermen of Scot's Landing, a hamlet below the sea cliffs, as it had done for centuries. They were the Ferriers of the Dead, who carried the souls of the newly departed out to Sena for the judgment of the Gods. Chief among them was Maeloch, owner and captain of the smack *Osprey*. He had been deeply devoted to Dahilis.

For two years things went generally well in Ys. Little Dahut fell overboard once, but a seal saved her. It was believed that the dead were sometimes reborn in this form, to watch over those they had loved; therefore seals were sacred and inviolate. Gratillonius's relationships with his wives became good, and one by one those who were able started bearing him children. He and Bodilis were particularly close. Dahut he adored; in his eyes, the child could do no wrong.

Maximus had forced a settlement which made him Augustus in Gallia, Hispania, and Britannia. He summoned his prefect to report to him in his seat of Augusta Treverorum. Accompanied by his remaining legionaries, whose deputy now was Adminius, Gratillonius set forth. On the way they rescued some travelers from a band of Bacaudae. These men were more than simple brigands; mostly they had fled Roman oppressiveness and developed a loose organization. As the leader of this group, Rufinus negotiated with Gratillonius. They felt a sudden liking for each other.

Later Gratillonius encountered Martinus, bishop of Caesarodunum Turonum and founder of a monastery near that city. Again there was quick mutual respect and friendliness. Martinus had been visiting Maximus to get mercy for the heretic Priscillianus and his followers, feeling it sin that Christians should persecute Christians even when someone was in error.

In Treverorum Gratillonius was arrested and interrogated under torture about his dealings with sorcery in Ys. Meanwhile Maximus broke his promise to Martinus and had the leading Priscillianists executed. However, the new Emperor, whose ambition was not sated, still needed Gratillonius in Ys to guard that flank of his. He released the prefect, charging him to extirpate witchcraft, and even allowed him to travel south, to recuperate and seek enlightenment.

Actually, what Gratillonius looked for was a surviving Mithraic congregation where he could be elevated to the rank of Father in the Mysteries. That would allow him to found a temple of his own in Ys. He had no illusions about the future of his faith, but wanted to offer its consolations to such believers as might come his way. Having achieved his purpose, he went on at Bodilis's request to call on the poet and rhetor Ausonius in Burdigala. There he met an exemplar of Roman civilization at its best—and also at its feeblest, unconcerned about the gathering threats to itself.

Back in Ys, he found a challenger waiting. This was a poor wretch who had intended simply to live well for a while and sneak off before the King returned. Gratillonius killed him easily, but was sickened. By now, too, he saw Maximus not as a deliverer but as a power-hungry, tyrannical usurper. Just the same, he would continue to do his best for both Rome and Ys.

Time passed. Children were born to him and grew. The Nine took turns caring for Dahut. Bright and beautiful, closely resembling her mother, she was often aloof and moody, though well able to charm when she chose. Men as rough as the legionaries or the skipper Maeloch became her slaves. There was always some-

thing strange about her—Forsquilis read signs of a
destiny, which might bring about a new Age—and
sometimes she was seen in company with a particular
female seal.

On the whole, Gratillonius's reign was highly successful. His naval, military, and political measures
brought safety from the barbarians, which in turn revived industry and trade. He gave justice to rich and
poor alike. Even his founding of a Mithraeum did not
shake his popularity. He had it constructed in the crypt
of the Raven Tower, one of those guarding the sea
wall.

Another religious matter he must take care of was
finding a Christian minister of Ys, to replace the old
one who had died. That was the minimum necessary to
appease Maximus. Traveling through the country of the
Osismii, the tribe who were the nearest neighbors of
Ys, he had become friends with Apuleius Vero. This
man, of senatorial rank, was the tribune of the small
Gallo-Roman city Aquilo, near the head of navigation
on the River Odita. On a later visit, Gratillonius rode
out alone along the tributary Stegir stream and in the
forest made a new friend, the hermit Corentinus, former sailor, later a disciple of Martinus and helper in
evangelizing the countryside. Eventually Gratillonius went
to Turonum and conferred not only with the Duke of
the Armorican Tract about military affairs but with
Martinus. The upshot was that Corentinus became the
new chorepiscopus in Ys: "country bishop," with more
powers than a priest though fewer than a full bishop.

Again Gratillonius mortally offended the Gods of Ys.
Another challenger appeared, who turned out to be
Rufinus, unaware that the centurion he had dealt with
was the King. Gratillonius bested and disarmed him,
but could no longer make himself butcher a helpless
man. Instead he offered a hecatomb, which Soren was
certain would not satisfy the Three. Rufinus became
Gratillonius's handfast man, coming and going widely
on his behalf, gradually recruiting Bacaudae to live in
the largely unpeopled interior of Armorica, give up

their banditry, and serve as scouts and irregulars for the King. This was violation of Roman law, but Gratillonius saw no alternative.

After all, the Empire was desperately weak. Frankish laeti—barbarian colonists—were not only in the area of Condate Redonum, supposedly supplying garrison troops, but openly carried on their pagan human sacrifices. Rufinus and some of his men rescued two slaves intended for this from the leader Merowech and warned that such practices would be suppressed altogether as soon as possible.

Maximus invaded Italy but was defeated and killed by Theodosius, Augustus of the East. With the help of Martinus, Apuleius, and other influential Romans, Gratillonius arranged for Maximus's veterans to be re-settled in Armorica, where they would provide a leaven in the civilian reservists and ill-trained native regulars. The old legionary units were depleted, and modern heavy cavalry had not yet been much seen in the West.

It seemed the Gods found their punishment for Gratillonius. Quinipilis died, and the Sign came upon Bodilis's daughter Semuramat. Gratillonius could not refuse to marry her without destroying his Kingship and everything he had worked for, but his faith required that henceforward Bodilis be simply his friend. It hurt them both deeply. In the course of years they learned how to live with it. As she grew older the new Queen also came to love him. She had taken the name Tambilis.

When he was not on a mission for Gratillonius, Rufinus lived well in Ys. Vindilis ferreted out what he kept hidden, that he was a homosexual, silently in love with his master. She counselled him to abstain from forbidden behavior in the city and to be discreet elsewhere. Unspoken was the fact that she now had blackmail power over him.

Hoping to win back the favor of the Gods, the Queens were raising Dahut to fervency in the ancient religion. She publicly and bitterly denounced Corentinus, and drifted away from her father, to his sorrow. Neverthe-

less, at her menarche he gave her a lavish Rite of
Welcome. Bodilis inducted her into certain secrets,
including the use of the Herb, which she would need to
know should she become a Queen herself. She was
now fully a vestal, though with ample leisure, a large
stipend, and freedom to live much as she chose provided she remain pure.

Over the years, Gratillonius paid numerous visits to
Apuleius in Aquilo. The tribune and his wife Rovinda
had two living children, the girl Verania and the boy
Salomon, whose honorary uncle Gratillonius became.
On one occasion the family presented him with a
splendid stallion colt, Favonius.

Time had also been at work in Ériu. Niall's foster-
kinsman Conual Corcc returned from years in Britannia.
The Roman general Stilicho was making life difficult
for those Scoti who had seized land there. Conual had
learned much, gained much, and brought back with
him engineers and artisans as well as warriors. After
calling on Niall in Mide, he went on to his homeland
Mumu, where he built a fortress on the Rock of Cassel
and started rapidly expanding his power. He did not
have Niall's implacable hatred of Ys, nor did he lead
plundering attacks on the Romans like Niall. Eventually
he began receiving envoys from King Gratillonius (or
Grallon, as the Ysans often rendered the name) and
discussing trade agreements. Rufinus led the first of
these missions. His guide was Tommaltach, a well-
born young man who had been in Ys—and, coming
back later, was smitten with blooming Dahut.

Niall had been fighting his wars in the north of Ériu.
He defeated his enemies the Lagini and demanded a
huge tribute. At the talks, Eochaid, a son of the Laginach
King Endae, flared up and insulted Niall's master poet
Laidchenn. Laidchenn's son and student Tigernach immediately composed a satire which, unexpectedly, raised
scarring blisters on the face of Eochaid and so forever
debarred him from becoming a king.

Niall went on to overrun territories tributary to the
Ulati, against whom his grand design lay. There his

son Domnuald was killed in a quarrel by Fland Dub, one of the defeated chieftains. Fland fled to the Ulati. Niall vowed revenge. He had not forgotten his curse on Ys, either.

First, though, he must subdue the Ulati. While preparations for this were in train, he made a massive attack on Britannia, whence Stilicho had departed. In his absence, equally vengeful Eochaid entered Mide at the head of an army and plundered it widely. Niall gathered his forces next year and broke the Lagini, ravaged their lands, and collected the ruinous Bóruma tribute. He also took back Eochaid and other high-born young men as hostages, and kept them harshly confined. This was contrary to his usual practice. He treated very well those from the north whom he had as sureties. They had earned him the nickname Niall of the Nine Hostages.

Gratillonius in Ys was maintaining an ever more uneasy balance, trying to keep his subjects content despite religious and other conflicts, to build up the strength of Armorica despite laws forbidding or bureaucracy discouraging what he saw as necessary actions, and at the same time to keep from provoking the Romans into invading the city. He made a number of domestic enemies, notably Nagon Demari, Labor Councillor, and had trouble conciliating other people, such as the mariners on whose smuggling he cracked down. Still, on the whole he was doing well, and finally decided to honor the visit of his friend Apuleius by holding a yacht race as part of the festivities.

Growing toward maturity, Dahut was becoming the belle of Ys. Yet her life continued its secret side. Some parts of it, even the Gallicenae saw little or nothing of, such as her meetings with the seal. Forsquilis took her out one night for a trial and ascertained that in her the ancient powers of the Nine were coming fully into being. Together they raised a wind, which none had seemed able to do since the destruction of the Scotic fleet before she was born. Dahut accepted the knowledge almost arrogantly.

However, she was all charm toward Aulus Metellus Carsa. This young son of a Burdigalan sea captain was staying a while in Ys to learn more about the city and make contacts, with an eye to getting a goodly share of the trade that was reviving under Gratillonius. He was enraptured when Dahut asked him to handle her boat in the yacht race. They started out cheerfully enough— but presently she grew somber, and at last ordered him to land short of the goal, at the sacked and deserted town Garomagus. Following her unbeknownst, he spied the seal bidding her farewell in a language she somehow understood. Not long afterward, out on the water, Maeloch and his crew saw the seal killed by an orca.

Dahut became altogether quiet and withdrawn. When the party returned to Ys, she hurried off by herself. Deeply concerned, Gratillonius found her after a search. She sobbed out on his breast a part of her bewilderment and despair. It seemed to her that the Gods had removed the seal from the world because otherwise she might not have done Their will in the future, whatever it was. More than that she could not or would not relate. Gratillonius assured her of his love and swore he would never deny her. Somewhat consoled, she went back home with her father.

I

— 1 —

Day came to birth above eastern hills and streamed down the valley. It flamed off the towers of Ys, making them stand like candles against what deepness lingered in western blue. Air lay cool, still, little hazed. The world beneath it was full of dew and long shadows.

This was the feast of Lug. Here they also kept the old holy times, but the great ones of the city called then on its own Gods. A male procession, red-robed, the leader bearing a hammer, mounted the wall at High Gate. They lifted their hands and sang.

"Your sun ascends in splendor
The brilliance of Your sky
To light the harvest landscape
Your rains did fructify.
These riches and this respite
From winter, war, and night,
Taranis of the Thunders,
Were won us through Your might!

"You guard the walls of heaven,
Earth's Lover, Father, King.
You are the sacrificer,
You are the offering.
The years wheel ever onward
Beyond our human ken.
Bestow Your strength upon us
That we may die like men."

13

Behind them, where the Temple of Belisama shone on
its height, female voices soared from Elven Gardens.

"Lady of love and life,
Lady of death and strife,
Maiden and wedded wife,
    And old in sorrow,
Turn unto us Your face,
Grant us a dwelling place
In Your abiding grace,
    Now and tomorrow!

"You are the Unity:
Girl running wild and free,
Hag brooding mystery,
    And the All-Mother.
Evermore born again,
You, Belisama, reign,
Over our joy and pain
    As does no other.

"You by Whom all things live,
Though they be fugitive,
Thank You for that You give
    Years to us mortals.
Goddess of womankind,
Guide us until we find
Shelter and peace behind
    Darkness's portals."

Ebb had barely begun and the sea gate of Ys remained
shut. Nevertheless a ship was outward bound. Eager to be
off while good weather held, her captain had had her
towed forth by moonlight and had lain at anchor waiting
for dawn. Mainsail and artemon unfurled, her forefoot
hissed through the waves. He went into the bows, killed a
black cock, sprinkled blood on the stempost, cast the
victim overboard, held out his arms, and chanted.

"Tide and wind stand fair for our course,
    but we remember that the set of them is often to a
        lee shore;

"We remember that gales whelm proud fleets
  and reefs wait always to rip them asunder;
"We remember how men have gone down to the eels
  or have strewn their bones white on the skerries;
We remember weariness, hunger, thirst,
  the rotting of live flesh and teeth loosened from jaws;
"We remember the shark and the ice,
  and the albatross lonely above desolation;
"We remember the blinding fog
  and the terrible sea-blink in dead calm:
"For these too are of Lir. His will is done."

The King of Ys, Incarnation and high priest of Taranis, was not in the city, for this was not so momentous a day as to release him from the Watch he must keep when the moon was full. With a handful of fellow worshippers he stood in the courtyard of the Sacred Precinct, by the Challenge Oak, looking toward the sun and calling, "Hail, Mithras Unconquered, Saviour, Warrior, Lord, born unto us anew and forever—" The silence in the Wood muffled it.

At the Forum, the heart of Ys, in the church that had once been a fane of Mars, Christians almost as few held a service. Nobody outside heard their song, tiny and triumphant.

— 2 —

Rain slashed from the west. Wind hooted. Autumn was closing in, with storms and long nights. If men did not soon take ship for Ériu, they would risk being weatherbound in Britannia until—Manandan maqq Léri knew when.

Two men sat in a tavern in Maia. That was a Roman settlement just south and west of the Wall, on the firth. Roughly clad, the pair drew scant heed from others at drink, albeit one was uncommonly large and handsome, his fair hair and beard not much silvered. Plain to see, they were Scotic. However, they kept to themselves and this was not an inn where people asked questions. Besides, the tiny garrison was in quarters; and barbarians went freely about, Scoti, Picti, occasional Saxons. Some were mercenaries recruited by Rome, or scouts or spies or informers. Some were traders, who doubtless did more smuggling than open exchange. It mattered not, provided they got into nothing worse than brawls. The Imperial expeditionary force had enough to do without patrolling every impoverished huddling place.

A tallow candle guttered and stank on the table betweeen the two Scoti. Its light and the light of its kind elsewhere were forlorn, sundered by glooms like stars on a cloudy night. Niall of the Nine Hostages gripped a cup of ale such as he would not have ordered pigs swilled with at home, were a king allowed to own them. Leaning forward, elbows on the greasy, splintery wood, he asked low, "You are quite sure of this, are you, now?"

Uail maqq Carbri nodded. "I am that, my lord," he answered in the same undertone. Most likely none else would have understood their language, but no sense in taking needless chances. "I'll be telling the whole tale later, my wanderings and all, first in this guise, next in that, ever the amusing newcomer who commanded a rustic sort of Latin—"

"You will, when we've time and safety," Niall interrupted. "Tonight be short about it. Here is a damnable spot to be meeting."

It had been the best they could do. Niall, waging war, landing where he saw it would be possible and striking inland as far and savagely as would leave him a line of retreat, Niall could no more foresee where he would camp than could peacefully, inquisitively ranging Uail. Maia was a fixed point, not closely under the Roman eye; men of Condacht and Mide had bespoken this tavern in the past; they could agree to be there at the half moon after equinox. Nonetheless Uail had had to abide two evenings until Niall, delayed by weather, arrived.

Uail shrugged. "As my lord wills. No men I sounded out, officers or common soldiers, none of them had any word from on high. We wouldn't await that, would we, now? But somehow they were all sure. The word has seeped through. Rome will fight one more season, hoping to have Britannia cleared of the likes of us by then. But no longer. Nor is there any thought of striking at Ériu. They will be needing the troops too badly across the Channel."

Niall nodded. "Thank you, my dear," he said. "I looked for the same. It sings together with what I learned myself, raiding them this year. They were never determined in pursuit when we withdrew. They've not moved against Dál Riata, nest of hawks though it is. We took in deserters, who told us they had no wish to fare off to an unknown battle away in Europe. Oh, it's clear, it's clear, we have nothing to fret about in our homeland from Rome."

"That is good to know, well worth the trouble of finding out."

Niall's fist thudded down on the board. His voice roughened. "I should have been aware already. I should never have havered like this, letting years slip by—" Abruptly he rose. His mane brushed the ceiling. "Come, Uail. Toss off that horse piss if you must and let's begone."

The mariner gaped. "What? It's a wild night out."

"And I'm wild to be off. The fleet lies on the north side of the firth, in a cove where no Roman comes any longer, two days' walk for us from here. If we start at once, we can pass Luguvallium in the dark."

"That would be wise," Uail agreed. Yonder city was the western strongpoint of the Wall. Both men took their cloaks and trod forth.

The rain was not too cold nor the night too black for such as they. Kilts wrapped them from shoulder to knee; at their belts hung dirks, and pouches with a bit of dried meat and cheese; once they were beyond the Roman outposts, no one would venture to question them.

They had walked a while when Niall said in a burst: "I have need of haste, Uail maqq Carbri. I hear time baying behind me, a pack of hounds that has winded the wolf. Too long have I waited. There is Emain Macha to bring down, and afterward Ys."

— 3 —

Among Celts, the first evening of Hunter's Moon awakened madness. In Ys, folk no longer believed that the

doors between worlds stood open then—if only because
in Ys, they were never quite shut—but farmers and
gardeners made sure their last harvests had been gathered, while herdsmen brought their beasts under roofs
and seamen lashed a besom to every craft not in a boat-
house. Within the city, it was an occasion for unbridled
revel.

Weather permitting, the Fire Fountain played. Masked,
grotesquely costumed—stag, horse, goat, goblin, leather
phallus wagging gigantic; nymph, witch, mermaid, hair
flying loose, breasts bared and painted—the young ca-
vorted drunken through the streets. Workers of every
kind were off duty, and none need do reverence to lord or
lady. The older and higher-born watched the spectacle for
a time, perhaps, before withdrawing to entertainments
they had prepared for themselves behind their own walls.
Those might or might not be decorous. Drink flowed,
music taunted, and no encounter between man and woman,
whomever they might be wedded to, was reckoned entirely real.

Certain classes observed restraint. The King kept Watch
in the Wood as usual. Such of the Gallicenae ashore as
were not with him held a banquet, and gave a prayer for
the ninth out on Sena. Down in Scot's Landing, the Ferriers
of the Dead bolted their cottage doors and their families
practiced rites that were austere; these were too close to
the unknown for aught else.

Yet all, all was pagan.

Corentinus left the torchlight and tumult behind him.
He had offered a Mass and sent his congregation to bed.
Now he was alone.

Out Northbridge Gate he went, and up Redonian Way
across Point Vanis. His long legs crunched the distance.
Save for him, road and headland reached empty. This
night was clear, quiet, and cold. Stars glimmered manifold before him, Hercules, the Dragon, Cassiopeia, at the
end of the Lesser Bear the Lodestar. The Milky Way was
dimmed by the high-riding moon and its frost halo. His
breath gusted white. Grass, brush, stones lay hoar.

Where the road bent east above the former maritime
station, Corentinus left it and made his way west. Soon he
came to an outlook over the sea, vast and dark and slowly

breathing. A grave was at his feet. He knew the head-stone. The one who rested here was no Christian, but had been an honest soldier. This did not seem the worst possible place to stop.

Corentinus lifted his arms and his gray head skyward. "O God," he called in anguish, "Maker and Master of the Universe; Christ Jesus, only begotten Son, God and man together, Who died for us and rose again that we might live; Holy Spirit—have mercy on poor Ys. Leave it not in its midnight. Leave it not with its demons that it worships. They mean well, God. They are not evil. They are only blind, and in the power of Satan. My dearest wish is to help them. Help me, God!"

After a silence, he bent his neck and bit his lip. "But if they are not worthy of a miracle," he groaned, "if there can be no redemption, and the abomination must be cleansed as it was in Babylon—let it be quickly, God, let it bo final, and the well-meaning people and the little children not be enslaved or burnt alive, but go down at once to whatever awaits them.

"Lord, have mercy. Christ, have mercy. Lord, have mercy."

II

— 1 —

The declaration of King Gratillonius hit the vernal Council of Suffetes like a stone from a siege engine. As prefect of Rome, he told them, he had lately received official word of that which he had been awaiting. The augmented legions in Britannia would take the field again this year, but only for a month or two. Thereafter they would return to the Continent and march south. Anticipating renewed barbarian incursions, mounting in scope and ferocity as time went on, Gratillonius wanted the shipyard of Ys to produce more naval vessels. Yet those would not become Ysan. That would be too provocative. Instead, he would offer them to the Duke of the Armorican Tract, to go under the command of the latter. Their crews would train Roman recruits to man them.

Outrage erupted. Hannon Baltisi, Lir Captain, roared that never would men of Ys serve under such masters, Christian dogs who would forbid their worship, who did not even ask the God's pardon before emptying a slop jar into His sea. Cothortin Rosmertai, Lord of Works, protested that such a program would disrupt plans, dishonor commitments to build merchantmen; in this time of prosperity, the facilities were bespoken far in advance. Bomatin Kusuri, Mariner Councillor, questioned where enough sailors could be found, when trading, whaling, slaving, even fishing paid better than armed service in the Empire did.

Adruval Tyri, Sea Lord, maintained that the King was right about the menace of Scoti and Saxons. They would

20

not be content to rape Britannia but would seek back to the coasts of Gallia. Yet Adruval hated the thought of turning Ysan ships over to Rome. What did Rome do for Armorica other than suck it dry? Would it not be better to build strength at home—quietly, of course—until Ys could tell Rome to do its worst?

Soren Cartagi, Speaker for Taranis, was also a voice for the Great Houses when he said, first, that to help the Christians thus was to speed the day when they came to impose their God by force; second, the cost would be more than the city could bear or the people would suffer; third, Gratillonius must remember that he was the King of a sovereign nation, not the proconsul of a servile province.

Queen Lanarvilis, who at this session was the leader of the Gallicenae, pointed out needs at home which the treasure and labor could serve. And was there indeed any threat in the future with which existing forces could not cope, as they had coped in the past? Had not the Romans now quelled their enemies and secured Britannia? Also in the South, she understood, peace prevailed; Stilicho and Alaric the Visigoth had ended their strife and come to terms. Rather than looking ahead with fear, she saw a sun of hopefulness rising.

Opposition to Gratillonius's desire coalesced around those two persons. When the meeting adjourned after stormy hours, he drew them aside and asked that they accompany him to the palace for a confidential talk.

In the atrium there, he grinned wearily and said, "First I wish a quick bath and a change into garb more comfortable than this. Would you care for the same?"

Soren and Lanarvilis exchanged a look. "Nay," the man growled. "We'll seek straight to the secretorium and . . . marshal our thoughts."

"Debate grew too heated," the woman added in haste. "You've brought us hither that we may reason with one another, not so? Let us therefore make sure of our intents."

Gratillonius regarded them for a silent moment. Tall she stood in her blue gown and white headdress, but her haunches seemed heavier of late, while her shoulders were hunched above a shrunken bosom. That brought her neck forward like a turtle's; the green eyes blinked and peered out of sallowness which sagged. He knew how faded her blond hair was. Withal, she had lost little vigor and none of her grasp of events.

Soren had put on much weight in the last few years; his belly strained the red robe and distorted its gold embroidery. The chest on which the Wheel amulet hung remained massive. His hair and beard were full of gray; having taken off his miter, he displayed a bald spot. Yet he was no less formidable than erstwhile.

Sadness tugged at Gratillonius. "As you will," he said. "I'll have refreshments sent up, and order us a supper. We do have need to stay friends."

—When he opened the door of the upstairs room, he saw them in facing chairs, knee against knee, hands linked. Taken by surprise, they started and drew apart. He pretended he had not noticed. "Well," he said, "I'm ready for a stoup of that wine. Council-wrangling is thirsty work." He strode to the serving table, mixed himself a strong beakerful, and took a draught before turning about to confront them.

Soren's broad countenance was helmeted with defiance. Lanarvilis sat still, hands now crossed in her lap, but Gratillonius had learned over the years to read distress when it lay beneath her face.

He stayed on his feet, merely because in spite of the hot bath he felt too taut for anything else. The light of candles threw multiple shadows to make him stand forth, for dusk filled the window of the chamber and dimmed the pastoral frescos, as if to deny that such peacefulness was real.

"Let me speak plainly," he began. "Clear 'tis to see, I hope to win you over, so you'll support my proposal tomorrow. That'll be difficult for you after today, because I put you on your honor not to reveal certain things I'm about to tell you."

"Why should we make that pledge?" Soren demanded.

"Pray patience," Lanarvilis requested gently. To Gratillonius: "Ere you give out this information, can you tell us what its nature is?"

"My reasons for believing the barbarian ebb has turned, and in years to come will flood in upon us. Already this year, seaborne Saxons occupied Corbilo at the mouth of the Liger. They're bringing kinfolk from their homeland to join them."

"I know," Soren snapped. "They are laeti."

"Like the Franks in Armorica," Gratillonius retorted. "Rome had small choice in the matter. I mentioned it for what it bodes. There is worse to relate. The reason why I ask for your silence about it is that if word gets loose as to what my sources are, it could be fatal to them."

"Indeed?" answered Soren skeptically. "I know you worry yourself about the northern Scoti, and doubtless you've been wise to keep track of them, but naught has happened aside from some piracy along the Britannic shores, nor does it seem that aught else will."

Gratillonius shook his head. "You're mistaken. I've nurtured relations with the tribes in southern Hivernia for more cause than improving trade. 'Tis a listening post. My informants and . . . outright spies would be in grave trouble, did it become known what regular use I have made of them. Yonder King Conual of the rising star, he has no hostility of his own toward us; but he is a sworn friend of northerly King Niall. The two wouldn't likely make alliance against Rome or Ys, but neither will wittingly betray the other. Now you may remember my telling you what I found out a while back, that Niall led the reaving fleet which we destroyed."

Soren thought. "I seem to recall. What does it matter?"

"He is no petty warlord. I've discovered that he was the master mind behind the great onslaught on the Roman Wall, sixteen years ago. Since then, and the disaster he suffered here, he's warred widely in his island. The latest news I've received makes me sure that this is the year when he intends to complete and consolidate his conquests there. After that—what? I expect he will look further. And . . . he has never forgotten what Ys did to him. He has vowed revenge."

Soren scowled and tugged his beard. Lanarvilis ventured: "Can he ever master naval strength to match ours? Besides a few crude galleys, what have the Scoti other than leather boats? Where is their discipline, their coordinated command?"

Gratillonius sighed. "My dear," he told her—and saw how she almost imperceptibly winced— "like too many people, you're prone to suppose that because barbarians are ignorant of some things we know, they must be stupid.

Niall will bide his chance. What he may devise, I cannot foresee, but best would be if we kept him always discouraged. I'm sending my man Rufinus back to Hivernia this summer. His mission will be to learn as much about what is going on as he can; and he's a wily one, you know. If he can do Niall a mischief, so much the better. You'll both understand that this is among those matters whereof you must keep silence."

She nodded.

"Aye," Soren agreed reluctantly, "but you've not shown us that Ys will have need of more navy, let alone that she turn it over to Rome."

Gratillonius drew breath. "What I have to tell you will become generally known in the course of time," he said. "However, by then the hour may be late for us. I've had passed on to me things that are still supposed to be state secrets. If we act on them, we must pretend we are acting on our own initiative. Else my sources will likely be cut off, and the heads of some among them, too."

Soren gave him a shrewd glance. "Apuleius Vero?"

"Among others. He wishes Ys well. Have I your silence?"

Soren hesitated an instant. "Aye," he said; and: "You know I am faithful, Grallon," said Lanarvilis.

The King took another long draught before he gripped the beaker tight, as if it were a handhold on the brink of a cliff, and told them:

"Very well. The peace betweeen Stilicho and Alaric is patchwork. It cannot last. Stilicho made it out of necessity. Trouble is brewing in Africa and he must protect his back as best he can while he tries to deal with that. He's terminating the campaign in Britannia not because the diocese has been secured but because he needs the troops in the South. He wants them as much for protection against the Eastern Empire as against any barbarians. Meanwhile Alaric and his kind wait only to see which of the two Romes they can best attack first. Stilicho is fully aware of that. He expects that within the next several years he must begin calling in more soldiers from the frontiers. Britannia, in particular, may be denuded of defenders."

Shocked, Lanarvilis whispered, "Are you certain?"

Gratillonius jerked a nod. "Most of what I've said is

plain enough, once you've given a little thought to the situation. Some of it, such as the African matter or the expectation of transferring legions—those are buried in letters to high officials. Lower officials who found ways to read them have sent the word along a network they've woven for the sake of their own survival; and one or two have passed it on to me. However, all in all, is it such a vast surprise? Is it not more or less what we could have foreseen for ourselves?"

She shivered. Soren grimaced.

Gratillonius pursued: "Think ahead, on behalf of our children and grandchildren. If Rome collapses, Scoti and Saxons will swarm into Britannia, Franks and their kin into Gallia. They'll breed like cockroaches. Here is Armorica, thinly peopled, thinly guarded. At this lonely tip of the peninsula, how long can Ys by herself hold out?"

Stillness took over the room. Night deepened in its window. The candle flames guttered.

Lanarvilis mumbled at last, her head bowed, "Yours is a grim word. I should see what documents you have, but—aye, belike we'd better think how I can change my stance tomorrow."

Soren's fist thudded on the arm of his chair. "You'd give the ships to Rome, though!" he exclaimed. "To Rome!"

"How else dare we build them at all?" Gratillonius replied, flat-voiced. "This is another warning I have from underground. Boy-Emperor Honorius starves for some way to assert himself. His guardian Stilicho is willing to indulge him, if the undertaking be such as Rome can afford. Indeed, Stilicho too would be glad of any accomplishment that impresses the West, the East, and the barbarians alike. To suppress a 'rebellion' in Ys would be easier than to dislodge the heathen Saxons in Corbilo. Nay, we must give no grounds for accusations against us, but keep ourselves too useful to Rome for it to make a sacrificial animal of us."

Soren cursed.

—He left directly after supper. "We've talked enough," he said. "Best I go home now." Gratillonius gave him a glance. The King had dispatched a messenger early on to inform Soren's wife that he would be absent this evening. "I want . . . to sleep on this." Gruffly: "Oh, I'll hew to my word. Tomorrow I'll urge that the Council consider your proposal more carefully, look into ways and means. But I must devise the right phrases, the more so after what position I took today, eh? Also, remember I'm not sure yet of your rightness, only sure that I disbelieve we've need of everything you want. However, goodnight, Grallon."

He took Lanarvilis's hand and bent slightly above the veins that lumped blue in it. "Rest you well, my lady," he said low. Releasing her, he stumped fast across the mosaic floor of the atrium to the exit. A servant scurried to let him out and hail a boy to light his way with a lantern.

"Good dreams to you, Soren," Lanarvilis had breathed after him.

These had been useful hours, Gratillonius thought, and the meal at the end was amicable. He had won about as much agreement as he had hoped. Next came further maneuvers, bargainings, compromises. . . . He might finally get half what he asked for, which was why he asked for as much as he did. . . . With luck, work might commence year after next, which was why he began asking this early. . . . Aye, time has made the bluff soldier into a very politician, he thought; and realized he had thought in Ysan.

He turned his gaze back to Lanarvilis. Time was being less kind to her, he mused. But then, she was a dozen years older than he.

"Wish you likewise to leave?" he dropped into a silence that felt suddenly lengthy. "I'll summon an escort."

"Are you weary?" she replied.

"Nay. Belike my sleep'll be scant. If you care to talk further, I'd—I have always valued your counsel, Lanarvilis."

"Whether or not I agreed with you?"

"Mayhap most when you disagreed. How else shall I learn?"

She smiled the least bit. "There speaks our Gratillonius. Not that argument has ever swayed him far off his forechosen path." She wiped her brow. " 'Tis warm in here. Might we go outside for a span?"

He understood. Sweats came upon her without warning, melancholy, cramps; her courses had become irregular; the Goddess led her toward the last of womankind's

Three Crossroads. "Surely. We're fortunate that the weather's mild."

They went forth, side by side. Soren had not actually required a lantern, for a full moon was up. When that happened on a quarter day, the King lawfully absented himself from his monthly stay in the Wood. Light fell ashen-bright on the paths that twisted through the walled garden, between hedges, topiaries, flowerbeds, bowers. At this season they were mostly bare; limbs and twigs threw an intricacy of shadows. The air was quiescent, with a hint of frost. Crushed shell scrunched softly underfoot.

How often had he wandered like this, with one or another of his women, since that springtime when first he did with Dahilis.

"Do you feel better?" he asked presently.

"Aye, thank you," said Lanarvilis.

"Ah, how fares Julia?"

"Well. Happy in her novitiate." Abrupt bitterness: "Why do you ask?"

Taken aback, he could merely say, "Why, I wanted to know. My daughter that you bore me—"

"You could have met with her occasionally. 'Twould have made her very happy."

"Nay, now, she's a sweet girl. If only I had the time to spare—for her, for all my girls."

"You have it for Dahut."

That stung. He halted. She would have gone on, but he caught her arm. They faced each other in the moonlight.

"Well you know, Dahut suffered a loss she cannot even talk about," he rasped. "She's needed help to heal her sorrow. I've provided what poor distractions I could think of, in what few hours I could steal from the hundreds of folk who clamor after me."

"She's had well-nigh a year to recover, and been amply blithe during most of it." Lanarvilis yielded. She looked off into the dark. "Well, let's not quarrel. She is the child of Dahilis, and we Sisters love her too."

Her tone plucked at him. He took her hands. They felt cold in his. "You are a good person, Lanarvilis," he said clumsily.

"One tries," she sighed. "You do yourself."

Impulse: "Would you like to spend the night here?"

How long since they had last shared a bed? More than a year. As much as two? He realized in a rush what small heed he had paid to the matter. He would simply hear from another of the Nine that Lanarvilis was giving up her turn with him. That happened from time to time with any of them, for any of numerous causes. They decided it among themselves and quietly informed him. When he did call at the house of Lanarvilis, they would dine and talk, but she gave him to understand that she felt indisposed. He agreed without disappointment. Return to the palace and a night alone had its own welcome qualities, unless he elected to go rouse someone else. Guilvilis was always delighted to please him, Maldunilis willing, Forsquilis and Tambilis usually downright eager.

Her gaze and her voice held level. "Do you wish me to?"

"Well, we did intend speaking further of this statecraft business, and, and you are beautiful." He did not altogether lie, seeing her by moonlight.

She blinked at tears, brushed lips over his, and murmured, "Aye, let us once again."

—They had left the window unshuttered, undraped. Moonlight mottled rumpled bedclothes and unclothed bodies.

"I'm sorry," he said. "I hoped 'twould give you pleasure."

"I hoped so too," she answered. " 'Twas not your fault."

He had, in fact, tried for some time to rouse her, until the Bull broke free of restraint and worked Its will. Her continued dryness had made the act painful to her.

"We've had a troublous day," he said. "Tomorrow morning?"

"Nay, better we sleep as late as we can. That meeting will be contentious."

"Nonetheless—"

"Confess we it to ourselves and the Gods, I have grown old."

Bodilis is just a year or two younger! speared through him. *She would be glad of me!*

It was as if an outside voice came: "Would you feel otherwise with Soren?"

Lanarvilis gasped and sat bolt upright. "What do you ask?"

"Naught, naught," he said, immediately regretful. "You are right, we should go to sleep."

He recognized the steel: "Do you dare imagine . . . he and I . . . would commit sacrilege?"

"Nay, never, certainly never." Gratillonius sat up also, drew breath, laid a hand on her shoulder. "I should have kept silence. I did for many years. But I do see and hear better than you seem to suppose. There is love between you twain."

She stared at him through the moon-tinged dark.

He smiled lopsidedly. "Why should I resent it? The Gods sealed your fate ere ever I reached Ys. You have been loyal. That's as much as a centurion can ask."

"You can still surprise me," she said as if talking in dreams.

"Indeed, I'd not really take it amiss if you and he—"

Horror snatched her. She clapped a palm across his mouth. "Quiet! You're about to utter blasphemy!"

To that he felt wholly indifferent. He grew conscious of how tired he was. "Well, we need never speak of this again."

"Best not." She lay down. "Best we try to sleep. Soren and I—we've left any such danger behind. It is too late for us."

— 2 —

"Nay," Keban said. "Don't."

"What?" Budic dropped his arms from her waist and stepped back. "Again?"

"I'm sorry," she said miserably. "I feel unwell."

The soldier stared at his wife. Several days of field exercises had sent him home ardent, the moment Adminius gave furlough. "What's the matter? A fever, a bellyache, what?"

Keban drooped her head. "I feel poorly."

He regarded her for a space. She stood slumped, her paunch protruding; jowls hung sallow down to the double chin; but that was no change from what she had become during the past four or five years. Nor was her hair, unkempt and greasy, or the sour smell of an unwashed body, or the soiled gown in need of mending. Yet the bones beneath, the eyes, the lips, remained comely; and he remembered.

"You are never quite sick," he mumbled, "and never quite in health. . . . Well, come on to bed, then. 'Twill not take long, and you can rest there afterward."

"Nay, please," she whimpered. "I would if I could, but not today, I beg you."

"Why not?"

She rallied spirit enough to retort: "Shall I puke while you're banging away in me? I am sorry, but I do feel queasy, and the smells—your breath, your cheese—Mayhap tomorrow, dear."

"Always tomorrow!" he shouted. "Can you no longer even spread your legs for me? You did for every lout in Ys when you were a whore!"

She shrank against the wall. He waved around at the room. Dust grayed heaped objects, strewn clothes, unscoured kitchenware. "May I at least have a clean house, that I needn't be ashamed to invite my friends to?" he cried on. "Nay. Well, be it as you will."

She began to weep. "Budic, I love you." He would not let himself listen, but stalked out the door and slammed it behind him.

The street bustled beneath a heartlessly bright sun. He thrust along its serpentine narrowness, through the shabby district it served. When acquaintances hailed him, he gave curt response. There were temptations to stop and chat, for several were female, wives or daughters of neighbors. . . . But that could lead to sin, and trouble, and possibly deadly quarrels. Let him just find a cheap harlot in Tomcat Alley or the Fishtail or walking these lanes.

Keban would understand. She'd better. She oughtn't to inquire where he'd been. Still, her sobs might keep him awake tonight—

Budic halted. "Christ have mercy," he choked in Latin. "What am I doing?"

It throbbed in his loins. Relief would allow him to repent. But the Church taught that God did not bargain. The pagans of Ys bought off their Taranis, Lir, lustful

Belisama with sacrifices; but only offerings made with a contrite heart were acceptable to the Lord God of Israel.

Budic turned on his heel and strode, almost running, to the Forum.

How wickedly merry and colorful the throng was that eddied and swirled over its mosaic pavement, around the basins of the Fire Fountain, between the colonnades of the public buildings! A merchant passed by in sumptuous tunic, a marine soldier in metal and pride. A maiden with a well-laden market basket on her head had stopped to trade jokes with a burly young artisan on his way to a job. A Suffete lady, followed by a servant, wore a cloak of the finest blue wool, worked with white gold emblems of moon and stars; her thin face was bent over a pet ferret she carried in her arms. Silken-clad and Venus-beautiful, a meretrix lured a visiting Osismian who looked moneyed as well as wonder-smitten. An old scholar came down the steps of the library bearing scrolls that must be full of arcane lore. A vendor offered smoked oysters, garlicky snails, spiced fruits, honeycakes. A shaggy Saxon and a kilted Scotian, off ships in trade, weaved drunkenly along, arm in arm. Music lilted through babble and clatter. It came from a troupe of performers, their garb as gaudy as their bearing, on the stairs to the fane of Taranis; flute and syrinx piped, harp twanged, drum thuttered, a girl sang sultry verses while another—shamelessly half-clad in what might be a remotely Egyptian style—rattled her sistrum and undulated through a dance. Young men stood beneath, stared, whooped, threw coins, burned.

The Christian forced his way forward. At the church he was alone.

That former temple of Mars had changed its nature more than once. Entering by the western door, Budic found the marble of the vestibule not only clean but polished. The wooden wall that partitioned off the sanctum in Eucherius's day had been replaced by stone, drylaid as Ysan law required but elegantly shaped and fitted. Inset murals displayed the Chi Rho, Fish, and Good Shepherd. Corentinus had left the sanctum austerely furnished, which he felt was becoming. However, the cross now on the altar had been intricately carved, with skill and love, by a Celtic believer, and was trimmed with beaten gold.

An organ had been installed. It was not that the present chorepiscopus had made many converts in Ys, though he had done much better than his predecessor; and those he had drawn to Christ—like Keban—were generally poor. But the resurgence of trade brought a substantial number of believers to the city each year; and there were some who took up residence as representatives of mercantile interests; and Corentinus was not a man whom one could fob off when he suggested making a donation.

The deacon who greeted Budic was a strong young Turonian whose call sent echoes ringing. "Hail, brother!" He used Latin. "May I help you?"

Budic wet his lips. "Can I see . . . the pastor?"

"You're in luck. In weather like this he's apt to go for a twenty-mile ramble, if he isn't ministering to the needy or whatever. But he has Church business to handle today, letters and accounts and such." The deacon laughed. "If he minds being interrupted, I've guessed wrong. Hold, brother, while I go ask."

Left by himself, Budic shifted from foot to foot, wondered how to say what he wanted to and whether he wanted to, tried to pray and found the words sticking in his throat.

The deacon returned. "Go, with God's blessing," he said.

Budic knew the way through corridors to the room where Corentinus worked, studied, cooked his frugal meals, slept on his straw pallet, praticed his private devotions. This likewise had seen improvement since Eucherius; it was equally humble, but shipshape. The door stood open. Budic entered timidly. Corentinus swiveled about on his stool, away from a table littered with papyrus and writing-shingles. "Welcome, my son," he said. "Be seated."

"Father—" Budic coughed. "Father, c-could we talk in private?"

"Close the door if you like. God will hear. What is your wish?"

Instead of taking another stool, Corentinus went on his knees before the big gray man. "Father, help me!" he begged. "Satan has me snared."

Corentinus's mouth twitched slightly upward, though his tone soothed. "Oh, now, it may not be quite that bad.

I know you rather well, I think." He laid a hand on the blond head. "If you have strayed, I doubt it's been very far. Let us first pray together."

They stood up. His voice lifted. Budic wavered through responses.

It was immensely heartening. Afterward he could speak, though he must pace to and fro, striking fist in palm, looking away from him who sat and listened.

"—we were happy once, she new in the Faith, we both new in our marriage—

"—since she lost our baby five years ago, and would have died herself, if you hadn't fetched Queen Innilis—

"—denies me. She pleads poor health . . . says that's why she's such a slattern—

"—lust like a beast's. Sometimes I've just forced her—

"—God forgive me if He can, I've thought how much easier it would be if she had died then—

"—today I set off in search of a whore—"

He wept. Corentinus comforted him. "You are sorely tried, my son. Satan does beset your soul. But you have not surrendered to him, not yet, nor shall you. Heaven stands always ready to send reinforcements."

—In the end, Corentinus said: "The harder the battle, the more splendid the victory. Many a man, and woman also, has suffered like you. But in trouble lies opportunity. Marriage was instituted by God not for pleasure but for the propagation of mortal mankind. Sacrifice of the pleasure is pleasing to Him. No few Christian couples, man and wife, have made this offering. They give up carnal relationships and live as brother and sister, that He be glorified. Can you do that, Budic? Certainly a childless marriage—and it's clear that poor Keban has gone barren —such a marriage thwarts—no, I won't say it thwarts the divine purpose, but it is . . . immaterial to salvation at best, self-indulgence at worst. If you and she, instead, unite in the pure love of God—it won't be easy, Budic. Well do I know it won't be easy. I cannot command you in this, I can only counsel you. But I beg you to think. Think how little you have now, how impoverished and sordid it is; then think how infinitely much you might have, and how wonderful, forever."

—Budic left the church. The sun had moved well down

the sky since he entered. Corentinus's benediction tolled in his head.

Blindly, he walked up Lir Way and out High Gate. Twice he almost collided with a wagon. The drivers swore at him.

He had made no vow. He believed he hoped he would grow able to, but first the turmoil in him must somehow come to rest. A dirt road, scarcely more than a track, went from Aquilonian Way on the right, toward heights above the valley. He turned off onto it, wanting a place where he could be alone with God.

Everywhere around him swelled the young summer. Air lay at rest, its warmth full of odors: earth, greenery, flowers. A cuckoo called, over and over, like the sound of a mother laughing with her newborn. Trees enclosed the path, yew, chestnut, elm, their leaves overarching it in gold-green; sunlight spattered the shade they cast. Between them he had an ever wider view across Ys of the towers, Cape Rach with its sternness softened by verdancy, tumultuous salt blue beyond. Birds skimmed, butterflies danced. Distantly, from one of the estates that nestled on the hillside, he heard a cow bellow; she was love-sick.

Hoofs thudded. Around a bend came a party of riders.

Budic stepped aside. They trotted near, half a dozen young men on spirited horses, their faces wind-flushed—Suffete faces, mostly, but Budic recognized Carsa's among them, the Roman youth who was spending another season here, studying under learned men of the city while he worked to get a commercial outpost well established. They were all lightly and brightly clad. Mirthfulness sparkled from them.

In the van was a horse that Budic also recognized: Favonius, the King's most splendid stallion, already the champion of races in the amphitheater and overland. He whickered and curvetted. The star on his head blazed snowy against the sorrel sheen of his coat.

Upon his back sat Princess Dahut. A woman should not ride an entire, Budic thought confusedly; it was especially dangerous at the wrong time of month. Gratillonius should not have allowed this. But who could refuse Dahut? She might have been a centauress, as fluidly as she and the animal moved together. Her clothes were a boy's, loose tunic and tight breeches, daring if not forbidden for a girl on an exiguous saddle whose knees guided as much as her hands did. Oh, blue-streaked alabaster tapering down to rosy nails . . . heavy amber braids, lapis lazuli eyes. . . .

She reined in. Her followers did the same. "Why, Budic," she called. At fourteen and a half years of age, she had lost the lark sweetness of voice that had been hers as a child; the tones came husky, but sang true. " 'Tis gladsome to see you. Had you not enough tramping about on maneuvers? What beckoned you hither?"

He stood dumb. An Ysan youth said glibly, "What but the chance of encounteering you, my lady?"

She laughed and dismissed the flattery with a flick of fingers. "How went the practicing?" she asked. Looking closer: "You've a sadness on you, Budic. That should not be, on so beautiful a day."

" 'Tis naught," he said. "Do not trouble yourself, my lady."

"Oh, but I do. Am I not the Luck of the legionaries?" Dahut's smile grew tender. " 'Twould be wrong to query you further, here. May Belisama be kind to you, brave man of my father's, friend of mine. . . . Forward!" And that was a trumpet cry. The party went on, recklessly fast, back toward Ys.

Budic stared their way a long while after they had vanished from his sight. It was as if a new fragrance lingered in the air.

When Innilis saved Keban's life, I swore I would always be at the beck of the Gallicenae, he thought slowly. Pastor Corentinus didn't like that. Could it be that God has punished me for it? But why? What can be wrong about serving you, Dahut, daughter of my centurion, Dahut, Dahut?

— 3 —

At last all was ready. On the mound of the Goddess Medb at Temir, Niall of the Nine Hostages held a mighty slaughter. Smoke rose to heaven from the fires where the

beasts cooked, and folk gorged themselves on the meat
until many had prophetic dreams. In the morning the host
assembled and went north.

Glorious was that sight. In the van rolled the chariots of
Niall and his three oldest living sons, Conual Gulban,
Éndae, and Eógan. Their horses neighed and pranced,
lovely to behold, each team perfectly matched in color of
white, black, roan, or dapple gray, plumes on their heads
above the flowing manes, bronze hangings ajingle and
aflash. The cars gleamed with gold, silver, brass, polished
iron. The skillful drivers were only less brilliantly garbed
than the riders, who stood tall beside their spar-high spears,
cloaks blowing back from their finery like rainbow wings.
Behind came the chariots of the nobles, and then on foot
the giant warriors of the guard, whose helmets, axheads,
spearheads shone sun-bright and rippled to their gait as a
grainfield ripples under the summer wind. The tenant
levies followed, tumultuous, and the lumbering oxcarts and
lowing, bleating herds of the supply train. On the flanks,
to and fro, galloped wild young outriders. Clamor rang
from horizon to horizon, horns, rattle and clank, shouts,
footfalls, hoofbeats, wheel-groan, and overhead the hoarse
ravens who sensed that war was again on its way.

At Mag Slecht, Niall paused for another sacrifice. It
depleted his cattle and sheep, but he would soon be in
Qóiqet nUlat and living off the country. The campaign
should not take many days, if all went well, though afterward he and his sons would be long occupied in bringing
their sword-land to heel. Meanwhile Cromb Cróche got
His blood-feast.

Summoned beforehand, the Aregésla joined him there in
numbers greater than he had brought himself. Their chieftains were eager for a share in the fighting, glory, and
spoils. Niall warned them sternly to keep obedient to him
and make no important move without his leave. Maybe
they would heed.

First the warriors traveled west, to bypass a huge stockpen
at the Doors of Emain Macha, for it was a strongpoint that
would have cost them precious time. A courier brought
word that allies were on the move, kinsmen of Niall's in
Condacht who had pledged him help. He hastened his
pace as much as could be. It was well and good for the Firi

Chondachtae to subdue the Ulatach hinterlands, taking their reward in booty, but he wanted to be in possession of the royal seat and its halidoms—the power—before they got there.

After he turned north and later east, sharp fights began, as tuaths rallied against the invaders. He went through them, over them, scarcely checked. More difficult were the many earthworks, the Walls of the Ulati. Garrisons sallied from the hill forts or sent arrows and slingstones in murderous flocks from the tops of earthen ramparts. Most lords would have squandered men trying to take each of these, while Fergus Fogae gathered force to himself at Emain Macha from his entire realm. Niall, who had learned from his battles with the Romans, simply bypassed them. Nowhere stood a cliff of stone from sea to sea, such as had balked him in Britannia. At worst, it was easier to struggle through woods and bogs than to overrun well-entrenched defenders. They could be left for later attention.

In the end, after pushing across the gently rolling countryside, leaving havoc behind him, Niall reached the outer guardian of Emain Macha itself. A few miles short of his goal, this wall reared high and green to right and left, as far as eye could see. Where the road made a break, fortifications hulked on either side, aswarm with armed men. They howled and jeered at the oncoming enemy.

Niall called a halt some distance off. As camp was being pitched, he summoned three of the Aregéslach leaders. "Now you shall prove your worthiness," he told them. "After dark, take a number of your followers aside—quietly, now. Go well off to north or south; we will decide which. At first light, storm the wall. Agile men can climb the embankment, and the seeing will be poor for Ulatach archers. With such a surprise, you can get across at not too great a cost. You will have a running fight, but hasten back to this road and attack at the rear."

It seemed a risky venture, but they could not show doubt before the tall, golden man. Their plans being laid, they in their turn egged on their folk until brawls broke out over who should have the right to go.

Before dawn, wind was driving rain in gray spear-flights. Niall had foreseen this by the clouds and made it part of his scheme. When scouts dashed back to tell of combat

noises, he had the horns blown, and his host advanced.
Unsure how big the troop was that had assailed them from
behind, the Ulati gave it more heed than was necessary.
While they were thus bewildered, Niall smote them
head-on.

Terrible was the struggle in that strait passage, but also
brief it was. With axes and swords athunder at the flanks
of their horses, the chariots rolled through and, once in
the open again, began harvesting. Romans would not have
boiled from their stronghold, desperate, but Niall knew
his Gaels. His men seized the chance, forced their way
into the works, and laid about them. After some unmeas-
ured time of uproar, he held the guardpoint. Rain ceased,
clouds parted, sunbeams struck, carrion birds feasted.

Niall stopped for a day, that he might take stock while
his people tended their wounded, buried their dead, and
celebrated their victory. The way to Emain Macha stood
open, but well he knew that word had flown thither and
warfare remained to do. He wanted his host fully prepared. This work included heaping praise on the three
Aregésla in the hearing of many and bestowing on them
gold, weapons, promises of dominion and high rank. He
was careful, though, to keep it clear that his sons would
always be above them.

Thereafter he moved onward. King Fergus came forth
against him. The armies met on a field which ever afterward bore the name Achat Lethderg—the Place of the
Red Goddess, Medb of Temir.

There did Niall break the Ulati. Throughout that day
the battle crashed and snarled. Edges grew blunt with
striking, men grew so weary that they staggered about,
horses that had been stabbed or hamstrung screamed while
wounded warriors fought to keep their pain to themselves,
wheels and hoofs and feet trampled earth into mud and
the fallen into shapelessness from which jutted shards of
bone. At last terror came upon the Ulati, and such of them
as were able fled any way they could while such of the Firi
Mide and Aregésla as were able pursued them like hounds
a deer, cutting at them and laughing in glee. Behind them
they left their King Fergus, dead in the wreckage of his
chariot, and comrades beyond counting. So did Niall prevail.

Too weary for more thanksgiving than a muttered dedication to the Gods of those Ulatach captives whose throats they cut, the warriors dragged themselves into fireless circles and slept where they dropped. In the morning Niall left most of them behind to rest and prepare proper honors for their fallen. With Conual Gulban, Éndae, Eógan, and enough guards to be safe from attack, he drove ahead for a look at Emain Macha.

This was a bright day. Wind whooped over meadows and shaws, which glowed intensely green. Small white clouds ran before it, and birds in their jubilant hundreds. Here and there, water gleamed like silver. Though the air was cool, along it flowed smells of loam, leaves, blossoms, growth—summer. Good it was to ride at ease, taking some stiffness out of the hard-used flesh by balancing against jounce and sway, calling merrily to each other, as charioteers tried which team could show the most paces and prances: they, the victors.

Smoke stained heaven. Niall scowled. "That can only be Emain Macha burning," he said. "Hurry now."

They topped a hill and looked across to the drumlin beyond. There on the ridge, behind its earthworks, the ancient seat of the Ulatach Kings was, and flames consumed the buildings within. "Stop," Niall told his driver Cathual. In a voice gone heavy: "The Ulati themselves have done this. They knew they could not hold it, and would not let us have it."

"So they are indeed brought low!" cried Eógan.

His father shook a silvering head and murmured, "I did not mean the war to end thus. Here something great is perishing. But you are too young to understand."

Higher and higher raged the fires. The smoke of them blackened half the sky. It roiled and swirled, that smoke; uneasy red light played on it from below; shapes came and went within it, darkling visions. Were they chariots that ascended on the wind, and in them Conchobar, Cú Culanni, Amargin, Ferbaide, and more and more, the heroes of the Red Branch departing forever? The sound of flames afar was like all Ériu keening for her beloved, her defenders.

Chill struck into Niall. He fought it off. "Well," he said, "for good or ill, this is the end of an age. The new one belongs to you, my dears."

Nonetheless he kept himself at the head of things. Notwithstanding that Conual, Éndae, and Eógan would be kings over these conquests, much was left to do before they were firmly in power. He must quell the Ulati who still resisted, and make allies agree to a share of spoils neither unfair nor overly large. Niall did not think he could return home before Lúgnassat, if then.

He even thought about pushing on after the enemy. It was against his better judgment. Driven into corners, the Ulati would be as dangerous as trapped wolves; meanwhile the Midach host would melt away, because men must go back for harvest and other work. What Niall and his sons had won should be ample for their lifetimes. To overreach would be to court the anger of the Gods. Yet . . . Domnuald was unavenged.

Thus it was with a certain relief that Niall received a present from one of his Condachtach kin when they met. This man had been in a clash to the southwest, where his folk overtook a ragtag company living off the land. Prisoners said its leader, who fell in the combat, was Fland Dub maqq Ninnedo, who had fled to league himself with Fergus Fogae. Remembering that Niall had set a price on the head of Fland, the Condachtach chieftain brought it as a free gift.

Niall made lavish return. Later, alone by lamplight in his tent, he stared long at the withered thing. Was it indeed what remained of his son's killer? Men lied, perhaps most often to themselves. They said what others wanted to hear, or their hearts did, and soon believed it. How could he know? In the meantime he could only bring home this head to show, which he had not taken with his own hands. It was a thin revenge.

III

— 1 —

Morning mist followed a night's rain. The Rock of Cassel reared out of it against gray heaven. Seen from below, blurred to vision, the castle on top no longer looked stark. It was as elven as Ys glimpsed across the sea.

Rufinus and Tommaltach paced the ruts of a road near the foot of the upthrust. Pasture lay empty, a drenched green on either side. Sometimes a sheep bleated out in the blindness that closed in after a few yards. The men could be quite sure that nobody overheard them.

Although each took every chance to practice the language of the other, today each spoke his own—if Ysan be reckoned as Rufinus's; for it is easier to be exact when the tongue moves in familiar ways. "You understand, then," the Redonian said. "I am not here, once again, simply to talk about further trade arrangements, now the Roman expeditionary force is departing Britannia. Trade could take care of itself. My mission is to gather intelligence for my lord, King Grallon."

Tommaltach's young visage writhed. He gripped his spear tighter. "I'll not be betraying of King Conual."

"Certainly never." Rufinus stroked fingers across the hand that held the shaft. "Have I not explained, have you not seen for yourself, there is no conflict? 'Tis Niall in the North who'd fain destory Ys—Ys where you keep memories and friends and dreams dear to you."

"But Niall and Conual are —"

"They are not enemies. Nor are they blood brothers.

41

They have a fosterage in common, little else. Besides, Grallon seeks not the destruction of Niall. He merely wants forewarning, so he can be prepared to fend off any assault."

"What you mean to do is, is underhanded!"

Rufinus laughed. "Truly? Think. Having learned that Niall will likely be gone for some while, I propose to fare up to his country and see whatever I can see, hear whatever I can hear. No more. 'Tis only that in his absence I, a man from Ys, can travel freer than would else be the case. Conual has already given me leave. Indeed, he's charged me with carrying gifts and messages to various people."

"But he supposes—"

"He supposes I will be exploring the possibility of peace and commerce." Rufinus shrugged, spreading his palms wide. "Well, is that a falsehood? Grallon would welcome the event. To you and yonder boulder, I confess 'tis unlikely in the extreme. Conual has told me the same. Yet there is no possibility whatsoever ere we know more about the circumstances at Temir. I am just staying discreet."

Tommaltach sighed and gave in. "You'll be needing guides," he said. "Sure, and I wish I could be that, but we have another season of war ahead of us here, until himself has gotten the oaths he wants."

"I know. May the Gods shield you." Rufinus was silent for a dozen paces. "Guides will be easy enough to engage. And I doubt anybody without powerful cause will attack a band of Ysan marines. I've confided in you, good friend, not because I wish your aid today, but because in future we can help one another."

Tommaltach gulped. "How can that be?"

Rufinus tugged the forks of his beard in succession. "You are son to a tuathal king, and a warrior who has won some fame. Men heed you. Our ships that lie waiting to bear us home—can they be protected by a gess as well as a guard? You could lay one. Also, I am no druid, to read the morrow. It could be that we return here under . . . difficult conditions. I know not what they may be, but a strong voice in our favor might prove invaluable.

"In exchange—Well, I've spoken with King Grallon. He'd like having a man from Mumu reside in Ys, to handle such matters as may arise concerning Scoti. 'Twould encourage commerce, and thus be to our advantage. Now we understand that this is a thought foreign to your folk, and so we would undertake to support such a man ourselves for the first several years, with a generous stipend— "

Tommaltach gasped. He stubbed his toe, nearly fell, came to a halt, and cried, "I could live in Ys?"

"You could that," Rufinus said, "and be welcome everywhere, among both commoners and Suffetes, on into the presence of the King and his wives and daughters."

— 2 —

By Hivernian standards, the estate of Laidchenn maqq Barchedo was magnificent. Southward it looked down a sweep of meadow to an argent streak that was the River Ruirthech; beyond, vague in vision as a fairyland, reached the country of the Lagini, which Rufinus had skirted on his way north. Elsewhere he saw more grazing for great herds of cattle and sheep; shielings near their small fields of oats or barley; woodlots, coppices, primeval forest in the distance. Rain-washed, the land gleamed smaragdine, incredibly lush, under a sky that had gone deep blue save for white flocks of cloud.

Rufinus had the idea from what he had heard that Laidchenn did not actually own this acreage in freehold, as a dweller in the hinterland of Ys owned his home ground, nor as a creature of the state like a Roman on his latifundium. Earth in Ériu was inalienable from the tribe that occupied it, unless a conqueror drove that tribe out altogether. However, King Niall had bestowed the trust here on Laidchenn, from which flowed rich proceeds. Likely the people were pleased. These barbarians revered learned men as much as had the olden Greeks. Laidchenn could safely dwell so near the ancient foes of Mide because a poet was inviolable.

Approaching from the west, Condacht now several days behind him, Rufinus saw a house, long, rectangular in form, loom above its surrounding outbuildings. Moss and flowers brightened its thatch, over peeled studs and white-washed cob. Hazel trees grew round about; Rufinus recalled that they were not only prized for their nuts, they were believed to be magical.

Hounds clamored but did not attack. Shepherd boys and the like had long since spied the Ysans and dashed to bring word of them. The few armed men who came forth did not act threateningly. At their head were two without weapons. One, thickset, bushy red hair and beard beginning to blanch, carried a rod from which hung pieces of metal that could jangle together, and wore a tunic and cloak whereon the number of the colors showed his rank to be just below the royal. The second was young, brown-haired, pockmarked, more plainly clad, but otherwise resembled the first.

Rufinus's followers kept their seats. It was politic for him to dismount. Leaping down, he raised an arm and said, "Greeting. I am Rufinus maqq Moribanni of Gallia across the water, come here from King Conual Corcc in Mumu, who asked me that I bear word from him to his dear friend, the ollam poet Laidchenn maqq Barchedo. Long have we traveled, inquiring our way. Have I the honor of addressing himself?"

"You do that," said the aging man. "From Conual, are you, now? A thousand welcomes!" He stepped forward, embraced the newcomer, and kissed him on both cheeks.

"You give me more respect than is my due," Rufinus said. "Forgive me if I, a foreigner, am ignorant of the courtesies proper for my great host."

Laidchenn took the bait, though quite likely he would in any case have replied: "You are indeed my guests, you and your men, Rufinus maqq Moribanni, and under my protection. Come, be at ease, let my household see to your needs. Whatever wishes you harbor that we can fulfill, you have but to let us know."

There followed the usual bustle. In the course of it, Laidchenn introduced his companion, who proved to be his oldest son and student Tigernach, and put some innocent-sounding questions about how the strangers had fared and what brought them to these parts. Rufinus appreciated the shrewdness with which his social standing was ferreted out. He took care to slip in a mention that besides speaking the Roman language, he could read and write it; the latter, at least, he would be glad to demonstrate if anyone was interested. This learning placed him immediately under a poet, more or less equal to a druid or a brithem judge. As for his purposes, that was a long story. Wisest was that he confer with his host before relating it at the feast which Laidchenn had ordered. Some of it might not be suitable for all ears. "Thus, blame not my followers if they are close-mouthed at first. They are not being unfriendly; they are under gess until I can give leave. Anyhow, they know little of the Érennach language, and nothing of the Midach dialects. You hear how awkward my tongue is."

"You do very well," said Laidchenn graciously, "while I lack all Latin."

He put no urgency on his guests, except in making them as comfortable as might be. Rufinus had taken hospitality as he found it in the island, from a herdsman's cabin to the hall of a tribal king, but not since leaving Castellum had he encountered any like this. After a bite of food and drink of ale, he was brought to a bath house to steam himself clean. On coming out, he found fresh clothes waiting. The attendant explained that women had taken his own down to a brook to wash, and these were his too. He would have private sleeping quarters: a small bedroom among several in the main building, formed by partitions that did not reach the roof but were amply high. The attendant said a girl was available if desired, and added she was pretty, skilled, and more than happy to make the close acquaintance of a man from abroad. Rufinus replied that he was grateful, but at the moment had too much wish to meet with the poet. He selected a carnelian brooch from the city's finest jeweler to take along, as a preliminary gift in return for the garments. At the feast he would make his real presentations.

Laidchenn received him in a hut offside, well furnished in a rough fashion. "This is for when I would be by myself to think and compose, or speak with someone privately," he said. "But since the day is beautiful, shall we walk about instead?"

No guards followed. He had no need of any. Those men of his who met the new arrivals had taken weapons simply to mark his dignity. Soon he and his visitor were saunter-

ing alone over the grass. Bees buzzed in clover, which
nodded white heads in answer to what the wind whispered. A lark caroled high aloft.

"Now what would you be telling me?" Laidchenn asked.

Rufinus had rehearsed his speech in his mind, careful
not to wax fulsome. "I have told how I carry greetings
from Conual Corcc. In my baggage are gifts he charged
me with bringing you. His affairs prosper, and he wishes
the same for his foster-kinsman King Niall and yourself. I
have much more to make known, but that can be said
before everyone.

"I cannot call on Niall. First, the word they have down
in Mumu is that he is making war on the Ulati and will not
likely return until late in the autumn, or even winter.
Second, it would be rash of me. I will not lie to you; that
would cast shame on us both. Here I tell that I am a Gaul
as I declared. But I live in Ys, whose King I serve, and my
companions are warriors of his."

"Ys!" burst out of Laidchenn. He stopped in midstride,
swung around, stared and then glowered.

"Hear me, I beg you."

"I must," Laidchenn growled. "You are my guest."

"Dismiss me if you will; but first please hear me out.
Remember, I come by way of King Conual. By and large,
Mumu has had good dealings with Ys; and you yourself are
a man of Mumu, are you not? My mission was to talk
about furtherance of trade and other such matters of common interest. Hearing of Niall's absence, I thought perhaps the Gods had brought me to Ériu in the same year.
Well does the King of Ys know what a bitter foe he has in
King Niall. He does not share that feeling. He would far
rather make peace and become friends. My thought was
that here I had a chance to fare north and speak with
leading men, who might afterward convey my message,
and meanwhile give me an idea as to what hope there is
for reconciliation. Conual did not believe it possible, but
he approved my intention, and suggested I seek you first,
you being the wisest." The scar on Rufinus's cheek contorted with his smile. He spread his arms, baring his
breast. "Here I am."

Laidchenn eased his stance. He nodded heavily. "I fear

Conual Corcc is right. Niall of the Nine Hostages does not forgive."

"Still, enemies also often exchange words."

"True." Laidchenn ruffled his beard and pondered. "May long life be glorious Niall's, he who has been so generous to me. Yet the Mórrigu has Her own dark ways—as all the Gods do Theirs—and each of us must someday die, and new men bring new times. . . . Knowledge is a drink that never quenches need for itself." Abruptly, enthusiasm blazed from him. "And you dwell in Ys! Ys of the hundred towers!" He seized both Rufinus's hands in his. "You shall stay with me as long as you desire, and we will talk, and—and maybe I can do more than that."

"You are—how does one say *magnanimous?*'—yours is a spirit as large as the sky." It was an odd feeling to Rufinus to realize that he meant it.

Thereafter he set himself to charm the natives. That was easy. For the most part, he told about the fabulous city. They bore no special hostility to it. Some had lost kinsmen in Niall's fleet, but that was fifteen years ago, seeming now a whim of war and weather; few remained whose memories of the perished were sharp. They would follow Niall if bidden, but the undying hatred was his alone.

Simply by virtue of what Rufinus had learned in Ys and the Empire—he, the runaway serf, bandit, scout, who had picked up his information in fragments, like a magpie —he was reckoned an ollam. Laidchenn conversed familiarly with him, Tigernach eagerly and deferentially, the visiting chieftains and judges almost shyly, everybody else humbly. At meat he received the chine of the animal, second to the thigh served kings and poets; and sat at the upper end of the hall, on Laidchenn's right, his seat just slightly lower; and had the privilege of passing to his host every third ale horn, while Laidchenn's wife sent each third of his to him. He could go wherever he chose, even to the holiest groves, springs, and rocks. His counsel and blessing were worth much more than any material goods.

His followers, the marines, benefited. Their company much sought despite their meager stock of words, they made merry with drink, women, hunts, rides, rambles, athletic contests. Rufinus's abstention from lovemaking raised no doubts about his virility, but instead increased

the awe of him. Thus it was doubly effective that most of
the time he was cheerful, amiable, as ready to greet the
lowliest tenant or rumple the hair of the littlest child as to
sit with the mighty and the wise.

In a few days he felt ready to drop a hint. Delightful
though this was, he said, the summer was wearing on. If
he wished to return home with his business completed, he
had better go about it, or else risk being weatherbound.

"You are right, my dear," Laidchenn replied. "I have
been thinking the same. In the absence of Niall and his
three oldest sons, their brother Carpre has the royal duties. He was a colt in the year of the evil, and so has scant
ill will toward Ys. Mind you, I would not be saying anything against his faithfulness; but it is no secret that he
chafes under his father's hand and longs to win glory for
himself. That whole brood does. The eagle's blood is in
them."

"Do you think, then, he will receive me?" Rufinus
asked.

"He shall that," Laidchenn replied, "for I myself will go
along with you."

— 3 —

In the high King's absence, Carpre could not reside at
Temir, only visit it for ceremonies. Progressing among the
homes the family owned around Mide, he was at present
a day's journey from the sacred hill, beyond a river which
the travelers crossed on a rude wooden bridge. That valley
was very fair, with much forest for hunters and swine-
herds. Similar to Laidchenn's, the estate stood by itself in
a great clearing to which roads led between the trees. A
palisaded earthen wall, a rath, ringed it in, causing people
to seek the grassy space outside for their sports.

Carpre, a young man with the blond good looks said to
be his father's, took Rufinus in at Laidchenn's request. His
reluctance the man from Ys deemed feigned. Though the
prince doubted Niall would ever take any éricc and honor
price for what had happened, and therefore no Maqq Nélli

could—while Niall lived—nevertheless he would consider Rufinus a herald, untouchable in anger, and hear
him out. Through the days that followed, Carpre asked
questions and listened as ardently as the rest of the Gaels.
Again the Ysans had no dearth of frolicsome fellowship.

Again Rufinus kept aloof from it. Besides maintaining
the dignity he found so useful, he did not care to waste
time in romping, especially with women—time all too
limited, during which he might accomplish something for
Gratillonius and could at the least gather intelligence. Let
him bring back such a bird, to lay at the feet of his master;
let him see a smile and hear a "Well done;" then he could
go rejoice in those ways that were his.

The blend of rigor and geniality continued to serve him
well. At first Laidchenn showed him around, when they
were free to stroll. On the second afternoon, coming back
from a hallowed dolmen in the woods, they saw half a
dozen men being led out the portal of the rath under
guard. It was a leaden, drizzly day. Rufinus stopped.
"Who are those?" he wondered.

Laidchenn frowned. "The hostages from the Lagini," he
said.

Rufinus looked closer. The men had nothing on but
tunics of the roughest material, ragged and scruffy; hair
and beards were unkempt, unwashed; faces were gaunt,
limbs lank, skin sallow. The equal number of guards urged
them offside and leaned contemptuous on spears while the
prisoners began dispiritedly exercising.

"Oh?" Rufinus murmured. He had seen the other hostages whom Carpre had charge of, well-fed, well-clad,
honorably treated. "Have they done wrong, that they must
live like penned animals?"

"They have not," Laidchenn sighed, "unless it be the
chief of them, and he a high King's son. He led a terrible
raid. Niall avenged that on his entire country, yet requires
this punishment too. He knows I think it wrong. A headstrong and unforgiving man, he, indeed, indeed."

Rufinus felt a tingle go up his spine. He knew a little
about the antagonism between the Lagini and their neighbors of Condacht and Mide—foremost Mide, whose found-
ers had carved with the sword most of its territory out of
theirs. "Tell me more, if you please," he said.

Laidchenn explained, laconically because they were standing in the wet and cold. At the end, Rufinus asked, "Would
it be possible for to go talk with that—Yo-khith, is that
how you pronounce his name?"

"Why would you?" inquired Laidchenn, surprised.

Rufinus shrugged. "Oh," he said carelessly, "you know
how it is laid on me to harvest whatever knowledge I can
for my lord." He laughed. "Who can tell but that Eochaid
will someday be the go-between for a real peace with
Niall?"

"On that day, swine will fly," snorted Laidchenn. He
considered. "Well, I see no harm in your curiosity. Come."

The hostages paused to stare, like their warders, as
the two approached. Rufinus's heartbeat quickened. The
one whom Laidchenn had pointed out, Eochaid, was beautiful. Three discolored patches marred his face, as well as
the thinness and grime of captivity, but underneath that it
could have been an Apollo's, straight nose, sculptured
lips, deep-set eyes whose blue seemed the more brilliant
against milky skin and midnight hair. He had kept his tall
body better than his companions theirs, doubtless by forcing some kind of gymnastics upon it while shut away;
muscles moved feline over the bones. Rufinus felt his
sullenness was not from despair, but defiance.

Laidchen accosted the guards. They could not refuse a
poet. Rufinus stepped over to Eochaid. "Greeting, King's
son," he ventured.

Breath hissed between teeth. "Who are you that hail
me?" The voice sounded rusty.

Aware of listeners, Rufinus declared himself. "I fear I
have no ransom for you, or anything like that," he added.
"But as a foreigner, who is also a herald, I may be able to
carry a word from you, and a word back, if you like."

The rest of the Lagini stood by like sick oxen. Eochaid
snarled. "What is there to say between Niall and myself,
or between myself and that man yonder whose son disfig-
ured me with a satire so that I can never become a king?"

"Well, you can perhaps become free again," Rufinus
answered. "Is that not desirable?"

Eochaid slumped. "Why should they ever let me go?"

"Perhaps to carry a message yourself. In Gallia and
Britannia, we have suffered from the Saxon. Will his long

ships never seek the shores of Ériu? Might it not be best that the Celts form alliance while they still can?" Rufinus reached to clap Eochaid's shoulder. A rent in the garment let his hand touch the flesh beneath. Despite the weather, it was warm—not feverish, but hot. Rufinus squeezed. "Think about it," he said. "I would like to speak further with you, if they let me."

He turned and departed, acutely conscious of the gazes that followed. At his side, Laidchenn muttered, "There was too much wisdom in your talk, my dear. Nobody will hearken."

Rufinus scarcely heard. His head was awhirl. It was not that he had any scheme. He had been acting on impulse. But maybe, maybe he could fish a prize for Gratillonius out of these gurly waters. And in any case, by Venus—no, by Belisama—it was sin to mistreat someone that beautiful!

In the course of the next several days, he sought out Eochaid whenever the Lagini were led forth. The hostage's moroseness soon melted. He became heartbreakingly grateful for news, gossip, advice, japes, whatever Rufinus offered. His fellow captives emerged a bit from their apathy, and the keepers enjoyed listening. All were disappointed when Rufinus asked permission to draw Eochaid aside where they could whisper, because he wished to put questions about the doings in Dún Alinni which Eochaid might not answer in the hearing of foemen. The chief of the guards gave his consent anyway. That was not stupidity. Besides his religious respect for a herald and ollam, he did not see how a meaningful conspiracy was possible.

Nor had Rufinus any in mind. He was merely laying groundwork for something he might well never build. And, of course, he got to stand with arms around Eochaid, feeling the thin but muscular body, cheek against cheek. His pulse throbbed.

What he asked caused Eochaid to say, "This is nothing they do not already know here."

"Doubtless," Rufinus answered. "What we have done is gotten the right to step away like this again. Tell nobody." He tightened his embrace, savoring the warmth. "The time may come when we have real business." He let go. "Be of high heart, my friend."

Throughout his stay he had cultivated the Midach lords

he met. A number of them openly wished matters were different. Yet they were sworn to their King, and clear was to see that while he lived there could be no peace with Ys.

The enemy of my enemy is my ally, Rufinus thought, over and over. He tried to imagine how Niall could threaten the city, or any place in Armorica, as long as the strength endured which Gratillonius had raised on land and sea. He failed. Nevertheless—contingencies—and Niall was certainly a scourge of Brittannia, Gratillonius's homeland. If he could not be done away with, the next best service to civilization would be to keep him occupied in this island. Would it not? Today he was triumphant (insofar as barbarians could be said to have triumphs) in the North of Hivernia; he was at ease with the West and the South; what was left to oppose him but the East, the Lagini's kingdom?

"Nonsense," Rufinus mumbled to himself in his lonely bed. "You know perfectly well the situation's more complicated than that. His younger sons are sure to go out conquering on their own, whether the old man will or nay. They'll attack other parts of the Ulati's country, and maybe parts of Condacht. He'll have enough to fret about. . . . Still, if the Lagini can add to his woes—his main hostage from them is Eochaid. The rest are well-born but don't count too much. Eochaid, though, free again—Eochaid, young stallion loosed to gallop, blessed by Epona—haw!" he gibed. Who did he think he was? Sophocles, or whatever they called the playwright whom Bodilis had spoken of?

The next day Laidchenn said he could not linger, but must get home and attend to things. The Ysans had better make haste themselves, back to their ship on the Mumach coast, if they wanted a safe sea passage. It was a pity that the peace mission had failed, but it was foredoomed from the start, and at least they would have plenty to tell.

That night Rufinus dreamed he made love to Eochaid in the smiling presence of Gratillonius. He woke in the darkness and lay furiously thinking until dawn grayed it. Then he dozed off, and when clatter in the hall wakened him anew, he saw what he was going to attempt. He might well fail, but the challenge, and whatever hazard might await him, sounded trumpets within his skull.

To Laidchenn he said: "This is a miserable rainy day, unfit for anything but sitting at the fire. If the weather is better tomorrow, I would like to take a last ride through these magnificent woods, where the Beings indwell as nowhere else I have been. Will you grant this? The day after that, we can go."

"I would not call today miserable, only a little damp," replied the Fer Érennach. "But indeed we must give our host proper notice, so he can send us off as befits his honor. Be it as you wish, darling."

After noon Rufinus declared that despite the rain, he felt cramped indoors and would take a walk. While he did, around and around the rath, the guards brought the Laginach hostages forth. Rufinus greeted them and presently drew Eochaid aside, as often before.

This time the captive came back shivering, afire beneath a tightly held face. "What is it?" cried his fellows, and "What did he say to you?" demanded the chief of his keepers.

Rufinus smiled. "Why, I told him of a ransom I think my lord the King of Ys may agree to offer, as a step toward uniting the Gaels with him against the Saxons," he answered blandly and grandly. "You will understand that I must not say more than this until later."

"No need to, ever," said the chief. "Red Medb Herself cannot swerve Niall from a sworn purpose."

"There are kindlier Gods," Rufinus told him, and went back inside the rath.

That night he slept very lightly, but awoke vibrant.

When he declined offers of company on his excursion, no one pressed him. From time to time, an ollam must go off alone and commune with his art. Nor did anyone think it strange that he belted a Gaelic sword at his hip. He could meet a wild beast or a crazed wanderer or an outlaw who did not know him for what he was. Carpre asked him to return well before dark for the farewell feast. Rufinus agreed, sprang onto his horse, and rode off merrily waving.

He was, in fact, back early in the afternoon, when the Lagini were being let out. He rode over to them. "In the morning I go," he announced, although that was generally known. "Eochaid, friend, come off a short ways with me, that you may freely tell me whatever is in your heart for me to convey."

This day was also chill, full of mist. The guards watched idly, shivering a bit within their warm clothes, as the prisoner in his rags followed the splendidly attired rider a few yards. Already there those forms became dim and dull. But what was to fear? Half starved, Eochaid could not outrun them; unarmed, he could put up no fight when he was overtaken—

He seized the ankle of Rufinus and pulled. Rufinus toppled from the saddleless blanket to grass. He lay as if half stunned. Eochaid drew Rufinus's sword from its sheath, grabbed the horse's mane, vaulted onto the back.

"Get him!" roared the chief. "Bresslan, Tardelbach, watch the rest!" He plunged forward, spear aimed. A cast shaft flew at Eochaid even as the Lagin was mounting. It missed. From horseback, knees gripping tight, Eochaid swung the blade he had taken. It knocked aside the foremost spear and sent the chief to his knees, blood dripping from a cheek slashed open. Eochaid put heels to belly.

Hoofs thudded away out of hearing. He was lost among the trees, the mists. Before pursuit could get itself together, he would be afar. Hounds or no, it was unlikely that they could find a wily woodsman.

Folk helped Rufinus up and led him to the hall. Laidchenn met him at the doorway. The news had gone ahead. Grimness congealed the poet's face. "Well," he rumbled, "and what have to say for yourself?"

"He t-took me by s-surprise," Rufinus stuttered. "I'm s-sorry."

Laidchenn drew breath. "I have my thoughts about that. But you are Carpre's guest, and under my protection, however unwise I may have been to give it. Now— man of Ys! —my counsel is that you call your followers and pack your baggage and be off at once. Do not wait to bid Carpre farewell, but thank whatever Gods are yours that he is elsewhere. For the sake of my honor, I will soothe him as best I may. But begone, do you hear?"

"Do you think I plotted—"

"I say nothing other than that the sooner you are out of Mide the better, and never show yourself here again."

"As my lord wills." Beneath his meekness and the whir-ring of what-to-do, how-to-go, Rufinus exulted.

— 4 —

Eochaid knew where the home of Laidchenn was. Everything about so famous a man spread widely. What he did not know was why he made for it.

That was not the shortest way to Qóiqet Lagini, though not overly many leagues longer. Of course, he must dodge about if he would throw his hunters off the track. Yet was this a well-chosen mark to set for himself?

His wonderment was faint, like a lamp flame in a cave where winds roared. His haste, later his wretchedness, made him unable really to think. He had lost count of days and nights, but hunger had ceased to torment him. Often thirst still did, for he dared not cast about after a brook or a spring but must wait to chance upon water. Sleepless-ness hollowed his head out; he took rest stops merely to keep from killing the horse, and crouched in his hiding places like a hare that has scented a fox. What naps he did snatch were made uneasy by cold. He was nearly naked. In the beginning, he had perforce kept the sword pressed to him by the arm whose hand clutched his ballocks lest the gallop pound them to mush. The edge cut him and cut him. When first he paused, he slashed up most of his tunic to fashion a crude loinstrap and a wrapping for the blade. Wind, rain, dew traveled with him and guested his fireless camps.

Thus was Eochaid emptied, perhaps to become the vessel of a Power.

At last, at last, from a sheltering grove, he beheld at a distance the house of Laidchenn, and well beyond it the Ruirthech, and beyond that his homeland. Daylight pre-vailed, though the sun was lost in grayness and a wrack of low-flying clouds. He tried, dully, to think whether he should wait till dark before crossing the open ground, or do so at once. After a slow while, he pushed ahead. No one was likely to get in the way of a harmless-looking wanderer. Besides, seeking to cross the stream at night could well be the end of him. He was not sure how, in his feebleness, he was going to do it by day.

The horse shambled and staggered, half dead. Eochaid hunched on its back. He felt so cold that it was as if the wind whistled between his bones.

Off on the left he saw the dwelling. There they sat warm and gorged over their ale horns, but he could not enter, he must pass by. Inchmeal he began to believe he understood what had brought him. Yonder was the one who had blasted his life. "I curse you, Tigernach maqq Laidchinni," he croaked. "A red stone in your throat. May you melt away like the froth of the river." They were curses poor and weak, such as a base tenant would utter. He himself was poor and weak. He rocked onward.

"Hoy! You yonder! Stop, if you please!"

The call resounded like a voice heard in dream. Eochaid turned his weary head. He heard his neck creak. The wind skirled. A man afoot was hastening toward him. A cloak in several colors blew back from coat and trews of rich stuff, golden torc, belt studded with amber. The man was unarmed, aside from a staff. Others appeared in the offing, out from under the trees around the buildings.

Eochaid's mount lurched ahead. "You must stop!" shouted the man. "For my honor's sake! I want to give you hospitality!"

There was something in the call that Eochaid had heard before. He could not remember what. He thought foggily that anyone trotting, not running, just trotting, could overhaul this wreck that he rode. Maybe he should heed. He drew rein. The horse whickered and stood with head and tail adroop.

The man laughed. "That's better," he said as he came nigh. "I was walking about, making a poem, and saw you. It would be shame if a wayfarer in need got by the house of Laidchenn—"

He jarred to a halt and gaped. "But you are Eochaid!" he exclaimed. "Eochaid the Fer Lagin."

Below him Eochaid saw the face of Tigernach, the satirist who had ruined *his* face. Those men who were bound toward him would take him prisoner and return him to the kennel.

He slid down off the horse. In his left hand was the

sword. He shook the wrappings off as he took it in his right. Did he or the Power strike? The blow was light, as wasted as his body was, but the iron sharp. Tigernach fell, blood spouting from his neck.

Horror yammered among the approaching men. Eochaid dropped the sword and ran. The Power had him. Husk though he was, he sped weasel-swift. Unable to grasp at once what had happened, and then frantic to care for the son of their master, the men were too slow in giving chase. Eochaid vanished into the reeds along the river. While every male in the household beat them as hounds bayed about, until nightfall, they did not find him.

— 5 —

Tigernach lived long enough to cough out the name of his killer.

Eochaid crossed the Ruirthech in the dark after all. Having skulked evasive or lain moveless under water with little but his nose above, he found a log that had drifted against the bank. With its help he swam the river. On the far side, he somehow walked until he came on a shieling. The family there was impoverished, but they took him in and shared with him what milk and gruel they had: for the Gods love this. He caught a fever and lay drowsy for days.

That may have been as well for him. A war band from the north side came over and ranged in search. They did not happen on the hovel, and must withdraw when the neighborhood mustered force against them. Belike he had drowned, they supposed, the which was too good for him.

In time, Eochaid became able to make his painful way to Dún Alinni. The news had gone faster. "You cannot stay here, you who have violated the home of a poet," his father King Éndae said. "All Mide and Condacht would come after you once they heard, and this Fifth would itself deliver you up to them." The breath sobbed into him. "Yet you are my son. If I must disown you, I will not forsake you."

And he gave Eochaid a galley of the Saxon kind, and let

it be known that men were wanted to go adventuring abroad. There were not a few ruined by the war or despairing of the morrow at home or simply restless and aspiring, who overlooked Eochaid's deed and risked any bad luck that might flow from it because they remembered what a peerless leader he had been. The upshot was that he departed with a full crew and several large currachs besides.

They fared south along Britannia, raiding where they could. That was not often, and pickings were lean. Stilicho's expeditionary force had lately withdrawn, but after expelling the Scoti who had settled there. Though it was against Roman law, the Ordovices and Demetae were now well-armed to protect themselves, while the Silures and Dumnonii had a legion not so far away to call upon. Eventually Eochaid and his men settled down for the winter on an island off Gallia, as various other sea rovers were wont to do.

During a spell of fairly good weather he sent a currach back to learn what had happened meanwhile. It returned with ill tidings.

Laidchenn had arrived home shortly before the killing. He was indoors when his folk brought him the news and the body of his son. Loud was the keening; but the poet remained silent until he had a lament ready to give at the funeral feast. The next day he went forth by himself. He climbed the raw earth of the barrow, faced south, and drew his harp out of its case. Sharp with early autumn, the wind at his back blew his words toward the river. Certain black birds circled overhead. When he was done, they also flew that way. Some workmen could not help hearing him. They shuddered.

"Lagini, I sing now.
Wing now to cravens,
Ravens; bespeak them!
Seek them will bold men.
Old men can only,
Lonely, send greeting,
Meeting them never:
'Ever to sorrow
Morrow shall wake you,
Take you like cattle—

Battle-won plunder—
Under its keeping.
Reaping is mirthless,
Worthless is sowing;
Growing dry thistles,
Bristles the plowland.
Cowland lies calfless.
Laughless the hall is.
All is turned sickly,
Quickly, O Lagini.' "

And every day thereafter, for a full year, did the ollam poet mount the grave of his son to satirize yonder country, its King and its people. And during that year, neither grain nor grass nor any green thing grew there. Herds starved in barren fields, flocks in sere forests, folk in foodless dwellings. When finally Laidchenn maqq Barchedo reckoned his vengeance complete, and the blight and the famine had lifted, that Fifth of Ériu took long to recover its health. Meanwhile pirates made free of the coasts, raiders and rebels of the interior.

Such was the tale that, above the fire of past wrongs, hammered the soul of Eochaid into a knife meant for Niall.

IV

— 1 —

In the dead of winter, people must rise hours before the sun if they were to carry out their duties. It was earlier than for most when Malthi, a maidservant to Queen Fennalis, entered the room where Dahut slept and gently shook her. "Princess. The time is come, as well as I can judge. Waken."

The girl sat up. Light from the lamp in the woman's hand glowed across tumbled hair, white silken shift, the cloven swelling of bosom. She scowled. Her tone came near to a snarl. "You dare! You called me from a dream, a holy dream."

"I am sorry, my lady, but you did order me yesterday evening—You must be in attendance at the Temple today—"

Dahut drew a measure of calm across herself. "Woeful it is, though, being wrenched away just when— Well, have you my bath ready?"

"Of course, Princess, and I'll be laying out your vestments. May I wish you a good morning?"

Rueful humor flitted across the clear brow, the soft lips. "Better 'twould be did I not have to arrive fasting!" Solemnity replaced it. Dahut flowed out of bed. "Honor to the Gods." Before an image of Belisama as Maiden, she offered her orison. At the end she whispered, "You will come again to me, will You not?"

Malthi had lighted a candle for her. She took it out into the hallway. That was less black than expected. The adjoining door stood open, and yellow radiance spilled forth.

Dahut looked in. Fennalis was abed but awake, propped up in a nest of pillows, a sewn stack of papyrus sheets open on the blankets. "Why, greeting, Mama," Dahut said with a smile. The old Queen liked to hear that name from the vestal's childhood. "How naughty. You should be asleep for hours yet, regaining your strength."

Fennalis sighed. "I couldn't. At last I called poor Malthi to arrange things." Her white head nodded at the cushions, the nine-branched bronze candelabrum on a table beside her, the booklet under her fingers. "I may as well use the time. Also, it takes my mind off— No matter."

Dahut entered. "Pain?" she asked, concern in her voice.

Fennalis shrugged. "Let's not speak of regaining my strength. It no longer exists."

Dahut set her candle down and regarded the high priestess closely. That stumpy body had been losing its stoutness fast of late. Skin draped emptily past the pug nose and over the withered arms. It was taking on a fallow hue. Nonetheless, her belly made a bulge in the covers. "Oh, dear Mama—"

"Nay, no sniveling. 'Tis high time I got out of the way, and ready I am to go. A kind of adventure, drawing close to the Otherworld. I begin to make out its shores."

Dahut's eyes widened. "In dreams?" she breathed.

"Often I cannot be sure if the glimpses come while I sleep or I wake." Fennalis gave her visitor a sharp glance. "Have *you* been dreaming?"

Dahut swallowed, hesitated, nodded.

"Sit down, if you'd fain tell me," Fennalis invited.

Dahut lowered herself to the edge of the bed. Fennalis reached unsteadily up to stroke her cheek. "How lovely you are," the Queen murmured. "And how strange. What was your dream?"

Dahut stared into the darkness that pressed against the window. " 'Twas more than one," she said low. "They began . . . two years ago, I think, after . . . my seal left me. I can't be certain, for at first they seemed little different from others, save that I always remembered them. I stood on a seashore. The waters were dark and unrestful beneath a gray sky. The air was windless. No birds flew. I was alone, altogether alone. Yet I was not afraid. I knew this strand and sea were mine.

"The dreams came far apart in the beginning, and I gave them little thought, when so much was happening in my life. Somebody slowly appeared, away off on the horizon. They came toward me, over the waves. Each time they got nearer. At last I could see they were three, a man, a woman, and . . . something else, a presence, a shadow, but I could feel the might within. . . .

"The dreams seek me more and more often. Now I can see that the man bears a hammer and wears the red robe and Wheel emblem of a King. The woman is dressed in blue and white like one of you Gallicenae. The third—I think has three legs and a single huge eye."

Dahut drew breath before she finished: "This morning, just ere the servant roused me, they were so close that I thought I could see what faces were theirs. It seemed to me that the man could be my father and the woman my mother—from what I've heard tell of my mother—"

Her words trailed off. She sat looking at the night.

"The woman may be yourself," Fennalis said.

Dahut twisted about to stare at her. "What? You can, can read it for me? I never thought you—"

"Divination, magic, the Touch, all such wonders, aye, they've passed plain little Fennalis by. Nor was I ill content with that. They are not human sorts of things. I felt no envy of Forsquilis, say. And as for you, my darling, I only wish—" The woman sighed once more. "Nay, I'm still too far from the Otherworld to understand this. I do beg you to be very, very careful."

Dahut straightened. "Thank you, but why should I dread my destiny?"

"You know what it is."

"I know it is *mine*." Dahut rose. Her gaze fell on the booklet. "What is that about? 'Tis new to me." Bending over, tracing with a fingertip, she read aloud: "—Blessed are the poor in spirit: for theirs is the kingdom of Heaven—"

She sprang back as if the papyrus had burned her. "Fennalis!" she cried. "That's Christian! I saw the name of Jesus!"

Calm descended on the woman. "It is. Corentinus has rendered some of his Scriptures into Ysan. He lent me this."

Dahut made a fending sign. "You've been with him?"

"Of late." Fennalis smiled. "At ease, child. We've merely talked a few times, at my request. He knows he'll never convert me. I'm too old and set in my ways."

"But why, then, why?"

"To learn a minim about what he believes, what so many people believe. Surely they have some truth, some insight, and I'd be glad to know what ere I depart."

"They deny the Gods!"

"Well, our Gods deny, or at least defy theirs. Who is the more righteous? Even when young, I—Dahut, my first King was Wulfgar, a rough man but well-intentioned, able, and—ah, a stallion of a man; and I was young. Stark Gaetulius slew him and possessed me. Moody Lugaid slew Gaetulius. I could not hate either; both gave me more children to love, and besides, this was the will of the Gods. Still, Hoel came like a big golden sun that drives out winter; and I was not yet too old to have a daughter by him. But horrible Colconor finally cut Hoel down. After five years, Gratillonius delivered us."

Exhausted, Fennalis sank back on the pillows. Her eyes closed. The girl could barely hear: "Someday those Gods you adore will send a man who kills your father. You may become his bride."

"I must go!" Dahut nearly screamed. With anger-stiff strides, she left the room. The candle shook and wavered in her grasp. Her free hand clenched and unclenched.

In a chamber of marble and fish mosaics, lights burned manifold and a sunken bath steamed fragrant. Dahut pulled off her nightgown, flung it on the floor, and descended.

Lying there, she slowly loosened. First her glance, then her hands glided over her body. Just past her fifteenth year, she was nonetheless entirely woman. She caressed the roundednesses, arched her back, mewed, with eyes half shut.

Malthi came in, recalling Dahut to the world. "Princess, 'tis getting late. Better we hurry." As the maiden stepped forth: "How beautiful you are. A pity I must towel you. Many a young man would trample dragons on his way to this task."

Dahut accepted the praise as she did all such words, something pleasant but unsurprising. Back in the bedroom —she had not paused to look in on Fennalis—the servant helped her into the vestal's gown: at this season, white with solar symbols embroidered in gold. Having combed out her hair, Malthi crowned it with a wreath of evergreen laurel, whereinto were woven red berries of holly. Red also were her shoes; but the girdle about her slenderness was Belisama's blue, with a silver clasp conjoining Hammer and Trident.

Taking a lantern, she left the house where she had spent the night and hastened along the street. In its district few had occasion to be up so early. She noticed two or three lights bobbing in the echoful lane. From these heights, she spied more of them down in the working parts of the city and along its avenues, glow-worm small. The air was cold and quiet; breath smoked. A half moon rode among uncountable stars. Towers raised black lances against them. At the top of one a window glimmered lonely. That was where Rufinus lived.

The Temple of the Goddess stood wan, its portico like a cave. Dahut gave her lantern into the care of the minor priestess who was keeping the door, and passed on into the sanctum. It was empty except for her. Lamps along the aisles made a twilight. She advanced to the altar at the far end.

There she lifted her arms. Her duties today would not be sacral, she would take her turn at maintenance and scribe work, but a vestal must always begin with prayer. Its form was not fixed; this hour was called the Opening of the Heart. Dahut looked up to the images of the Triune, Maiden, Mother, and Hag. In the dim and uneasy glow, they seemed to stir. "Goddess, All-Holy," she said under her breath, "come to me. Make known Your will. Embody Your power. Belisama, be Dahut."

— 2 —

The men whom Niall had sent south found him at the hostel of Bran maqq Anmerech, on his way to Temir for the festival of Imbolc. A brief and murky day was drawing to its close. Firelight barely kept shadows at bay in the

long room where the King sat among his chief warriors.
Bran would not offend that nose with the stench of grease
lamps, and instead heaped the trench full of sweet fir
wood. Gold gleamed, eyeballs glared. Having eaten, the
company were at drink while a bard gave them a ballad
about an adventure of Niall's great ancestor Corbmaqq.

One did not interrupt an ollam poet, but this was a
much lesser sort of fellow. Wet and muddy, the travelers
tramped in and greeted their lord. "It's welcome you are,"
he said. His tone lacked heartiness. He had more and
more been brooding these past months. "Bran, fetch what
they need and prepare them quarters." That could be
done somehow, for the party numbered only ten.

"We have brought such a man as you sent us to find,"
declared the leader. "Come forward, Cernach maqq
Durthacht."

A short but square-shouldered, slightly grizzled person
responded. He had a cocky manner and a mariner's gait.
Niall's gaze probed him. "You are indeed he who can
teach me the tongue they speak in Ys?" asked the King.

"I am that, lord," Cernach answered. His dialect of
Mumu was heavy but understandable. "And this is my
wife Sadb. I will not be leaving her by herself a year or
worse." He beckoned her to join him at his side. She was
younger than he, full-breasted, broad-hipped, her hair
red and her face comely though freckled. When she smiled,
Niall thawed a bit.

"Well," he said, "sit down, the pair of you." A girl
brought stools for them, placed at his knees where he sat
benched. After mead cups were in their hands, Niall commanded, "Tell me about yourself, Cernach."

"I am a trader captain with my own small ship, harbored
in the mouth of the River Siuir. For years I have taken
cargoes to and from Ys. I have abided in it, and in my
house at home I have received merchant seamen from it,
on their way to our fairs or to Cassel. I know it as well as
any outsider can know a place so full of magic and poetry;
I speak the language with an accent, but readily."

"And you are willing, for rich reward, to share your
knowledge with me?"

"I am, also for the glory of having served Niall of the
Nine Hostages."

The King peered. "Think well," he warned. "I am the bitter foe of Ys. What harm I can wreak there, I will, and reckon it far too little revenge for the wrongs done me. They began with the shattering of my fleet and the slaying of my son, when he meant Ys no trouble at all. They have gone on through the unloosing of my foremost hostage, which led to the murder of a son of my head poet and his own withdrawal from my household. That made ashen in my mouth the taste of my victory over the Ulati."

"I have heard this."

"Then you must know that I will learn of Ys as a means toward my vengeance. How that is to happen I know not, but happen it shall, unless I die first or the sea overwhelm the world. Now you have friends yonder, as well as business and, surely, good memories. Would you help sharpen my sword against these? Answer honestly, and you shall go home with gifts for your trouble. A man ought to stand by his friends."

"I will indeed say freely, my lord." Cernach grinned, a sailor's impudence. "I have sworn no oaths with anyone. That is not the way of Ys, unless maybe among the fishers down at the place they call Scot's Landing, and those are an uncanny lot. True, there are men of Ys—and women, ah, women—whom I like; and I have profit of my trade. It would grieve me to see Ys ruined the way Alba is being ruined. However—lord, I said I would be frank—I do not believe you can harm it. It is too strong, its masters too wise and wary. Even mighty Niall could break his heart against that rampart. Maybe I can do you the service of making you see this. Whether or no, well, why should I not play druid and instruct you?"

The warriors stiffened, half appalled. Niall himself tensed. His lips pulled back over his teeth. Then he slackened, rattled forth a laugh, lifted his goblet. "Boldly spoken! It seems I can trust you to do what you agreed, in full measure. Come, drink; and I see that the hostelkeeper is carrying out food after your journey."

—But later, as the fire guttered low, his mood darkened again. "Never seek to turn me from my vengeance," he muttered. "It would spill our time. It could cost you your head. Remember that."

Cernach's wife Sadb leaned toward him. "You have an

inward sorrow, Niall maqq Echach," she said softly. "Could
I be relieving of it a little this night?"

Niall considered her. At last he smiled. "You could
that," he answered. "Let us away."

They said their good evenings and left for the enclosed
space given him, his arm about her waist. Cernach looked
after them with an expression that became pleased. Bran
cleared his throat and said, "I think we can still find a girl
awake for you, guest who has gotten such an honor."

On the face of Bran's wife were disappointment and
envy. Niall was not only powerful and handsome. The
word went among the women of Ériu that he was a lover
without compare.

— 3 —

When the Suffetes met at vernal equinox, a thing occurred that Ys had never known before. The King brought
charges against one of their number.

"—Nagon Demari, Labor Councillor. It has been noto-
rious how his bullies terrorize the waterfront and beat
insensible men who resist the demands he makes of them
through the guild he heads. Direct evidence has been
lacking. . . . Now Donnerch, son of Arel, the independent
carter who was taking the lead in forming a new and
honest guild, he has been murdered, set on as he passed
through the Fishtail after dark and stabbed. This is common
news and has caused widespread mourning. What did not
come out hitherto is that Donnerch was so robust he did
not die at once. He regained awareness and named his two
assailants to the patrolmen who found him lying in that
alley. Fate made these be legionaries, and therefore they
reported directly to me. The Captain of Marines is honest
and able, but restricted in what he may do. Without
impartial witnesses, the killers need only maintain that
Donnerch must have been mistaken, and they would go
free. I had them quietly seized and privately interrogated.
Torture was not necessary. To me, the Incarnation of
Taranis, they confessed as soon as I promised to spare

their lives—a pledge the Captain of Marines does not have power to give. They have told me, as they will tell you, that they acted on the order of Nagon Demari."

Uproar. Horror. Oratory. The grindstone that was procedure.

" 'Tis a foul bargain, letting hired murderers keep their heads," protested Bomatin Kusuri, Mariner Councillor.

"They shall be taken in chains to Gesocribate and put on the Roman slave market," Gratillonius replied. "The proceeds shall go to Donnerch's widow and children."

He cast all his force and all his power of persuasion and, aye, intimidation into the effort to destroy Nagon. That man had been a thorn in the side of Ys, and the wound suppurating, far too long.

"The testimony's not good enough," declared Osrach Taniti, Fisher Councillor, himself a hard-bitten old salt. "We can't condemn him on the word of two lampreys like those. Mind ye, I'm no friend to Nagon. My Brotherhood's often had to work with his Guild, but we've nay had to like it. However, Nagon has gotten betterment of the longshoremen's lot. Else yon fellows could ha' whistled for a share in this prosperity we're supposed to've gained. That speaks for his character."

"It says merely that every tyrant or demagogue must needs do some service for somebody," retorted Queen Vindilis. "The King has confided in the Nine. We are agreed Nagon is evil."

"We would never wish to ruin the Guild itself," said Forsquilis. "Let honest leadership rebuild it."

"Ah, but who shall name that leadership?" demanded Soren Cartagi. "The King? Beware!" He raised a hand. "Nay, hear me out. None will deny that Gratillonius has wrought mightily on behalf of Ys. Yet time and again he has overreached himself, he has broken bounds that were ancient already when Brennilis lived. He has not been content to be high priest, president of this Council, and war chieftain. He would become dictator. I say this to his face, more in respect than in anger. He is a well-intentioned man, ofttimes mistaken but mayhap more often right. However, what of his successor? What could, say, another Colconor do with power such as Gratillonius would put in the hands of the King?"

There were those, the accused among them, who flatly denied the charges. Argument roiled on throughout the day.

Finally, wearily, a majority voted a compromise. The evidence was deemed insufficient to convict Nagon Demari of a capital crime. The killers might have taken his instructions wrong, or become overexcited. Still, they were henchmen of his, and bad men. His association with them was by itself a grave violation of trust, and gave credence to many more allegations. Nagon Demari was therefore stripped of every office and forbidden to hold any for the rest of his life.

"Stand forth," Gratillonius bade him, "if you have aught to say ere I confirm or dismiss this judgment of the Council."

Left untouched had been the question Soren raised, whether the King himself had exceeded his rights and established a dangerous precedent.

The stocky, sandy-haired man stepped up. He kept his back to the assembly, in scorn. It was the one on the dais whom his chill gaze defied, and the soldiers behind, and perhaps the eidolons of the Three looming above them.

"What is there to say?" he rasped. "You've hounded me for years, and at last you have me between your jaws. Ill was the fate that brought you to the Wood. May a challenger soon come and kill you. You shall not crush the workers who will be cursing your name, nor shall you break my spirit. But here I will not linger, where thanks to you my innocent family can no longer hold their heads high. You will be rid of me, Grallon, because I will take myself away from your pestilential presence. You will not be rid of divine justice."

Gasps went around the chamber. Gratillonius said merely, "Go, then, and live among the Romans. You'll take enough loot with you." The struggle had exhausted him. It was worse than combat. On the battlefield you at least usually had a clear-cut victory or defeat.

He adjourned the session and departed amidst his guards, waving off every attempt to speak with him. Bodilis followed the squad. This was to be a visit he paid her.

Dusk brimmed the city with blue when they reached her house. The soldiers left them and they entered. Bodilis took him to her scriptorium, pending supper. That large room—crammed with her books, writing materials, artistic work in progress, specimens, objects of beauty—was their refuge, now that the bedchamber was denied them. Candleglow fell on small refreshments, wine, water, tisane kept warm by a lamp.

"Won't you shed cloak and robe?" she suggested in the Latin they commonly used when alone together. "They must hang heavy this evening."

"They do that," he sighed, pulled them off and laid them over a stool. Her cat promptly sprang up and sat on the raiment. Bodilis's look followed Gratillonius as he went to pour himself a glass of wine, undiluted, and take a lengthy draught. His light undertunic hung across shoulders still broad and back straight, leaving bare the powerful limbs. Bits of silver glinted in the auburn of his hair and close-trimmed beard. Her locks were quite gray.

"I'm glad this is your evening," he said. "I need your strength."

"Others among us have as much," she answered softly. "and comfort to give you besides."

"But not your . . . calm, your fellow-feeling. And your wisdom. You can see beyond the politics of what we did today and help me discover what it really means." He sat down and stared at the floor.

She took a cup of herbal brew and a chair facing his. "You speak extravagantly."

He shook his head. "No. I'll set my clumsy words aside, though, and ask for your opinions." It was not the first time in the past decade. The pain of the barrier he had perforce raised between them had long since become familiar; they could talk freely as of old, until he bade her goodnight and sought his bed at the palace.

"Do you wonder what we can best do about Nagon's partisans?" she replied. "We know there will be much resentment. Most of his working men believe that, whatever his faults, he was on their side."

"That was considered beforehand," he said impatiently. "Don't fear any riots. Patrols will be doubled at the waterfront for the next several days. I do wish the Gallicenae would help cool things down."

"You know we mustn't take sides. We serve the Goddess on behalf of everybody."

"I meant in reconstructing the Guild. If the Nine were counselors and overseers of that, who could doubt the job was done as honestly as human beings are able? . . . But we've covered this ground already. I'll do what I can with what tools are allowed me."

"Well, I can propose to my Sisters that we reconsider, but it'll surely be futile. We went as far as we should in condemning Nagon. You must have something else on your mind."

"I do." His expression was troubled, almost bewildered. "What certain staunch men said—Oh, I'd given the matter thought before, but hastily. Always there's been too much to do, at once, no time for reflection; and afterward it's too late. But am I being wise, wise not for myself but for Ys? You've made me think back to my history lessons when I was a boy. Marius, who saved Rome from the Cimbri, meant to do well by the people but undermined the Republic—which Caesar demolished in all but name, meaning to repair the state—Am I sapping the wall of Ys? What about the King after me?"

"Oh, darling!" she cried, leaned forward and seized his hand. "Don't talk like that!"

"I'd better," he said grimly. "I'll leave so many behind me, Dahut, Tambilis, the children, maybe you—"

"But you have years ahead of you," she insisted, "as strong as you are. Who has even challenged you since Rufinus, more than a decade ago, in spite of your sparing him? And all the omens foretell a new Age for Ys. It could well bring an end to, to that which happens in the Wood."

His bleakness did not ease. She hurried on: "Meanwhile, true, we do have serious matters to deal with. You understand—understand fully, don't you?—you will be getting a new Queen."

He hesitated. "Poor Fennalis is ill," he admitted. She had not attended the Council, nor any function of the Gallicenae.

Bodilis studied him. "You shy from this," she murmured.

"Oh, now, I call on her whenever I can. She's cheerful."

"She puts on a good face. But how often have her servants asked you to turn back at her door, saying she's asleep or whatever? That's been at her orders. Gratillonius, lately she's begun vomiting thick, gritty black masses. We know what those mean. She will soon die. We can only try to ease her way a little. You must not hide from the truth."

"What can I do, though?" he groaned. "Which of the vestals will be next? There's no foretelling."

"There can be forethought. What if the Sign comes upon one of your own daughters?"

He stiffened. After a silence that grew long he said, flat-voiced, "That would be very unwise of your Gods."

"Well," she said, more hastily than before, "we Sisters have been considering the girls of the second and third generations. They have their family connections, generally to Suffetes. Whichever of those clans gets the high honor —well, some members will stand aloof, but some will try for this or that advantage. Lanarvilis can best advise you about it."

"Hm." He rubbed his chin. The beard felt wiry. "I'll seek her out."

"First," Bodilis urged, "you should give reverence to the Three. What happened today was truly an upheaval. It may win Their favor, and certainly it'll help calm both Suffetes and commoners, if you recess the Council tomorrow and hold a solemn sacrifice."

He shook his head. "I can't."

She was shocked. "Why not?"

"I've made another promise. It should have been kept earlier, but the word reached me in the middle of my preparations for this day's business, and . . . Tomorrow at sunset I'll be leading a high rite of Mithras. It would make me impure if I offered first to Anyone else."

"But why is this?" she whispered. "No holy day of His—"

"My father in Britannia has died," he told her. "My initiates and I must give his spirit its farewell."

"Oh, my dear." She rose and reached for him. He got up too. They clung to each other.

— 4 —

Joreth kept an apartment on the third floor of that tower called the Flying Doe. She had had its walls done over so that motifs of the sea played across them, waves, dolphins, fish, seals, kelp, shells. Sea-green were the draperies along the windows and the coverings of her bed. Small erotic sculptures decorated the main room. The incense that wafted about lacked the heavy sweetness common in places of this kind; it was subtly wild.

When Carsa entered, he stopped and caught his breath. Daylight through glass limned Joreth's lissomeness against heaven. It smoldered in the amber masses of her hair. She wore a silken gown, close about breasts and hips, flowing of sleeves and skirt, gauzy save where embroidered vines curled tantalizing. "Welcome," she purred, and undulated forward to take his hands in hers. "Be very welcome. What a lovely youth you are."

He swallowed dryness. His heart thuttered.

Enormous blue eyes looked up out of the delicate face. "Aulus Metellus Carsa, nay?" she said with a smile like daybreak. "A Roman from far Burdigala, dwelling among us in Ys. Oh, you must have many an adventure to tell of."

He remembered vaguely how her ancilla had received him two days ago in an upstairs room. Before taking his money and setting this hour, she had engaged him in amiable conversation. It was known that Joreth did not receive men whom she would find unpleasing; she had no need to. Now Carsa realized that the information about him had been passed on, doubtless including the fact that he was sturdy, with curly dark-brown hair and features broad, blunt, but regular. Well, he thought, foreknowledge helped her charm her patrons.

The sight of her was enough, though. Glimpsing her in the streets, hearing enraptured stories from friends, he could at last no longer resist. The price was scarcely within his means, but—

But she was so like Dahut.

She led him to a couch, bade him sit down, poured a fine wine for them both, settled herself beside him. "Come," she proposed, "let us get acquainted. Unlock that tongue of yours."

"You're beautiful!" he blurted, threw his arm about her waist and sought to kiss her.

She held him off with a gesture of her whole body that was not a repulsion but a promise. "Pray wait," she laughed.

"You shall have your desire, but I would fain give you the greatest pleasure therein. This is no cheap tavern where you must wolf your girl as fast as your food. You have time ahead of you. Let your . . . appetite . . . grow at leisure."

"Looking at you," he mumbled, "I can hardly rein myself in. I was hoping—twice, ere my time had drained out of the clepsydra—"

"Well, we'll see about that. Young men are quickly ready again. But Carsa, I tell you afresh, this is no whorehouse. I want to know my lovers in spirit as well as flesh. Else they and I are mere beasts in rut. That is wrong."

He fumbled for words. "Aye. The more so when, when you are of royal birth."

She arched her brows. "You have heard?"

"Somewhat. I cannot really untangle it," he admitted. "These many Queens and Kings through the years. But I'm told you are kin to—to Queen Bodilis."

Joreth threw back her head and laughed anew, a peal in which he thought he heard a certain thinness. "To Princess Dahut, you mean. Deny it not. 'Tis my good fortune that I resemble her."

"And mine," he sprang to say.

"La, you're swift to learn our pretty Ysan ways, Roman," she teased. "I'll enjoy teaching you further. Shall I begin by explaining my descent?"

"Whatever you wish," he answered humbly.

"Well, in the days of King Wulfgar there was a Queen who had taken the name Vallilis. The first child she bore him was to become Queen Tambilis—not the present Queen of that name, but her grandmother. Near the end of her life—she died accidentally, unless 'tis true what some believe, that the Gods Themselves decide the doom of all the Gallicenae—Vallilis bore Wulfgar another daughter, Evana."

Carsa winced. He could not forget the story of Wulfgar. At the death of Vallilis, the Sign came upon Tambilis, his daughter by her. Helpless in the grip of a Power, Wulfgar had possessed her, and she bore him Bodilis. It was not reckoned incestuous in Ys, when the Gods had made the choice. But Wulfgar was said to have been haunted by guilt. He fell to the sword of Gaetulius, though he should have prevailed over the Mauretanian.

Tambilis lived on. When Hoel had taken the crown, she bore him that Estar who became Dahilis after she, the mother, passed away. And Dahilis became, by Gratillonius, the mother of Dahut.

Now a daughter of Bodilis, also by Hoel, reigned as a new Tambilis. . . . A shiver went through Carsa. This history was as dark, as twisted as that of the house of Atreus. What was he, a Christian man, doing in Ys?

Joreth's voice called him back from his fears: "Evana served out her vestal period and was released. She married a merchant of Suffete class, a man of the Tyri, who are themselves kin to that line of descent. I was her last child and only daughter who lived. Since my grandmother had been a Queen, I too must become a vestal, though that requirement ends with me. My term concluded two years ago, from which you can reckon out that my age now is twenty—not too much more than Dahut's."

"And, and when you became free?" He felt his face grow hot.

Her answer was cooling: "I rejoiced. Poor Dahut, if she is like me in her heart. Aye, in her leisure time she shines brilliant, she is the center of a whirlpool of doings; but 'tis cruel to keep a spirited lass virgin that late. I'd already determined I'd be no household drudge, nor even a fine lady whose husband winks at her lovers. I'd be my own woman, and how else than as a courtesan?"

She paused before adding softly, "Why dissemble, Carsa? I know quite well that I am the desire of men, the envy of my sisters in the life, less for my own sake—albeit I flatter myself I am attractive—than for my likeness to Dahut. Golden Dahut, quicksilver Dahut, who enthralls by her beauty and liveliness, but more, I think, by her strangeness, that slight sea-wind whisper of the Unknown, which she always bears about her."

He remembered the seal, and certain other things. "You . . . understand much, Joreth."

" 'Tis my business to." She leaned close. "What I offer you, Carsa, is a dream. You can keep your eyes open while you pretend to yourself I am Dahut; and I have skilled myself in her ways. But first I must know you as well as she does. Tell me, Carsa."

For a moment he recoiled. How could he thus besmirch

that snow-pure maiden? Then he recollected her glances and motions, the wickedness of her wit. Oh, she was pagan through and through, and in all likelihood she knew about Joreth and was amused or, maybe, triumphant.

"Speak," Joreth breathed in his ear. Her fingers went lightly seeking over him.

—He had not stayed abstinent. That was well-nigh impossible for a foreigner resident in Ys, unless he be a very holy man; many of the city's women actively pursued variety. Three of Suffete rank had seduced him in turn. Corentinus had sighed to hear his confessions but not upbraided or penalized him much. Carsa had learned how to boast without being oafish: of the antique splendors and modern diversity in Burdigala, of his education and travels, of how he with his sling had once helped drive pirates away from his father's ship. The ladies had drawn him out and listened with every sign of fascination. They were knowing as well as sightly, those ladies.

They had nothing of Dahut about them.

—Dazed, he stumbled down the stairs. When could he return? He had at least a year before him. This spring his father had left him off, commissioned to establish an office of the firm now that he was familiar with Ys and had useful connections there. He was also supposed to help propagate the Faith. . . . He would justify the trust, he would work like a horse to enlarge the business, so that out of his share he could afford to visit Joreth often. And, God forgive him, he would keep it from Corentinus. . . .

As he stepped into the ground-floor hall, astonishment smote him. Another man was entering. He recognized that medium-tall, supple figure, that countenance blue-eyed and snubnosed, that hair and youthful beard startling black against the white skin. Both walkers halted and stared.

Tommaltach broke the silence. "Well, well!" he said. His Ysan carried a lilting accent. "Sure, and this is a surprise." He grinned. "Or is it?"

Carsa flushed. "What do you want here?" he demanded.

"The same as you just had, I am thinking. Since I'm settled down in Ys—" The Scotian shrugged. "Jealousy would be foolish. We both are only biding of our time, along with the rest like us."

"Time?"

"Come, boy, Joreth can't have robbed you of your mind." Since people were moving to and fro, Tommaltach stepped close and lowered his voice. "In two years, less a few months, Princess Dahut will be free."

"But who will she wed? Not you or me!"

"Oh, I doubt she'll content herself with any one man, ever. —Hold your anger! Don't be striking me. You've seen her more than I have, you lucky rascal. Will you not join me in hoping we shall both be among those she blesses?"

V

— 1 —

Although it was an offside room in the basilica at Turonum, for confidential conferences, the space where Gratillonius stood seemed chosen to dwarf him. Quite likely that was true. It would ordinarily have held ten or twenty men. Instead, he was alone—how alone—before two. The amanuensis who sat at a table and recorded words spoken did not count. He was a slave, less real than the images on shadowy walls. Those were recent, in fresh plaster covering whatever paganisms had formerly been depicted. The artist had lacked training. Yet the angular, elongated shapes staring out of their big eyes, Christ with His angels and saints, somehow radiated power; they judged and condemned.

Curtly summoned to report, the King of Ys stood before the governor and procurator of Lugdunensis Tertia. They sat in chairs large and ornate enough to be thrones, their togas warm around them, garments whose antiquatedness made him feel the weight of Imperial centuries. He had now been long on his feet. Entering out of mild weather, he had found his tunic and trousers inadequate against the chill here; it was gnawing inward as his knees wearied.

"You remain obdurate?" asked the governor. Titus Scribona Glabrio was a fat man, but underneath jowls and paunch he carried hardness to match that of his gaunt associate. "In light of the Augustus's decree, handed you to read for yourself, that worship of false gods is banned, Their temples and revenues confiscated for the use of the

78

state—you refuse your duty to promote the Faith or even to embrace it?"

Gratillonius choked back a sigh. "With due respect, sir," he answered, "we have discussed this at length today. I repeat, Ys is a sovereign nation. Its law requires that the King preside over the old rites. Your Church has an able minister there; he and his congregation have my protection; more I cannot do, and remain King."

"You can be recalled, prefect, and as of now."

"Sir, I know. You can arrest me. But I ask you again, what then? Ys will be outraged. It will withdraw from the cooperation that I make bold to say has been priceless to Rome. As for the next King, Ys will do what it's done in the past, when it lost one in some irregular way. It'll find a new man to guard the Wood: purchased slave, volunteer tough, outlaw seeking refuge, makes no difference. What does matter is that he'll be the creature of the magnates, because he'll be ignorant and without cause for loyalty to Rome. Whether you let Ys pull back into isolation or you come and lay it waste, you'll have lost the bulwark of Armorica."

Quintus Domitius Bacca, procurator, sent his words gliding serpentine: "How conscientious have you proven, though, Gratillonius? You encourage trade with the barbarians of Hivernia. I have thrice written to you, explaining how the influx of gold is upsetting the Imperial order, inducing people to hold the Emperor's currency in contempt, bypass normal commercial channels, evade taxes, flout regulations, and seek with increasing frequency to flee those stations in life to which God has called them. But you will not cut it off."

"Sir, you have my dispatches," Gratillonius replied. "I've done what I could about smuggling, but I still think the first job of our sea patrols is protection against piracy and aid to mariners in distress. It is not to stop merchant vessels for random searches. Meanwhile, traveling around, I've seen how by and large the people—all the Armorican tribes—how much better off they're coming to be year by year, safer, healthier, decently fed and housed—"

"Silence!" interrupted Glabrio. "We know of your activities throughout the western half of the peninsula, far in excess of any mandate ever given you. What ambitions do you nourish for yourself?"

Gratillonius stiffened. Anger ignited in him, to burn away fatigue. Nonetheless he chose his phrases with care. "Sir, I've explained that, over and over, not just today but through my letters and visits to your predecessor. I can't understand why you insist on seeing me. Well, I did know what you'd ask and came prepared to answer." Apuleius Vero had warned him four years ago, and repeatedly afterward; he had inquired on his own, and pondered what his discoveries meant. "I believe I did that the first hour today. Why have you been dragging me through it again —I've lost count of how many times, how many different ways—with never a chance to rest or a share in the refreshments brought you? Do you hope to wear me down? Sir, you're wasting your time. I was interrogated under torture once, and that was also a waste of time, for the selfsame reason. There simply is nothing more to tell."

Glabrio flushed. "Are you being insolent?"

"No, sir. I am being truthful, as a soldier should. I *am* still a centurion of the Second."

"A-a-ah," murmured Bacca. The least smile played over his lips. "Shrewdly put. You are not altogether the blunt veteran you act. But we knew that already, didn't we?"

Within himself, Gratillonius eased slightly. They were accepting his reminder, these two, that their authority was limited to civil affairs. His position in Ys had always been anomalous, ambiguous, especially after the fall of Maximus who appointed him. It embraced both military and diplomatic functions. Breaking him would require—to a properly cautious official mind—the concurrence of the Duke at least, and quite possibly of higher-ranking men, perhaps Stilicho. Would those personages really think it worth a cost that might prove enormous?

"There is a certain justice in your complaint, too," Bacca went on. "We may have been thoughtless. Governor, shall we dismiss this man for the nonce? I do have other matters to take up with you in private."

Glabrio put on an appearance of considering before he said: "Very well. Gratillonius, you may go. Hold yourself in readiness for further interviewing tomorrow, should I decide that that is necessary. Farewell."

Gratillonius saluted. "Thank you, sir. Farewell." He wheeled and marched out, aware that he had won his case —for the present, at any rate—and could soon start home. He was too tired to rejoice.

When the door had closed behind him, Glabrio turned to Bacca and demanded, "Well, what is this you want to discuss?"

"It requires privacy, I said," replied the procurator, and sent the amanuensis off.

Thereupon he leaned his sharp features close to his superior's and continued: "That fellow did speak truth. I've been investigating virtually from the day you and I took office, and I know. The only reason to call him here was to take his personal measure. It's formidable."

"I agree." Glabrio frowned. "I do not agree that's good."

"Nor do I. What could happen eventually to our careers, or our own selves, if Ys remains independent, with its influence growing for every year that passes? Now that's been largely the work of Gratillonius. I do believe he has no desire to become another Maximus. He has merely made Ys—alien, pagan Ys—indispensable to the security and well-being of this flank of the Empire. If Rome destroys him, she undercuts the whole bastion he has built for her. And yet the activities and the very existence of Ys subvert the Imperium." Bacca laughed. "Forgive mixed metaphors, but his is a Gordian knot indeed."

"Alexander cut the first Gordian knot across."

"Do you think of having Gratillonius done away with? I'd wager many solidi that any such attempt would fail. His escort, the old Roman legionaries and the young Ysan marines, they keep a close eye on their King. Win or lose, an effort to eliminate him would be recognized for what it was. In fact, I'm afraid that even his accidental death hereabouts would be assumed a murder commissioned by us. No, my friend, we'd better take special care to see that Gratillonius returns intact."

Glabrio shifted his broad bottom on the chair. "I know you," he growled. "You have something in mind. Don't shilly-shally the way you like to. I'm hungry."

"Well, then," Bacca said, rather smugly, "in the course of my duties I have agents keeping track of what happens, and I follow up the more interesting clues myself. Lately there has arrived a malcontent from Ys who was quite high in its affairs until Gratillonius got him removed. We've had a couple of talks, he and I. Today I ordered that he come to the basilica and wait for our summons. Shall I call a slave to fetch him?"

—Bitterly and fearlessly, Nagon Demari confronted the Romans and told them: "Of course I want that brotherfucker dead. Of course I've thought about how to do it."

"Remember," said Glabrio, "we mustn't alienate Ys. We must rather bring the city to obedience."

Nagon nodded. "Right." His Latin was atrocious but understandable and improving daily. "Bring it to Christ. Right. I'm taking Christian instruction, sir. But if you don't want to go in and outright conquer Ys—and that would leave a ruin, with my poor benighted longshoremen killed fighting against you—why, you'll have to send your own man to chop Grallon down. Once he's King, he can work with you to change things gradually."

Glabrio stroked his clean-shaven double chin. "We'll have to be crafty about it," he said, "though we can secretly direct his actions. It helps that Gratillonius himself has much strengthened the Kingship."

"The trouble is," Nagon warned, "you get the Kingship by killing Grallon in the Wood, and he's a troll of a fighter. How long's it been since anybody dared challenge him? A dozen years? In spite of the fact he broke the law to spare that man. He wouldn't spare the next; and meanwhile he keeps in practice. Word gets around."

"Furthermore," Bacca said, chiefly to Glabrio, "some adventurer who did succeed in overcoming Gratillonius would not necessarily be the man we want in Ys. What foreknowledge of him would we have, what hold on him? What rewards could we promise for his cooperation, greater than he might find there for himself?"

"Also," the governor fretted, "if we sent the right man, how do we know he'd win?"

"A succession of men," Bacca said. "I've looked into the law of Ys. It's not unlike the ancient rule at Lake Nemi in Italy. Our guest there has been most helpful in explaining. The King is required to meet every challenger, though just one per day. If he's sick or badly hurt, the engagement is postponed till he's well. Now if a contestant appears *every* day, without surcease, hardy and battle-trained men who have no fear of death—day after day after day, while his lesser wounds and his weariness accumulate—he'll be done."

Glabrio grunted. "A pretty notion. Tell me where we'll find this string of undiscourageable warriors."

"I can!" Nagon cried. "I know!"

"Indeed? Well, before you name them, think. People in Ys are not stupid. Present company excepted, they seem on the whole rather attached to King Gratillonius. An influx of trained fighters such as you propose—no, it would much too obviously be at Roman instigation. It would have the same effect as killing him in this city. Or worse, because the victor, our man, would face a constitutional crisis like that which Brutus did after he met Caesar on the ides of March. The consequences are unforeseeable."

"The maneuver need not be at all obvious," Bacca answered calmly. "Nagon has had a brilliant idea."

Standing before them, the Ysan raised a finger. Vengefulness made ice floes of his eyes. "You may lose a few to start with," he admitted. "But before long you will get the kind of victor that we—you—that Rome can use, and safely, too, everything looking perfectly natural. Listen. Only listen a minute."

—At the hostel, Gratillonius went to its stable. There he saddled Favonius, after which he rode the stallion full speed to the Greater Monastery. He wanted to call on Martinus. Doubtless he'd have to wait till the bishop finished whatever devotions were going on, but then, for a while, he could enjoy the company of an honest man.

— 2 —

"**Y**a Am-Ishtar, ya Baalim, ga'a vi khuwa—"

The aurochs bull lifted his head. Sunlight gleamed off his horns and ran hotly down the great shoulders. Secure under his ward, cows and calves went on cropping the grass in the glade.

"Aus-t ur-t-Mut-Resi, am 'm user-t—"

The young summer filled the forest with greenness and

fragrance. Bees buzzed, touching noonday silence no more
than did the whisper out of shadows. The bull blinked,
drooped his neck, settled down to rest.

*"Belisama, Mother of Dreams, bring sleep unto him,
send Your blind son to darken his mind and Your daughter whose feet are the feet of a cat to lead forth his spirit—"*

The bull's head sank. He slept.

Behind the growth of saplings that screened her, Dahut
lowered the hand that had pointed at him as she cast the
spell. "I did it," she breathed, half unbelieving. "The
Power flowed into me, through me, and—and for that
space I was not myself, or I was beyond myself."

Forsquilis nodded. "You have the Gift in full measure,
as far as we have tried you," she answered, equally low-
voiced. "I failed to throw the net of slumber the first time
I sought to after learning how, and likewise the second
time. But you—"

She stopped, because the maiden had darted off, around
the small trees, between a pair of giants, out into the glade
and sunlight. There, gleefully, crowing laughter, Dahut
sprang onto the back of the bull, gripped his horns, rocked
to and fro as if riding him. Her hair flowed wild over the
woods-runner's kirtle that, with breeks and sandals, clothed
her. For a short space the cows regarded her drowsily,
then one took alarm and lumbered in her direction. She
jumped from her seat and scampered back under the
forest roof. The cow returned to her calf.

Forsquilis seized Dahut by the shoulders. Anger made
the Queen's face more pale than before and deepened the
fine lines that had of late appeared around eyes and mouth.
"Are you mad?" she gasped. "You knew not how deeply
he sleeps, nor how long he will. He could have been
roused, and that would have been the end of you, little
fool, tossed, gored, stamped flat."

"But he wasn't," Dahut exulted. "I never feared he
would be. The Gods wouldn't let him."

Forsquilis's fury calmed down to grimness. "Are you
truly that vainglorious? Beware. Erenow They have found
cause to disown mortals They once loved, and bring those
persons to doom." She paused. "My fault, mayhap, my
mistake. I should have made your trial of this art some-

thing less, like putting a sparrow or a vole to rest. But I let you persuade me—"

"Because I am born to the Power, and you know it!"

"Come," Forsquilis said. "Best we start back, if we'd reach the city ere sundown." They had traveled a number of leagues east, beyond the boundary stones, well into Osismiic territory. There were woods in the hinterland of Ys, near the Nymphaeum, but those held too much mystery, too many Presences, for an apprentice witch to risk disturbing.

Side by side, Queen and vestal walked toward the halting place of their escort. Brush was sparse beneath the trees, kept down by grazers such as they had found. Last year's leaves rustled underfoot. Sometimes a bird winged across sun-speckled shade, bound to or from its young in their nest.

"You must learn to be more careful, dear," Forsquilis sighed after a while. "Aye, and more humble. Set beside you, a lynx is cautious and meek."

Dahut flushed. "Not when caged, ardent to be free." She tossed her bright head. "Do you know this is the farthest from home I have ever been, this wretched daytrip? Why would father not take me along to Turonum?"

"Blame him not. He would gladly have done so, but we Nine together told him he must not yield to your wheedling. You'd have been too long agone from your Temple duties. He has shown you Audiarna more than once."

"That dreary pisspot of a town? Nay, not a town; a walled village, naught Roman about it save a few soldiers, and they natives."

"You overstate things. You often do."

"Outside, a whole world waiting! Ah, it shall be otherwise when the new Age begins, I vow."

"Bide your time," Forsquilis counselled. "Master yourself. Today you bestrode an aurochs. When will you ride your own heart on roads wisely chosen? 'Tis apt to run away with you."

"Nay, 'tis I who choose to ride full speed—Hush!" Dahut snatched at Forsquilis's arm and pulled her to a halt. "Look."

Ahead of them was another opening in the forest, where a spring bubbled forth. Here, too, new growth around the edges hid the pair from sight. Horses cropped, spancelled. Half a dozen men sat or sprawled idle. Metal shone upon them. They were legionaries of Gratillonius's, guards of the royal two on this excursion. Reluctantly, they had obeyed the Queen's order to wait while she led the vestal onward afoot.

Mischief sparkled in Dahut's glance. "Listen," she hissed, "what a fine trick 'twould be to spell them to sleep. Then we could dust them with ants from yonder hill."

"Nay!" exclaimed Forsquilis, shocked. She made the girl look straight at her. "Worse than an unpleasant prank on those who deserve well of us. A base use of the Power, a mockery of the Gods Who granted it. Oh, Dahut, remember you are mortal."

The princess shrugged, smiled wryly, and proceeded ahead. As she came into view of the soldiers, the smile turned dazzling, and she answered their relieved greetings with a flurry of blown kisses.

Budic trod near. His fair skin reddened while he asked awkwardly, "Did it go as you wished, whatever you came here to do, my lady?"

"Wondrous well," she caroled. "Now let's be off. Let's get into a road and put spurs to our beasts."

He went on one knee and folded his hands, to provide her a step up into the saddle. It was as if the weight he raised were holy.

— 3 —

Theuderich the Frank held broad acres some miles out of Condate Redonum. He farmed them not as a curial but as he pleased; the Romans had long since decided it was prudent to wink at their own law rather than try to enforce it upon laeti of this race. After a fire consumed his hall, he rebuilt it on a grand scale, for he had waxed wealthy.

Thus he was at first unprepared to give more hospitality to a single traveler than his honor demanded—a place at the lower end of his board and a pallet on the floor for the night. If not a beggar, the man was plainly clad and indifferently mounted. If not a weakling, being short but broad, he was armed with only a Roman infantry sword and looked no more accustomed to its use than he was to riding. When he asked for a private talk with the master, Theuderich guffawed. Thereupon the fellow drew forth a letter of accreditation. Theuderich recognized the seal and did not trouble calling his slave accountant to read him the text. "Come," he said, and ordered ale brought.

He and the stranger, who named himself Nagon Demari, left the smoky dimness of the hall and walked through a drizzle of rain to a lesser building nearby. "The women's bower," Theuderich said. "It will do for us." Large windows covered with oiled cloth made the single room within bright enough for his wife, his lemans, and their serving maids to work at the loom it held or sit on the stools sewing, spinning, chatting. He shooed out such as were present, closed the door behind him, and turned to his guest.

For a short span, the men studied each other. In his mid-thirties, Theuderich was hulkingly powerful. A yellow beard spilled down from a ruddy face wherein the eyes glittered small by the broken nose. His garments were of excellent stuff but his smell was rank. "You're neither German nor Gaul," he grunted. "What, then?"

"A man of Ys, now in the service of Rome like yourself," Nagon answered.

"Ys?" Theuderich's countenance purpled. He lifted his ale horn as if to strike with it.

Nagon barked a laugh. "Easy," he said. "I've no more love for the King of Ys than you do. That's why I've sought you out."

"Um. Well, sit down and tell me. Speak slow. Your Latin's hard to follow."

Nagon forbore to remark on his host's accent. They hunched on opposed stools. Nagon tasted his ale. It was surprisingly good; but so quite often were Frankish fabrics, craftworks, jewelry. "I can understand your grudge against Ys," he began. "Were you not among those who were set on by what turned out to be agents of its King— eleven years ago, I've heard?"

"Yah," Theuderich snarled. "My father Merowech vowed revenge. On his deathbed, he made my brothers and me swear to pursue it. Not that we needed haranguing. We've suffered more than that one hour of dishonor. Those tame Bacaudae are everywhere about these days, in the woods, the hills, the countryside. They turn our serfs against us. Again and again they've disrupted our preparations for sacrifice, till Wotan no longer gets men on His high days, but only horses. When we've gathered war bands to scour them out, they've faded away, to come back and shoot us full of arrows from cover, or cut the throats of our sentries after dark. And Rome will give us no help. None!"

"Rome has her hands full," Nagon said. "She finds the King of Ys . . . troublesome." He leaned forward. "Hark, my lord." His life had taught him when and how to flatter. "I have a plan to broach. I come first to you because, while you may not be the supreme leader of the Franks—since this colony of your free-souled folk scarcely has any such man—and you are not even the eldest living son of your great father: still, everybody tells me you are among the strongest and most respected in Armorica. They say also that you are wise, discreet, well able to keep silence until the time be ripe for action."

Theuderich puffed himself out. "Go on."

"Let me ask you a question. Considering what valiant men the Franks are, and what wrongs the King of Ys has done them, and what wealth and glory are to be had yonder, why has none of you ever gone to challenge him?"

Theuderich glowered. His hand dropped to his dagger. "Dare you think we're afraid?"

"Oh, no, never. Surely you have a sound reason."

"Um. Well." Theuderich drank deep, belched, and scratched in his beard. "Well, the fact is that Grallon hound is a legionary of the old kind, what you can hardly get anywhere any more. I've looked into this myself, I have. Men have told me how he's minced his opponents like garlic cloves, and always wins over his sparring partners. What gain in letting him chew up others? Whoever did take him would likely be too badly hurt to get much use out of being King of Ys. Besides, challengers would pester him to his own death."

"This could be changed," Nagon said softly.

Theuderich sat upright. "How?"

"What if Grallon had to fight a man every day? The first

few might die—gloriously—but soon he would be tired and battered, easy prey."

Theuderich slumped. "That's been thought of. Can't be done. Ys would never let so many armed strangers in at once; and she's got the force to keep them out. Anyhow, we can't make war on Ys. It's a Roman ally, and we're Roman subjects. Stilicho would be quick to punish us. He may not be too fond of Ys either, but he doesn't stand for that sort of disorder, as—we've learned."

"It could be arranged," Nagon purred. "Suppose the Ysan troops were elsewhere. Suppose then the Franks marched in and established themselves. It would not be an act of war, for how could the Ysans put up a fight? It would be without Roman permission, but also without official Roman knowledge. By the time these doings could no longer be ignored, Grallon would be dead. The new King of Ys would find the Imperial authorities quite willing to pardon any offense against their law, in return for a payment that he could easily make out of the city treasury. Thereafter he could go about lifting the burden off you, his people, that Grallon laid on you. He would be a hero. So would those be who died to prepare the way for him. Their fame would be immortal."

As he talked, Theuderich had begun shivering and panting. At the end, the Frank bayed, "How can this *happen?*"

"We will talk about that," Nagon said. "Pray understand, my lord, the new King need not—must not—become a sacrificial animal waiting for slaughter. His aim shall be to change everything there, piece by piece, until at last he can bequeath the city to Rome, the way I've heard the kingdom of Pergamum was. The Romans will quietly guide him. They won't interfere with his pleasures. Think, nine lovely wives, and the fabulous city itself! In the end, Ys will be Christian, but this King we're talking about cannot be, if he's to lead the rites as he must, unless maybe in his old age he chooses baptism. Oh, a Frankish warrior would be perfect. He'd be an omen foreshadowing the future of all Gallia."

Theuderich stared.

— 4 —

One evening before midsummer, a sunset of rare beauty kindled above Ocean. For a timeless time clouds shone with rose and gold and every hue between, against a clear blue that slowly deepened toward purple. The waters breathed calm, giving back to heaven those changeable colors. Whenever it seemed the splendor was about to fade into that night which had already led forth the first eastern stars, fieriness broke free again. Entranced, folk throughout Ys swarmed onto the wall; their murmurs of wonder were as low as the sea's.

Rufinus was one of them. He could have watched from the Polaris, but not as well. On his way, he knocked on the door of Tommaltach, who occupied rooms below his. Together they hastened by the shipyard and up the staircase there. Being important men, they won admission past the guards at the Raven Tower, away from the crowd and onto the stretch where the war engines were. Only a few Suffetes and ladies had done likewise. Those couples or individuals kept well apart, desirous of nothing except the miracle before them. The two comrades recognized Queens Bodilis and Tambilis at some distance, but did not venture greetings.

Finally glory smoldered away forever. People grew conscious of chill in the air and began to descend while they still had light. More and more stars trembled above inland hills. The western clouds had gone smoky.

"Ah, that was a sight of the Beyond, and I thank you for calling me to it," Tommaltach said. "The flames of Mag Mell—though it may be what we have glimpsed is from somewhere greater, from One Who is above the Gods."

Rufinus laughed. "You're too serious for a young lad," he answered. "Come along to my apartment and we'll pour a stoup and be our proper, roisterous selves."

Tommaltach's vision strained into the gathering dusk. "Was Princess Dahut here to see? I do hope so."

As they approached the Raven Tower, several men came from its door. They wore vestments above their clothes. It was not yet too dark to discern the features of Cynan, Verica, Maclavius, a few Ysans—and, in the lead, King Gratillonius, Father of the Mithraic congregation.

Feet halted. Rufinus and Tommaltach touched their brows. "Hail, lord," they said. Gratillonius responded.

Rufinus's teeth flashed in the blackness of his fork beard. "A pity this was a holy day of yours," he remarked. Clearly it was, for ordinarily a believer would just say a prayer wherever he happened to be at nightfall. "While you were underground worshipping the sun, he gave the rest of us the most marvelous spectacle."

" 'Twas Mithras we communed with," Gratillonius reminded him, "and His light shone upon our souls." A certain exaltation lingered in him. "My friend, if you would only listen—"

Rufinus shook his head. Pain edged his tones. "Nay, I'll not pretend what is false . . . before you. Never can I be a communicant of your faith."

"You've told me that erenow, but will not say why. Surely—"

"Never."

Tommaltach quivered. "But I, sir!" burst from him. "I would try my best to understand."

Gratillonius regarded him as closely as the dimness allowed. "Think well," he said. "This is naught to trifle with."

"Nor do I mean to." Tommaltach's voice had lost his usual confident cheer. "What I've been watching—Oh, but 'tis more than that. Since coming to Ys and knowing —you—well, the city, the world beyond, enough to see that I really know nothing—The gods of Ériu are far off, sir, and They seem so small."

"Mock Them not. However—" Gratillonius smiled. He reached forth to clasp the Scotian's arm. "Of course we'll talk, you and I, and if you come to believe in all honesty that Mithras is Lord, why, I myself will lead you into His mysteries," said the father of Dahut.

VI

— 1 —

Rain had left the air humid. As the sun declined, vapors reddened its disc, but fog would not likely roll in to cool Ys before dawn. Gratillonius was almost glad to come off the street into the house of Maldunilis.

Zisa, her daughter and his, admitted him with a perfunctory "Hail." This year the girl had had her Welcoming, but to her that stage of life had brought sullenness, perhaps because it first brought fat and pimples.

"How went your day?" Gratillonius made himself ask.

She grimaced and shrugged. "A day at the Temple. You're late. The servants are trying to keep dinner from getting ruined."

"I'd duties of my own," he snapped. Before he could go on to rebuke her for insolence, Maldunilis entered the atrium. That was just as well. Gratillonius stalked to meet her and join both pairs of hands as was fitting.

The Queen looked closely at him. "Again you have a thunderstorm in your face," she said. "What's gone awry this time?"

He gazed back. Over the years she had added flesh to flesh, though her frame was large enough that as yet she did not appear quite gross. Her features remained good in their heavy fashion and her hair was still a burnished red-brown. It was untidily piled on her head, like the raiment on her body. He had grown used to that. He had also grown acceptant of the fact that her interest in civic affairs, or in most things, was weak; she passively accepted the decisions her Sisters reached.

"No need to trouble you now," he said, as often before. "You'll soon hear."

If only this were Bodilis, Lanarvilis, Vindilis for counsel; Forsquilis, Tambilis for instilling fire; Innilis, even Guilvilis for the peacefulness that nurtures. But tonight was Maldunilis's turn with the King. Well, she had her rights, and she was by no means a bad person, and a man ought to shoulder his burdens without whining about them.

She nodded. "Come," she said, "food waits."

She, or rather her cook, set an excellent table. This evening Gratillonius scarcely noticed what was before him, except for the wine. Of that he took several helpings. Maldunilis chattered for both of them; that too was common in their marriage. "—Then Davona—do you know Davona? She's that blond underpriestess who renewed her vows after being widowed two years ago, but believe me, she's a husband-hunting hussy—Davona claimed the foxglove had lain stored too long and lost its virtue, and that was why that poor gangrel we took into the hospice died, but I know she wants to be the one who goes with the gatherers to bless the herb, because there'll be handsome young marines along—

"Grallon, why did you scowl so?"

He shook his head. "'Tis naught. Go on."

"What else? Oh. Well, later that same day I saw my dressmaker. I do need a new outfit for Midsummer, and the price she named—"

Zisa was silent, systematically feeding. Always she watched her parents. Her eyes were small; they made Gratillonius think of a sow's eyes.

Sometimes he wished he could like, or at least not dislike, this child of his. The rest were pleasant, certain of them more than that. Bodilis's Una, newly fifteen, and Tambilis's Estar, four, almost rivaled Dahut as she was and had been. Of course, they were her close kin. He shied from that remembrance. Vindilis's Augustina was turning a little strange in her vestalhood, doubtless taking after her strong-willed, aloof mother. The same might be said of Forsquilis's Nemeta, but she was a spirited lass and often cheerful. Tambilis's older girl, Semuramat, and

Lanarvilis's Julia were rather solemn, yet never withheld affection from him. Guilvilis's six, ranging from fifteen to three, were very ordinary people who accorded him the same awe, and some of the same love, she did. . . .

Maldunilis finished her dish of comfits. "Are you through, dear? Time for sleep," she said archly.

Gratillonius rose. The wine buzzed faintly in his head, bees in a clover meadow where a youth and his sweetheart had found solitude. "Aye," he answered, "I must be up early."

She giggled. "Indeed you must be up."

He turned his face from Zisa, lest the girl see him flush. Maldunilis had always lacked reticence. He knew what his daughter was thinking—*you are going to futter now*—and would not have cared save that she appeared to gloat over it. Glimpses he had had, looks she cast him, tones and gestures, caused him to suspect she was given to listening at the bedroom door.

Ahriman take that! If what he wanted most was a life free of folk peering, guessing, gossiping, sniggering, proclaiming how much better than he they could do his work, why, then he should long since have slipped away from Ys and become a hermit like Corentinus aforetime. But when his God spoke, Corentinus had had the manhood to obey orders.

Gratillonius accompanied Maldunilis from the triclinium. The wine in his veins helped him ignore everything else. Likewise did the heat that began licking at his loins. Once a Queen of Ys had the King to herself, the Gods entered them both; and Belisama held supremacy over Taranis.

Immediately after the door had closed behind them, Maldunilis flung her mass against Gratillonius. She kissed avidly, mouth wide open, tongue searching. " 'Tis been a weary while," she groaned.

His hands wandered. His mind did also, under less control. For the thousandth time, he puzzled over the ninefold marriage that was his. Did the powers of the Gallicenae spring from their pent-up needs? Yet this bulk that he held could belong to any fishwife. Nor did the others claim much more—Innilis's occasional healing, Forsquilis's occasional visions or minor spells—than some barbarian witch might. Together they had summoned him, overthrown Colconor, wrecked the Scotic fleet, or so they believed; but that was, O Mithras, sixteen years ago, and they were frank in their doubts that they could do anything of the kind ever again. They did not *feel* they could. The Age of Brennilis was dying away.

Gratillonius disengaged from Maldunilis and fumbled at his clothes. Let him find whatever surcease was in her, quickly. Most evenings they blew out the lights before they bedded. That was not so common among Ysans of the upper classes, including his other wives, but this one didn't care and in the dark he could pretend, after a fashion. At this season, though, daylight dawdled. She cast her own garb on the floor. Well, his member responded, and he would pillow his face in the softness between those heavy breasts.

"A moment," she laughed. Matter-of-factly, she slipped the lid off the pot and sat down. Somehow, the gurgling excited him further. No, not all the power of the Nine had left them.

—It was as if lust were a dam, and when it had been broken, care flooded back through him. Lying there in the sweat-dampened sheets, he gagged on a breath.

She stirred beside him. "What's wrong?" she asked.

"Naught, naught," he demurred.

Sometimes she could surprise him. Raising herself to an elbow, she looked down into his eyes and said diffidently, "I know I am a lackwit, but if you want to talk, if that will help, I can keep silence about it."

He sighed. She smiled and stroked his brow, ruffled back his hair. Maybe, if he spoke the matter forth, he really would sleep better.

"No need for that," he told her. "No secret. I'll be setting it before the Council. A message came today from Turonum."

She caressed his head and waited.

"The Romans—" He must gulp and search for words. "The Duke and the civil governor together have sent me a command, me, the prefect of Rome. About a month hence, there'll be military exercises lasting for . . . a while, they say. It's to be jointly with the regular forces of Ys. Our marine corps and such of our naval vessels as are not out are to report at Darioritum Venetorum and place themselves under the Roman general for the duration of the maneuvers."

"What? Has that ever happened erenow?"

"Never. And Armorica faces no threat these days."

Maldunilis frowned into space. "I don't see—What is bad about this?"

"Why, that it is such a new thing, without any clear cause. Oh, the letter speaks of preparing against the future, and cites our offer to train crews for the ships we'll build for Rome. I cannot refuse obedience and appeal to higher authority. As King of sovereign Ys, I must persuade Ys to do as I, the prefect of Rome, am bidden. The timing is skillful, this soon before our Midsummer Council. I'll catch the Suffetes unprepared and ram an agreement though. I must."

"I'll vote however you want, of course. But surely this is naught bad. Won't our men make a grand showing! Will you go too?"

He shook his head beneath her fingers. "Nay. The order is clear on that. I stay home to look after my 'responsibilities'—Imperial interests. What are they planning, those men?"

"Mayhap only what they say they are."

"You wish to believe that. I'd like it myself. Well, I see no choice before me."

"Then stop fretting." Maldunilis lay back down. Her hand roved across his chest and belly, and onward. "Tonight, be simply Grallon the man."

— 2 —

Flowing into the sea about ten road miles from Ys, the River Goana marked the southeastern frontier of the city's hinterland; beyond lay Osismia. Nonetheless, Rome claimed Audiarna, the town on its right bank. The inhabitants were almost entirely Gauls, including the small garrison. It had been directed to report with the Ysan marines at Venetorum. That seemed peculiar, since the whole western tip of the peninsula would then be stripped of troops. However, Ysan naval patrols ought to keep pirates away, and there was nothing to fear from inland, was there? Rather, the exercises would be another step toward rebuilding an effective defense for all Armorica.

The day was bright when the newcomers entered Audiarna. Sunlight flashed off pikeheads, high helmets, cuirasses whose lines and ornamentation called deep-water waves to mind. A breeze blew, making banners snap and plumes ripple brilliant. Though numbering a mere few hundred, the marines of Ys were the most impressive sight the sleepy little city could remember. They tramped through its gate and down its principal street in a unison that was not mechanical but flowed, like the movement of a single many-legged panther. Their officers led them on blooded horses. The pack animals that followed were nearly as mettlesome, the supply wagons graceful, playfully decorated, akin to chariots. No tubas brayed; drums thuttered, pipes shrilled, in rhythms whose alienness was of the tides and the winds.

At their heads blazed beauty, a young woman on a great sorrel stallion. Her hair streamed free, gold and amber. Flamboyant as well as impudent, silver-worked blue tunic and kidskin breeks hugged the curves of her; a red cloak winged from her shoulders; a circlet set with gems glittered around her brow. When she drew rein in the forum, a kind of susurrus went through the people who had gathered to watch.

The native company and its Roman cadre had been waiting. Abruptly their outfits looked shabby and their formation ragged. The chief centurion, himself mounted, lifted an arm in salute. The Ysan leader did likewise before clattering over the pavement to utter greetings. At his side rode the maiden, and it was she who spoke first. Being commissioned by a suzerain state and in charge of the superior force, the Ysan would have command over both as far as Venetorum; that concession had helped reduce unwillingness to go. When the centurion formally proffered a vinestaff, it was the maiden who took it and in turn gave it to her companion.

Thereupon she wheeled her steed, rode back to the front of the marines, and cried while the stallion snorted and stamped beneath her: "Comrades of the road, farewell! Now I must return and you continue onward. Yet in spirit I will fare with you always. The legionaries who came to Ys with my father the King call me their Luck. Let me be yours too, as you travel among foreigners and hold high the honor of Ys."

"Dahut!" roared from the men. "Dahut! Dahut!"

"The Nine Gallicenae will watch and pray and work their spells on your behalf," she vowed. "So will every vestal, myself the foremost. Come home in joy. In the names of Taranis, Lir, and Belisama Queen of Battles, be you our strength!"

Again they cheered.

The centurion frowned. It was too much for the chorepiscopus at Audiarna. Although Dahut had used her own language, most of the onlookers knew enough of it to follow; it was not enormously different from theirs. A few registered indignation or made signs and muttered prayers. But many seemed excited, certain among them even uplifted. These also raised a shout.

The chorepiscopus left his church, from the porch of which he had been watching, and pushed through the crowd around the market square. A heavy man, his gray hair tonsured in the style of Martinus, he strode until he stood before the towering horse and the beautiful rider. He raised his arms and bawled in Latin: "O people of Audiarna, soldiers of Rome, what is this work of Satan? Beware of your souls! This pagan witch is not content to flaunt herself in man's clothing like a harlot, she invokes the demons she worships, here in our very midst, we, the subjects of the Augustus. Cast her from you before she leads you down into the fires of hell!"

The Ysan marines growled. Most of them had understood. Hands clenched on weapons.

Dahut quelled the trouble. She threw back her head and pealed forth laughter. Looking down at the cleric, she replied, also in Latin: "Have no fear, old man. If I lead anybody, it will be to nowhere hot, but the sea that is Ys's. Besides, I am leaving now. Let me suggest first, out of kindness, that you study your grammar. What you did to your conjugations was utter horror. But then, your Jesus wouldn't know the difference, would He?"

Before the Ysans could whoop, and so make the Romans angrier, Dahut called to them: "Again, farewell! Fare ever well!" She spurred Favonius and sped from the forum. Her four-man escort had difficulty keeping up. In moments she was gone. The sound of hoofbeats on stone dwindled away. Men blinked at each other, mute, uncertain, as if they had just awakened from a dream.

— 3 —

"—Then as the fog lifted, taking soundings we found bottom at forty fathoms. Here fish abounded. We saw thick shoals of little fish like sprats, and rushing to eat them before they dispersed were multitudinous cod of twenty or thirty pounds. For three days we fished, cleaning and salting the catch until we bore ample food. Meanwhile, though rarely as yet, we sighted such birds as to make us think land must not be overly far. Our water casks were low and foul, since rain had not come for us to gather in our mainsail as had happened earlier. Therefore we bore on westward."

Bodilis paused in her reading aloud. Gratillonius looked across the table where he and she shared a bench. "Does this still ring true?" he asked.

Maeloch, opposite, nodded his shaggy head. "Aye," he rumbled. " 'Tis pretty much a learned man's words, but ye can hear through them that 'twas a plain fisher captain who told him the story. No mermaids, no magical isles, only a nigh endless waste of sea till at last yon crew came to a shore."

Gratillonius thrilled. It was not that he doubted the men of Saphon's smack Kestrel had had a strange adventure, three generations ago. Throughout the history of Ys, craft had fared helpless beyond the horizon when a freakish storm sprang out of the east. Kestrel was among the few that won back. What kept the tale alive was that the return had been after months, as if from the dead. Gratillonius saw no reason either to question the claim that those men had found land. What he wondered about was how much their description had grown with the telling, year by year, lifetime by lifetime.

When he spoke of it to Bodilis, she said that quite possibly someone had taken down the account in writing, soon after Saphon came home. She offered to search the library. That required patience; scrolls and codices were heaped on shelves in uncounted thousands. Finally, triumphantly, she found the one document. Having perused it himself, Gratillonius wanted an opinion from a master mariner, preferably also a fisher. *Osprey* happened to be in port unloading a haul.

The library was a curious place for such a tale. High windows between pillars admitted sufficient light into the cool dimness to read by. A mosaic floor depicted the owl and aegis of Minerva. If the Goddess Herself was represented on a wall, bookcases that reached to the ceiling had long since hidden Her. A caretaker padded about, dusting. At another table, a man sat reading and a vestal copied something from a tome, probably at the orders of a minor priestess who wanted the information in convenient form. No sound penetrated from the Forum outside. Here was a cavern of mute oracles.

"Go on, my lady, I pray ye," said Maeloch eagerly.

"You may not like what follows," Gratillonius warned.

"Ha? Why not, sir?"

"Because it makes false those wonders that are in the mouths which today tell the story. There is no giant eel, no elven queen in her palace of illusion, no herd of unicorns—naught of the Otherworld at all."

Maeloch grinned. "Why, I'd be surprised if there was. What I've seen of weirdness—and that's more than most—beggars men's brags and boys' daydreams. Ye'd nay ha' bid me hither did the yarn lack *real* wonders."

"Wonders indeed," murmured Bodilis: isles clustered in hordes along the ruggedness of a coast which stretched on and on, immensity behind it, forests of spruce and fir and birch, teeming with elk, bear, beaver, otter, and beasts and birds unknown to Europe, tribespeople broad-faced and black-maned who carried tools of stone. She cleared her throat.

"Hark well," Gratillonius directed Maeloch. "Afterward, think hard. It appears *Kestrel* reached a country huge, rich, and virginal. How much so, we can but guess; yet surely, as you said, the truth will dwarf any imaginings of ours."

The sailor gave him a keen stare. "Ye'd fain outfit an expedition."

"Aye. Two or three ships built especially for the voyage. It seems the way west is difficult but east is much easier, as if Ocean were in truth the world-engirdling river the ancients supposed. Knowing that, we can plan wisely. However, first I need experienced men to tell me if this can likely be done or is a mere fever-dream of mine."

"Ye're nay given to wild notions, King Grallon. Carry on, my lady."

The hope flamed in Gratillonius. Yonder a new land, no, a new world—waiting for Ys, whose seafarers alone had the skill and boldness to reach it—colonies free of hoary hatreds, tyrannies, poverties, menaces, where civilization could be reborn and a palace worthy of elves might arise for Queen Dahut!

"More and more birds did we see," Bodilis read, "and presently driftwood."

A man entered the room and hastened to the table. "Begging your pardon, sir," he muttered in Latin. "Urgent."

Annoyed, Gratillonius twisted about on the bench and recognized his legionary Verica. The two dozen Roman soldiers had stayed in the city when the marines left, to be the core of guardians on its wall and peacekeepers in its streets. Of course, he thought wearily, someone always knew where the King was to be found. "Well?" he rapped.

"Sir, the beacon's lit. Beyond Lost Castle. Nothing's at sea except fishers and a couple of merchantmen. A party worth worrying about must be coming along Redonian Way."

Gratillonius tautened. Few of the signal towers wrecked by barbarians had yet been rebuilt, in these years of peace, but he had worked to have bonfires ready for kindling in a chain along the shoreline. They were intended to warn of pirates. If no hostile fleet was in sight, then an Ysan watcher had been alarmed by what he saw bound overland. Yet apparently no sign burned in Osismiic territory. Such would have been visible from Point Vanis. Which meant the Romans had observed nothing to fear.

Which most likely meant that this was all harmless. And yet—and yet the fighting men of Ys were afar.

Gratillonius rose. "I must go," he said. "You two can continue."

"I'd have trouble listening," Maeloch answered grimly. Anguish crossed Bodilis's countenance. For a moment, her hand clutched Gratillonius's.

Verica at his heels, he went out into the Forum and up Lir Way to Warriors' House by High Gate. The bustle and color around him had gone curiously distant, not quite real. He told himself he was foolish to conjure phantoms, that everything could well be a mistake, or benign; but he was no philosopher. He was a military man who needed to make contingency plans.

The barrack echoed emptily to his footfalls. Only a couple of youths were there, from among those newly recruited as auxiliaries in the absence of the regulars. It took a while to devise instructions for them to carry out or pass on to the others, with the aim of getting all his legionaries together and providing some kind of replacements on the wall. Thereafter they were gone for a maddeningly long spell. He sent Verica to fetch his horse Favonius from the palace, and then in Dragon House had the man help him into his armor. Still he must wait.

One by one, though, they arrived, his Britannic Romans. It struck him sharply how none of them was a young man any longer. Even Budic had furrows in his face, while Adminius the deputy was grizzled, nearly toothless, and gaunt as a twig in winter. Just the same, they snapped to their duties and followed him out the gate with a smartness he doubted the Imperial units now at Venetorum could show.

By that time the strangers were in sight, headed down Redonian Way from its southward bend at the old station on Point Vanis. As Gratillonius led his handful to meet them, he saw a score or so detach themselves and leave the road, slanting southeast across the trails that crisscrossed the heights.

This day was sunny. Wind chased small white clouds off an olive sea full of whitecaps that burst against skerries. Intensely green with summer, grass billowed over the headland, around its boulders and megaliths and shelters;

sheep made flecks in the distance, driven away by frightened herders. The wind skirled. It bore salt odors. Gulls rode it beyond the cliffs, and a hawk immensely above.

Nearing them, Gratillonius estimated the invaders at a hundred and fifty. It would have meant little—so few would not have dared—when Ys had her usual defenders on hand. Nor could he send to Audiarna for help. That fact chilled him with the knowledge that this must be nothing coincidental, nothing peaceful. Those were Franks.

Big men, mostly fair-haired and blue-eyed, they walked in loose formation behind a few mounted leaders. They had not many pack animals either, nor any wagons, which suggested they did not plan on a long campaign. Some wore nose-guarded helmets and chainmail coats, some kettle hats and boiled leather, but all were well-armed— sword, ax, or spear, and at every belt the terrible francisca. Hairy, slouching, stenchful, they were nonetheless a nightmare sight; it was as if the Roman road shuddered beneath their tread.

Gratillonius reined in and lifted an arm. After a moment, a Frank afoot hoisted a peeled white pole. Gratillonius took that for a sign of truce. Commands barked hoarse and the laeti grumbled to a halt. One on horseback clattered forth from their van. Gratillonius went to meet him.

They sat glowering at each other. "I hight Theuderich, son of Merowech," said the Frank in wretched Latin. He was big, coarse, and golden. "I speak for these men of Redonia whom I lead."

"You speak to Gratillonius, King of Ys, prefect of Rome. What are you doing here? Trespass on an ally is a violation of Imperial law."

Theuderich spat laughter. "Complain in Turonum, or Treverorum or Mediolanum or wherever you like," he gibed. He raised his palm. "Don't be scared. We mean no harm. Let us camp for a bit and you won't have any trouble. We're only here to make sure things go right— that justice is done," he added, a wording he had doubtless rehearsed.

The tension in Gratillonius slacked off a little. It often happened thus, when waiting had finally ended and confrontation was upon him. Alertness thrummed. "Explain yourself."

"Well, my lord," said Theuderich smugly, "the King-ship of Ys is for any foreigner who challenges and slays the old King, like you did, hey? We Franks think the time is overpast for one of our nation to take this throne and set matters right. So we've come in a body. That way, can't be any of your sly Ysan treacheries against our challengers— one each day, right, my *lord?* The Gods will decide. We've already asked Them: drawn lots to see who goes first and second and so on. Chramn, son of Clothair, Wotan picked him." He glanced toward the darkling circle of the Wood below them. "I think he's arrived by now."

As if in answer, faint against the wind, from the Sacred Precinct there tolled the sound of the Hammer striking the Shield.

VII

— 1 —

"**R**emember," Gratillonius told Adminius and his other legionaries, "if he wins, he's King. Don't rebel or try to kill him in your turn or do anything but your duty. That is to keep Ys safe and orderly. You're the framework of what watch it's got till the marines and navy men come back. After they do, you can go to Turonum and put yourselves under the garrison commander there."

"We don't want to, sir," the deputy answered. "We got families 'ere, and— And you'll take this swine any'ow, sir, we know you will."

Unspoken behind the faces: But what of the next, or the next, or the next?

Gratillonius had not allowed himself to think about that. He dared not do so yet. Events were moving like a runaway horse; it was less than an hour since the challenge sounded. He turned from the soldiers. In the absence of the marines, theirs was the task of keeping folk who had swarmed to the scene at a good distance down the road. Nobody had brought hounds to pursue a man who fled, but that was unnecessary today. Gratillonius marched at the measured Roman pace to the trees of battle.

The Franks who had accompanied Chramn waited by the rail fence of the meadow across Processional Way. That was just as well. To have them near the Ysans could easily have brought on a riot. As it was, the yells that reached their ears caused them to glare and grip tightly the spearshafts on which some of them leaned. Doubtless they could not make out the words, but threat, defiance, revilements were unmistakable. If a Frankish King brought comrades of his to Ys, they must needs dwell there like an army of occupation. They'd be less disciplined, though; killing, maiming, rape, and robbery would become everyday occurrences.

Chramn stood under the courtyard oak. Red-robed and black-browed, Soren held ready the bowl of water and sprig of mistletoe. From the porch of the Lodge the staff watched, appalled. Behind, wind soughed mightily through the grove.

Chramn leered at Gratillonius. He was young, perhaps twenty, taller by two or three inches and heavier by perhaps fifty pounds of bone and hard muscle. Reddish whiskers fuzzed an incongruously round, apple-cheeked countenance within which the small blue eyes seemed doubly cold. For weapons he bore throwing-ax, dagger, and a longsword scabbarded across his back. A little circular shield was protection incidental to helmet and knee-length hauberk. He would be difficult to get at inside that iron.

Gratillonius halted. Soren must cough before he could ask, "Are you both armed as you desire?" The Frank scowled, and Soren repeated the required questions in Latin. Chramn replied with a noise that must be an affirmative. Gratillonius simply nodded.

"Kneel," Soren directed. The contestants obeyed, side by side as if this were their wedding. Soren dipped the mistletoe in the water and sprinkled them. He chanted a prayer in the Punic tongue Gratillonius had never learned.

The Roman wondered if his enemy was inwardly calling on some heathen God. He formed words in his own mind. *Mithras, also a soldier, into Your hands I give my spirit. Whatever befalls me, help me bear it with courage.* The plea clanked dull, meaningless. Abruptly, of itself: *To You I entrust Ys, my children, my wives, all who are dear to me—because Who else is left to care for them?*

"Go forth," said Soren in Ysan, "and may the will of the God be done." His gaze trailed the pair out of sight.

Chramn joined Gratillonius in passing between the Lodge and a shed, into the grove. Soon huge old boles and densely clustered leafage hid the buildings. The ground was almost unencumbered, except by occasional fallen trees moldering away in moss and fungus. Dead leaves crackled underfoot. Sun-speckled shadow filled the spaces among the oaks, below their arching crowns. For some reason, no squirrel or bird was about, but the wind blustered through branches, making them creak as well as rustle. It smelled of dampness.

At a glade near the center, where grass rippled within a narrow compass, Gratillonius stopped. "Shall we begin?" he said. "Here I killed my two earlier men"—and spared the third; but he had no desire to let this one depart alive.

"Good," replied the Frank. "You think you will kill me too, ha? You will not. You are a dead man."

His voice had taken on a curious, remote quality. Likewise had his expression. The spell of combat was upon him, Gratillonius realized. It did not take the Celtic form, that utter abandon which flung Scoti howling onto the points of their foes. Gratillonius had heard that this could seize Germani too, but Chramn was different. He had not become a Roman machine either. He seemed a sleepwalker, lost in dream, as if already he were among those fallen warriors who feasted and fought in the hall of their Gods, awaiting the last battle at the end of time. Yet he watched and moved with total alertness, all the more dangerous because of having put aside his soul.

Gratillonius drew blade and brought up his shield, ready to shift it as need arose. The two men circled warily, several feet apart. The Frankish ringmail moved supple as snake scales. Chramn's free hand hovered.

It pounced. The francisca leaped from his belt and across the wind. Gratillonius just caught it. He felt the impact through shield, arm, shoulder. The ax stuck in the wood, hampering. Chramn's sword had hissed forth in nearly the same motion as the cast. He bounded forward and swung.

Gratillonius blocked the blow. Chramn tried for a cut lower down, on the leg. Gratillonius fended him off with the big Roman shield while his own short blade worked from around it, probing.

The fighters broke apart. Again they stalked, each in search of an opening. Their looks met; once more Gratillonius felt a strange intimacy. He had given Chramn a slash in the left calf, blood darkened that trouser leg, but it was a flesh wound, the Frank had likely not even noticed.

Chramn charged anew. Shield against shield, he hammered above and sickled below. Several times his edge rang on Gratillonius's helmet or scraped across armor. The Roman could only defend himself, parry, push, interpose, retreat step by step.

The flurry lasted for minutes. Gratillonius felt his heart begin to slam and his breath rasp dry. Sweat drenched his undergarments, reeked in his nostrils. He saw the Frank smile sleepily, well-nigh serenely.

He is a generation younger, Gratillonius knew. He has more strength. He means to attack me like this over and over, till I'm winded and my knees shake and the weight of my hands drags on me. Then I am his.

Gratillonius's glance flickered right and left. He saw what he needed and edged toward it, a tree with lower boughs close to the ground at the rim of the glade.

If he drew well into the grove, the longsword would be hindered, the shortsword not. Chramn knew that. He rushed while his foe was still in the open.

Gratillonius slipped below a branch and went to his left knee. His shield he held slantwise. The limb caused the Frankish metal to strike it awkwardly. He himself had a clear thrust upward from the ground.

His point went under the hem of the byrnie. He guided it with care—time had slowed, he had abundant leisure for precision—and felt it go heavily into a thigh and worked it around to make sure of severing the great blood vessel there. After that he sank it into the belly just above the genitalia.

Chramn pulled free. He lurched back. Gratillonius rose. With his dripping sword, he slashed across the right hand of his opponent, cutting finger tendons. The long blade dropped into the grass. Blood spurted from beneath the hauberk.

"Well," panted Gratillonius, "that's one."

He lowered his heavy arms. Chramn stared and staggered. He would crumple in another half minute or so.

He screeched something and threw himself forward. The shield fell from his left hand, which was still useable. With that hand he grabbed the centurion at the back of

the neck. He was losing his footing now, sinking to earth.
He kept the hold while he crashed his helmeted head
upward, against the chin of his killer.

Blackness erupted.

—Gratillonius gaped at the sky. He looked around, bewildered. A corpse sprawled beside him where he lay.
"He was dead," he mumbled. "He hit me." Blood matted
his beard. "He was dead. He hit me."

He tried to get up and could not, but crawled between
the trees, homing like an animal. Often he collapsed, lay
huddled, stirred and crept a little further.

He came back out into sunlight, from behind the house
that was red. Men gathered around. "He was dead,"
Gratillonius whimpered. "He hit me."

Soren called for the physician. Gratillonius was borne
inside. A moan lifted from the Ysans, a howl from the
Franks. Then Fredegond, son of Merowech, laughed aloud
and crossed the road into the Sacred Precinct. He took the
Hammer and rang the next challenge.

— 2 —

A boat had fetched Tambilis from Vigil on Sena, because at an hour like this all the Gallicenae must be on
hand. They met in the house of Fennalis, for the old
Queen could no longer leave her bed.

Eight standing crowded the small, simply furnished room.
It was hot. Sunlight filled the glass of the west-side window as if with molten brass. Everyone spoke softly; the
loudest sound was the labored breath of Fennalis.

"A messenger from Rivelin at the palace reached me as
I was leaving home to come hither," Bodilis reported. "I
had ordered him to send me immediate word of any
change."

"I should have thought of that!" blurted Guilvilis. Tears
trickled down her cheeks.

"Cease blubbering," said Vindilis. "What news?"

"Gratillonius has fallen into a deep slumber," Bodilis
told them. "Rivelin expects he'll have his wits back when
he awakens."

Lanarvilis nodded. "I looked for that from the first," she said. "A blow to the chin—aye, one that did not dislocate or break his jaw—should not do harm like a cudgel at the back of the skull." Her glance went affectionately down to Fennalis. "True? You were ever good with the wounded."

The dying woman achieved a nod and a whisper: "But he'll—be weak—subject to giddy spells—in need of rest and care—for days."

"He mustn't fight again till he's hale," decided Maldunilis, pleased with her own wisdom.

Vindilis frowned. "There's the question, Sisters. *May* he wait that long?"

"Of course he shall," cried Tambilis. Red and white chased each other across her young face. "Else 'twould be no fight. The Gods do not want that."

"But the Franks do," said Lanarvilis bleakly, "and we're ill prepared to deny them."

"What have they been doing since—." Tambilis could not finish. She had run straight here from the dock.

"Those at the Wood returned to their fellows on Point Vanis, bearing the slain," Lanarvilis answered. "At Soren's protest that we had a rite for him, they jeered. They're camped near the bend of Redonian Way. A band of them went down with a cart to fill jugs at the canal, and our folk could do naught about the defilement of the sacred water but curse them from the battlements. Nor can we keep them from ravaging the hinterland and murdering whomever they catch, if they grow impatient with us."

"What of their dead?" wondered Innilis with a shiver. "Will they burn or bury those—on the forbidden headland? Taranis will smite them for that. Won't he?"

Vindilis compressed her lips before stating, "Grallon held a burial out there long ago. Only today was he stricken down."

"I watched from a Northbridge Gate tower," Forsquilis said. "Nay, I cannot make a Sending by daylight, but a charm did briefly sharpen my sight. The Franks have several coffins with them. Yon corpse lies shut away. Those men who had been at the Wood with him—the chosen against our King, I think—stood around the box. They drew blood from their veins and sprinkled it, then they

crossed swords above and roared what must have been a
vow of revenge."

"Let us send a herald and appeal to their honor," Tambilis
urged.

"Where will he find it?" sneered Vindilis.

"Well, their pride, their boastfulness," said Bodilis. "I
follow your reasoning, dear. Tell them that he who insists
on doing battle with a man not fully recovered is himself
no man at all."

"They might well scoff," Lanarvilis warned. "At best, we
do but gain a short reprieve for . . . him."

"Dare we even seek that—we, the whole of Ys, and we,
the Nine who uphold the law of the Gods?" replied Vindilis.
"Had the King's foeman not been at point of death when
he delivered that blow, he would have finished Grallon
off; and that would have been the will of the Gods, the
Frank the new Incarnation of Taranis. How can Grallon
delay merely on account of being somewhat weakened,
and not violate the law?"

Lanarvilis swallowed hard. "I have talked with Soren,"
she said as if each word were a drop of gall on her tongue.
"He believes this. He says the King must answer the
challenge as soon as he can walk to the scene, or be no
longer King. There are . . . many who'll agree, though
they love Gratillonius and abhor the barbarian."

Innilis covered her eyes. "Another Colconor?" she
moaned. Vindilis laid an arm around her slight shoulders
and drew her close.

The older woman's features had gone rigid. She stared
before her. "We are foredoomed in any case," she said,
flat-voiced. "Give him back his full health, and still Grallon
cannot possibly win every combat before him. He will
grow wearied, and bruised, and— Sisters, what we must
do is take counsel among ourselves as to how we shall bear
what is coming onto us, and how keep Ys alive while we
search for deliverance."

Tambilis wept on her mother's breast. Fennalis sighed
on her pillow. Compassion overrode the suffering in her
countenance.

Forsquilis lifted her arms. Her voice rang: "Hear me.
Not yet are we widowed and enslaved. Each victory of our

King wins *us* another day and night; and who knows what might happen? We can take a hand in shaping our fate."

"Nay," protested Lanarvilis in something like terror, "we may not cast spells against a contender. 'Twould be sacrilege. The Gods—"

"We were not altogether passive about Colconor, toward the end," said Bodilis, rallying.

"But this—"

"Our lord lies injured. Had it been by cause of war or mishap, we would tend him as best we could and heal him by whatever means we command. Shall our care, our duty, be the less because the harm came to him in the Wood?"

"My thought," Forsquilis agreed. "Innilis, you have the Touch, and I—can fetch certain materials that sometimes help. Let us go to the palace. Nature would give him back his strength in a matter of days. We will simply lend nature our aid."

The fear ebbed from Lanarvilis, but trouble remained: "Is that lawful, now?"

"If not, the Gods will decree we fail," Forsquilis said. "Come, Innilis. I know you have the courage."

Mutely, the other left Vindilis and followed the witch out of the room.

— 3 —

The long light set ablaze the gilt eagle atop the dome on the royal house. Farther down, garden wall and the mansions opposite filled the street with shadow, like a first blue wave of incoming night. The crowd gathered outside the main gate waited dumb; rare were the mutters within that silence. Some had stood thus for hours. Most were humble folk, though here and there glowed the cloak of a Suffete or sheened the silk of a well-born lady. Rufinus the Gaul was clad with unwonted somberness. A young Scotian in a kilt stood side by side with a young Roman who had put on a robe for this. They lingered in hope of any word about how their King fared.

"Make way!" called a sudden clear voice. "Way for Dahut his daughter!"

Her vestal gown billowed white around her slimness, so hastily she strode. The hair streaming loose from under a chaplet of laurel seemed almost a part of the deep-yellow rays from across the western sea. In her right hand she carried a twig of mistletoe and a stalk of borage.

People saw her and pressed together to give room as she demanded. A few breathed greetings. Nearly all touched hand to brow. Awe sprang forth on their visages. In several it mingled with adoration.

The four guards at the entrance were legionaries. "Open for me," Dahut said.

"I'm sorry," Cynan replied, "but our orders are to let nobody in."

She bridled. "Who told you that?"

"Rivelin, the physician. He says your father should not be disturbed."

"I countermand it, in the name of the Goddess Who whispered to me while I prayed in Her Temple."

"Let her by," Budic exclaimed. The other two men growled assent. Their years in Ys had taught them that what was lunacy elsewhere could be truth here. Cynan hesitated an instant longer, then turned about and undid the portal himself.

Dahut passed through, up the blossom-lined walk of crushed shell, between the stone boar and bear on the staircase, to the bronze door. She struck fist against the relief of an armored man as if he were an enemy. His breastplate, hollow, rang aloud. A servant swung the door aside. Before he could speak dismay, Dahut had swept past, into the atrium.

A graybeard in a dark robe advanced across the charioteer mosaic to greet her. "Bring me to him," she said.

"He sleeps, my lady," Rivelin demurred anxiously. "His prime need now is for rest. No one should touch him, unless perchance a Queen—"

"Ah, be still, old dodderer. I know where he must be. Abide my return."

Dahut went onward. He started to follow. She spun about, glared, hissed like a cat. Fear took him and he rocked to a halt.

She let herself into the main bedchamber. Drapes made it crepuscular, obscuring the wall's representation of Taranis directing His thunderous, fecundating rain over the earth. Gratillonius lay in a spread-eagled posture, naked beneath a sheet. He had been shaven so his hurt could be examined, washed, bandaged. That would have made him seem years younger, despite the lines plowed into his face, had it not been for a waxy pallor under the tan. Only his breast stirred. He snored heavily, which he scarcely ever had done before.

Dahut stood a while gazing down at him. Her left hand stole forth to take hold of the sheet. She peeled it back and stared a while longer, lips parted over the white teeth.

Thereupon she touched fingertips to him and held them, very lightly, above the heart. With her free hand she stroked the sacred plants across him, brow, eyelids, cheeks, mouth, jaw, throat. Murmuring arcane words, she raised his head and laid the cuttings under it. Stooped over him, she ran both hands along his body, circling motions through the crisp hair on his chest, down the belly to pause at the navel, on until they came together and cupped him at the loins.

"Father, awake," she said low.

Stepping back, she pointed at his head and spoke again, "Awake, awake, awake!" in a voice that sang with assurance.

Gratillonius opened his eyes. He blinked, glanced around, saw her at the bedside, and sat up with a gasp, "Hercules! What is this?"

Dahut leaned close. "Are you well, father?" It was scarcely a question.

"Why, I think—I seem—" He felt of his head. "What happened? That Frank, I did for him but then I remember no more—but—" He noticed that he was exposed and snatched at the sheet. A healthy red suffused his skin.

Dahut laughed. "You killed him, but in his death throes he gave you a blow to the jaw that cast you from your senses. 'Tis the hour of sundown." Her tone grew steely. "You'll have call for your full strength. The Goddess told me, within myself, to come restore you."

"You have the Touch—you, already?" he asked wonderingly.

"I have my destiny."

He stroked his padded, smooth chin, flexed his muscles, abruptly swung feet to floor and stood up, the sheet draped around him. His look encountered hers.

She lifted her head higher. "My destiny is other than a filthy barbarian wallowing on me," she said.

"You are no Queen," he responded slowly.

"Well, I would be—" Dahut caught his arm. All at once she was a young girl pleading. "Oh, father, you can't fall to those horrible men, you mustn't, everything would fall with you! Drive them off! I know you can."

His features set. "Fennalis will soon leave us," he said in an undertone. "If the Sign does come on you, when I also am dead— Nay!" he bellowed.

Military habits revived. "Go out and wait for me to dress myself. We shall most certainly see about this."

Dahut obeyed exultantly. In the atrium she met Forsquilis and Innilis, who had just arrived and forced admittance. "I've made him whole," she said.

Innilis whitened, her eyes grew enormous. "What? Oh, nay, darling, you cannot have, you shouldn't have—"

Sternness came over Forsquilis. "Hush. There *is* a fate in her, whatever it be."

Gratillonius entered in tunic and sandals. He barked a few inquiries about the situation. "Come with me," he said then, and went onward.

Trailing after him, wringing her hands, Innilis wailed, "What do you mean to do?"

"Gather a force and destroy them," he flung back.

Forsquilis caught a breath.

"But you've been *challenged!*" Innilis expostulated in horror.

"If we tarry, we'll lose any chance at surprise, and Mithras knows we need every advantage we can scrape up," Gratillonius said.

"The Gods are with us," Dahut added at her father's side.

Forsquilis bit off a reply.

At the gate, Gratillonius spoke tersely to his soldiers. They laid down a shield for him to stand on. Each took a corner and raised him high, his auburn locks catching the sunset, like a Gallic chieftain of old. The people shouted.

"Hear me," he trumpeted. "Ys, your city, her Nine holy Queens, and you her children shall not fall prey to brigands through any vile trick of theirs. Carry this word for me. Every man of Ys who can fight and who cherishes honor, freedom, and his own household, every such man should meet with me at moonrise, bringing his weapons!"

— 4 —

The rendezvous was the manor of Taenus Himilco, Landholder Councillor, on the fertile northern slope of the heights, somewhat beyond the Wood. Had the Ysans come in a body they would have betrayed themselves to the Franks, whose fires glowed baleful on the headland above the sea cliffs. Instead, they slipped out by ones, twos, threes as the summons found them and they reached decision and made ready. It stretched over hours, for the moon, waning toward the half, did not appear till almost midnight.

Gratillonius could not have made himself sit still in the darkened house. That would have been unwise of him, anyhow. He went to and fro through the gloom outside, welcoming newcomers, talking, getting the men roughly organized and informed, radiating a confidence that was a lie. He knew how forlorn his venture was. It had nothing in its favor save that it was better than waiting to be crushed.

The time finally came. He read it in the stars and heaved his armored mass onto Favonius. The stallion stumbled occasionally, pushing along under trees. Gratillonius heard more horses move likewise at his back, those ridden by such well-to-do men of fighting age as had been inspired or shamed into joining him. The bulk of his army—he had no good idea how large—was ordinary folk, sailors, artisans, laborers, farmers, shepherds, carters, shopkeepers, a few foreigners who chanced to be on hand and willing for a brawl. He heard the soft swearing of his legionaries as they threaded back and forth, trying to keep the crowd in some kind of order.

When he came out on the nearly treeless promontory, vision got clearer. The moon, wan above eastern hills, with stars and Milky Way turned gray the grass, bushes, rocks, and silvered the waters beyond. A breeze whined chill. Glancing behind, he saw his followers straggle from the orchard they had passed through. Pikes and the infrequent ax or mailcoat glimmered amidst shapelessness. He estimated three hundred men. That well outnumbered the Franks, but those were soldiers by trade, properly equipped and strongly encamped. Gratillonius felt sure it was shrewdness rather than fear of ghosts that had made Theuderich ignore Lost Castle. The ruined earthworks and ditch would aid defense, but without a hinterland for support, a band like his could too easily be trapped and starved on the small jut of land.

Still, the Ysans were no lambs either. As they regrouped, Gratillonius spied Maeloch's bulk and heard him rumble, "Usun, take ye your post here; Intil, ye over here—and the twain of ye remember what ye owe your King, ha? —And the rest of ye—so, so, so—crossbowmen and slingers at the middle—" The mariners of Ys were trained to fight pirates. Many landsmen had also once prepared against bandits, and had maybe not let their skills decay too much during the past peaceful years. Rufinus had taken charge of several woodcutters and charcoal burners; word had gone a ways out into the hinterland. His former Bacaudae would have been infinitely welcome, but—

Adminius approached the centurion. "We're 'bout's ready as we'll ever be, I think, sir," the deputy said.

"Very well," Gratillonius answered. "Let me repeat, the quieter we move, the likelier it is that most of us will be there to revel around the Fire Fountain tomorrow evening."

"We will, sir, we will! Us boys'll go around shushing the civilians. God be with yer, sir."

Gratillonius clucked to his mount and started off. His chosen route was not to Redonian Way and then due west, but slantwise across the promontory. Though slower and more difficult, it offered a hope of not being noticed too early.

As always when battle drew nigh, doubts and qualms fell away from him. He was committed to action now, and rode at peace with himself. If he lost, if he fell in the fray—well, during the hours at Taenus's home, he had spoken with Maeloch, and the Ferrier had promised passage to Britannia for Dahut and the other princesses, from himself or any surviving son of his. The Gallicenae—the Gallicenae would abide and endure, because they must, but this they had done before, until finally they witched forth a stranger to free them.

Behind his right shoulder, summer's dawnlight crept after the moon.

Time and a mile ebbed away. The Frankish camp grew plainer in sight. Horses and mules were secured at intervals around it. Cookfires were banked, each a small red constellation surrounded by men rolled into their cloaks. A watchfire danced yellow and smoky at the center, and the spearheads of sentries threw back the eastern glow.

At any instant, someone would see the Ysans and cry alarm. Gratillonius swung sword on high. "Charge! Kill them!"

With a yell that went on and on, a growl beneath it, like wind and wave on a shingle beach, the Ysans plunged forward. Gratillonius checked his horse, which neighed and reared. He must hold back, try to oversee what happened, lead his Roman cadre wherever it was most needed, as he had done on that day when Eppillus fell, Eppillus who slept just beyond the bivouac of this new enemy.

The young Scotian Tommaltach dashed past, battle-crazy, shouting and brandishing his blade, wild to be first in the onslaught. Gratillonius could only briefly hope the boy would live. The chances of the young Burdigalan Carsa looked better; he was bound for a slight rise of ground, a commanding position, where he could use the sling that whipped to and fro in his hand.

The men of Ys swept by Gratillonius. They were not altogether a rabble. Shipmate ran beside shipmate, neighbor beside neighbor.

The Franks boiled out of slumber, grabbed their weapons, sprang to form a square. The Ysans should have thrust straight in to prevent it. But they lacked officers. They surfed against the array as it was taking shape, and those in front got in the way of those that followed, and men recoiled and milled about.

They did well even so. Few Franks were in armor. Ax, knife, sword, pike, club, missile worked havoc. Defenders fell and for a moment it was as if the attackers would break the square. Then Theuderich winded a horn in signal, and his men charged in what became a wedge. Slaughter churned. The Ysans withdrew in confusion, leaving their dead and badly wounded to be trampled underfoot or lie ululating. The Franks closed up afresh, howled threats and taunts, moved around as one to collect what mail they had left behind.

Tommaltach went among his comrades like wildfire, blade and war cry aloft. Maeloch spat on his hands and beckoned his followers to pull back together. Rufinus got his to take stance nearby. Crossbow bolts and arrows began to sigh into lightening heaven, seeking prey. More wicked were the slingstones of sailors, herdsmen, and Carsa, splintering temples or knocking out eyes, from every quarter around the foe.

Yet Gratillonius saw from his distance that whatever slight military order his men had had was fast going out of them. They clamored and prowled like a pack of dogs. At best, a few groups retained cohesion, and those could merely keep their places and shoot the last missiles remaining to them. The legionaries at Gratillonius's back cursed aloud.

Theuderich understood equally well. His horn sounded anew. The Franks moved forward and began hewing. Ysans fell, stumbled off, scattered. Gratillonius saw the barbarians bound his way. He was the goal. With him and his veterans down, the Franks could kill at their leisure until their opponents fled. And if he retreated, Ysan resolution would break at once.

He jumped to earth, cast the reins of Favonius over the muzzle, unshipped his shield. "We'll meet them halfway and cut them apart," he said, knowing they would not unless a miracle occurred. They knew it too, but closed ranks and marched with their centurion.

Behind them, the sun cleared the inland hills. It flared off Frankish iron.

Mithras, also a soldier—

What can I promise You for Your aid, not to me but to my Ys, now in this hour without mercy? he thought in an odd, detached fashion. He was not bargaining, but explaining. —Mithras, God of the Light that holds off the Dark of Ahriman, Your chosen sacrifice is a pure heart, and this I do not have; but in token and to Your honor I vow a bull, white and perfect, that in the slaying of him I may tell the world how You at the sunrise of time made it come alive, and that You abide still, Mithras, also a soldier.

What radiance burst forth? The sun should dazzle the Franks, not the Romans.

Gigantic under the sudden blue, the figure of a man strode in advance of the legionaries, on the seaward flank so that they could see he was beautiful and smiling. He was armored like them, in his right hand a shortsword whereon it seemed that flames flickered, in his left grip a shield whereon stood the Cross of Light, and it too blazed; but on his head was a Phrygian cap, which fluttered in the morning wind like a flag.

"Taranis, Taranis!" Gratillonius thought he heard dimly from the strewn Ysans. He knew otherwise, and yet he did not know, he was lost in the vision, all he could do was lead his men onward against the enemy. What it said for them that they held firm and got to work!

The vision was gone. The Franks were shattered. Bawling in terror, they broke ranks, ran, stood their ground when cornered and died piecemeal as the Ysans came over them. Someone—not Theuderich, who lay with his brothers gaping fallen-jawed at the sky while the gulls and scaldcrows circled low—someone winded a horn again and again. In some chaotic, valiant fashion he drew his surviving comrades together, into formation, homeward bound on Redonian Way.

After disposing of the hostile wounded, the Ysans gleefully pursued. They did not seek another clash, but were content to harass from the sides, with arrow and slingstone. Few Franks got as far as the Osismian border. There they could only save themselves by dispersing, in threes or twos or alone, into the woods, and thus straggle back to their kinsmen and the widows outside Redonum.

VIII

— 1 —

In the Council chamber of the basilica, before his ranked soldiers beneath the eidolons of the Three, Cratillonius stood on the dais, robed, the Key out on his breast in plain sight above the emblem of the Wheel, Adminius holding the Hammer near his right hand; and he said to the Suffetes:

"I did not call this meeting in order that we chop law, as some of you have been seeking to do. My position is simple. Let me state it.

"We attacked the Franks because they were invaders, come in violation of the Oath that Brennilis and Caesar, Ys and Rome, swore these four and a half centuries agone. Barbarians, they befouled the water that flows from the Nymphaeum, blocked traffic on our main highway, and would surely soon have been wreaking worse. True sons of Ys rallied behind their King to cast them out, and succeeded, with fewer casualties than would have been reasonably awaited.

"Aye, it seems the challenger I should have met in the Wood fell in that battle, to a hand unknown. What of that? He fell on his own misdeeds. Had he survived and come back like an honest man, of course I would have fought him myself. If any living Frank wishes vengeance, let him arrive by himself and strike the Shield; he shall have the full protection of our law until the combat.

"The people cheer. Though it has cost them losses and wounds, they know what they freed themselves from. Will

121

you, my lords, tell them they should have submitted? I warn you against that.

"On the face of it, ours was a desperate venture. Nonetheless it was victorious, and overwhelmingly." (Surely many believe this.) "That shows the Gods of Ys fought with us, and are well pleased. You have heard how most who were there saw a shining vision—I did myself—a sight that dismayed the enemy so that his line broke before us. I, a plain soldier, albeit the high priest of Taranis, I venture not to say more about this. Bethink you, though.

"Enough talk. We should put quibbles aside and get on with coping with the very real troubles and dangers ahead of us."

" 'Quibbles,' you call them?" cried Hannon Baltisi, Lir Captain. "If you'd led the attack *after* doing your second combat in the Wood, aye—but you flouted the sacred law. Dare you tell us the Gods smile on your plea of military necessity? They are more strict than that, Grallon. Their patience is great, but sorely have you tried it."

Lanarvilis, who spoke today for the eight Queens that could be present, rose to respond. "We Gallicenae have debated this, and prayed for insight," she said quietly. "It appears to us that our King chose what, in his mortal judgment, was the lesser evil. Oh, far the lesser evil. So must men of good will often do. Had the Gods been angered, They could have let him suffer defeat and death on Point Vanis. Aye, They could have made it that the man who slew him was his challenger. Instead, he stands here a conqueror.

"There shall be a festival of thanksgiving as soon as possible, as great as Ys has ever seen. There shall be rites of purification and a hecatomb. Then surely will the Gods forgive whatever sins Their Ys was forced to commit for Their sake as well as her own.

"Thus declares the Temple of Belisama."

"Lir is not that easily appeased," Hannon said.

"The Speaker for Taranis supports the King and the Nine," declared Soren Cartagi.

"And I too, for one," added Bomatin Kusuri, Mariner Councillor.

"And I," joined in Osrach Taniti, Fisher Councillor,

"and I make bold to say we twain have some knowledge of Lir's ways."

Once Hannon might have argued further, but old age was overtaking him. "So be it," he mumbled, and sank back. A murmur of assent ran around the benches.

"We do have more perils," reminded Adruval Tyri, Sea Lord. "How could yon Franks have come in, exactly when our forces are elsewhere, save by Roman connivance? What will the Romans try next?" His look was not unfriendly, but it was straight, at the prefect.

Gratillonius sighed. "As yet I know little or nothing about that," he told them all. "I'll be searching out whatever I can." He refrained from mentioning how helpful he hoped Corentinus, through Martinus, could be in that. "Belike some officials overreached themselves, and higher authority will hold them to account for it. Meanwhile, naught else should threaten us in the near future, and our marines and ships are due back soon. What I need from this Council is its agreement that I—that we are on the right road."

He got it. The result could scarcely have been otherwise, especially given the temper of the common folk. This meeting had been a formality, although a necessary one.

Following the benediction he must give—how leadenly it always sounded in his ears!—the Councillors went off to their various businesses with scant further talk. As Gratillonius passed the seats of his Queens, Forsquilis left their group and took his arm. "What?" he asked, surprised.

"Come to my house," she said low.

"But the day is yet young, I've much to do, and—Tambilis—?"

"Her courses came upon her yesterday, earlier than usual. She will be the one who resumes the Vigil tomorrow, also out of turn. For we took this as still another portent, we Sisters, when we met ere coming here today."

His immediate feeling was pleasure. He knew it for unworthy, but events had kept him abstinent for several days and nights now, and this was the most passionate of his wives. Forsquilis recognized as much. A faint flush crossed the severely chiseled countenance. It drained away at once, her cool reserve in public took her over, and he realized that they had chosen her for cause, whatever it might be. "We must talk, you and I," she said.

There had been no opportunity before. He got back from pursuit of the Franks, day before yesterday, in time to make speeches of thanks, sincere to the men, mechanical to the Gods; and kindle the Fire Fountain at dusk before addressing the wildly celebratory crowd; and, finally alone, give Mithras what devotion he was able. Then sleep rammed him. The following day went to a whirl of work, such as the situation demanded. The Gallicenae had been fully engaged too, conducting services, helping the hurt, comforting mourners.

Forsquilis was not the most learned, wise, or devout among the Nine; but her soul dwelt nearest the Otherworld and sometimes, it was whispered, crossed that frontier. A chill crawled down Gratillonius's backbone. "Very well," he said.

When they emerged on the basilica steps, hurrahs surfed over them. Though Ys was picking up its daily life again, people still thronged the Forum, waiting for a sight of the victor, their rescuer. Gratillonius warmed.

A lean, long-legged figure broke from them and bounded toward him. A legionary made to wave the intruder off. "Let him come," the King ordered.

Rufinus made salutation to him and the Queen. The Gaul wore a sleeveless tunic, for swaddling covered a gash in his left forearm that had required stitches. He moved as lightly as ever, and the green eyes danced with all the wonted mischief. "You said yesterday you'd urgent work for me, lord," he reminded, "but the telling would need privacy. I took this chance."

"Aye. Good," replied Gratillonius. "My lady, would you abide here a moment with the guard?" She nodded slowly. He could see how she tightened beneath the blue gown.

He led Rufinus back upstairs and into a corner of the portico. "I want you to find me a bull, white and perfect," he said in Latin. "Do it discreetly. Bring him to a hiding place nearby—you'll know one, my fox—on the eighteenth day before the September calends, and notify me. Pay whatever it costs. I'll reimburse you."

The sharp, scarred visage grew wary. "Well, that should give time enough. But why just then?"

"That's my affair," said Gratillonius roughly.

"Forgive me, sir." Rufinus steadied his gaze. "I meddle,

but a man often has to if he's to serve his master faithfully. The following day is sacred each month to Mithras. I know that much. You plan a thank-offering."

Why did I think I could fool him? wondered Gratillonius. "I pledged it when the Franks were about to break us. You saw what next happened, that sunrise."

"I saw something very strange," Rufinus murmured, "but Ys is a den of strangeness." He frowned, tugged his fork beard, said abruptly: "You'd never get an ungelded bull down into that crypt of yours."

"I know. Regardless of the Christian slanders, blood sacrifices to Mithras are rare and solemn. We—we believers will make ours on the battlefield."

"No, please, I beg you. That'd enrage too many worshippers of the Three."

"I've thought about this too. A man of Mithras does not sneak around. But we need not be offensively conspicuous. By the time our act becomes known through the city, it will have happened, it'll be in the past. I rely on you to help see to that. Afterward I'll defend it against any accusation, and I'll win."

"You will that . . . among men. The Gods—"

"What, are there Gods that you fear?"

Rufinus shrugged. "I'll do what you want, of course."

Affection welled up in Gratillonius. He leaned the Hammer against a column and clasped the Gaul by the shoulders. "I knew you would. You're as true as any legionary of mine. And you've never done a service higher than this. Why won't you enroll with the Lord of Light? You deserve to."

Sudden, astonishing tears stood in the feline eyes. "That would be a betrayal of you."

"What? I don't understand."

"I'd better go." Rufinus slipped free and hurried down the stairs to lose himself in the crowd.

Gratillonius rejoined Forsquilis. "You're troubled," she said.

" 'Tis not a matter for women," he rasped. At once he fretted about whether he had given away too much. However, she kept silence, and her face was unreadable.

At her house he dismissed the soldiers and changed his robe for a tunic. This was a warm, cloudless noontide. He stored garments in the homes of all the Nine. Tucking the Key underneath as he was wont, he felt it hard and heavy upon his breastbone. Ordinarily, after these many years, he didn't notice.

He found that she too had donned light, plain garb, a linen gown. It lay pleasingly across curves that somehow blent well with her panther ranginess. Her feet were bare on the reed matting she had over her floors. To him that suggested she did not want the bother of unlacing sandals. Desire throbbed. "Well," he said as merrily as he could, "I suppose your cook has something in preparation, but first—?"

"First we talk." She led him to her secretorium. Window drapes dimmed it. That gave an eerie half-life to the objects round about, archaic female figurine from Tyre, symbol-engraved bones, flint thunderstones, cat's-skull lamp, ancient scrolls. . . . They sat opposite each other. Her eyes, gray by full light, seemed huge and filled with darkness.

"What was that apparition during the battle?" she asked softly.

"Why, why, who knows?" he stammered, startled. Recovering balance: "Such visions have come often erenow. Homer tells how the Gods appeared to heroes who fought under the walls of Troy. The old Romans saw Castor and Pollux riding before them at Lake Regillus. Constantinus claimed the Cross that is Christ's stood once in the sky, and in that sign he went on to make himself supreme. We too, when we met the Scoti in the first year of my Kingship, we'd have slain them to the last man, save that a huge and horrible crone seemed to be there. I thought I saw her myself. You remember. Was it a God, a demon, a delirium? Who knows?"

"You evade my question," she said, unrelenting. "Who, or what, was this?"

"I've heard Ysans say it was Taranis. The Christians among my legionaries speak of an angel. Who knows?"

"You, though. You called on your Mithras, did you not?"

He mustered defiance. "Aye. As was my right. And I am free to believe He answered."

"The attributes of that Being—from what I can discover—."

Her calm dissolved. She trembled. "Let it b-be Anybody else Who was there, Anybody."

"What?" He leaned forward to take her hands. They were cold. "How can you say that? When Mithras Himself came to save Ys—"

"Like an outlaw to the last farm where dogs are not at his heels," she gasped. "Oh, Grallon, this is what I have to tell you, that the omens are evil, evil. The Gods of Ys have endured so much. Put down your pride!"

Rage swelled in him. "I ask only that They take heed of my honor, as Mithras does." Her distress checked his mood. "But what are those omens, my dear? Your Sisters looked unafraid enough this day."

Forsquilis gulped. "I did not tell them, nor can I tell you, for 'tis naught so clear as a star falling above the necropolis or a calf born with two heads or even a sortilege or a face in the smoke. Nay, dreams, voices half-heard in the wind and the waters, a chill that gripped me when I sought to pray—I could only tell the Queens that the Gods are troubled, and this of course they knew already. I did not say to them how it *feels*."

She cast herself from her seat, onto his lap, and clung, her face burrowed against his shoulder. "Oh, Grallon, Grallon, be careful before Them! We must not lose you!"

He held her close, stroked her and murmured to her, aware the while that what she wanted was below his reach; but he need not say it in so many words, need he? Let him comfort her as best he might, and afterward stand guard again over her and Dahut and Ys, in the quietly spoken name of Mithras. Her embrace turned into wild, lip-slashing kisses, with clawings to get rid of garments, until they were on the floor together.

— 2 —

Torches in the avenue and lanterns up the street, night become a sunrise glow about their eager feet, lit the way for golden youth bound forth to celebrate, and Dahut was awaiting them within her father's gate.

Plangency of harp and flute, the heartbeat of a drum,

pulsed in Ys to welcome those whom she had bidden come
dance away all darknesses, that morning sun might see
how brightly Dahut's dower shone—her father's victory.
Golden flashed the eagle wings and bronze the open door,
chariots careered within the burnished palace floor, tall
the sentry columns reared through incense-dreamy air,
and lamplight turned to living gold in Dahut's loosened
hair.

Silken gowns and purple edges rippled, flowed, and
swirled, silver gleamed and amber smoldered where the
dancers whirled. Music laughed and laughter sang around
their skipping feet, and Dahut went before them all, the
fleetest of the fleet. Fair the well-born maidens were and
handsome were the men treading out the merry measure,
forth and back again. Close embrace or stolen kiss could
cast a sweet surprise; but Dahut was the star that shone
before the young men's eyes. Kel Cartagi, Soren's grand-
son, touched her hand and waist. Then the dance be-
reaved him of her with its lilting haste. On she swayed to
Barak Tyri, on to many more. So Dahut left a swathe of
joy and woe across the floor.

When the music paused a while and gave the fevered
guest time to cool or drink or chat or flirt or simply rest,
Carsa strove to keep a Roman impassivity while Dahut in a
ring of other men made jubilee. Tommaltach the Scotian
boldly shouldered through to her, cowing with a wolfish
grin whomever would demur, ready with such words as
run when bardic harpstrings thrum; then Dahut gave him
half a glance, and he was stricken dumb. Legionaries
duty-freed who hastened at her call, honor guard for her
their Luck, stood ranked against the wall, armed and
brightly armored from the war that they had won, and
Budic's gaze trailed Dahut as the new moon trails the sun.

Soon the music woke again, the dance began afresh.
Red and gold and purple twined, unrestful rainbow mesh,
till the western stars grew pale and silver streaked the
east, when Dahut bade the youth of Ys come follow her to
feast.

Afterward she led them out to breathe the sunrise air.
Light caressed her slenderness and blazed within her hair.
Up onto the city wall she took her company, and Dahut by
the Raven Tower looked across her sea.

— 3 —

The moon was still down when Gratillonius and his followers went out Northbridge Gate, but starlight sufficed. Redonian Way glimmered ashen and resounded hollowly under their tread. After they passed the bend and turned east, though, murk grew before them. Clouds piled huge over the hills, womb-black save where lightning kicked. Ever strengthening, wind skirled cold as it drove them and the sound of thunder westward.

Muton Rosmertai, Suffete of Ys and Lion of Mithras, shivered. "Yon's no natural storm, bound this way this hour," he said. They were going by Lost Castle. He made a warding gesture at the ruins. A wave-burst on the cliffs below bawled answer.

"We fare in the service of the God," Gratillonius rebuked him.

"Other Gods are angry."

"There is always war among Them," Cynan said. "We are soldiers."

"I am not afraid—not daunted," Muton insisted. By the vague, quivery light they saw him puff himself up. He had been a zealous convert, advancing rapidly in the Mysteries because of good works and quick mastery of the lore. However, he was otherwise a dealer in spices, who had never crossed the water or fought a battle. "I only wondered if we are altogether wise, if the cause may be better served by heeding the warnings of Those who likewise are entitled to honor."

"A soldier questions not his orders," said Verica, whom Gratillonius had made his Runner of the Sun. "He carries them out."

"And saves his grumbling for the commissariat," Cynan laughed.

Gratillonius felt uneasy at the talk. Cynan's fellow Persian, Maclavius, delivered the Father from having to command silence and let men brood: "What say we sing? A good route song shortens the miles. *Fratres, Milites*, eh?"

That was in Latin, as most Mithraic hymns were throughout the Western Empire. One by one they took it up, the men of the four high ranks and the half dozen Soldiers, Occults, and Ravens behind them.

"Brothers, soldiers of the Army, now the marching has begun.

And aloft before our ranks there go the Eagles of the Sun—"

The deep cadences laid hold on hearts. Soon it mattered less how the sky above was darkening and the wind had started to sting faces with flung raindrops.

It was not overly far to the meeting place Rufinus had described. Where a trail from inland met the pavement stood a shepherd's shelter, usually deserted at night. Another four lower initiates waited there, under captaincy of the Osismiic Lion Ronach. They had the two mule carts ready which Gratillonius wanted. One was full of articles brought inconspiciously out of the city the previous day, the other carried an abundance of firewood. From the shelter, Rufinus led the bull he had purchased in Osismia. With him was the new member of the congregation, Tommaltach the Scotian, as yet only a Raven but picked to come along on this mission because he could best cope with the beast if it got dangerous.

It was indeed a magnificent animal, Gratillonius discerned, heavily muscled, mightily horned, snow-pure of hue. "Well done," he said, taking the chain to the nosering from Rufinus. "See me at the palace about noon and I'll repay your outlay."

Snag teeth flickered in the fork beard. "May that include what I spent on wine? I'd have to guess."

"Whatever you claim, I'll pay. You'd never cheat me, Rufinus."

"I japed, I japed." Sudden pain was in the voice. It turned matter-of-fact: "Niveus here is gentle for a bull, but watch out if a horse gallops by in sight. He'll want to charge. He tries to go inspect every cow he sees, too, I suppose in hopes she's hot. Tommaltach knows him by now. Goodnight." He withdrew so swiftly that it was as though he had melted into the wind.

"We'll scarcely meet either of those troubles the rest of this walk," Gratillonius said. Anything to lighten the mood. He tugged carefully. "Let's go, fellow."

Their progress grew slow. The weather outpaced them. Stars vanished. Lightning leaped, first behind, later overhead, blue-white savagery—no help against the dark. Thunder-wheels boomed down unseen heaven. Wind droned and whined. Raindrops came thicker. Somebody got a couple of lanterns lit, which bobbed cheerless and barely showed the way. The bull snorted, tossed his head, occasionally pulled on the chain. Tommaltach went at his side, spear in right hand, left hand stroking the creature, scratching it behind the horns, while he crooned a Gaelic herdsmen's melody.

"You do have a gift for this," said Gratillonius after a long time wherein nobody spoke. "I've heard about your skill, how you've sported on farms. Will you secure the sacrifice?"

"I'm too lowly, I think," Tommaltach replied.

Gratillonius shook his head. "Nay. This will be the Mystery of Creation, when all men are one." Maybe so. It seemed plausible. The books and memories he had ransacked said hardly anything about Tauroctony in the flesh; the rite was too seldom performed. He had actually discovered more about the Tarubolium of Cybele, but it was a disgusting thing, fit for a cult in which men had often gelded themselves.

His band was to redeem a sacred promise in clean and manly wise. Surely Mithras would also want it done sensibly.

" 'Tis honored I am, Father," Tommaltach said.

"You may find you've won the riskiest part," Gratillonius warned.

"Sure, and that helps make me the handfast man of my King."

Gratillonius fled from the worshipfulness in that soft accent, into talk about how best the matter could be carried out. From days on the family farm he well remembered the ways of slaughtering large animals. But it would not be right to stun this bull first with a sledge hammer. He should be fully alive when he died for the God and the people.

Worse, the Hammer was Taranis's, whose high priest the King of Ys was. . . . Lightning ignited the whole sky. Thunder struck brutal blows.

The procession came out on Point Vanis and reapproached the bend of Redonian Way. A sickle moon should have gleamed at their backs and the last stars ahead of them as whiteness entered the east. Instead, night raved. Ys was invisible, save in livid blinks which made the sea ramping under its wall shine like enemy weapons. Gratillonius would only be able to guess at the moment of sunrise.

He lifted his glance. *Mithras shall have His honor*, he told Them.

At the grave of Eppillus he stopped. "Here will we make the offering," he said. A part of the fight against the Franks had spread this far, and in any event, no spot on the headland could be more hallowed. "But the feast— Ronach, you know. Start the fire."

The Osismian saluted and led the woodcart onward, to a dip near the brink that gave some slight lee. Gratillonius stood by with his fellow officers, holding his cloak tightly to preserve what dignity he might, while Ravens, Occults, and Soldiers groped about, unloading the second cart. Doubtless curses got muttered, strewn seaward by the blast. Much of the freight was furniture and ritual objects, to be carried after Ronach, but vestments and sacred implements were there as well.

Gratillonius needed scant change of garb. For this ceremony, unlike those in the crypt, he, the Father, already wore tunic of white wool, sandals, and sword, like Mithras at the first Slaying. He simply doffed his cloak and donned a Phrygian cap. Fleetingly, he thought of taking off the Key. But no, in an obscure fashion he felt that that would be a betrayal. He left it against his breastbone.

The Runner of the Sun, the Persians, and the Lions had more elaborate outfits, which required help. The fumbling seemed to go on for hours. Tommaltach found it ever harder to keep the bull soothed.

Fire glimmered and flapped. Ronach returned. Was the world ever so faintly less black? Sometime about now, somewhere beyond the stormclouds, the Companion of Mithras rose in immortal glory. "Gather, gather," Gratillonius called into the wind. "We shall begin." A flurry of rain struck his face, half blinding him.

The three lower ranks drew away and turned their backs on the Mysteries they must not witness until they had been elevated—apart from Tommaltach, and his attention was on the restless bull. Eyes rolled white, horns made motions of goring, hoofs pawed turf, breath gusted with a sound like waves breaking across reefs below.

Lanterns stood dim under the headstone of Eppillus, which Gratillonius made his altar. The prayers and enactments were stripped-down, simple, because men heard the full rainstorm striding closer, and hailstones skittered ahead of it.

Gratillonius went toward the bull. He drew his sword. "Mithras, God of the Morning—" Wind ripped the words away.

Tommaltach did what he had said he could do. Catswift, he seized the great horns and twisted. The bull bellowed. He went down. Earth boomed. Tommaltach sprang back and snatched for his spear, ready to thrust.

The bull rolled off his side, onto belly and knees. Gratillonius pounced. His left hand seized the nose-ring and hauled. The huge head followed, with a roar of agony and rage. Gratillonius struck home, just in front of the right shoulder. The impact was thick. Blood spouted over him.

He got clear before a horn could catch him in the beast's death struggle. Panting, he stood and watched. There were more prayers to say, but not till the bull lay quiet; sooner would be indecent, like gloating.

Lightning smote near Lost Castle, a bolt many-fingered, as if it sought. Thunder drowned trumpetings that turned to sobs, gurgles, finally silence. Hail whitened the headland. Rain came in a wind-harried torrent.

Gratillonius consecrated the sacrifice. He caught blood from it in a chalice, drank, shared with Verica, on behalf of all. The liquid was sticky, hot, and salt. He cut slabs of meat, which his underlings carried off to roast. Much more remained than this tiny gathering could eat. The carcass must be dismembered and burned before the worshippers left. The Ravens would come back later and get rid of the calcined bones.

Unless the storm quenched the fire. His concelebrants trudged after Gratillonius. Those who stayed to tend the fire had stoked it high. Flames rumbled and streamed from a white-hot core. Rain struck, steamed, hissed away. The sacred meal could be cooked at least partly. Father, Runner of the Sun, Persians, Lions could lie drenched on the benches and be served by their slogging Soldiers, Occults, and Ravens, bleakly chewing and gulping in laud of Mithras.

And yet, and yet, they did! When they had finished, Gratillonius rose to give benediction. Suddenly, uncontrollably, he threw his head back and laughed into the sky, at the Gods of Ys.

— 4 —

"He refuses to call a Council for dealing with the matter," Vindilis related. "He claims 'twould be needlessly divisive when—he claims—no desecration occurred. If we must bring it up, he says, we can do so at equinox."

"Shall we?" asked Innilis timidly. Held out on Sena these past three days by the storm and heavy seas that were slow to die down afterward, she had only returned to Ys this morning. Vindilis had kept herself informed, and sought the rosy house as soon as possible. She had wanted to be the one to break the news. Even so, it would strike hard at her beloved.

"Ha!" The tall woman prowled the conference room as if its trim of blue and gold, floral murals, fragile objects of beauty were a cage. Her haggard countenance kept turning to the window, full of cloudy noontide. "A month hence? Well does he know how futile that would be, after such a time. Whatever indignation most of the Suffetes now feel will have damped out into indifference. Already, my listeners tell me, already the common folk are with Grallon. Most say, when they trouble—or dare—to talk about his deed in the taverns or shops or streets—most say he must be right. For is he not their wonderful King, on whose reign fortune has always smiled?"

Innilis, seated on the couch, looked down at the fingers that writhed in her lap. "Could it be true?" she whispered. "Why should the Gods, our Gods be jealous that he sacrifices to his?"

"A blood sacrifice on Lir's clifftops, beneath Taranis's heaven? Nay, my darling, you're too loath to condemn."

"What do . . . our Sisters think?"

Vindilis sighed. "Bodilis, Tambilis, Guilvilis in her half-wit fashion, of course they defend him. Maldunilis is passive as ever, weakly frightened, hopeful this thing will go away. We're keeping word of it from poor Fennalis. Lanarvilis was as shocked as myself, but soon decided political necessity requires smoothing the scandal over. She's trying to mollify Soren Cartagi."

"Soren?"

"Oh, he was wild with fury. He feels this was a treachery against him, after he'd sided with Grallon in Council about the attack on the Franks. Lanarvilis undertook to soothe him enough that he'll at least continue working with the King on matters of public concern, as erenow. 'Tis better than Grallon deserves. I could almost wish those two, Lanarvilis and Soren, would finally share the bed they've longed for all these years."

Innilis gasped.

Vindilis smiled starkly. "Fear not. They never will. There's been too much sacrilege done. *He'll* thrust himself into her—Grallon—as he will the rest of us. Unless we deny ourselves to him. I've done that." A yelp of laughter. "He was polite. Accepted instantly. Aye, relieved." Vindilis halted before the other woman and peered downward at her. "You, though," she murmured, "could punish him thus."

"Oh, nay, I, I'm such a little bag of bones—"

"Beautiful bones, beneath exquisite flesh," Vindilis breathed.

Innilis paled, reddened, paled. Her eyes fled to and fro, never lifting. "He likes me. He's gentle, and, and sometimes—Nay, I beg you, make me not hurt him. . . . What of Forsquilis?"

"She was shaken, took omens, would not tell us what they were but said—if Lir and Taranis strove that dawn to stop the deed, then Mithras prevailed over Them. For her part, she'd stand by her King, whatever may befall him. And off she went, defiantly, arrogantly, to the palace where he was; and nobody saw them again till morning."

Innilis shuddered. "Could she . . . have spoken sooth?" she whispered.

"It may be. It may be. Taranis and Lir—But Belisama bides Her time. I think She will not wait long."

Seeing terror, Vindilis sat down, laid an arm around the waist of Innilis, drew her close. "Be brave, sweetling," she said low. "She Whom we serve will not strike at us, surely, for his wrongdoings. We must stay together, we Sisters, share our solace, strength, love."

Her free hand caressed the small breasts, then traveled upward to loosen the knot of the silken cord that fastened Innilis's gown at the neck. Her lips fluttered over a cheek, toward the mouth.

"Nay, please," Innilis asked, "not at once. I'm too— horrified—I cannot—"

"I understand," Vindilis answered quietly. "Nor do I myself want more than your nearness. I only long to have you by me, hold you in my arms, and you hold me. Will you give me that hour of peacefulness?" Abruptly she seemed frail, vulnerable, old.

— 5 —

Dahut arrived at the house of Fennalis while the moon was rising over the eastern hills, ruddy and enormous. As yet its rays streamed unseen, for the sky was still blue, Ocean still agleam with sunset; tower heights flared brilliant, though beneath them dusk had begun to steal like a mist through the crooked streets of Lowtown. Bodilis opened the door for her. An instant the two stood silent, regarding each other. The vestal had not paused to change from her white dress of Temple duty. That, and tresses high-piled, caused her to shine amidst shadows, a lighted candle. The woman was plainly clad, in garb that carried a smell of sweat, her own hair disarrayed. She slumped with weariness.

"Welcome at last," she said tonelessly. "I hoped you could come straightaway when I'd sent for you."

Dahut spread her palms. "I'm sorry. I might have asked leave, but I was to take part in evensong and . . . this is no time to slight the Goddess, is it? Now when She may be wrathful, and Her moon has reached the full."

"Mayhap. Yet I cannot believe She'd want Her Fennalis to suffer lengthened pain."

"I *am* sorry!" Dahut exclaimed, on the least note of impatience. "I thought Innilis—"

"Oh, Innilis had been here, and failed. You were the final hope. I should have told Malthi to tell you that, but I was tired, I forgot." Bodilis stood aside and beckoned. "Come."

Dahut entered the atrium. It was turning crepuscular. "You, you do realize I know not if I can do aught either?" she said. "When a Queen, a healer Queen, cannot. There was just that moment with my father. Of course I pray the Goddess lend me power to help. Fennalis was always kind to me."

"To everybody." Bodilis led the way toward the bed-chamber.

Dahut plucked at her sleeve and asked, "Are none of our simples of any avail?"

Bodilis shook her head, "Nay. Formerly, the juice of the poppy; but she can no longer keep anything down. Hemp smoke gives some ease still, but only when the pangs are not too sharp."

"I knew not. I should have come to see her oftener."

"That would have gladdened her. She loves you. But the young are ever wont to shun the dying."

Dahut lowered her voice. "Death is the single remedy left, isn't it?"

"Aye." Bodilis stopped. She gripped Dahut's arm hard. "I've even thought of giving it to her myself. The books tell that hemlock is gentle. But I was afraid. Belisama calls Her Gallicenae to Her when *She* wills. Pray, though, pray for an ending."

"I will." Dahut's eyes were moon-huge in the gloom.

A seven-branched candleholder illuminated the room. The air was close and full of murk; it stank so badly that the maiden almost gagged. Lately changed, the bedding was wet again, sweat, urine, foul matter that dribbled out despite Fennallis not having eaten for days. Hair lay thin and lank over the blotchy face. The skin of the jowls sagged away from a nose that had finally become prominent. She breathed in uneven gusts. Now and then she made a mewing sound. It was impossible to say whether she recognized when Dahut bent above.

The virgin looked off to the image in a niche beyond the foot of the bed. It showed Belisama the Crone, though not hideous as offtimes; this aged lady smiled serene and lifted a hand in blessing. Dahut gestured and murmured. Bodilis reverently raised her arms.

It was yarrow that Dahut stroked Fennalis with and laid beneath the head of. The princess could not altogether hide repugnance while she bared the swollen body and passed fingers over; her words stumbled.

Nonetheless, as she ministered, Fennalis grew quiet, closed her eyes, and slowly smiled. Dahut straightened. "I believe you have done it," Bodilis whispered in awe. "Yours is the Power of the Touch. What other potencies do you bear within?"

Triumph rang softly: "I'm glad. The Goddess chose me."

A water jug, washbasin, soap, and towel were in the room. Dahut cleansed her hands fastidiously. "Sleep well," she said to Fennalis, but did not kiss her before leaving.

Bodilis accompanied Dahut to the door. "Please come back tomorrow early," the Queen requested.

"Certes. It will be a free day for me."

"Where are you staying?"

"At Maldunilis's. Did you not know?" In the past year, Dahut had taken to occupying the home of whoever had Vigil. Her clothes and other possessions she stored at the palace, for servants to bring upon demand. Just the same, she talked ever oftener about getting a place of her own.

"I'd forgotten, as tired as I am." The Gallicenae had been caring for their Sister by turns. However, for several days now a fever had confined Lanarvilis and Guilvilis. It was not grave; word was that they would be back afoot tomorrow; meanwhile, double duty fell on the rest. Bodilis had assumed the entire nursing, since she could postpone a number of her usual tasks, such as directing the library or advising on the esthetics of public works.

Dahut hugged her. "May you soon be relieved."

"May Fennalis. Goodnight, dear."

When the door had closed on the girl and the moon-brightened twilight, Bodilis leaned against it a while, eyes nestled into the crook of her arm. "Semuramat—Tambilis," she muttered, "I hope *you* are having pleasure this even-tide." Straightening: "Nay, that was self-pity." She laughed at herself for thus talking to herself and returned to the bedroom. "Malthi," she called, "we need you again."

Reluctantly, the serving-woman came to assist in washing Fennalis, changing the bedding, carrying off the soiled stuff. The patient had become able to help a bit, rolling over as needed, drowsily, without showing pain. "I think you can go sleep," said Bodilis at the end of the task.

"You, my lady?" inquired the maid.

"I'll keep watch for a span." Bodilis dossed in an adjoining chamber, the door between left ajar. "I've thoughts to think ere I can await the blind God."

She settled herself in a chair and reached for one of the books she kept on a side table. She had spoken truth. There were certain disturbing questions to consider, after what had just happened. But first she would seek easement. Epictetus lay three centuries dust; it did not matter; his implacable calm spoke still.

"All things serve and obey the laws of the universe: the earth, the sea, the sun, the stars, and the plants and animals of the earth. Our body likewise obeys the same, in being sick and well, young and old, and passing through the other changes decreed. It is therefore reasonable that what depends on ourselves, that is, our own understanding, should not be the only rebel. For the universe is powerful and superior, and consults the best for us by governing us in conjunction with the whole. And further, opposition, besides that it is unreasonable, and produces nothing except a vain struggle, throws us into pain and sorrows."

"Bodilis."

Though she barely heard, a part of her had stayed alert. She put the book aside and went to the bed. Fennalis smiled up at her.

"How fare you?" Bodilis asked.

"I feel at peace," Fennalis whispered.

"Oh, wonderful. Dahut wrought that."

"I have a dream-memory of her, but all was so confused then. Now the world is clear. Clear as the sacred pool—" Words faded away.

"Can I bring you aught? Water, milk, soup, bread?"

Fennalis feebly shook her head. "Thank you, nay." She lay mustering strength until she could say: "I would like—do you remember the story about . . . the girl, the bird, and the menhirs? My mother used to tell me it when I was little. . . ."

Bodilis nodded. "A Venetic tale, no? Do you care to hear it again?"

"That would . . . be pleasant—"

Bodilis brought her chair to the bedside and settled back down. "Well," she began, "once long ago there was a girl-child who lived near the Place of the Old Ones, where the cromlechs stand tall and the dolmens brood low and the menhirs are marshalled in their hundreds, rows of them reaching on and on and on. This was so long ago that the great bay there was dry land. Forest grew thick upon it. That was a lonely place to live, loneliest of all for her, because she was the sole child of her father, whose wife was dead, and he a charcoal burner whose hut stood quite by itself in the woods. The girl kept house for him as best she was able. For playmates she had only the breezes, the daisies, the sunflecks that flit on the forest floor when wind stirs branches, and the butterflies that dance with them. She often wished for friends, and longed to go to the Place of the Old Ones. Her father had never let her. When she asked, he said it was haunted. But she dreamed of elvenfolk, unearthly beautiful, who came forth by moonlight and danced, still more gracefully than butterflies, among the solemn stones.

"Now one day when her father was off to his work, the girl took a jar to the spring that bubbled some ways from their hut. She had not gone but three steps times three when she heard a peeping sound. She looked, and there was a nestling bird on the ground, a tiny sad scrawny thing that had fallen out. Soon it would die miserably, unless a fox or a badger found it first. The girl felt sorry for it. She picked it up. Looking about, she saw the nest high overhead—"

Bodilis stopped, for Fennalis had closed her eyes and was breathing evenly. "Are you awake yet?" Bodilis asked low. No answer came. After a minute or two, Bodilis was sure the woman had fallen asleep.

Weariness dragged at her. She yawned, blinked, decided she too might find some oblivion. From the holder she took a candle to light her way.

—She woke. Moonlight streamed steeply through a window to make a pool on the floor. The candle guttered low. Hours must have passed, more than she had intended.

Sighing, she rose and shuffled in to see how her patient was.

When she got there, Fennalis opened eyes. As Bodilis watched, the pupils dilated. Sweat broke forth. Breath rattled shallow.

An instant, Bodilis stood motionless. "Were you waiting for me?" she murmured. She sat down on the edge of the bed, leaned over to embrace Fennalis. Sometimes she prayed, sometimes she crooned, while the death struggle ebbed out.

Finally she could stand up, close the eyes, bind the jaw, kiss the brow. Thereafter she groped to the window and stood long staring into the white inexorable moonlight.

— 6 —

Sleep had altogether evaded Dahut. At last she wandered forth.

She stood in Lost Castle, Cargalwen, at the outer verge. Behind her hulked mounds that were crumbled houses, ridges that were fallen walls. Darkness lay thick in between, but hoarfrost on grass and stones glimmered along the tops. Beneath her the cliff dropped nearly sheer. Surf boomed and snarled, an incoming tide. Light from the westering moon sheened across black surges, exploded white where waves burst over rocks. In that direction it dimmed stars, but above the hills they were many, Auriga, Gemini, ever-virgin Pleiades, bloody-eyed Bull. A wind wandered, bearing the first bite of autumn. Dahut's garments fluttered. She never noticed that, nor the chill. She had bided thus for a time outside of time.

A flame passed through her, above the cleft of her breasts. She cried out. Then: "A-a-ah. Now, now."

With shaky fingers, she unlaced the bosom of her dress and pulled the cloth aside. By straining her neck backward, she could see what had appeared. Under the moon, the crescent showed not red but black.

She swung about, raised her arms, shouted into the moon: "Belisama, I am ready! Gods, all Gods, I thank You! I am Yours, Belisama, You are mine, we are One!"

The wind strewed her call across the sea.

She stripped the clothes from herself. Naked, yelling aloud, she danced beneath the stars, before the Gods of Ys.

IX

— 1 —

"O-o-oh," Tambilis moaned. "Oh, beloved, beloved, beloved!" By the first faint dawnlight Gratillonius saw her face contorted beneath him, nostrils flared, mouth stretched wide, yet ablaze with beauty.

He never quite lost awareness of Forsquilis's caresses, they were in the whole of the tempest, but it was Tambilis whose hips plunged to meet his, whose breasts and flanks his free hand explored, until he roared aloud and over-leaped the world with her.

Afterward they lay side by side, she dazedly smiling from a cloud of unbound hair. Her body glimmered dim against the darkness that still filled most of the chamber. His heartbeat slugged down toward its wonted rhythm.

Forsquilis raised herself to an elbow on his left side. Her locks flowed to make a new darkness and fragrance for him as she lowered her head and gave him a kiss. It went on, her tongue flickering and teasing, before she said from deep in her throat: "Me next."

"Have mercy," he chuckled. "Give me a rest."

"You'll need less than you think," Forsquilis promised, "but take your ease a while, do."

She crouched over him. Hands, lips, erected nipples roved. He lay back and savored what she did. Not for a long time had he brought more than a single Queen to the Red Lodge. Indeed, the last few months he had stood his Watches alone, save for men with whom he did business or practiced fighting, as troublous a year as this had been.

Now, though, he had his victories. Of course a difficult stretch was ahead; but he felt confident of coping. Let him celebrate. Let him, also, affirm to Ys that King and Gallicenae were not estranged. Vindilis alone—but he suspected she had largely been glad of an excuse to terminate a relationship they both regarded as mere duty. If anything, she ought in due course to feel more amicable toward him than erstwhile. The fears that Lanarvilis and Innilis nursed would dwindle away when nothing terrible happened. As for the rest of the Nine—

Forsquilis straddled his thighs and rubbed his organ against her soft fur. By the slowly strengthening light he saw her look at him through slitted eyes and her tongue play over her teeth. Eagerness quickened in him. He reached to fondle her. Tambilis, having gotten back some control over her own joints, rolled onto her belly and sprawled across the great bed, watching with interest. There was no jealousy among the Sisters.

Astonishingly soon, even for a King of Ys, Gratillonius hardened. Forsquilis growled, raised herself, moved forward and down again, slipped him in. She undulated. Presently she galloped. Tambilis slid over to lie across him, give him herself to hold close while he thrust upward. Forsquilis's hands sought her too.

In the end they rested happily entangled and let the sun come nearer heaven. He wondered if his sweat smelled as sweet to them as theirs to him. The chill of its drying was pleasant, like washing in a woodland spring. Well, he should soon be free again to range the woods, far into Osismia, riding, hunting, or simply enjoying their peace. The peace for which poor Corentinus yearned. How Corentinus would regard the scene here! Wicked, damned Ys. Gratillonius smiled a little sadly. He had grown fond of the old fellow. And grateful to him for counsel and help over the years. A strong man, Corentinus, and wise, and in touch with Powers of his own; but this he would never allow himself to understand. . . .

"When shall we start anew?" asked Tambilis from Gratillonius's right shoulder.

"Hold on!" he laughed. "At least let's break our fast."

Forsquilis took her head off his left shoulder. "Aye," she said, "we may start getting visitors, insistent dignitaries, early from the city. 'Twould disadvantage us did our stomachs rumble at them."

They sought the adjacent, tiled room. Its sunken bath had been filled but not yet heated. They frolicked about in the bracing cold like children. Having toweled each other dry, they dressed and went out into the hall. Servants were already astir, hushed until they saw that the master had awakened. The carvings on the pillars seemed sullenly alive in the gloom, which hid the banners hung overhead.

"We will eat shortly," Gratillonius told the steward. To the Queens: "Abide a span, my dears." That was needless. They had their devotions to pay, he his.

He went outside. Dew shimmered on the flags of the Sacred Precinct, leaves of the Challenge Oak, brazen Shield. A few birds twittered in the Wood. He walked forth onto Processional Way, where he had an unobstructed view of the hills. Streamers of mist smoked across the meadow beyond. The sky was unutterably clear. Between its headlands, Ys gleamed, somehow not quite real—too lovely?

Gratillonius faced east. The sun broke blindingly into sight. He raised his arms. "Hail, Mithras Unconquered, Saviour, Warrior, Lord—"

Praying, he began through the silence to hear footfalls draw near, light, a single person's, likely a woman's. Abruptly they broke into a run, pattering, flying. Did she seek the King to ask justice for some outrage? She must wait till he was done here. He ought not think about her while he honored his God.

"Father! Oh, father!"

She seized his right arm and dragged it down. Dumfounded, he turned. Dahut cast herself against him. Embracing him around the neck, she kissed him full on the mouth.

He lurched. "What, what?"

She stepped back to shiver and skip before him. Her gown was dew-drenched, earth-stained, her tresses swirled tangled, her cheeks were flushed and radiance was in her eyes. "Father, father," she caroled, "I am she! I could wait no longer, you had to know it from me, father, beloved!"

For a moment he could not feel the horror. It was like being sworded through the guts. A man would stare, uncomprehending. He would need a few heartbeats' worth of blood loss before he knew.

"Behold!" Dahut took wide-legged stance and tugged at her dress under the throat. The lacing was not fastened. The cloth parted. For the first time he saw her breasts bared, firm, rosy-tipped, a delicate tracery of blue in the whiteness. They were just as he remembered her mother's breasts. The same red crescent smoldered between them.

Whatever was on his countenance sobered Dahut a trifle. She closed the garment and said, carefully if shakily, "Oh, 'tis sorrow that Fennalis is gone, but not sorrow either, she suffered so and now she is free. The Gods have chosen. Blessed be Their names."

Again joy overwhelmed her. She snatched both his hands. " 'Tis *you* will be my King, you, you! How I have dreamed, and hoped, and prayed—I need not lose you. Ys need not. Nay, together we'll make the new Age!"

The ice congealed within him, or the molten metal, it did not matter which. "Dahut," he heard himself say, word by dull word, "daughter of Dahilis, I love you. But as any father loves his child. This thing cannot be."

She gripped his hand harder. "I know your fear," she answered fiercely. "I've been awake all night, and—and earlier I've thought about it, oh, how often. You recall what happened to Wulfgar. But you're no ignorant Saxon. You know better than to cringe before a, a superstition. The Gods chose you too, you, father, King, husband, lover."

Was she Dahilis reborn? Dahilis had been almost this same age. No, he must win time for himself. "Go," he said. "Into the house. Two of your—two Gallicenae are there. Is it not seemliest you declare it first to them? There are rites and— Meet me later this morning, you Sisters, and we'll talk of what's to be done."

He pulled free of her and shoved her toward the Sacred Precinct. She seemed bewildered at his action. Before she could recover he was striding off, as fast as might be without running, to Ys. Abandoning the Wood before the three days and nights of full moon were up was mortal sin, unless urgency arose. He must assemble the legionaries at once, and any other men he could trust.

— 2 —

The barge that carried Maldunilis back from Sena had not brought Innilis to replace her. Instead, the Nine foregathered at the Temple of Belisama. "Aye, the Nine," said Vindilis grimly.

Summoned, Gratillonius arrived about noon. He came alone, onto the Goddess's own ground, but in red robe with the Wheel emblazoned on his breast and the Key hanging out of sight. A hush fell wherever his big form passed along the streets. None dared address him. Rumors buzzed through Ys like wasps from a nest kicked open. He hailed no one.

Elven Gardens lay deserted under the sun. The blossoms, hedges, topiaries, intricate winding paths where sculptures sprang forth, were outrageously beautiful. The towers of Ys gleamed athwart the horns of land, the sea reached calm and blue save where it creamed over skerries or among the rocks around the distant island. Hardly a sound arose other than his tread on the shell and gravel.

He climbed the steps to the building that was like the Parthenon though subtly alien to it. Between the bronze doors he passed, into the foyer adorned with mosaics of the Mother's gifts to earth. Underpriestesses and vestals waited to greet the King. Their motions were stiff and those that must speak did so in near-whispers. Fear looked out of their pale faces.

Gratillonius followed the corridors along the side, around the sanctum to the meeting chamber at the rear. Gray-green light from its windows brought forth the reliefs in stone that covered the four walls: Belisama guided Taranis back from the dead to make His peace with Lir; amidst bees and airborne seeds, She presided over the act of generation; She stood triune, Maiden, Matron, and Crone; she rode the night wind on the Wild Hunt, leading the ghosts of women who had died in childbed. Almost as phantom-like seemed the blue robes and high white headdresses of the Nine who sat benched before the dais.

The door closed behind him. He mounted the platform.

No word was spoken. He let his gaze seek left to right. Maldunilis, fat and frightened. Guilvilis, onto whose homely visage a smile timorously ventured. Tambilis, taut with woe. Bodilis, hollow-eyed, slumped in exhaustion. Lanarvilis, poised aquiver. *Dahut.* Vindilis, stiff, glowering. Innilis, huddled close beside her, striving not to shudder. Forsquilis, who had been aflame this dawn, a million years ago, gone altogether enigmatic.

Dahut could scarcely sit still. It was as if she were about to leap up and speed to him. Her fists clenched and unclenched. He saw her robe swell, wrinkle, swell to her breathing.

Six of those women had lain in his arms, again and again and again, from the first year of his Kingship; one since the end of that year; one, in shared pain, eleven years ago, then for the past eight years in joy. They had walked at his side, talked gravely or merrily, dealt food and wine and worship with him, quarreled and reconciled and worked with him for the guidance of Ys and the raising of the children they had given him. Now, because of the last and loveliest, they had become strangers.

"Greeting," he said finally.

"Oh, greeting!" piped from Guilvilis. Lanarvilis frowned and made a hushing gesture.

She would force Gratillonius to speak first. So be it. He braced himself. His back ached between the shoulderblades. That was no way for a soldier, tightening up, but this was no battle such as he had ever fought before. His mouth felt dry. He had, though, marshalled some words beforehand, as he had marshalled his fighting men—Christians, Mithraists—who stood by at the palace. Let him deploy them.

"We've a heavy matter on hand," he said. His voice sounded harsh in his ears. "I do not weep for Fennalis, nor suppose you will. She was a good soul who lay too long in torment. We can be glad she is released, and hope she is rewarded. Many people will miss her, and remember how she served them."—in her cheerful, bustling, often awkward, always loving way.

Vindilis's countenance showed scorn. He could well-nigh hear the gibe: Are you quite done with your noble sentiments?

"Because I respect you, I'll come straight to the point," he told her and her Sisters. "Your Gods have seen fit to lay the Sign upon my daughter Dahut. They surely know—as you do who've known me this long—that I cannot and will not wed her. My own God forbids. It is not a thing on which I may yield or compromise. If we all understand this at the outset, we can go on to understand what your Gods intend. You yourselves have found portents of a new Age coming to birth in Ys. This must be its first cry. Let us heed, and take counsel together."

Dahut snatched for air. Tears brimmed her lapis lazuli eyes. "Nay, father, you cannot be so cruel!" Her anguish was a saw cutting him across. He held himself firm between the sawhorses.

Lanarvilis caught the girl's hand. "Calm, darling, calm," the Queen murmured. To Gratillonius, coldly: "Aye, we foreknew what you would say, and have already taken counsel. Now hear us.

"What the Gods ordain for Ys, we dare not seek to foresee. Yet the purpose of this that has happened is clear. It is to chasten you, traitor King, and bring you back to the ancient Law.

"In your first year you broke it, you sinned against each of the Three. You refused the crown of Taranis. You buried a corpse on Lir's headland. You held a rite of your woman-hating God in water sacred to Belisama. Patient were They—though little you ken of what the Gallicenae underwent to win Their pardon for you.

"Your behavior could have been due to rashness, or ignorance; you were young and a foreigner. Likewise, one might overlook your contumacies throughout the years that followed. There were necessities upon you, Rome, the barbarians, even the requirements of that God you would not put from you.

"But thrice again have you sinned, Gratillonius. Against Taranis—aye, 'twas years ago, but you denied Him His sacrifice when you spared your Rufinus—Taranis, Whose own blood was shed that earth might live. The chastisements that came upon you, you shrugged off."

"I should think Taranis wants manliness in men," Gratillonius interrupted. "If we had a dispute, 'tis been composed."

Vindilis took the word: "The Gods do not forget. But They kept Their patience. Lately you defiled Lir's grounds with your bullslaying, in the teeth of His storm. Still the Gods withheld Their wrath. Now, at last, They require your obedience. This maiden They chose for the newest queen of Ys—and belike the brightest, most powerful, since Brennilis herself. Dare you defy Belisama too?"

"I seek no trouble with Gods or men," he protested.

"You'll have it abundant with men also," Lanarvilis warned. "The city will tear you asunder."

Gratillonius hunched his shoulders, deepened his voice: "I think not. I *am* the King, civil, martial, and sacral." Quickly, he straightened where he stood and mildened his tone. "My dears—I dare yet call you dear to me—how can you know this is true what you've said? Why should the Gods force a crisis that splits us, just when we need unity as seldom erenow? For the dangers ahead are nothing as simple as a pirate fleet or a brigand army. I say Dahut is indeed the bearer of a new Age; but 'twill be an Age when Ys puts aside the savage old ways and becomes the Athens of the world."

The girl bit her lip; blood trickled. She blinked and blinked her eyes. He longed, as he had rarely longed in his life, to hug her to him and comfort her, the pair of them alone. "Dahut," he said, "hear me. I w-w-want your well-being. This thing would, would not be right. Nay, you'll be the first princess, the first Queen, who was free to, well, to let her own prince find her."

At the edge of attention, he saw Lanarvilis wince. Dahut shook her head and cried raggedly, "My King is the King of the Wood!"

Bodilis spoke, flat-voiced: "The wedding should be this day. Go through with it. That will calm the city. Afterward we—you will have time to decide."

He felt heat in his brows, chill in his belly. "I know better than that. We twain would be led to the bridal chamber, and once there I would be helpless. First will I fall on my sword. Bodilis, I looked not for you to try and trick me."

She shrank back into herself.

Tambilis stirred. "But *is* it so dreadful?" she pleaded. "You and I—we grew happy. 'Twas at my mother's cost, but—why, Grallon? Why should we not welcome Dahut, whom we love, into our Sisterhood?"

"The law of Mithras forbids," he answered with a surge of anger. "A man without a law is a beast. Enough. I told you, this stands not to be altered. Shall we go on making noise, or shall we plan what to do for Ys?"

Vindilis bared teeth. "Because of your sacrilege on Point Vanis, I have denied my body to you," she flung. "What if all we Nine do likewise? You can have no other woman."

"And you, you would not be like Colconor, you would not," Innilis quavered.

Gratillonius was mainly conscious of his sadness for Dahut. He made a one-sided smile. "Nay," he said, "but I told you, a man ought to be more than a beast. I'll have my duties to occupy me."

"I'll never forsake you!" Guilvilis half screamed.

Before anyone could reprove her, Forsquilis leaned forward. It was like a cat uncoiling. "Grallon, you have right, as far as you've bespoken it," she said. "We do not know what this portends. I fear 'tis a war between Gods, but we do not know. King and Queens, Sisters, night is upon us, the stars have withdrawn and the moon has not risen. We must tread warily, warily.

"Grallon speaks truth. He cannot wed Dahut, not while he abides with Mithras. We may in time persuade him otherwise; or we may learn that his insight, into the Gods Who are not his, was better than ours. Neither outcome is possible for enemies. We can only find our way, whatever our way is, we can only find it together.

"I have no new omens. Mayhap none of us will be vouchsafed any. But this much I *feel.*"

" 'Tis plain good sense," Bodilis murmured.

"What should we do, then?" Maldunilis ventured, pitiably hopeful of an answer.

Forsquilis gave it: "Since this is a thing that never erstwhile came upon Ys, we have a right to be slow and careful. We must be honest before the people; I think then they will accept, although—" she actually flashed a grin—"the words we use to tell them, the show we put on for them, those must be artistry. Give Dahut her honors and dues as a Queen, of course; but let the wedding be postponed until the will of the Gods is more clear. Meanwhile, let us not weaken the sacred marriage by an open quarrel.

"I feel that thus we may win through to a resolving, to the new Age itself. But—"

Suddenly Forsquilis rose. Her skirts rustled with her haste as she went to Dahut. The girl got up, bewildered, to meet her. Forsquilis clasped Dahut close. "Oh, darling child," she said, "yours will be the most hurtful part. I sense, it whispers in me, all that is to come will spring from you, how you bear your burdens and, and what road you choose to fare."

Gratillonius saw his daughter cling hard to his wife, then step back with strength. His spirit went aloft, more than was really reasonable. "Gallicenae," he said, "soon I must meet with spokesmen of the Suffetes. Can we decide what I shall tell them?"

— 3 —

In the event it was Soren whom he first saw, the two men by themselves in the private room of the palace.

"Nay," Gratillonius declared, "I will not call another Council."

"Why not?" Soren fairly snarled. They stood within fist range of each other and glared. Evening made dim the chamber, which brought forth the whiteness of Soren's eyeballs, streaks in his beard, bald pate. "Dare you not go before us?"

"I'll do that regardless later this month, at equinox. By then we'll know better what's to come of this, and we'll have been thinking. I hope you and your kind will have been thinking. If we gathered earlier, 'twould be a shouting match, not only futile but dangerous."

"You speak of danger, you who'd bring the curse of the Gods down on Ys?"

"Ah, do you sit among Them, that you are sure what They will do—what They can do? Have the Turones fallen to famine or plague since Bishop Martinus tore down their old halidoms and made Christians of them? Here I am, a mortal man; and I go daily out beneath the sky. Let the

Gods strike at me if They choose. My business is with my fellow men."

"Those may well become the instruments of the Gods, lest the whole nation suffer."

Gratillonius shook his head and smiled without merriment. "Beware, Soren Cartagi. You think of the worst sacrilege, the murder of the blood-anointed King. I do not believe any Ysan would raise hand against me. That would destroy the very thing you'd fain preserve. Nay, I expect instead the people will rally behind me once they've heard my case and thought on it. For I am their leader, and I am their mediator with Taranis."

"I've something else in mind," Soren rasped.

Gratillonius nodded. "Aye. Another sequence of challenges from outside. Sooner or later I must fall. 'Tis been done in the past, when a King grew intolerable. But you will not do it; you will seek out your colleagues and make them refrain too, as the Gallicenae have already decided to refrain."

Soren folded arms across his massive chest and compressed his lips before he said, "Explain why."

"You know why, if you'll stop to think. Ys is in peril from worse than Gods. I cannot provoke Governor Glabrio further by accusing him of connivance at the Frankish invasion, but there is no doubt. When I sent him a complaint against them, the reply was days late in coming, surly in tone, and dictated by Procurator Bacca—a studied insult. It berated me for attacking and killing subjects of the Emperor, rather than negotiating any differences between us. It said my 'murderous blunder' is being reported to the vicarius in Lugdunum, together with a list of my other malfeasances."

Soren stood quiet while dusk deepened, until he said low: "Aye, we know somewhat of this."

"You'd have seen the letter for yourselves as soon as my Watch in the Wood was up."

"What do you propose to do?"

"Send a letter of my own to Lugdunum, by the fastest courier Ys can supply. I may well have to go in person later and defend myself. That will be tricky, mayhap impossible. The Franks were unruly, but as laeti they provided Redonia its strongest defense. Now the flowers of them are reaped, the spirit of the rest broken. Ys remains obstinately pagan, its traders cause folk to desire more than the Empire provides, its freedom undermines subservience.

"Nevertheless, I am a Roman officer. Let Rome's prefect here be slain, and that will be the very pretext Glabrio longs for. He could well persuade the Duke to order an invasion. At worst they'd be reprimanded afterward for exceeding their authority, and their part of the booty would doubtless be ample compensation for that.

"If you are wise, you will do whatever you can to keep challengers out of the Wood!"

"Can you win your case before the vicarius?" Soren asked slowly.

"I said 'twill belike prove harder than any combat for the Key. I am no diplomat, no courtier. But I do somewhat know my way through that labyrinth the government. And I do have influential friends, Bishop Martinus the nearest. It all makes me the sole man who has any hope of keeping Rome off."

"Suppose you fail with the vicarius."

"Well, I'll not tamely let him revoke my commission. Above him is the praetorian prefect in Treverorum, to whom I'll appeal," Gratillonius reminded. "And beyond him is Flavius Stilicho, ruler of the West in all but name. He's a soldier himself. I think likely he can be made to agree that Ys is worth more as an ally against the barbarians, however annoying to the state, than as a ruin. But he will want a fellow legionary overseeing it. And I am the only prefect who, as King, would command the support and obedience of the Ysan folk—and, at the same time, try to preserve the rights, the soul, of the city. Ys needs me."

Soren brooded for a long spell. Gratillonius waited.

Finally the Speaker for Taranis said, "I fear you are right. I must get to work on your behalf, and afterward with you."

"Good!" Gratillonius moved to give him the clasp of friendship.

Soren drew back. Sick hatred stared from the heavy visage. "Need drives me, naked need," he said. "Perforce, in public I shall hold back the words about you that are in my heart. But know, beyond your damnable usefulness

against your Romans, you have my curse, my wish for
every grief in the world upon your head, blasphemer,
traitor, wrecker of lives."

He turned and departed.

— 4 —

The funeral barge stood out the sea gate on a morning
ebb, bearing death's newest harvest in Ys. Weather had
turned gray and windy. Whitecaps on olive-hued waves
rocked the broad hull and cast spindrift stinging across its
deck. The evergreen wreath on the staff amidships dashed
about at the end of its tether. Under the spiral-terminated
sternpost, two steersmen had the helm and the coxswain
tolled his gong, setting rhythm for the oarsmen below. By
its copy forward, the captain kept lookout. Somberly clad
deckhands went about their tasks. The dead lay shrouded
on litters, a stone lashed to each pair of ankles, along the
starboard rail. Elsewhere their mourners sat on benches or
gathered in small groups, saying little. Among them on
this trip were the King and the Gallicenae, who would be
the priestesses because a Sister of theirs was going away.

Gratillonius stood apart, looking off to the dim streak
that was Sena. Thus had he often traveled over the years,
when someone fallen required special honor, since the day
they buried Dahilis. Always at least one Queen had been
at his side. Today none of them had spoken a word to him.

When out on deep water, the captain signalled halt. The
gongbeat ceased, the rowers simply holding the vessel
steady. A trumpeter blew a call that the wind flung away.
The captain approached the Gallicenae and bowed to
Lanarvilis, who was now the senior among them. Ritually,
he requested that she officiate. She walked into the bows,
raised her hands, and chanted, "Gods of mystery, Gods of
life and death, sea that nourishes Ys, take these our
beloved—"

When the invocation was done, she unrolled a scroll and
from it read the names, in order of death. Each time,
sailors brought that litter to a chute, Lanarvilis said, "Fare-

well," the men tilted their burden and the body slid down over the side, into the receiving waves.

How small was Fennalis's. Gratillonius had never thought of her like that.

At the end, the trumpet sounded again, a drum beneath. There was then a silence, for remembrance or prayer, until the captain cried, "About and home!" Oars threshed to the renewed gongbeat, the barge wallowed around, it crawled back toward the wall and towers of Ys.

Gratillonius felt he must pace. As he commenced, he saw that the Nine had partly dispersed. Dahut was alone at the starboard rail. His heart thuttered. Quickly, before he could lose courage, he went to her. "My dearest—" he began.

She swung avidly about. "Aye?" she exclaimed. "You've seen what's rightful? Oh, Fennalis, may the Gods bear you straightway to my mother!"

Gratillonius retreated, appalled. "Nay," he stammered, "you, you misunderstand, I only wanted to talk between us—when we land, a chance to explain—"

Her face whitened. So did her knuckles where they gripped the rail after she turned her back on him.

He left her and trudged, round and round, round and round.

A hand touched his. He grew aware that Guilvilis had joined him. Slow tears coursed over her cheeks. "You are so unhappy," she said. The tip of her long nose wiggled. "Can I help? Is there aught I can do for you, lord, aught at all?"

He choked back wild laughter. She meant well. And this could be the start of healing the wound. Whether or no, at least with her he would not fail or flag, he could lose himself in the Bull—even closing his eyes and pretending, maybe—until he lost himself in sleep. "Aye," he muttered. "Excuse yourself from any duties that wait and come to me at the palace." It was where his armed men were. He did not require protection any more, if ever he had, and soon he would dismiss them, but meanwhile their presence enabled him to overawe some of his angry visitors. "Be prepared to stay a goodly time."

She sobbed for joy. That was the most sorrowful thing he had seen this day.

— 5 —

The marines and navy men returned, full of stories about their experiences. Their friends met them with tales to overwhelm those.

Herun Taniti came upon Maeloch and Cynan, among others, in a tavern. This was not their disreputable old haunt in the Fishtail, but the Green Whale. The skipper had prospered over the years, like most working men of Ys, while the naval officer and legionary had pay saved, together with proceeds from modest businesses they and their families conducted on the side.

After cheery greetings and a round of drink—

"Do folk truly, by and large, feel the King does right?" Herun asked. "I should think many would be cowering in fear. How shall the world now be renewed?"

"Well, the fish ha' been running as plentiful as ever I saw, and no storms spoiled the crops, nor did rot strike once they were in, nor a murrain fall on the kine," grunted Maeloch. "I'd say nature steers a straight course yet."

"Such as I've talked with, whether Suffete or commoner, and they're not few in my line of work, they're becoming content again," added Zeugit the landlord. This being a slack time of day, he could sit a while and gossip with these customers. "Many were alarmed at first, but when naught untoward happened, well, they're apt to reckon that dealings with the Gods are for the King, and surely this King, before all Ys has had, knows what he does."

"Young men sometimes get downright eager," put in the courtesan Taltha. She was there as much for her learning and conversational abilities as for beauty and lovemaking. "They talk of a new Age, when Ys shall become glorious, aye, mayhap succeed Rome as mistress of the world."

Zeugit glanced around. The room was spacious, clean, sunny, muraled with fanciful nautical images. Only one other of the tables had men benched at it, intent on their wine and a dice game. Nevertheless he dropped his voice.

"Truth is, few will avow it, but I think the faith of most has been shaken by what's happened; and it could not be shaken so much had its roots not grown shallow. Well, this is a seaport. Under Grallon, 'tis become a busy seaport, strangers arriving from everywhere, with ways and Gods that are not those of our fathers, back when Ys lay for hundreds of years drawn into its shell. More and more of us fare abroad, and carry home not just goods but ideas. Aye, change is in the air, you can smell it like the sharpness before a lightning storm."

"Men who've come to think 'twas not Taranis but Mithras Who appeared on Point Vanis, they're starting to seek initiation into that cult," Taltha said. "Myself, I'll stay with Banba, Epona— They are female, They will hear me." She signed herself. "And Belisama, of course. But it may well be that She has a unique destiny in mind for Princess Dahut."

"Well, between us, I might seek out Mithras too," Zeugit confessed, "save that 'twould harm my business. Also, I'm a bit old for learning new mysteries, or for that little branding iron. No disrespect, sir," he said to Mithraist Cynan.

"No offense taken," replied the soldier in his solemn fashion. "We seek no converts like the Christians, who'd conscript them. The legionaries of Mithras are all volunteers." He paused. "Indeed, lately the King sent a man back who'd fain enlist."

"What, was he unworthy?" asked Herun. "I've heard the cult will take none who're guilty of certain crimes and vices."

Cynan smiled a bit. "We're not prigs. You ken me. Nay, this is an old comrade of mine from Britannia, Nodens, we've marched and messed and worked and fought and talked and gotten drunk together for twenty years or more! I'll name no names. But he is a Christian, like most in our unit. After the battle, he having seen the vision, he went and sought acceptance by Mithras. Gratillonius—I was there, as it happened—he told this man nay. He was very kind, the way our centurion can be when 'tis called for. But he said, first, this man has a wife and children to think about, here in Ys. If he should travel into Roman country, or the Romans come hither, and they learned he was apostate, it might go hard with his family as well as himself. Second, said Gratillonius, this man is sworn to Christ, and on the whole has had a good life. A man should stand by his master or his God, as long as that One stands him true."

"Well spoken," murmured Herun. He stared into his cup. "Although I must think, I must think deeper—" Raising his glance: "What say you, Maeloch?"

The fisher shrugged. "Let each do what he deems right, whatever it be, and we need think no less of him," he answered. "Me, I'll abide with the old Gods. To do else would be to break faith with the dead."

— 6 —

Dahut inherited the house that had been Fennalis's, and immediately set about having it made over. For any purpose she chose, she could draw upon the Temple treasury without limit—she, a Queen. Those of her Sisters who saw the accounts thought her extravagant, but forbore to protest at once and commanded that minor priestesses keep silence likewise. Let Dahut indulge herself this much; she had enough difficulties.

Tambilis called on her the day after she moved in. Dahut made the guest welcome, without quite the warmth there had formerly been between them. Tambilis looked around the atrium in amazement. Ceiling and pillars were now white with gilt trim; the walls were painted red, black spirals along the tops; furniture of precious woods, inlaid with ivory and nacre, bore cushions of rich fabric, skins of rare animals, vessels of silver and cut crystal, exquisite figurines, with less regard to arrangement than profusion.

"You have . . . changed this . . . made it yours, indeed," Tambilis ventured.

Dahut, clad in green silk whereon inwoven serpents twined, a pectoral of amber and carnelian in front, her hair in a tall coiffure caught by a comb of pearl-studded tortoise shell, Dahut made an indifferent gesture. "The work's scarcely begun," she said. "I'll have this shabby mosaic

floor ripped out; I want an undersea scene. I'll have the
finest painter in Ys come in, when I've decided whether
that is Sosir or Nathach; he'll do me panels for the walls,
the Gods in Their aspects; and more."

"Ah, that's why you've not yet had us here for a
consecration."

"Work alone will not make this house ready for that."
Dahut curbed her bitterness. "Come, follow me." On the
way back, she ordered a maidservant to bring refreshments. Sounds of carpentry in progress clattered, but screens
blocked sight of the men.

Since some among them were in what was to be her
private conference room, Dahut led Tambilis to her bedchamber. It too had a tumbled, unfinished look, in spite of
its new sumptuousness. A niche-image showed Belisama
helmeted, bearing spear and shield, though not like
Minerva; the gown clung to voluptuousness, the countenance stared ahead in unabashed sensuality. It had been
stored in the Temple for generations. No Queen since the
original owner had wanted it, until Dahut. She bowed
low. Tambilis confined herself to the customary salute.

"Be seated," Dahut said brusquely, and tossed herself
onto the bed, to lie propped on pillows against the headboard. Tambilis took a chair.

"Well, dear, certes you've been busy," she remarked
after silence had stretched.

"What else had I to do?" Dahut replied, scowling.

"Why, your duties—"

"What are they? I am no more a vestal. Nor am I a
graduate set free, nor a Queen, mauger they give me the
name. They know not what to do with me."

"You can help where asked. Besides, you have your
schooling to finish. I was a child at first; I remember how
it was, and thought you did too, such friends as we were."

"Aye, the Sisters can invent tasks, meaningless things
that any underpriestess could do. I can sit through droning
hours of lessons. Is that being a Queen?" Dahut's forefin-
ger stabbed toward Tambilis. "And you, you were at least
wedded, already then. And after a while, when you were
as grown as I am—" She strangled on rage.

"Oh, my dear." As she leaned forward, reaching to
touch, Tambilis reddened.

Dahut saw. She held back, fleered, and asked in a tone gone wintry, "When were you last in his bed? When will you next be?"

"We—you know we decided hostility to him would be . . . self-defeating. I'll plead for you, Sister mine. I'll work on him as cunningly as I can—as a woman can who does love her man and so has learned how to please him. Be patient, Dahut. Abide. Endure. Your hour shall come."

"My hour for what? When?" The maiden stirred, sat straight, gave her guest the look of a hawk. "Be warned, I will not wait quietly very long. I *cannot*. Belisama summons me."

Tambilis shivered. "Be careful," she begged. "You can . . . you can engage yourself for a while yet, surely. This house and—well, I know how you've gone forth to hunt or sail or, or otherwise spend your strength till you can rest. Come, borrow that splendid stallion of your father's, as often erenow, and outpace the wind."

That was a wrong thing to say, she saw at once. Dahut paled. Slowly, she replied, "Another horse, a horse of my own, mayhap. But never, unless the King give me my rights, never again will I fare on his Favonius."

— 7 —

A sudden gale sprang out of the west. Wind hooted, driving rain through streets that became gurgling streams. Waves bawled, tumbled, dashed themselves and its floats against the sea gate; but the King had locked it.

Budic sat alone with Corentinus, in the room that the chorepiscopus had for himself at the back of the church. A single lamp picked its scant furniture out of shadows. Shutters rattled; rain hissed down them. Chill crept inward. Corentinus did not seem to notice, though his robe was threadbare and his feet without stockings in their worn-out sandals. Highlights glimmered across shaven brow, craggy nose and chin, eyes as deep in hollows of murk as were his cheeks. "And what then?" he asked.

The soldier had come in search of spiritual help.

Corentinus promised him it, but would first have a report on the lately concluded Council. Several men had already told him things—incompletely, however, and Budic had been present throughout as a royal guardsman.

"Well, sir, there isn't much more to tell. Those like Lir Captain, who would not withdraw their opposition, they got their words entered in the chronicle. Queen Lanarvilis, speaking for the Gallicenae, said they'd keep public silence about the marriage issue, for the time being. The Council in general, it voted down censure of the King, which was the least of what the zealous pagans wanted. It didn't approve his action, either. Instead, it entered a prayer into the record, a prayer for guidance and compassion from the Gods. It did declare its support for Gratillonius in his politics, especially his dealings with Rome. That was the end of proceedings. They'd ordinarily have considered other matters, you know, public works, taxes, changes in the laws that this or that faction wants—but nothing of it seemed important. It could wait till solstice, when everybody will know better where he's at."

Corentinus nodded. "Thank you. I'd say Gratillonius got as much as he could possibly have hoped for, at this stage. God aid him onward." His tone softened. "Daily I pray he see the Light. But sometimes—sometimes I don't really pray, because it's not for a mortal man to question God's ways, but I wish for a place outside of Heaven and hell, a kindly place for such as Gratillonius, who hear the Word and do not believe, but who remain upright."

Budic's voice cracked across. "God bless him—for his, his forbearance. He *must* not marry Dahut, God must not let him do such a thing to her, but what's to become of her, then? Father, that's what I'm here about, the wilderness in me—"

Corentinus raised a palm. "Hold! Quiet!" The command snapped like a hawser drawn taut when a ship plunges. Budic gulped and trembled on the stool where he sat.

For a space, only the storm spoke. Corentinus unfolded his knobby length and loomed up toward the ceiling, arms and face raised, eyes shut.

Abruptly he opened them, looked down at Budic, said, "Follow me," and went to the door.

The legionary obeyed, bewildered. Corentinus let them

out into the deserted Forum. Rain slashed and runneled. Wind keened. Dusk was setting in. Corentinus strode so fast that Budic could barely keep alongside him.

"What, what is this, sir? Where are we bound?"

Corentinus squinted ahead. His reply was barely to be heard through the noise. "A vessel lies wrecked. Women and children are aboard. We've no time to gather a rescue party before it's pounded apart. But the vision would not have come to me in vain."

Budic remembered a certain night in his home, and stories he had heard from elsewhere. Nonetheless he must exclaim, "What can two men do? The gate is barred. The dock at Scot's Landing—"

"Too far. Too slow." And in fact Corentinus was bound not south, but north on Taranis Way. "God will provide. Now spare your breath, my son. You'll need it."

Tenements of the well-to-do yielded to mansions of the wealthy. Statuary stood dim in the failing light, along either side of the avenue, a seal, a dolphin balanced on its tail, a lion and a horse with hindquarters of fish—Epona Square, a glimpse of the equestrian idol—Northbridge Gate, the battlements of the Sisters like fangs bared at unseen heaven—water ramping among rocks under the bridge—the short road that climbed onto Point Vanis to meet Redonian Way—the highroad wan, rimmed by wind-swept, rain-swept grass and bush, empty of man or beast, here and there sight of a menhir or a dolmen—near the end of the headland, where the road bent east, a blur in the blackness, a gravestone—

Corentinus took the lead down the trail to the former maritime station. Budic stumbled after, drenched, jaws clapping, feet slipping and skidding in mud. Surf crashed against the jetty that it was year by year gnawing away. Under the cliffs, gloom lay thick, the ruin shapeless. Budic tripped over a fragment, fell, skinned his knee. "Father, I cannot see," he wailed into the thunders and shrieks.

A globe of light appeared at the fingertips of Corentinus's uplifted right hand. It was like the ghost-glow sometimes seen at the ends of yardarms, but bright and serene. By its radiance Budic spied a jollyboat banging loose against what remained of the dock. It must have broken its painter or been washed off a strand where it rested and drifted here. Three or four oars clattered in the water that sloshed in its bilge.

Corentinus beckoned. Budic could do no else than creep forward, into the hull, onto the middle thwart. Corentinus climbed into the stern and stood erect. "Row," he said, softly but heard with the clearness of a voice in a dawn-dream.

Dreamlike too was Budic's placing a pair of oars between their tholes and pulling on them. Even in dead calm, a single man should not have been able to make a boat that size do more than crawl along. For him to row in seas like this, into the teeth of the wind, was beyond the strength of a madman. Yet as Budic put his weight to the task, the hull bounded forward. It mounted the billows to their crests and plunged down their backs like a hunting cat. Corentinus balanced easily. His right hand carried the phantom lantern, his left pointed the way to go.

Night blinded the world. The lonely light swayed onward.

Finally, finally it picked out its goal. A slim craft of some thirty feet lay hard on a skerry, held by snags onto which it had been driven. Waves dashed clamorous over the rock. They were breaking the strakes and ribs of the vessel, bearing those off. Groanings and crackings passed through surf-bellow, wind-howl. Already no refuge was left for the people aboard, save the section amidships. They clawed themselves to the stump of the mast, the tangle of its cordage.

This had been a yacht, Budic recognized. A couple of Suffetes must have celebrated the end of Council by taking their families out on a day cruise; all Ysans reckoned themselves familiars of the sea. The gale had caught them by surprise.

While he himself was no sailor, living here he had inevitably been on the water often enough to have gained a measure of skill. The surges ought to have cast him helpless onto the reef. He maneuvered in and kept his boat as steady as if it were a skiff on a mildly ruffled lake.

Something passed by, on the verge of sight. A shape half-human, foam-white, riding a monstrous wave like a lover? A screech of mockery, through tumult and skirl?

The thing vanished into the haze of spindrift. Budic shuddered.

Corentinus hitched up his robe and made a long-legged step to the reef. There he stood fast, though waves boiled higher than his knees. With his left hand he helped the victims clamber from the wreck and scramble over to the boat. Budic would pause in his labors to haul one at a time across the rail.

They filled the hull when all were huddled together. Their weight left bare inches of freeboard. Corentinus came back to take stance astern. By the light he bore, Budic discerned half a dozen men—ha, Bomatin Kusuri, Mariner Councillor—with two middle-aged women who must be wives—the other men were surely crew—and four small children—doubtless the youngest belonging to the Suffete couples, taken out as a holiday treat—exhausted, chilled blue, terrified, but alive.

Rowing did not seem very much more difficult, nor did the boat take on very much more water, than on the way out. Well, now he had the wind behind him. Face full of rain, he could barely see Corentinus give directions. The pastor's robe flapped around his gauntness like a sail that has slipped its sheets; but the light glowed ever steady.

It vanished after they had made landing at the station, and helped the people up the trail, and were safe on Point Vanis.

Abruptly another shadow, Corentinus called in Ysan—not quite steadily, for weariness was overtaking him too—"Give thanks to the Lord, Who has delivered us from death."

"'Twas a demon," babbled a crewman, "I swear 'twas a sea demon lured us, I'd never have let us anywhere near those rocks but we couldn't see the pharos, I think the wind blew it out, and then there was a shining—oh, the white thing that laughed while we went aground!"

Corentinus grew stern. "If you have looked into the abyss and still not seen the truth, at least keep your pagan nonsense to yourself." Milder: "Can everyone walk as far as the city? This darkness hoods us, but we'll keep pavement under our feet. Best we carry the children." He groped about. "Ah, here's a little girl for me. Rest you, sweetling, rest you, all is well again and God loves you."

The party staggered forward. Budic felt how drained of strength he was. Barely could he hold the boy who made his burden. The rescued men must often stop and exchange the other two youngsters. Corentinus paced steadily at his side.

"You've wrought a miracle tonight," Budic mumbled. "You're a saint."

"Not so," the chorepiscopus answered with brief vehemence. "This was God's work. We can only thank Him for the honor He gave us, of being His instruments."

"But why—ships are wrecked every year—why this one?"

"Who knows? His ways are mysterious. A Suffete who embraced the Faith would be valuable in winning salvation for Ys. Or God in His mercy may simply have granted these innocent children their chance to receive the Word and enter Heaven. It's not for us to say." A laugh barked. "And yet—I *am* no saint; may He forgive me—maybe He decided that after everything else that's been happening, high time Ys saw a Christian miracle!"

"Salvation. . . . Princess Dahut, sea-child. . . . D-d-do you suppose this—while she's still free of the deadly sin—this will change her heart?"

Starkness answered the appeal. "We may pray so. I know this much, Budic, I have this much foreknowledge. If Dahut does not come to the Light, she will do such ill that it were better she had died in her mother's womb."

X

— 1 —

The gale damped down to a high wind and frequent, violent showers. Seas crashed on the wall and gate of Ys. Bodilis would be confined on Sena for another two or three days, it seemed.

That morning Guilvilis was to lead sunrise rites at the Temple. A rainsquall struck while she mounted the steps—on the far right side of the staircase, as it happened. Near the top she lost footing on a tread which centuries of traffic had beveled and the wet made slippery. She slid, staggered, and went over the edge to the flagstones below. Once and horribly she screamed, then lay moaning like an animal.

A vestal who had also been on the way up saw and scurried to her. Having seen how she writhed and how her left foot thrashed but the right did not, the girl sped back after help. Such few as were present at this hour came in haste. An old underpriestess took charge; she had long been married to a physician, and upon taking new vows after she was widowed had become an instructress in the healing arts. They got Guilvilis onto an improvised litter and into a side room where there was a bed.

"Father must know," said her daughter Antonia, who chanced to have duty. Before anyone could naysay it, the fourteen-year-old was off at full speed to find the King. The old priestess grimaced, and sent others to inform the rest of the Gallicenae and fetch the royal chirurgeon Rivelin.

Gratillonius arrived first. He dropped his sodden cloak

in the portico and strode aggressively through the vestibule. The Key could be seen to swing on his breast under the tunic which, with sandals, was the only other garb he had taken time to don.

Dim light seeped into the little chamber. A younger priestess and a vestal kept watch. They shrank aside as he entered. He lifted the heavy blankets beneath which Guilvilis lay shivering, and her gown. It became clear to him that her right thigh was broken. He lowered the blanket and stooped above her face. Sweat studded it. She breathed rapidly and shallowly. He looked into her half-open eyes. "Pupils seem all right," he muttered in Latin. In Ysan: "Guilvilis, do you ken me? This is Grallon."

Her gray lips tried to twist into a smile. He kissed them very lightly. "Poor Guilvilis," he said, "you've never had much luck, have you? But you're as brave a lass as ever I knew. Have no fear. You'll be hale again." He stroked the thin hair, stepped back, took stance where she could see him, folded his arms, and waited.

Vindilis and Innilis came in together. The tall woman stiffened at sight of Gratillonius. She glared. "Get out, you bird of woe," she said, regardless of how she shocked the attendants. "What can you do here save call more misfortune down on her?"

He stood fast. His reply was flat. "Do you, then, accuse your Gods of penalizing loyalty?"

"Please, please, I pray peace," Innilis implored from the bedside. Her fingers were deft, drawing forth jars, cloths, implements from a bag she had brought. "Beloved, you can best help by standing outside. Let nobody in other than the medicus. Tell the Sisters this is grievous but not mortal, Our Lady of Solace willing."

Gratillonius began to move but Vindilis left ahead of him, in a susurrus of skirts. He paused a moment startled, then thoughtful. He winced a bit when Guilvilis made a jagged noise. Innilis was cleaning and anointing the abrasions, into which fibers from the garment had gotten. "I'm sorry, dearest, I'm sorry," she murmured. "This must be done to stave off infection. I'll be quick, I'll be as gentle as I can."

Rivelin appeared, saluted her and the King, made his own examination. "I fear we have no clean break, but a splintering," he said. "She'll be slow to heal, at best, and mayhap crippled. The sooner we put traction on it, the better. I've need of a colleague to help, a man with strong hands."

"Here I am," said Gratillonius.

"What?" The physician mastered his surprise. Whispers had long gone about concerning surgery the King performed once on Sena; and many had seen him competently treat injuries due battle or accident. "Well, my lord, let me describe for you what force must be applied, and put you through the motions, while we send after the necessary materials."

—When Gratillonius emerged, he found six women gathered in the corridor. His shoulders sagged and he had begun to tremble a bit. Sweat made blots on his tunic below the arms and reeked around him. "It went well," he told his wives and daughter, dull-voiced. "Rivelin is finishing now, with Innilis's help."

"Would you give her naught for the pain? Would you not allow that?" Vindilis snapped.

"Nay, Sister," Tambilis protested.

"Innilis dared not drug her when she had gone so cold," Gratillonius said. "Besides, when we began the work she swooned. Later she'll get something so she can rest quietly. I did not . . . enjoy myself." His glance sought Dahut. "It must needs be done."

The maiden made no response. "Oh, Grallon," Tambilis whispered, and moved toward him, her hands outheld. Lanarvilis pulled at her sleeve and hissed in her ear. Tambilis halted. Tears in her lashes caught what light there was.

Dahut stirred. "Let me go in to her," she said. "I will give her the Touch. She'll suffer less and heal properly."

Forsquilis frowned. "Nay, best not. Not now, not here. The house of the Goddess, and you unconsecrate—Mayhap later, when Rivelin's let her go home."

"I may not help my Sister, I may not keep Vigil—I may not be Queen, thanks to you!" Dahut shrilled at her father.

"I'm leaving," he said. "Have someone keep me informed and tell me when I can call on her."

He walked off. Tambilis half moved to follow, but checked

herself. "Patience, my dear," Lanarvilis admonished after
the man was gone.

"But he is so alone, so unhappy," Tambilis pleaded.
"You act as if this were his fault."

"Was it not?"

"Let that be. Unwise it is to talk about such things,"
warned Forsquilis. She went to embrace Tambilis. "I understand. All that you are cries out to go to him. I miss
him too, the big sad sobersided lost soul. But this is the
sacrifice we must make."

"Punish him," Vindilis said, "starve his lust, punish him
until he gives in. Not that he will ever again have me. But
you others, make him pay. You are the instruments of the
Gods."

"He may force himself on us, now that he can't have
Guilvilis," said Maldunilis, not altogether fearfully.

Lanarvilis shook her head. "Nay. Give him his due. He
is no Colconor. He will not squander the respect we still
have for him, nor antagonize us worse at a time when he
needs every ally he can find."

"But what shall we do?" asked Tambilis miserably.

"What we have been doing since he spurned his bride—
naught. Give him no invitations. Decline any he gives us.
Be coldly polite in conference. When at last he seeks us
out, receive him likewise. When he speaks of bed, tell
him calmly that he has broken the sacred marriage, not
we, and we think the Gods have made an example of
Guilvilis. That should deter him—that, and his injured
male pride. If not, if he does press suit, well, 'tis for each
of us to decide, but if outright refusal fails, then I think we
should lie down and send our minds away. He is not such
a blockhead that he will not know it."

"If I can do that," Tambilis whispered.

Forsquilis bit her lip. " 'Twill not be easy," she said.
"Remember, though, we do it for him too, that he be
brought to make his peace with the Gods."

"How long must we?"

Forsquilis spread her hands. "As long as necessary—or
as possible. Meanwhile hope, pray, seek what small spells
we might cast. Who knows what can happen? . . . Dahut,
what's wrong?"

The princess had started. She recovered herself. "Nothing," she said. Acridly: "Nothing and everything. A thought passed through me."

"What was it?" Vindilis asked.

Dahut looked away. "A fleeting thing. Let me pursue it further."

"Have a care, child. Take counsel with your Sisters. Ever were you prone to recklessness."

Dahut flushed. "The Gods will watch over me," she said, and stalked off.

— 2 —

Weather continued windy, cloudy, raw. The sun blinked in and out of sight while shadows swept a darkling sea where white horses went at gallop until they reared up against the reefs. The noise pervaded Ys, a murmur in Hightown, a rumble and boom and monstrous sighing where the wall stood off the waters. The gate was open, but pilots gave its floats a wide berth.

Tommaltach and Carsa paced the top between North-bridge and the Gull Tower. They had been drinking in Carsa's apartment and decided some sharp air was in order before they supped. Save for the posted guards, nobody else was there. Surf roiled among the rocks below, burst, recoiled in swirls and smothers of foam.

"I wonder that the people take not this as a sign their Gods are angry," said the Roman. His gesture encompassed the bleakness and the time through which it had prevailed. He spoke in Ysan, the language the two young men had in common; as yet, Tommaltach's Latin was halting.

"Why, 'tis naught unusual," the Scotian replied. "You've not dwelt here long enough. At home we'd call it an autumn mild and dry."

Carsa brightened. "Then you think 'twill not make things harder for Gratillonius?"

"Ah, is that what gnaws at you? Well, me too, me too."

"No offense meant, my friend, but you are a pagan, albeit not of the Ysan kind. You understand these folk better than a Christian from the South can."

"I am an initiate of Mithras," said Tommaltach stiffly.

"I know." Carsa laid a hand on the other's arm. "Would that you had taken the true Faith! But what I meant was that you, hailing from among heathens, you can see how the evil works within the souls of men. And you've relieved me. Thank you."

Tommaltach regarded him a while as they walked before he said, slowly, "You hope Grallon will—be able to—hold out against marrying his daughter."

"Hope?" Carsa exclaimed. "I pray! Daily, more than daily, prostrate, I implore God to keep her pure." He snapped after breath. "Do you not?"

Tommaltach searched for words, which was unlike him. "Well, if Dahut becomes truly a high priestess in Ys, there goes many a dream. I've never heard that any of them ever took a lover. And if her father says Mithras forbids it, I believe him, though I'm still ignorant of most of the Mysteries. Yet what's to become of the poor darling? How can she ever be free to make her own life? Wonderful beyond wonder, could she become the sort of Queen we have at home. How likely, though, is that? First and foremost comes her welfare."

"Mean you," asked Carsa harshly, "that if her father yields and—the defilement—happens—you would let it go unavenged?"

"He is *my* Father in Mithras," Tommaltach said with difficulty.

"I have sworn before God," stated Carsa, "that if he does it to her, I will kill him."

— 3 —

The full moon fled through clouds. They were silver where it touched them, elsewhere smoke and swiftness. The light shuddered over earth. Wind blew icy down the valley, a hollow whistling. It ripped dead leaves off trees and scourged them along the road where Dahut ran.

She turned in at the Sacred Precinct and stopped. Breath gusted in and out of her. A cloak flapped about her shoulders. Its cowl had fallen back and stray locks fluttered from hastily woven braids. The paving of the yard flickered wan as light came and went, between three hulks of blackness. The Challenge Oak and the Wood behind groaned. Now and then the Hammer swung against the the Shield and a faint ringing thrilled forth.

Dahut raised her arms. The Red Lodge lay darkened, King and attendants were asleep, but somebody might easily awaken. She began to chant. "*Ya Am-Ishtar, ya Baalim, ga'a vi khuwa*—"

The spell cast, she moved forward soft-footed. A moonbeam showed her lips drawn back, teeth bared, the grin of a warrior in battle.

Nonetheless she paused whenever the old wooden stairs creaked beneath her weight; and she moved the doorlatch with utmost caution, and opened the door an inch at a time. As soon as the gap was wide enough she slipped through and at once closed it, as quietly as might be.

A while she listened. Through night sounds muffled by walls, she heard a couple of snores from the benches where men lay. At first the hall was tomb-dark, then she gained sufficient vision to make them out, barely. The pillar idols loomed clearer, more real than they. "Taranis, lover of Belisama, be with me, the beloved of Lir," she whispered.

Cat-careful, she made her way over the floor. A banked fire in a trench warned her off with a few blood-colored stars. At the interior door, she must feel about until she found its latch. The passage beyond was less murky, for windows had been let into this rebuilt half and the weather was not so tumultuous as to require that they be shuttered. Their glass shifted between moonlight milkiness and gaping black, but always blind, nothing truly seeable through them, as if she had gone outside the world.

The door to the royal bedroom stood ajar. She shut it after she had passed through and, again, poised wary for several score heartbeats. The single window here was on the west, and the moon had not yet reached the zenith; thus the brightest that entered was an uneasy gray. She could just see Gratillonius. He lay on his side. An arm and shoulder above the blanket were bare. In the middle of the huge bed, he seemed very alone.

Dahut sat down on the floor to take off her sandals, lest

she make a noise. Rising, she unfastened the fibula that held her cloak and lowered that garment, likewise her belt. There remained a gown, which she pulled over her head.

For a moment she looked at her body, ran hands across the smooth curves, smiled. Thereafter she spent minutes studying how the chamber was arranged, estimating distances and directions, planning each movement. Finally she padded to the window. When she had drawn the drape that hung beside it, sightlessness engulfed her.

She glided to the bedside, found the top edge of the sheet, pulled it back, slipped onto the mattress, lay until she was sure Gratillonius had not moved, then pulled the covers over her and edged across to him. He breathed slowly, deeply. The slumber spell held, and for hours it would take more than a touch to awaken him.

His back was to her. She brought her belly close against the warm solidity. A shiver passed through her. She writhed. Her hips thrust. He stirred a little. She drew slightly back and waited for him to sink anew.

Thereupon she raised herself to an elbow and brought her mouth down to his ear. A male odor entered her nostrils. His hair and the regrowing beard brushed her lips.

"Gratillonius," she whispered, "I am here. I could no longer keep from you, Grallon, my darling, take me now." Her free hand slid by his waist, across the ridges of muscle, to the loins. She closed fingers on what she found and moved them. The flesh stirred, thickened, lifted. Heat pulsed. "Grallon, King, lord, lover, here is your Queen."

"Wh-what?" His voice rumbled unsteady, dazed. "Who? Tambilis?" He rolled around, groped, cupped a breast. "You?" Joy throbbed.

She flung herself at him, stopped his tongue with hers, cast a thigh over his. Her hand quivered and tugged, urging the bigness whither she wanted it.

He got to his knees and one palm. "Quickly, mount me quickly," she said an undertone that could be any woman's.

His other hand stroked. Abruptly it halted. "But you, you're not Tam—Fors—who?" he stuttered. It ripped from him: "Dahilis!"

He pulled out of her clasp. His trembling shook the

mattress. "Aye, this is Dahilis come back to you," Dahut keened and sought after him. He scrambled, thudded to the floor and across it. Dahut yowled.

Gratillonius hauled the drape downward. The heavy fabric ripped free of its rings. Clouds had briefly parted around the moon. Light cast its patina over Dahut where she crouched on the bed.

Whoo-oo, said the wind.

Dahut clambered to her own feet. Tears torrented, agleam in the night. "I would save you," she implored, "I would have you do the will of the Gods. 'Tis not too late."

She stumbled toward him. He lifted crooked-fingered hands. "To this have your Gods brought you, child of mine?" His tone was dead.

"Oh, father, I'm afraid for you, and I love you so."

"You know not what love is, you who . . . who supposed a man would not know his dear one in the dark. Go. Depart. Now."

"Father, comfort me, hold me—"

She had come nigh enough to see his face turn into a Gorgon mask. "Go!" he roared. "Ere I kill you!"

Like a bear enraged, he advanced on her. She whirled and fled. Behind her she heard him cry out, "Dahilis, Dahilis!" and began to weep, with the racking sobs of a man unpracticed in it.

Naked, Dahut ran down the road to Ys. She wept also.

More and more, the clouds were swallowing the moon. She should be able to pass unseen through High Gate, always open in peacetime, as she had left.

The wind whipped her with cold. Dead leaves tumbled and rattled before her feet. Wings passed overhead, an eagle owl. It vanished with the moon.

— 4 —

Vindilis called on Lanarvilis at the home of the latter. They sought the private room. Lamps burned to offset the dullness of a rainy noontide. Their glow brought out the blue and vermilion of lush fabrics, ivory and wood grain of fine furniture, sheen of silver and gleam of glass. Vindilis's gaunt figure, black-clad, was like a denial of it. She sat rigid in a chair facing the couch on which Lanarvilis half slumped.

Vindilis went straight to the attack: "Already the time is overpast for decision. Those of us who honor the Gods and fear Their wrath must close ranks."

"That is . . . all of us . . . though we may disagree on what course is wisest," Lanarvilis said.

"There can be no question of wisdom. Prudence is madness. Better Ys defy the whole might of Rome than forsake her Gods."

"What would you have us do?"

Vindilis sighed, while her gaze smoldered the fiercer. "Pray for a sign; but meanwhile make ready for it. I've sought you first because you are pious, my Sister, far more than some among us. Yet you support Grallon."

Lanarvilis straightened. "In his capacity as intercessor for us with Rome. That requires upholding his authority in other respects too. I need not like this nor intend to continue it forever."

Vindilis nodded. "I do not say we should denounce him immediately and call for his overthrow. Nor should we suffer his desecrations much longer. Unless he repent and make Dahut, the Chosen one, the mother of the new Age—make her Queen, and do it soon, then somehow he must be broken. Otherwise Rome will have conquered Ys without drawing one sword."

Lanarvilis frowned. "Go on."

"Let us begin by rallying those of the Nine whom we can. It is bitter to say, but he has deluded certain of us. Poor, stupid Guilvilis; well, the Gods have taken her out of the game for a while. Bodilis—Bodilis wants to believe, with him, that the new Age will be altogether different from the past. Those two we dare not confide in."

Lanarvilis bit her lip. "Shall we plot against Sisters of ours? Nay!"

"I did not call for that. To go on, Innilis is devout, obedient, but she is such a tender and loving person, she hopes this will somehow end happily. We can count on her loyalty, but we must spare her as much pain and anxiety as we can."

Lanarvilis smiled wistfully.

"Maldunilis too wants an easy way out," Vindilis went on, "though in her 'tis due sluggishness and a sort of lazy lust for him. Another King would serve her as well."

"You speak ill of your Sister," Lanarvilis reproached.

"I speak truth."

"Are you quite sure you do?"

"Well, we lack time for pussyfooting. Come a crisis, Maldunilis will stand with us, but not firmly. At best, we can reckon she will not take sides against us, now or later.

"Tambilis is shattered. I fear she loves Grallon more than she adores the Gods. She's young, healthy, will recover and ask herself if she should go on denying him. We must try to make her find the right answer. She feels closest to Forsquilis, unless it be to Dahut. I think you and I, Lanarvilis, should seek the aid of Forsquilis in rallying Tambilis to us."

The other Queen looked uneasy. "But what of Forsquilis herself?"

"Aye, there's ever been an enigma there. We can only appeal to her, in whatever way we deem likeliest to succeed."

"And afterward?"

"The Gods will grant a sign in Their time. We who are entirely true to Them should prepare ourselves; then when we know what must be done, *do* it."

— 5 —

Toward evening of the second day after full moon, Dahut appeared at the home of Bodilis. Hitherto she had kept within her own house and bidden her servants turn visitors away.

Weather had abated, going colder but calm, clear in the east and overhead. Westward, though, cloud masses piled blue-black and the sky around the sun was a bleak green. Shadow was beginning to fill the bowl of Ys.

Dahut knocked. Bodilis opened the door. "Welcome," said the woman low. "Oh, thrice welcome, child. I'm so glad you heeded my message. Come in."

Dahut entered. Her stance, face, entire body bespoke resentment. "What do you want?" she demanded.

"That we talk, of course. I've dismissed the staff. Here, give me your cloak, let's seek the scriptorium."

Dahut slouched beside Bodilis through the atrium painted with dolphins and sea birds. "I came because 'twas you who asked. But try me not too hard."

Bodilis squeezed the girl's shoulder. " 'Tis life and fate are doing that to you, darling. Have you the courage to meet them calmly?"

Dahut's nostrils flared. She tossed her head.

They passed into the long room full of scholarly and artistic materials. Dahut halted. Breath hissed between her teeth.

Gratillonius remained seated. He offered a smile. "Be of good cheer," he said. His voice was hoarse. "I'm sorry if I frightened you . . . earlier. You are the daughter of my Dahilis, and I love you. Bodilis lent herself to this little ruse because else you might not have agreed to see me for much too long. We want naught save to make peace."

Dahut stared at the Queen. "You knew?" she asked.

Bodilis nodded. "Your father bared his heart to me."

"I have to none other," Gratillonius said with the same roughness. "Nor will I. Sit down, dear one. Have some wine if 'twill ease you."

Dahut sank to the edge of a chair. Bodilis took a third. They sat in a triangle. Silence clamped it tight.

Bodilis broke though. "Dahut," she said gently, "what you sought to do was wild. Thank the Mother, thank Her throughout your life, that it failed. But your father is not angry with you. Not any more. You are young, wounded, distraught. Come back to us and let us heal you."

A flush passed across the pallor that lay like a mask on the face of the maiden. Fury spat: "What did I wrong? I would have claimed my rights, and the rights of the Gods. *He* refuses them!"

"Would you have consummated the marriage ere the wedding?"

"Since I must."

"That was surely why the Power of the Goddess was not in you."

Dahut moistened her lips and looked into her father's eyes. "You can still make it well between us," she said.

Gratillonius clutched the arms of his chair. "Not in the way you call for," he stated. "Bodilis persuaded me 'twas folly in you, rather than wickedness. Well, learn from your mistake. Take thought."

"We know not what form the new Age shall bear," Bodilis added. "Can we shape it ourselves? We can strive, at least. Imagine a Queen who chooses her King freely, has him to herself, will not lose him in a fight against some wanderer who beds her with the blood scarcely off his hands."

"What would you have me do?" Dahut retorted.

"Be patient while we make our way forward."

"Into what?"

"The unknown."

"Nay, I'll tell you whither you're bound." Dahut sprang to her feet. Poised before them, she jeered: "You'd have me renounce the Gods, the whole meaning and soul of Ys. Where then shall I seek? Your Mithras will not receive me. Cybele is dead. Christ waits. You'd make Christians of us!"

"If need be, aye," said Gratillonius starkly. "I've lain awake nights bethinking this. 'Twould ease most of our troubles. There are worse Gods."

"Nay!" Dahut screamed. She pounced across the floor, snatched the wine flagon off a table, cast it against the wall. It cried aloud as it smashed. Shards flew. Redness like blood spattered over books. Bodilis moaned and half rose.

Dahut crouched back. Her countenance had gone inhuman with rage. "Christ be cursed! Lir haul me under ere I give myself to Christ! But I'll be Queen, true Queen, foremost of the Nine, and the name I take shall be Brennilis!"

She flung the door open and sped from them, out into the sunset.

— 6 —

Next day Gratillonius spoke privately with Rufinus, in the palace.

"We must look to our defenses," he said, using the Latin that was customary between them.

The Gaul regarded him. "You've no idea of making war on Rome," he murmured. "However, if Ys should become a very hard oyster to open—"

"Ys can become an ally more valuable than it has been," Gratillonius interrupted. "We've sea power, but hardly any on land. The Franks may have learned what their proper place is, but they'll forget eventually, and meanwhile there'll be Germani—Alani, Huns, who knows? —pushing westward. What I have in mind—this will take years, obviously, and won't be easy—it's to mesh ourselves with the Armorican tribes, especially our Osismiic neighbors, somewhat as we've done navally with Rome. They supply most of the manpower, we supply cadre and much of the weaponry."

"Hm." Rufinus tugged his fork beard. "How will the Romans take to that?"

"We'll have to show them how much better it'll work than slovenly mercenaries and raw reservists. Maximus's veterans have made a difference already, and the former Bacaudae will be priceless in case of invasion. What we can do for a start—a start toward forming a true regional militia—is simply to tighten and enlarge that fellowship. You'll be essential to this. But tell me frankly if you think the idea has merit."

"Quite a conundrum, sir!" laughed Rufinus. The discussion that followed occupied a couple of hours. They decided the plan was at least worth pursuing further . . . after present difficulties had been resolved.

As he was readying to leave, Rufinus gave the King a long look. "You're grieved," he said slowly. "More than just your conflict over Dahut should warrant. Would you care to talk about it? You know I'm a miser where it comes to secrets."

Gratillonius reddened. "How did you get any such ridiculous notion?" he growled.

"I've come to know you over the years," Rufinus answered, almost sorrowfully. "Your tone of voice—oh, everything about you of late—" He formed a wry half-grin, "Well, I'll be off before you boot me out. If ever I can help, I am your man." He sketched a Roman salute and departed.

— 7 —

Tambilis visited Guilvilis. Bedridden still, the injured Queen was seldom free of pain, which lifted in her like a spear, but endured it dumbly. Her children, the younger ones in particular, provided distraction of a sometimes chaotic sort. Nonetheless she welcomed her Sister.

"You're sweet to come," she said from the pillow. "They don't all, you know."

Tambilis's gaze went uneasily around the room. Dusk was fading the gaudy, foolish trinkets Guilvilis liked. "Well, they, they do have many duties," she mumbled.

Guilvilis sighed. "They are afraid. I know they are. They fear I got hurt because the Gods were angry with me."

"Oh, now——" Tambilis took hold of the hand that plucked at the blanket.

"Well, I am not afraid," Guilvilis said. "Grallon isn't."

"He comes here too?"

"Aye. Didn't you know? He comes when he can find time. 'Tis kind of him. We've naught to say to each other. He can only sit where you're sitting. But he does come see me. I think his Mithras God will protect us."

Tambilis flinched and drew a sign. "Well," she said with forced cheer, "let me give you the newest gossip from the marketplace."

"Nay, please," Guilvilis replied earnestly, "tell me how he fares."

"But you told me he visits you."

"We can't talk." Guilvilis swallowed tears. "He's been . . . heavy. Something hurts him. What is it, Tambilis?"

"I have not . . . seen him, spoken with him . . . save as affairs of the city or the Temples require. . . . He goes about his rounds. Aye, he keeps very busy."

"Is it this thing with Dahut? How is Dahut?"

"She holds aloof. Ranges alone into the countryside, gone for hours at a stretch. Shuns or scamps all tasks. How can we compel her, if we reckon her a Queen? I tried to speak with her, but she told me to go away. And we were good friends once. May that come again."

"If only Grallon— Could you make Grallon wed her, Tambilis? Then everything would be well, would it not? You're beautiful. He might listen to you."

"Not while I— But I know not if I can continue thus, when he's so sad." Tambilis shook her head violently. After a moment she brightened her voice. "Come, this is useless. Let me tell you of a comic thing that happened yesterday at Goose Fair."

— 8 —

The moon waned toward the half. Each night was noticeably longer than the last.

Fog stole in from the sea during one darkness. At dawntide it hid heaven and blinded vision beyond a few yards. It also damped sound; the noise of surf under Cape Rach drifted in its gray as a remote *hush-hush-hush*. Sere grass dripped underfoot. Dankness gnawed.

Out through the swirling, between a lichenous tomb and a canted headstone, came Forsquilis from the necropolis. Her gown and cloak were stained, drenched, her hair lank and eyes bloodshot. A tall form waited. Nearing, she recognized whose it was, and halted. For the span of several wavebeats she confronted Corentinus.

"What do you here, Christian?" she asked finally, tonelessly.

The ghost of a smile stirred the stiff gray beard. "I might inquire the same of you, my daughter."

"I am no lamb of your flock." Forsquilis made to pass by.

Corentinus lifted his staff. "Hold, I pray you."

"Why?"

"For the sake of Ys."

Forsquilis considered the rugged features. The sea mumbled, the fog smoked. "You have had a vision," she said.

He nodded. "And you."

"I sought mine."

Compassion softened his words. "At terrible cost. Mine sought me out of love."

"What did it reveal?"

"That you had gone to beg a remedy for the sickness devouring Ys. I know better than to tell you, here and now, that what you did is forbidden. In your mind, it is not. But I know that you asked for bread and were given a stone."

Forsquilis stood moveless a minute before she asked, "Will you give me your oath to keep silence?"

"Will you accept a Christian vow?"

"I will take your word of honor."

"You have it."

Forsquilis nodded. "You've been many years among us," she said. "I believe you.

"Well, what I may relate is scant. It concerns Dahut. She attempted something. It was impossible, you'd call it fearsome, but she was desperate. I, through my arts, had some forewarning, and . . . followed along. Dahut failed. She has not yielded, rather she is bound on her purpose though hell and Ocean lie before her."

"Possessed," said Corentinus grimly.

Forsquilis spread her hands from under the waterlogged mantle. "In Ys we would say fated. Be that as it may, this night I sought to learn what I might do toward the rescue of us all."

Corentinus waited.

The Athene face twisted in anguish. "I can do nothing! I *may* do nothing. My lips are locked, my skills are fettered, lest I seek to thwart the revenge of the Gods on Grallon. So did it command me."

"What if you disobey?" asked Corentinus.

"Horror upon Ys."

"As the pagan Gods visited plague on Thebes because of the sin of Oedipus. But yours would do Their harm because of the righteousness of Gratillonius. The true God is otherwise, my daughter."

Forsquilis clenched her fists. "Hold back your preaching!"

"I will, I will. You must, then, stand aside while Gratillonius goes to his doom?"

Forsquilis swallowed, blinked, jerked forth a nod.

"Why do you appeal to me?" Corentinus went on, still quietly.

"Can you help him, somehow, anyhow?" she cried.

The fog was parting, dissolving. A sunbeam lanced through.

"That lies with him," the pastor said. "And with God."

Forsquilis snapped a breath and strode from him. Soon she was lost in the mist. He remained behind to pray for mercy on every soul gone astray.

— 9 —

Dusk deepened. More and more stars glimmered into sight. Processional Way was a ribbon of pallor between meadow and heights on the right, the Wood of the King on the left, where wind mourned through the oaks. Ys gleamed faintly ahead.

Dahut rode homeward. Formerly her father would have required an escort for her, safe though the hinterland was these days, but now she claimed independence—not that they had met of late, those two.

A man bounded soft-gaited from the edge of the Wood and loped along at her foot. She clucked to the horse before she knew Rufinus and eased. "What will you?" she greeted him.

Eyeballs and teeth caught what light lingered, sulfur-yellow in the west. "I've a warning for you, Princess." He spoke as coldly as the wind blew.

Dahut sat erect in the saddle. "Well, say on."

"Your father, my King, to whom I am sworn—he is in pain on your account. He is not at war with you, but you are with him."

"Be off, mongrel!"

"I will not until you have heard me. Listen, Princess."

"Queen."

"Listen to me. I've my ways of finding things out. We needn't go into what I've learned and what I've reasoned—not yet—not ever, if you behave yourself. But hear me, Dahut. There shall be no plotting against my King. I make no accusations. I merely say it is banned. I am ready to defend him however necessary or—" a dagger slid forth—"if necessary, avenge him. Do you understand, my lady?" Rufinus chuckled. "Surely you, his daughter, are glad to hear this. Let me bid you a very good evening."

He slipped into the shadows. Dahut spurred her horse
to a gallop.

— 10 —

The day was calm and crisp. Waves rolled almost
softly against the wall of Ys and scarcely troubled its open
harbor basin. Inland, autumn colors dappled the hills.

Gratillonius stood on the top, above the sea gate, with
Cothortin Rosmertai, Lord of Works. "Nay," he told the
fussy little man, "the sample taken shows the doors continue sound. However, it does hold dampness. Dry rot
will start creeping under the metal. Within—oh, ten or
fifteen years, the wood will be weakened. We must replace it ere then."

"Of course, of course." Cothortin pulled at his chin.
"Although that's a huge task. 'Tis not been done in living
memory."

"I know. Yet the records show how, and we've time to
train craftsmen and divers, everyone we'll need. What we
should set in train soon is the cutting and seasoning of the
oak."

Cothortin pondered. In his fashion, he was competent.
"Aye, you've right, my lord. The Osismiic forests—and
when conditions are as unsettled as they regrettably are,
'tis wise to be beforehand."

"As it happens," Gratillonius told him, "I've need to
visit Aquilo and discuss various matters, such as our policy
toward Rome, this month. I can also raise the question of
timber."

Cothortin gave a small, anxious sniff. "Should you leave
Ys, my lord, under . . . present circumstances?"

" 'Tis a short trip. I'll be back in time to stand my
regular Watch."

The longing swelled inside Gratillonius—to be off, away,
however briefly, to someplace where the Gods of Ys had
no dominion.

XI

— 1 —

It was two years since he had last seen Apuleius Vero, when the tribune came to Ys, and four since he had last been in Aquilo. They had corresponded, but sporadically. Gratillonius was no writer, and besides, language must be guarded, in case a letter fell into certain hands. Entering the small city, he observed new construction, streets fuller and noisier, a pair of coasters at the wharf despite the late season. The hinterland had also looked still more prosperous, better cared for, than formerly. What a shame if this should be lost, he thought.

Dismissing his escort to quarters and giving Adminius charge of Favonius, he went on afoot to the house of the Apuleii. A crowd eddied around, people knew and hailed him, the air of welcome was almost overpowering after his loneliness. Word had flown ahead, and Apuleius waited in person at the door. They clasped arms tightly.

"How good to see you again, friend," the tribune said with as much warmth as he ever allowed into his tones. He had grown more gray and his hairline had receded further, but the finely chiseled features were free of any slackness. "Come in, do." He beckoned a slave to take the luggage which an Ysan marine had carried after the King.

They entered the atrium. The same chaste floral patterns as before decorated it, except that one wall panel had been done over; now stems and blossoms entwined a Chi Rho. Gratillonius noticed, too, that while Apuleius's tunic remained of fine woolen fabric, carefully tailored and

185

meticulously cleaned, it lacked olden touches of color and elegance. "I trust you can stay for several days and get well rested," the host said. "You look terribly fatigued. Was it a hard journey here?"

"Not at all," Gratillonius answered. "In fact, refreshing. But you must have seen in my message that I've got serious matters to talk over with you, though I didn't spell them out. We—"

A ten-year-old boy erupted from the inner doorway and sped across the mosaic. "Oh, sir, you're here!" he cried.

Apuleius lifted a hand, smiling. "Hush, Salomon," he reproved. "Where are your manners?"

Gratillonius grinned. "Warriors will charge forward," he said, "if you're still like what your father was telling me in Ys. Caution, however, caution is always in order. We may get in a bit of shieldwork this trip, you and I." He was fond of the lad. Abruptly, a blow to the throat, he felt how like a son of his own this of Apuleius was, the son that nine times nine Gallicenae could never give him.

Salomon's blue eyes widened. "You've brought me a shield?" he blurted.

"For shame," his father said. "Greed is a sin, and barbarous as well."

"I don't want to undermine your authority," Gratillonius said, "but it did occur to me that this fellow must have outgrown the sword I gave him last time, and be about ready to make acquaintance with other gear. Later, Salomon. Uh, how's the rest of the family?"

"In excellent health, by God's mercy," Apuleius replied. "Verania is to market with her mother. They should return soon. Meanwhile, shall we get you settled in? Salomon, go back to your lessons. I will expect better answers this evening than yesterday, when I question you about your Livius, or there will be no excursion to the farm for you tomorrow." He took Gratillonius's elbow. "Come. Wine awaits, and first a slave to wash your feet."

Gratillonius regarded that ceremony as pointless, when he had arrived on horseback wearing boots, but he was long since used to the other man's antiquarian practices. At that, warm water and toweling hands, followed by slippers, soothed. He would have liked a chair with a back to it and undiluted wine, in the bookful room to which

Apuleius conducted him, but such things were ordinary only in Ys.

The tribune signed his beaker before drinking. That had not been his custom earlier. "Do you care to tell me at once, in brief, what brings you?" he asked. "If not, we have enough everyday memories to exchange. But you may find relief in speaking forth."

"I would," Gratillonius admitted. "Not but what you can have guessed pretty well. I know how you keep abreast of developments, also beyond Armorica. That's why I've come, for your thoughts and, maybe, your help."

"Suppose you describe the situation as you see it."

Gratillonius did, in words he had carefully chosen and condensed on the way here—the situation with respect to the Imperium. Dahut and the rest, no, he could not talk about that. If rumors had drifted this far, Apuleius had the kindness not to mention them. The whole story might shock him, and Gratillonius needed him calm, Euclideanly logical. Besides, what had any of it to do with Rome?

In the end the listener nodded, cupped his chin, gazed out the window at the pale autumn sky, where rooks rode a bucking bluster of wind, and murmured: "Approximately what I expected. I've already given the matter thought— since hearing of that scandalous Frankish affair, in fact— and made various inquiries. We must talk at greater length, of course, but I think I know what I will recommend."

"Well?" Gratillonius exclaimed. He curbed himself. "I'm sorry." He tossed off a draught. It was Rhenian, tartly sweet. He was a little surprised that he noticed; he had not done so before.

"Best I speak bluntly," said Apuleius with some difficulty. "Your prospects of winning a favorable judgment in Lugdunum are poor. Your enemies in Turonum have connections you lack; and, to be sure, they can make a not unpersuasive case for your having allowed Ys to become a subversive influence. You plan to appeal step by step until at last you reach the Augustus—well, between us, as you yourself put it, Stilicho. This would be a mistake. It could cause proceedings to drag on for two or three years, during which you must often go in person to defend yourself, first here, then there. Such absences would weaken your standing in Ys. You could lose what control you have over events, or it could be pried away from you. Or . . . anything could happen. Stilicho, for example, is not so almighty as he seems. Greater men than he have fallen overnight; or God may call him from this world. Do not delay."

Gratillonius looked into the hazel eyes. A tingle passed through him. "You do have a recommendation for me."

"We must explore this," Apuleius warned. "However, I feel we will reach much the same conclusions. Send a letter directly to Stilicho. I'll help you compose it and give you one of my own to accompany it, for whatever that may be worth. Far more valuable will be a testimonial from Bishop Martinus, which I believe we can get, and perhaps other prominent Armoricans.

"We do *not* do this behind Glabrio's back. You inform him of your action, as soon as it is too late for him to halt it somehow or dispatch a courier who'll arrive ahead of yours. He then has no grounds for complaint about plots against him, nor any reason to get you summoned to Lugdunum. You may quite likely have to attend a hearing in Treverorum, but that won't be for months, when Stilicho's reply has come. God willing, it should dispose of the business."

"Stilicho may not be easy to reach," Gratillonius said, mostly because he wanted everything laid out plain to see. "The way he moves around, holding the Empire together."

Apuleius nodded. "Like the carpenter on a foundering ship, who dashes about as timbers and cordage come apart in the storm," he answered sadly. Brightening: "But this will be Glabrio's problem in equal measure. Meanwhile you have time to strengthen your position, marshal your advocates."

"You think Stilicho will give me a favorable judgment?"

"At least, he ought not to condemn you out of hand. Your reasoning about him appears sound to me. He is a soldier himself, a practical man, experience in starcraft; and, I hear, being half a barbarian, he nourishes a wistful admiration for everything civilized—as Ys is, in its perverse fashion."

"What do you mean by that?" asked Gratillonius, startled.

Apuleius sighed, leaned forward, laid a hand on the knee of his guest, smiled like a herald offering truce. "No intent to offend you," he said. "Ys is a wonder of the world. I came back from it so enchanted that it was only after much thought, prayer, austerity I fully understood how it trembles—dances, in its heedlessness—on the brink of hell. And I had been there—" He paused. "*You* are not corrupted, dear friend. In you the antique virtues survive. But you should realize how Ys appears when seen not by its own many-colored lights but by the Light. Pray God it be redeemed before too late."

"Meanwhile," said Gratillonius stiffly, "my job is to keep it on guard duty for Rome."

"True, good soldier. Come, let us put this aside for now, let us drink together and talk of happier matters. Surely you'll have time to share a few innocent pleasures with us?"

—As the men returned to the atrium, Rovinda and Verania entered. The woman was still comely, if somewhat faded. At thirteen the girl had lengthened into thinness, with curves of hip and breast shy beneath her plain gown. She could barely whisper greetings to Gratillonius, while staring downward. Afterward, though, from beneath billows of fawn hair, whenever she thought he was not looking, her gaze followed him always.

— 2 —

Wearying of confinement—his work, which had been undemanding in summer, became nil after Mumach traffic shut down—Tommaltach left Ys, as often before, for a ramble in the countryside. Sometimes on these excursions he was days agone, far into Osismia. On his back were sword and bedroll, in his hand was a spear that doubled as a staff, at his belt hung a few necessities including a packet of food and a sling for knocking down small game. Most evenings, though, he could charm a family into giving him supper, a doss, perhaps a companion for the night.

This morning was clear and chill. Outside High Gate there rose a clamor from smithies and carpenter shops, pungency from tanneries, dyeworks, soapworks, all such industries as were banned in the city, bunched along

Aquilonian Way. Their buildings were mostly small, many primitive, cob or wattle-and-daub with thatch roofs, but cheerful well-being bustled in and out of them. A number of men recognized Tommaltach and called greetings. He responded affably. Once their long isolation had ended, Ysans soon became apt to make much of any foreigners.

Having traversed the section, Tommaltach had the amphitheater on his left. Just beyond. Aquilonian Way bent south and went up onto the heights. He followed it. That was a stiff climb. At the top he halted, less to catch his breath than for a look around. From here the road would bear him out of sight of Ys and then, turning again east, presently to Audiarna, at the frontier of the Empire.

Gorse grew thickly at his feet, rustly beneath the wind that shrilled off the sea. Below reached the valley, closely hemmed in but nonetheless, in its peace and wealth, radiating a sense of spaciousness. Harvests were gathered, leaves fallen, pastures sallow; the sobriety of the land brought forth its sculpturing and made the homes on the hillsides gleam like jewels. Exquisite, too, at this distance, lay the amphitheater, the canal a silver thread behind it. The wood of the King squatted there, but one could look away from its darkness.

Westward swept Cape Rach, out to a spire that was the pharos. The tombs in front seemed a mere huddle, moldered into meaninglessness. Closer by, grazing sheep and an occasional wind-gnarled evergreen livened the tawny earth.

Point Vanis was scarcely visible. The towers of Ys crowded it from view. They soared in brilliance, as if cut from crystal, over the city wall, which itself became a ruddy chalice for them. Seafowl were flocking yonder—drawn by the carts that lumbered out with offal at this time of day, but still a storm of wings which the towers pierced on their way to the sky. Beyond surged Ocean, sapphire, emerald, and leaping ivory, onward to worldedge where holy Sena lay. Sails danced; the sons of Ys were not yet ready to withdraw for the winter from her sea.

"Glorious you are," Tommaltach said. "Would I were a poet, to chant the praise of Dahut's home."

A while later, realizing in surprise how much later, he was pulled from his dreams by a sound of hoofs. The rider approached from the east at a gallop. Sunlight flashed off armor. When he drew close, Tommaltach identified him as a Roman legionary—Guentius, he was. As he came in earshot, the Scotian cried, "What's the haste this fine day?"

"Gratillonius returns," called back the newcomer, and went on downhill.

Tommaltach nodded. He should have remembered who had accompanied Dahut's father to Aquilo. They liked to have a proper reception ready for their King in Ys.

He squinted. Following the horsemen, his gaze had encountered a runner just emerged from the industrial cluster. A woman, young, to judge by speed, grace, and shapeliness. A white gown fluttered loose about her ankles, a blue cloak from her shoulders, as hastily as she went through the wind. Her left hand gathered the mantle at her throat so that the cowl should not fall back but, instead, keep screening. She lowered her head while Guentius neared and went by; his curious glance did not find her face.

Tommaltach ran fingers through his hair, puzzled. The woman stayed on Aquilonian Way. He decided to wait till she reached him. Maybe she had need of male help, and was bonny.

She reached him, stopped, drew away the hood. Sunlight blazed off her braids. The spear dropped from his grasp.

Dahut smiled. A trace of moisture gleamed over a fair skin only slightly flushed. She breathed deeply but easily. "Why, Tommaltach," she said, "would you have left with never a farewell to your friends?"

"My, my lady—" It was he whose heart and lungs shuddered. "Sure, and I'd not—But I'd no idea. . . . How may I serve you?"

"Come, let us stroll onward, ere folk below notice us and gawk," she laughed.

Numbly, he retrieved his spear. She took his free arm. They paced down the middle of the road. Ys sank from sight. It was as if they had the world to themselves, they and the wind and a pair of hawks wheeling high above.

"Did you intend one of your lengthy wanderings?" she asked.

He gulped and nodded.

"I feared that, when I saw you go past outfitted like this," she said. " 'Twas sheer chance I did, unless it be the will of some kindly God. I was off to fetch a horse and make a solitary trek of my own for several hours. But then, instead, I covered me and went on afoot like any nameless girl. Let those who spied her breaking into a dash wonder why." She squeezed his arm against her side. "Belike they think what a lucky scoundrel yon Tommaltach is, that his women pursue him."

His countenance burned. He stared directly frontward. " 'Tis well I decided to wait, my lady," he pushed out of his gullet.

"Oh, I think I could have overhauled you, long though those legs be. You see, I was determined. Of a sudden, a half-formed thought that had been in me sprang from my brow full-grown."

"Wh-what is that?"

"Did you truly mean to be elsewhere at Hunter's Moon?"

"At—? Oh, Samain. Well, I'd not *meant* to, my lady. It only happens that in Ys I'll have no rites to take part in as at home, and this seemed a good time to travel, before the days grow too short and wet. I'd find me somebody's roof to spend the eve under."

"Are you ignorant of our celebration that night? 'Tis the maddest, merriest revel of the year."

Tommaltach frowned. "I have heard tell," he answered slowly.

"And you'd miss it, a lively young man like you?"

He walked in silence for a while.

"Why this? Why?" Dahut insisted.

Tommaltach summoned resolve. He released himself from her, halted, turned and leaned on his spear, holding it fast with both hands. " 'Tis the worst of nights for being abroad," he stated. "Then the doors between the worlds swing wide. All kinds of beings wander free, síd dwellers, the Sky Horse, the Fire Hounds, bogles, werebeasts, evil witches, vengeful dead. The Law stands down and black sorcery rules over the earth. 'Tis the next day and night are joyous, when the wickedness is gone again and the year passes from the Goddess to the Horned One."

Dahut raised his brows. "Oh, surely you've put spooks

behind you," she said. "You, who've traveled, met educated people, lived these past months in Ys, and wintered here ere then. Why, you worship Mithras."

"That doesn't mean a man cannot or should not pay respect to the Gods of his fathers and, and the old usages," he replied unhappily.

The slightest scorn tinged her voice: "I've heard that some of the Scotic tribes make a human sacrifice that eventide, to appease the demons. Have you such plans?"

"I have not!" He perceived his own indignation and stood bemused.

Dahut trilled laughter, stepped close, laid hands over his, looked up at him. "Well, set the rest of it aside too. In Ys the time is simply occasion for festival, and has been for centuries. Yet Ys flourishes, Ys is free of ghosts."

" 'Tis less sure I am of that than when I first came here—. But I'm sorry, I beg my lady's pardon, and her pardon for my rash tongue as well."

She dimpled and beamed. "Ah, you can jest. I forgive you on condition you turn back and keep the night with me."

He could only gape.

"You are not afraid to, are you?" she challenged.

"I am not!" He shook his head violently.

Dahut grew yearning. "Hear me, Tommaltach. Take pity on me. You know how torn my life has been of late. Nay, you cannot truly know, but mayhap you can guess. I, who was young, glad, hopeful, am as trapped and alone between the worlds as any homeless phantom. What shall I do? What can I do? What will become of me? Or of Ys, whose King defies its Gods?" She let go of him, stood with fists doubled at her bosom, and went on bravely: "But I'll not bewail myself. Rather, I'd fain by merry once more, though it be for the last time ever. Why should I sit in my empty house and weep while Ys holds revel?"

"Oh, my lady." Pain made raw his voice.

Dahut blinked her eyes free of tears and smiled anew, a smile that turned mischievous as she spoke. "Going forth to sing, dance, carouse the night away, that will hearten me, will be my message to fate that I am yet unbroken. Who knows? It may turn my fortunes around. The Gods favor the bold. I've heard that you Scotic warriors often kiss your spearheads ere a battle, and go into it laughing. Then you must understand me." (He nodded, stricken mute.) "Now I cannot very well join the frolic openly. Even as a vestal, I was supposed to keep discreet. As one who claims to be a Queen, I should attend the solemn banquet of the Gallicenae, but I can beg myself free of that. My wish is to go out masked, unbeknownst, and mingle with the throng. For both pleasure and safety, I need an escort, a strong young man who'll afterward keep my secret. I could not trust any of Ys with it, but you, Tommaltach, you I trust utterly.

"Will you be my companion on the eve?"

"My lady," he croaked, "I would die for you."

"Oh, that should not be needful. Thank you, dear sweet Tommaltach, thank you!"

" 'Tis you I must thank—"

"And you're handsome and lovable too!" Dahut skipped into a dance, there on the highway, arms raised to the sun. She caroled. He stood in his daze and stared.

She took his arm again at last, and got them walking onward. "We'd best start back home erelong, separately," she said. "However, this little while is ours, and so will the whole night be, two moonrises hence." He having partially regained balance, they chattered blithely about plans.

A noise from the rear interrupted them, hoofbeats. They stepped to the roadside and Dahut shadowed her face with the cowl. A woman sped by. She barely glanced at them as she passed, perhaps not recognizing the man either. They knew her, light-brown hair streaming back in disarray from delicate features, tall body that years and two child-births had matured without causing to grow ungainly— clad in haste, careless of appearance, and her mount doubtless taken from the livery stable among the indus-tries in the same hurry—. She thudded on down the road.

"Queen Tambilis," Tommaltach said in wonderment. "What might she be wanting? Oh, of course. Today the King comes home. She's off to meet him."

"I should have known," Dahut hissed. "When I met Guentius, I should have known. But I did not stop to think."

Looking sideways, he saw her gone white; the very

irises of her eyes seemed to have paled. Abruptly she whirled from him. "I don't want to see them together," he heard. "I *will* not. Not him and her."

She strode back toward Ys, her pace just short of becoming a run. He followed. "My lady—" he gobbled in his helplessness.

She threw her command behind her: "Abide a while. I must return by myself. Say naught. You will hear later— concerning Hunter's Moon." He jerked to a stop and watched her go from him.

— 3 —

Samain Eve was bitterly clear. That was good, for there was much to do. Great folk and their attendants opened the seasonal fairs held for three days all over Ériu. Most tenants could not arrive that early. They must first finish bringing in their flocks for the winter and dig up any root crops still in the ground, lest the terrors of that night wither these. They must douse every hearth and meet on hilltops to take new fire from the blazes freshly kindled, after their chieftains had led them in sacrifice. Meanwhile their wives and children must make houses ready, plaiting together withes of hazel, rowan, and yew to fasten across doorways and windows, setting food outside for the dead who would come wandering by, fetching water from sacred springs or pools, preparing a porridge of certain wild grains and seeds for the family, making sure of enough lamp grease or rushlights to last out the dark.

As the sun lowered, well-nigh everyone hastened indoors. Tomorrow and the day after, they would welcome in the new year. On this night they huddled away from Those who then went abroad. A few of the mightiest druids stayed out to take omens; a few covens met to carry out rites and cast spells handed down from the Firi Bolg and Fomóri; outlaws and gangrels cowered in the bracken; but otherwise the hours of the moon were given over to what was unhuman.

Save for Niall of the Nine Hostages and his charioteer.

Folk at Tallten shivered, muttered, made fending signs. They were not many, mostly warriors on watch in the fortress raths round about. The great fair here took place at Lúgnassat. Samain fair was at Temir itself, and the King should have been there.

Instead he had entered with guardsmen and menials the day before, opened and occupied the royal house, sent messengers to and fro, conferred in secret with those who came; and an eldritch lot they were. His fighting men were picked: tough-hearted old bullies who had followed him for long years, some to the wall of Ys. Likewise the servants were such as recked little of Gods and less of ghosts. The feast had been savage; a quarrel over the hero's portion led to a slaying, which had not happened in living memory.

Niall denied that that was an evil portent. He gave out that his tanist Nath Í could well preside over the first day's sacrifices and games at Temir. He, Niall, would return there at dawn of Samain—the distance was only ten leagues or so—to partake in the Sharpening of the Weapons, the Wedding of the Year-Bride, and whatever else required himself. But this eve he must be at Tallten.

For that was where the Kings and Queens of Temir lay buried.

During the day, his men brought wood to a grave he named. Toward sunset, three women lighted it. Nobody dared watch what more they did. Besides, the mounds hampered sight, though except for the barrow of Lúg's foster-mother at the middle they were not long or high. Unlike the Children of Danu at their Brug, these descendants of Ír and Eber rested each in his or her own chamber, alone and prideful.

The sun dropped down to a black wall of forest in the west. It had turned the river fiery. Purple beyond the plain, eastern heaven began to lighten as the moon climbed from below. Bats flitted about. The chill made early dew glimmer on grass and stones.

Through silence came a trampling of hoofs and rumble of wheels. Niall drove forth from the hall. He stood splendidly garbed in a chariot that sheened with bronze. A cloak worked in seven colors rippled from his shoulders. The head of his spear caught the last rays of sun, as did the fading gold of his hair. Also richly attired, Cathual had the reins of two matched gray stallions, animals of Southland breed such as were seldom seen in Ériu and beyond any price.

Ahead of Niall loomed the grave of the Goddess, amidst the ridges that covered his own kin. Shadows blurred them, but wavered as he neared the balefire at the foot of one. There flames roared upward from a white-hot bed. Three black-clad women stared into them.

Cathual drew rein. He must stay where he was, because the horses were uneasy, snorted, nickered, stamped, chafed. Niall descended. He dipped his spear to the women. "Have you made ready?" he hailed them.

"We have that," said the maiden.

"Herself will listen," said the wife.

"Ask no more," said the crone.

"But this I intend."

"It is for you," said the maiden.

"Make your bargain yourself," said the wife.

"You shall not see us again," said the crone.

They departed, went behind the barrow, were perhaps lost in the nightfall; for just then the sun slipped away. Bleak greenish glow lingered a while. The moon rose monstrous.

"Lord," said Cathual, and the firelight showed sweat aglitter on his face, "best you be quick. Sure, and I know not how long I can hold these beasts."

Niall advanced to the head of the grave. He held his spear level above it. "Mongfind, stepmother mine," he said, "wake." The fire brawled. "Behold who has dealt with witches such as once you were, he whose death once you sought. I call you back to the world. I give you blood to drink. I make my peace with you, now at last on this night, that you may turn the hatred that was ever in you against my foes."

He leaned over and thrust the spear downward till it stood at the middle of the mound like a lean menhir deeply implanted. "By this I rouse you, I please you, I compel you!" he cried.

Swiftly, then, he went to stand before the horses. They neighed aloud and snapped at their bits. "Steady, Cathual," Niall commanded. From his waist he drew a shortsword that he had taken off a slain Roman in the year of the Wall. He stepped in and smote. Blood spurted from the neck of the right-hand stallion. The left-hand animal screamed, reared, lashed his forehoofs. Barely did Niall avoid a blow that would have shattered his skull. He wielded his weapon, there between the huge thrashing bodies, and scrambled clear.

Cathual fought the reins while the horses bucked, lurched, stumbled, shrieked in their death throes. Blood reddened the grave. The noises rattled off into stillness. They struggled a while yet, down on the earth, before they lay quiet. The moon mounted higher. It turned the land ashen.

"Now," said Niall. He cut the bodies free. Meanwhile Cathual unloaded a wine cask, two beakers of gold, and a battle ax. Racket lifted anew as he hewed the chariot into pieces which he cast on the fire.

Niall butchered the carcasses. He slashed off steaks and chops; the rest he divided roughly, chunks such as a strong man could lift. Blood-besmeared, he stood at the tumulus and said, "Mongfind, wise-woman, take your sacrifice and be slaked. I am Niall whom you hated, and you are she whom the people so fear that at Beltene and Samain a druid has come to do that which will keep you under. But your sons are long since my faithful followers; and at this turning of the year I have sent the druid away, and instead called witches to my aid and yours.

"Mongfind, come! Help me. Tell me how I may destroy Ys, the city that slew my first-born son, Ethniu's child. Give me this, and I will unbind you for aye. I will make the law that folk shall offer to you at the turnings of the year, quench your thirst, ease your hunger, and beg your blessing. Mongfind, come to this, the first of your feasts!"

He took back the spear and skewered meat. While he roasted it, Cathual kept the fire fed and broached the wine cask.

Thereafter the two men squatted to eat until they could hold no more and drink until they could barely walk. They said nothing; this meal was not for pleasure.

When at last they were done, and the moon high and small and icy in a frost-ring, they cast the remnants of the horses on the fire. It sparked, sputtered, sank low. Tomorrow the birds of the Mórrigu would gorge. Niall planted the ruined spear in the coals. Flames ran up its shaft like the wreathings of a Beltene pole. "I am going to bed now," the King said drunkenly. "Mongfind, follow me."

He and his charioteer helped each other through the moonlight to the hall. Reeling and staggering, all but helpless, they still met no creatures of the night. Guardsmen who sat awake greeted them with shouts of relief, then stepped back, dumbstricken, for these two were entranced. They fell into their beds and toppled into sleep.

In the morning Cathual, hammers and chisels at work in his head, groaned that he had dreamed about a river. There had been woods, and an arrow, and the river flowing forever west into the sea. Everything was confused and senseless, mainly he felt sorrow, grief unbounded, but he did not know why, unless it was that the river flowed always west into the sea. Perhaps he had only had a nightmare. Prophecy was not for the likes of him.

Niall said nothing. Calm though pale, he returned to Temir and carried out his duties. Indeed, he seemed unchanged; men could see that he thought about some great undertaking, but this he had often done.

Only afterward did he reveal that his stepmother had sought him out while he slept. She looked newly dead; a wind he could not feel or hear tossed her gray locks and fluttered her gown; the hands that touched him were cold. Yet she grinned as well as a corpse can and told him, "Seek the Queen who has no King."

— 4 —

As ever, the first evening of Hunter's Moon filled Ys with bacchanalia. Then the lowliest laborer became equal to the highest-born Suffete, owed no reverence, incurred no blame. Even among temperate families, a gathering in someone's home could well lead to stealing off with somebody not one's spouse, or turn into an outright orgy. If weather was at all bearable, the young took to the streets, unless parents were so strict as to forbid a virgin daughter's going out. Wine, ale, hemp smoke, and giddying mushrooms ruled the night. Lowtown was apt to become dangerous, but violence was rare in the prosperous parts of the city; there were better things to do than fight.

The Fire Fountain played in the Forum. Colored gushes and spurts of burning oil threw uneasy radiance and shadows over the throng that milled about, almost hiding the moon that rose above the hills. Nobody felt the cold. All were too closely together in each other's perfume and sweat, all were too active. Most wore either finery overdone to the point of gaudiness or fantastical costumes. They capered, danced, hugged, kissed, frequently at random; they laughed, shouted, howled, sang. Instruments rang, brayed, tinkled, clicked, hooted, squealed, throbbed, altogether wild.

A goblin mask leered at a girl who pranced wearing swirls of gold skin paint beneath a couple of flimsy veils. Feathers covered a man from head to foot. A lass and lad had partnered their attire to form a bare-breasted centauress. Two youths, the first outfitted as a satyr, the second with antlers and deerskin cape, wagged leather phalluses of matching immensity. A hideous old witch revealed well-turned ankles as she danced with a fellow gotten up to resemble, he imagined, a Hun. A girl with the Suffete face giggled as a burly sailor held her by the waist and felt inside her splendid gown. A visiting Osismiic tribesman carried in his arms an Ysan lady who could not walk because her legs were encased in a fish tail; she rewarded him with a cup brought to his lips and ingenious caresses. The tumult seethed on beyond any person's sight.

One could see what was on the steps of the buildings around the square. Three different groups of musicians played regardless of conflict. Here pipes wailed and drums pulsed frantically in the Phrygian mode, there two kitharas resounded in the Ionian with a drinking song, yonder a trumpet blew a stately Dorian measure—but the words being sung to it were very far from stately. Two lithe

women in scanty Egyptian garb rattled their sistrums and
undulated. A juggler practiced his art. Several couples had
spread their cloaks and were in various stages of lovemaking. In the portico of the Christian church, a man stood
naked except for a crown of thorns and held his arms
straight out to the sides while at his feet three women,
wearing exiguous suggestions of Roman legionary gear,
shook dice.

Tommaltach frowned when he noticed that. It could be
unwise, and was certainly ill-bred, to mock anybody's
God. For his part he wore tunic and trews of good stuff,
and a gilt mask over the upper half of his face. He cheered
himself with a fresh squirt of wine from the leather bottle
slung at his shoulder.

"Yaa! Give me some of that!" cried Dahut. She opened
her mouth and cocked her head back. He laughed and
obliged her. She was in clothing similar to his, sufficiently
loose that she could pass for a boy. A full mask covered
her head except for jaw and lips (like rose petals they
were, those lips). It was an owl's-head image, hollowly
staring.

She darted from him, up onto the steps where the
dancers were. There she skipped, swayed, snapped her
fingers, no less fleet or graceful than they. He gaped in his
marveling. She had been wildly gleeful from the sundown
moment when they met. Each time she had caught his
hand, stroked his back, leaped and trilled before his eyes,
burned in memory.

"To High Gate!" called a voice through the uproar.
More joined in: "To High Gate! To High Gate!" The
processional dance along Lir Way was traditional, after the
moon had mounted enough to light it.

Dahut bounded back down. "We go, let's begone," she
sang, and tugged at her escort's arm, urged it around her
waist. For an instant he was alarmed. Folk who saw a man
and a boy thus together— But nobody would care tonight,
and he and she were both nameless, and besides, she had
remarked that many women would be in male disguise.
And she was Dahut and he held her.

The musicians scampered to take place at the front of
the line that was confusedly forming. They composed their

differences and began the saucy "She Sat Upon the Dolmen." Forth they went, and the young of Ys rollicked
after. Their dances were manifold. Some sprang or whirled
by themselves, some in pairs or rings or intricate inter-
weavings. Dahut and Tommaltach, side by side embraced,
kicked their way, with much laughter. When the line had
straggled a distance, she signalled to him—somehow he
understood—that every few minutes they should link their
free hands and gyre around cheek to cheek. He drowned
in the warm fragrance of her, spiraled down and down a
maelstrom forever.

From its frost-ring the moon silvered towertops, dappled pavement, made the stone chimeras appear to stir as
if they too would fain join the lunacy. Echoes boomed. As
the avenue climbed, revelers who glanced backward saw
past the wall and sea gate to a slowly rolling immensity,
obsidian dark but bedazzled by the moon.

Dahut guided Tommaltach. They moved away from the
line and into a side street.

"We're, we're drifting off," he faltered.

Her hand in the small of his back, her eager feet bore
him onward. "We two," she said deep in her throat.
"Follow, follow."

Stunned amidst thunder, he danced with her up the
winding narrowness. Music and shouts reached him ever
fainter, until they were dream-noise beneath moon-hush,
where only the tap-tapping of Dahut's shoes over stone
could speak. Houses walled him and her in darknesses
broken by glimpses of a pillar or a brass knocker, sometimes a yellow gleam escaping a window shuttered against
the cold of Samain Eve.

"Stop," she said, and was gone from him like mist in a
wind. But no, she was at a particular door, she turned its
latch and swung it wide, lamp-glow spilled forth amber
across her. She beckoned. He stood stupefied. "Come,"
she called, "be not afraid, here is my home."

He stumbled into the red atrium. She slipped off her
mask and tossed it onto a chair. The low light died and was
reborn in her braids. She smiled at him and returned to
take his hands in hers, to look into his eyes. "On this
night, aught may happen," she murmured. "I wearied of

that vulgar spectacle. Let us celebrate the moon by ourselves."

"My lady," he stammered, "this is—I dare not—I'm but a barbarian, a foreigner, and you a Queen of Ys—"

Her nails bit into him. Lips drew back from teeth, blood drained from cheeks and brow. "Queen," he heard. "This day Queen Tambilis went out with the King to the Red Lodge, and this night she sleeps at his side. How long till the rest betray me too?"

Then immediately she laughed again, crowed laughter, hugged him and laid her cheek to his for one surge of his heart. Withdrawing, she said, "Nay, forgive me, I've no wish to plague you with our politics. Let us merely be gladsome together." Reaching up, she pulled his mask off. "Be seated. My household has this time free, of course, so let me serve you, friend and guest. Forget whatever else we have ever been."

There was actually little to do. Wine and goblets waited on a table, with delicate small foods. She ignited a punk stick at a lamp and brought it to an incense burner likewise prepared. Thereafter she held it in a brazen bowl full of leaves parched and crushed, which she must blow into smoldering life. Placing herself on the couch beside him, she said, "This smoke has its virtues, but it does bear a harsh odor which I hope the perfume will soften. Now pour for us, Tommaltach."

He obeyed. They regarded each other over the rims of the vessels and sipped.

She chatted merrily. After a while he became able to respond.

When she had had him inhale the smoke several times, he felt a boundless, tingling ease and joy. How wonderful the world! He could fling off a whipcrack quip or he could sit and watch her dear lips for a hundred years, just as he chose.

"Wait," she whispered. "I will be back."

He gazed at a lamp flame. There was a deep mystery in it, which he almost understood.

Dahut re-entered. Her hair flowed free, down over the lightest and loosest of belted robes. Blue it was, sea color, a hue that lapped beneath the lapis lazuli of her eyes.

Blue also was a pinch of dried blossoms she cupped in her left hand. She raised her goblet in the right. She bent her head and kissed the borage. She licked it up and washed it down with a mouthful of wine. This was another mystery on this night of mysteries.

She coiled herself at his side and laid her head on his shoulder. "Hold me," she breathed.

He never knew which of them began the kiss, or when.

She took him by the hand and led him to the bedchamber. Moonlight poured through unshuttered glass to mingle with candlelight from a table, quicksilver and gold.

Gravely, now, she guided his fingers to her girdle and thence to the robe.

He knelt before her.

She reached, it was as if she lifted him back to his feet, and that kiss went on and on.

She giggled, though, while they both fumbled with the fastenings of his clothes.

But thereafter she caught him to her, and presently drew him onto the bed, and purred to him, "Yea, oh, yea."

—He did not know if he had caused her pain. "You are the first, the very first, beloved," she told him, shivering in his arms; and a dark spot or two said the same; but she drew him onward, and was quick to learn what pleased him most and to do it.

—Dawn grayed the window. Dahut sat straight in the rumpledness and clasped her knees. Above, her breasts were milk and roses, save for a bruise he had made in his ardor and she had simply bidden him kiss for a penance. She looked down on Tommaltach where he sprawled.

Suddenly her gaze and her voice were an oncoming winter. "Done is done," she said, "and splendid it was, and may we have many more times in the same heaven. But you know—do you not?—that ours was a mortal misdeed, and we must both die, unless you do the single thing that can make the world right again."

— 5 —

Gratillonius woke slowly. Fragments of dream criss-crossed his awareness, glittery, like spiderwebs in a forest seen bedewed by the earliest sunlight. They faded away after he opened his eyes. He did not know what hour it was, but brightness seeped by the drapes to make a luminous twilight in the room. Well past dayspring, he guessed drowsily.

And the day? Aye—he chuckled within himself to note that he was thinking in Ysan—Hunter's Moon ongoing. Tonight it would be completely full. He thought that if this calm weather held, he and Tambilis might walk a ways on the road and enjoy its beauty. That should not count as abandonment of his Watch, provided they return here. Last night they had been too busy.

She slept still, curled toward him, her face dim beneath a tangle of hair. How lovely she was. Most women showed at their homeliest now. He stretched his mouth in a smile while he stretched his muscles—carefully, not to rouse her—and breathed the warmth of her. Let her rest. They had today, tonight, and the following day and night before this retreat ended and he must go back to being King, prefect, centurion. After she met him on Aquilonian Way they had delightedly conspired how he could slough off obligations during this while. . . .

Poor lass, she would have her own troubles to cope with. But together, shield beside shield, they would prevail, make enemies into allies, restore what was lost, and, aye, in the minds of men conquer territory for Dahut, for her to reign happy too.

He slipped out from under the blankets. Air nipped him. He would dress and, after prayers, run around the Wood before they broke their fast.

A sound struck through. He froze in place. It had been faint, muffled, he must have mistaken some clatter from the hall. . . . It sought him again, and again: the hammer-tolling of challenge.

— 6 —

At first he could not believe who stood there at the oak. Had he fallen back asleep and into nightmare? No, he thought in a remote place, that could not be. He was too clearly conscious of leafless boughs overhead, scratchiness of the woolen tunic he had flung on, the breeze flowing cold around his bare legs and the flagstones cold beneath his bare feet. Next he thought a mistake must have happened. If Tommaltach was drunk, say, one need not take a childish prank seriously. But Tommaltach stood steady before him, arrayed in a Scotic kilt which was neatly wrapped around his otherwise naked lean muscularity, a long sword scabbarded across his back and a small round shield in his left hand; the black hair was combed to his shoulders, the handsome visage newly scrubbed, the gaze fire-blue—

All at once it wavered. Tears glimmered forth. "Will you not say a word to me?" Tommaltach screamed like a man under torture.

"What can I say?" Gratillonius answered woodenly.

"You could ask me why." Tommaltach sobbed breath after breath into himself. "Or curse me or, or anything."

"You mean to fight me?"

"I do that." In tearing haste: "It must be. You will not do what you should. You will not let Dahut be what the Gods have chosen her to be. You must die, Grallon, though my own heart die with you."

"I, your Father in Mithras." Immediately Gratillonius regretted his words. He had not imagined they would be so cruel. Tommaltach cowered back from them.

He recovered his courage fast. Gratillonius admired that. "I have eaten your salt too," Tommaltach blurted. "Mithras witness, this thing is none of my wish. But men have risen against unjust rulers erenow. And you refuse justice to Dahut."

He loves her, Gratillonius thought. He loves her in the headlong way of young men, the way I loved Dahilis. I

knew that already. It was graven on him, as it is on others
I could name. But I did not think it would send him crazy
like this. Well, he is a barbarian.

Aloud, slowly: "Suppose I agree I've been wrong, and
wed her. Will you take back your call to battle?"

Tommaltach's mouth fell open. After a moment he
slurred, "Would you be doing that, really?"

"Suppose I do."

Tommaltach rallied. "I cannot be withdrawing, can I?"

Gratillonius gave him a rueful smile. "Cannot, or will
not? Well, it makes no difference. *I* cannot yield."

"Then we must fight." Tommaltach fell on his knees. He
covered his face and wept. "Father, forgive me!"

Almost, Gratillonius did. But no, he thought, that would
be unwise. Here was an opponent young, skilled, vigorous. Let him at least remain shaken.

"I will dispatch a man to Ys at once," said the Roman
tactician. "Making ready will take an hour or two. Be here
in time." He could not quite bring himself to add, "Traitor." He turned and went back into the house.

Tambilis waited. Heedless of staring servants, she fell
against him. "Oh, Grallon, Grallon!" He embraced her,
stroked her hair, murmured that she should not cry because everything was under control.

She drew apart and asked desperately, "Shall I bed with
your killer? How could I?"

"Your Gods will strengthen you," he said.

She blenched, as Tommaltach had blenched; and like
the Scotian she recovered, to tell him: "Nay, I misspoke
myself. I'd not matter. 'Tis you that would be no more."

He constructed a laugh and chucked her below the
chin. "Why, I've every intention of abiding in the world
for many another year, annoying the spit out of countless
fools."

Thereafter he issued his orders and commenced his
limbering up—no food, no drink except a little water,
before combat. His further thoughts he left unvoiced.

The marine guards with their horses and hounds, and
those who held off a clamorous populace down the road;
Soren in his vestments; the legionaries in their armor and
their distress—it had a ghastly familiarity, another turn of

a millstone. Tommaltach seemed calm now; he even bore a faint smile on his lips. Gratillonius wondered how Dahut would receive him unto her, should victory be his. Surely she would grieve at losing her Papa. . . . But she was not going to.

Soren finished the ceremony. He added: "May the will of the Gods be done." Startled, Gratillonius glanced at the heavy features. Implacability responded. In his eyes, Gratillonius realized, *I have become another Colconor. That was a lonely feeling.*

He dismissed it and led the way into the Wood.

At the glade, he halted. "This is where we usually work," he said. Shake the opponent from any Celtic sense of fate, of possession by his people's female God of war. Remind him that this Roman sword had terminated earlier lives among these huge winter-bare trees. Heaven overhead was nearly white, the sun a frost-wheel casting skeletal shadows. Grass underfoot lay drained of color.

"For Dahut," Tommaltach crooned. "We both fight for Dahut." The words were Scotic, but sufficiently akin to Britannic or Gallic that Gratillonius understood.

"Let us begin and be done," he answered in Latin. He drew his blade, slanted his big Roman shield, shrugged once to make sure his mail was properly settled on him.

Tommaltach's iron gleamed forth. He still bore a smile, and in his eyes an otherworldly look. It was not the sleepwalker's look of Chramn the Frank, but a gaiety beyond anything human. Nevertheless he edged about with the sureness and alertness of a wildcat. Clearly, he meant to offset the mobility of his near nakedness and the length of his weapon against his enemy's armor. Also youth, wind; he could wear Gratillonius down, until the King lacked strength to bring shield up fast enough.

The old badger and the young wolf. How very young a wolf!

Tommaltach kept his sword back, warily, while he circled. Gratillonius turned to face him: smaller radius, easier executed. Clearly, Tommaltach hoped for a chance to strike past the Roman's guard from a rearward angle, into neck or thigh. Clearly, he understood that as he did, he must have his own shield ready to catch the Roman probe. It was light, quickly maneuverable.

Gratillonius retreated inchmeal. If he could lure Tom-maltach under a tree, as he had lured Chramn—

Tommaltach refused the bait. He let the distance between them grow. Finally he stood his ground and waited. After all, the King must fight.

So be it. Gratillonius walked forward.

The Scotic blade whirred, whined, struck, rebounded, hunted. Wear the badger down.

But the badger knew how to gauge every oncoming impact, how to shift his shield about and meet it, oh, such a slight shift, consuming hardly any force, while the body kept itself at rest, conserving breath, endlessly watchful.

Tommaltach backed off, panting. Gratillonius marched in on him.

Their eyes met, again the strange loverlike intimacy. Tommaltach yelled and cast a torrent of blows. He forgot about his shield. Gratillonius saw, made a roof of his own, suddenly advanced—by slacking off one of the knees he had held tense, so that he swung forward as if on a wave—and struck. The sword went in heavily, above the left hip. Gratillonius wormed it around.

Tommaltach sank away from the iron. There was an extravagance of blood; there always was. Gratillonius stood aside. Tommaltach gasped something or other, which might or might not have made sense. He pissed, shit, and died.

XII

— 1 —

A maidservant admitted Bodilis. Dahut heard and came forth into her atrium. "Welcome," she said tonelessly. The Queen had sent word ahead, and the younger woman had decided to receive her.

Bodilis hurried across the floor and embraced the other. "Oh, my dear, my dear," she said low.

Dahut stood unresponding and asked, "What do you want?"

"Can we talk alone?"

"Come." Dahut led the way to her private room. Bodilis had hitherto only heard tell of it. She looked around at the clutter of opulence and suppressed a sigh.

Dahut flung herself into a chair. She was ill-kempt, in a rich but rumpled green dress. Her eyes were reddened and dark-rimmed. "Be seated," she said, her tone as brusque as the hand-wave that accompanied it. She had made no mention of refreshment.

Bodilis gathered her gray skirt and settled onto a couch opposite, sitting especially straight. "I feared I'd find you like this," she began. "Child, can I help? May I? A friend to listen to you, if naught else."

Dahut stared past her. "Why think you I need help?"

"The terrible thing that happened this morning. Tell me not 'tis left you untouched. The marks are branded on you."

Dahut slumped silent. Outside, wind shrilled through fitful evening light. The room was overheated.

"Your father came so near death," Bodilis said after a while, "and at the hands of your young friend, who did die, at your father's. You must be torn between joy and grief. Worse—let me be frank—you surely understand that the Scotian challenged for love of you, in hopes of winning you. Naught else can explain his action."

Still Dahut withheld any answer.

"Beloved, put away guilt," Bodilis urged. "How could you be at fault that he went mad? As well blame the reef where a ship strikes, driven by storm and tide. I do hope you can be—nay, not more careful in future—that you can keep this from happening again. Of course, you could not foresee what he would do. But if you make clear that 'twas never your desire, nor ever could be—" Her voice faded out.

Yet she refused to admit defeat. Presently she went on: "Meanwhile, and always, know you have our love, the love of your Sisters. I speak first for myself and Tambilis—"

Dahut stirred. Her look speared at the visitor. "You've seen Tambilis?" she demanded.

"Aye. After the news reached me, I went out to the Sacred Precinct. We talked long together, she and Gratillonius and I. Most of what we said concerned you. Our foremost wish is for your happiness. It truly is. Will you speak with him after he returns? You know not how your coldness pains him."

Dahut turned sullen. "He can end that whenever he chooses. Until then, nay, I will not see him."

"Think further. You'll have time ere he comes back."

"Why, 'tis only tomorrow that his Watch ends."

"But immediately afterward, he intends a Mithraic funeral for the fallen man."

Dahut leaped to her feet. "He *dares?*" she shrilled.

Bodilis rose too. " 'Tis not the custom, but he forced assent, pointing out that the required rites are separate from the burial. Tommaltach's will be well away from the city, in earth whose owner gives permission."

"Where will the King find such a farmer?" Dahut asked, calming a little.

"In Osismia. His man Rufinus knows several who'd be glad, thinking that they gain a guardian spirit. He'll guide the party. They'll be gone three or four days—Child,

what's wrong?" Bodilis reached to clasp Dahut's shoulders.
"You seemed about to swoon."

The young woman sat back down and stared at the floor.
" 'Tis naught, " she mumbled. "You reminded me—But
no matter. I am indeed weary. This has been a . . . trying
day for me." She forced herself to smile upward. "You're
kind to come and offer comfort. 'Tis like you. But I'd
liefest be alone."

"Let me brew you a sleeping potion. Then tomorrow
when you have rested, remember your father loves you."

Dahut made fending gestures. "Aye, aye, aye. But if
now you'd be helpful, Bodilis, go and let me deal with
myself."

The Queen bade a sad goodbye and trudged off.

Dahut paced the house, twisted her fingers together or
struck fist in palm, snarled at any servant who passed
close. Finally she snatched a cloak off its peg, drew it
about her, and went out.

The sun had just set. Sea and western sky glimmered
yellow. Overhead and eastward the sky was already as
dark as a bruise. Tattered clouds smoked before the wind.
They filled Ys with dusk. No other people were in sight,
but somebody's pet ferret scuttered across Dahut's path.

The way was short to the home of Vindilis. An amazed
attendant let Dahut into its austerity. The Queen entered
the atrium from within, saw who this was, and said, "Give
the maid your wrap. You will stay for supper, no? But
we'll talk at once."

She had been busy in her scriptorium. Candlelight fell
on Temple accounts and writing materials. The air was
cold; she had her hypocaust fired up only in the bitterest
weather. She took Dahut's elbow, guided her to a seat,
and brought another around for herself. Face to face,
knees nearly touching, they leaned forward.

"Why have you sought me?" Vindilis inquired. Her tone
was impersonal.

Dahut ran tongue over lips. "I need . . . counsel, help."

"That's plain. But why me?"

"You are—I think in many ways you're the strongest of
the Nine. Certes you're the most—the most devoted. To
the Gods, I mean."

"Hm, that's a matter of judgment. I'd call Lanarvilis, at

least, more pious than myself. Also, she's ever been the readiest to act in the world as it is, best equipped by temper and experience. She's on Sena, you know, but tomorrow—"

Dahut shook her head. "Please, nay. Mayhap I should confide in her too. But she has ties that I think you're free of."

"True, she sometimes puts political considerations above what I might deem to be more important," Vindilis agreed. "Well, say on, dear, and be quite sure I can keep a secret. 'Tis about the combat today, I suppose."

Dahut nodded.

Vindilis studied her before continuing: "You wish the outcome had been different." Dahut caught her breath. Vindilis raised a palm. "You need not reply to that. Grallon is your father, who bore you in his arms when you were little, made you toys and told you stories and showed you the stars."

"But he's wrong now," Dahut cried, "wrong, wrong!"

"I myself wish Tommaltach had won," said Vindilis. "The will of the Gods is working more strangely than I can fathom." Her words softened. "Oh, understand me, I do not hate Grallon. I am angry with him beyond measure, but when he does fall I will mourn him in my heart ere I brace myself to endure whatever evils he spared me and the new King does not. Yet he was never a friend of the Gods, and he has become Their avowed enemy. Dahut, you will be far from the only Queen whose King slew her father. Think of him, if you will, as having gone off to dwell with his Mithras."

Dahut had regained composure. "Some of the Gallicenae believe we need him still, against Rome." Her voice was harsh. "Do you?"

"Lanarvilis maintains that," Vindilis answered obliquely. "She is reluctant about it, though. Certain among us are whole-hearted; they'd fain he never die. And certain others—. As for myself, I see the reasoning; but the Gods are not bound by reason."

"And you own that you wanted Tommaltach's victory! I knew you would. 'Tis why I came to you."

"Have a care," Vindilis warned. "You were ever reckless. This is perilous ground we walk."

"That's what I most need counsel and help about." Dahut went on in a rush: "I fear Rufinus. Tommaltach did what he did for love of me, desire of me. Rufinus knows that. He'll wonder if more young men may go the same way. He's threatened me already. He drew knife and vowed to kill me if I plotted against his King. Will he believe I have not? Or will he suppose my mere presence is a mortal danger to Grallon? I fear that smiling man of the woods, Vindilis. Oh, I fear him. Help me!"

The Queen brought fingers to chin and narrowed her eyes. "Rufinus is no fool," she murmured. "Nor is he rash. However, he is very observant . . . and, aye, very much devoted to Grallon."

"What shall I do?" Dahut pleaded.

Vindilis took both her hands. "Be of good heart, beloved child. Your Sisters will keep you safe. I hear Rufinus will be going off with the King to bury Tommaltach. Those few days' absence should dampen any . . . impulses. Meanwhile, and afterward, you must cease either brooding alone in your house or haring forth alone into the countryside. Resume your duties as a high priestess. 'Twill be healthful for your spirits. 'Twill also keep you surrounded by people, and in the favor of the Gods. Then in Their chosen time, They will see to your destiny."

Dahut shivered. "But what if, if a man does win the crown—might Rufinus blame me—somehow—and, and seek revenge? 'Tis like a shadow forever across the sun— having him about—after what he told me that twilight."

Vindilis sat quiet for a spell. Then she straightened and said, "I believe something can be done, if you wish it so much. Afterward, let's pray, the will of the Gods can be done. I'll see to this."

She rose. "Enough," she finished. "You did right to come here. Now let us go warm ourselves with a stoup of wine ere we sup. When you return home, I'll have my sturdy manservant Radoch escort you. But first of all, come with me to the tiring room and let me make you presentable. I'll rub your hands and feet, and comb those lovely locks, and you'll feel hope rising anew."

— 2 —

Rain lashed from the west, as if Ocean were taking wing. Even Rufinus's aerie was caught in the blindness and noise of it. A single lamp guttered in the main cham-

ber. It stirred up misshapen darknesses more than it relieved
them. That lent a ghostly life to the portrait busts of a
centuries-dead boy and of Gratillonius. The Gaul sat in a
chair, almost on the middle of his spine, legs cocked over
a table, and regarded the images while he played on a
pipe of narwhal ivory. The notes wailed below the wind.

The door, which had been unbarred, swung open. Instantly he uncoiled, sprang to his feet and backward, stood
poised near his weapon rack. A figure entered and closed
the door. "Be at ease," said a female voice. It was a
command. The newcomer trod forward and retracted the
cowl of her drenched outer garment. Black hair turning
white in streaks, severely drawn back, and whetted features flickered into sight.

"Queen Vindilis!" Rufinus exclaimed. He saluted her.
"What brings you, after—ten years, has it been? How
knew you I was in this place?"

"The King returned today. 'Twas a safe wager you'd be
with him," she answered dryly. "I thought belike after the
journey you'd wish an evening alone; and for my part I
wanted this visit known to none but us two."

He hastened to take her cloak and hang it up. "What
was that you were playing?" she asked. "An alien mode."

"Scotic, my lady. I learned the tune in Hivernia, where
I also got this that can whistle it." He showed her the
pipe. The intervals between the stops were greater than
on those instruments with which she was familiar.

"What does the music signify?"

He hesitated. " 'Tis a threnody."

"For Tommaltach?"

"Aye." His tone harshened. "I know not what possessed
him. If it be a human, not a demon, who somehow lured
him to his death, I will find out and—"

"But you are not vengeful toward Grallon, are you?" she
interrupted.

He grew somber. "Nay, of course not. He did what he
must, in agony of soul. He too was betrayed . . . by
someone."

"Did you get Tommaltach well snugged down?" Vindilis
asked quickly.

Rufinus nodded. "The King did, with such reverence
you'd never have known he was the slayer. I dare hope

the prayers lifted the sorrow off him a little. . . . But be seated, my lady, I beg you. May I offer wine?"

Vindilis took a chair and signalled him to do the same. "Mine is no amicable errand," she told him curtly. "You have terrorized Queen Dahut, daughter of the King you profess to love."

"I have not!" he protested. "I only—"

"Silence. We could spend half the night on your slippery contortions around the truth. The fact is, I care not what the truth may be. It suffices that Dahut has plenty to bear without going in fear of you. Therefore you will depart Ys forthwith."

"Nay, now, I'll have justice," he said, appalled. "We'll take this before the King. He'll hear me out."

"We will not. You will not. You know why—you, who call yourself his handfast man."

He lashed back: "You and the rest who deny him, you call yourselves his wives."

Her tone held steady. "Aye, gossip is rife. It is as empty in this case as would be any chatter about justice. Rufinus. I want you away from here, far away. Give Grallon any pretext you like, or none, but go. In return, I'll spare him certain facts which *include* your menacing of Dahut."

He sagged. "I would not have harmed her," he whispered. "I warned her off something she might do in desperation."

"So you say. I am not so sure. If Grallon had perished in the Wood—well, Tommaltach was your comrade, but one wonders, one wonders. No matter. You may be guiltless, but you must begone."

"Not forever," he implored.

She considered. "M-m-m. . . . I've a feeling this will work itself out, in whatever way it does, within a year. Aye. A twelvemonth hence, you may send me a letter. If I send back permission, you may return, on the understanding that you will never cause Queen Dahut the slightest anxiety." Relenting a bit: "During that span of time, she may well lose her fear of you, especially if the troubles upon us have ended. I may try to soothe her myself."

"I thank your graciousness," he said bleakly.

She rose. "You have a sennight," she told him. "Give me my cloak."

She left. He stared long at the door. Finally he screamed, "Bitch!" He snatched a javelin from the rack and cast it at the wood. It sang when it struck.

Rufinus filled a goblet and began thinking.

— 3 —

Weather cleared. The morning sun stood low to southward. Its rays felt nearly heatless. They shivered over the waters and glinted off hoarfrost ashore. Otherwise land rolled dun, leafless apart from the occasional evergreen, beneath pallid heaven.

Hoofs rang on pavement as a band of men set forth on Aquilonian Way. They were eight marines, whose armor and pikeheads flashed, and at their head, clad in plain wool, Gratillonius and Rufinus. A couple of pack mules followed. Four of the group were young, unwed; they would be gone for months. The rest would accompany the King back to Ys from Audiarna.

Riding on his left, Rufinus cast the rugged countenance a glance. White marbled that auburn beard. "Do you still have misgivings, sir?" the Gaul asked low.

Gratillonius gave him a lopsided smile. "Not really," he said in the same Latin. It was as well for the other man to practice the educated, rather than serf's version, despite Rufinus having read extensively since he learned how. "I did have my doubts when you volunteered for this mission, but you convinced me." He gestured at a sealed pouch which hung from the adjacent saddle. "The letters are in good hands."

They were his own, and Apuleius's, and ones lately received from such persons as Bishop Martinus and the military commandant at Turonum: whatever prominent Romans had responded to his request for commendations. All would go to Stilicho.

Wherever Stilicho was. If new wars had called the general out of Italy, reaching him would well prove arduous and devious. While Rufinus lacked experience of the Empire beyond Armorica, he should make up for that in toughness and quick-wittedness. Not that he would likely have to fight. Rather, given the credentials he bore, the Imperial highways, hotels, supply stations, and remounts ought to speed him forward. The marines going along were more an honor guard, meant to impress, than a bodyguard. They'd return with whatever courier bore Stilicho's reply north. However, in part they were precautionary. These days you never knew beforehand what might come at you.

"I do question the wisdom of your staying on down there," Gratillonius proceeded. "The more I think about that notion of yours, the less it seems to me that it'll do any good—and you so bloody useful hereabouts. Why should they even allow you to hang around?"

Rufinus sighed. "I've tried to explain, sir, and failed, because I don't have any plan. How could I? But I think I can one way or another talk myself into some kind of appointment, if only because I amuse a few high officers. It'll be lowly, but I'll keep my ears open, and from time to time put in a word on your behalf. I believe the news I'll eventually carry back—the overall picture, the feel of things at Stilicho's headquarters—I do believe you'll find that worth waiting for."

"Never mind. We've covered this ground before. You're bound and determined, and I've no way to prevent, so I may as well accept." Gratillonius laughed. "Frankly, I think you want time for a proper sampling of the pleasures in the South. Cool wines, warm clime, hot girls."

Rufinus's mouth stretched wide. "Sir, no! When I've known Ys? It's you, sir, you I want to serve."

Gratillonius slapped him on the back. "I know. I was joking."

"Grallon—lord—be careful while I'm gone. You're in terrible danger. Watch out for—Sir, if you'd just go through with what they want—"

Rufinus's head drooped. "But of course you won't," he ended.

"Watch out for your tongue," Gratillonius snapped.

The road turned and climbed. A hare bolted from the gorse alongside. A crow cawed from a bough.

"Well, well," said Gratillonius, "no sense in this. Let's be cheerful. We'll toss a cup together in Audiarna before we make our goodbyes; and I envy you the adventures you'll be having."

The scar twitched as Rufinus sketched a grin. "Well you may, sir. I'll see to that."

They reached the heights. Gratillonius drew rein. "Stop a moment," he suggested. "Take your last look at Ys."

Rufinus sat a long while gazing back at the city where it gleamed against heaven and Ocean.

— 4 —

The afternoon grew mild. Such folk as were able left their work and sauntered about on streets, the wall, the headlands, enjoying its briefness. There would be few more like it, now that the Black Months were setting in.

Carsa meant to be among the strollers. He had little to do once shipping season was past, and often felt restless. Warehoused goods required periodic inspection, and sometimes attention, in this Armorican dankness. Infrequently, a letter arrived from Burdigala, or he sent a report on his own initiative. He was supposed to investigate possible new markets and routes, keep track of existing ones in the region, and familiarize himself with Ys. To that end he talked with what men he found—but outsiders were scarce in winter—and had become a student under certain scholars, pagans though they were. Those were inadequate outlets for his energies.

He was donning outdoor garb in his apartment, on the fourth floor of the tower called the Waterfall, when his knocker clattered. Opening the door, he saw a boy whose brass pendant, a skimming gull, proclaimed him a public messenger. Carsa took the folded papyrus handed him and, alone, unsealed it. Curvily inked Latin characters said: "Meet me at Menhir Place. D."

D? His heart bounded. He told himself this was nonsense, but nonetheless had difficulty securing his sandals.

—She kept him waiting by the ancient stone for a time that felt endless. When she arrived, she was drably clad and hooded, head bowed. Passersby took her for a plebeian girl. None accosted her. This was a poor quarter but not lawless, and besides, sunlight still cleared the city battlements.

When she reached him and looked up, he breathed, "My lady?" while the world spun. He started to bring hand to brow. Dahut caught his wrist and guided the gesture to his breast, salutation between equals. "Nay," she said in an undertone, "betray me not."

"I'd n-n-never," he stuttered.

She bestowed a smile on him. "Of course. But let us be an ordinary couple, pacing along as we talk."

"On top of the wall?"

She shook her head. "I might too easily be recognized there. We can follow the winding ways to Skippers' Market. 'Tis nearly deserted."

"What do you want of me, my lady? Name it, and if I have it, 'tis yours."

Dahut's lashes fluttered long above her cheekbones. "Would that I could give you a simple answer. 'Tis much harder to confess I'd like your company today. You think I'm shamelessly forward. But I am so lonely." She clutched his hand. "So lonely, Carsa."

"You should not be, you."

"I am beset, Carsa, by Gods and men. I know not where to turn. The grisly thing that happened with Tommaltach—I too was fond of him, I miss him, but his ready laugh is stilled and—You are a Roman, Carsa. You stand outside all this. But you are also a kindly friend, a strong man. . . . Will you listen to me, speak to me, till sunset? I must go to the Temple then, but if we could walk about first and quietly talk—"

He took her arm, awkwardly. "I am not worthy," he said, "but, but here I am."

She uttered a forlorn laugh. "Beware. I may call on your company again."

" 'Tis yours, always, my lady."

They went on down a lane of violet shadows.

XIII

— 1 —

Clouds drove low on a wind that howled as it hunted. Their leadenness blew in streamers around the towertops of Ys. Sometimes a few raindrops stung. Hardly anyone was about in the streets who could have walls between him and the cold.

Though the tide was out, waves battered heavy enough that the King had locked the sea gate. It was doubtless unnecessary. However, little or no waterborne traffic moved at this season, and if the harbor basin was free of chop, vessels within would not chafe at their moorings.

The shipyard lay nearly deserted too. Days had grown so short that it was not worth paying wrights to appear. They sought work indoors, where there were lamps. Maeloch was alone with his drydocked *Osprey*.

His crewmen needed employment during the shorebound months, but he no longer did. Over the years he had modestly prospered; the rebirth of trade increased demand for fish and also enabled him to make some investments that had paid well. Now he wanted to assure himself that the smack would be seaworthy when next required.

He was examining the hull inch by inch, chalking marks where he should caulk or otherwise restore things. A man passed by on the ropewalk. Maeloch recognized him. "Budic!" he roared. "Hoy, old tavern mate, come have a swig!"

The soldier stopped. He was in Ysan civil garb, tunic, trews, cloak, half-boots, but he had ever kept his hair short and his face clean-shaven. The fair locks fluttered. Standing, peering, he swayed a bit. "Oh," he called back. "You. Well, why not?"

Less than steadily, he advanced to the gate and let himself in. Maeloch guided him to a shed which gave shelter but, with its door open, had light to see by. Budic plumped down onto a stack of planks. From a shelf crowded with tools and supplies, Maeloch fetched an ale jug. Budic quaffed deep.

Retrieving the vessel, Maeloch gave him a long look. Budic's chin was stubbly and his eyes bloodshot. " 'Tis early to be drunk," Maeloch said.

Budic shrugged. "I began ere dawn. Well ere dawn." He hiccoughed. "Why not? No duty today for me. Naught at all."

Maeloch settled onto a cluttered worktable and took a pull of his own. "Ye should natheless wait till others are free," he advised. "Drinking without fellowship be a drabble-feathered thing."

"Well, I was on my way into the Fishtail. I'd find somebody. I'd used up what was in my house, you see." Budic reached.

Maeloch hesitated an instant before handing the jug over. "More in a house than cups for passing the time," he said.

"Ha! In my house?"

The bitterness took Maeloch aback. He ran fingers through his white-flecked beard. "Hm. I'd heard—Gossip does go about. But I'd nay pry."

"Why not?" retorted Budic belligerently. "You pried in the past, you, aye, pried, poked, prodded, banged her. She was good then, eh?" He glugged.

"Your friends put that from their minds years ago," said Maeloch in pity.

"Born anew in Christ, aye, aye, that's our Keban."

"We'd ha' honored your wife if ever we'd been guests in your home."

"With her housekeeping? Nah. But she has become a good Christian woman, her. Yea verily, she has that. How gladly she 'greed we sh'd live t'gether like brother and sister, for the glory of God."

Maeloch attempted a laugh. "Now yon's a mighty sacri-fice!" He sobered. "Mistake me nay. Poor girl, if she's been as ill as I've heard, 'tis well done of ye. I've off and on found it kindest or wisest to leave my Betha be for a while and seek elsewhere. Ye remember."

"No more. Not for me." Budic shook his head. "I vowed I'd stay pure too. That was after the miracle of the boat. Could I do otherwise, I who'd been in God's own hand?"

Maeloch frowned. "Mean ye that rescue two-three months agone, Bomatin Kusuri's yacht? What tales have come my way ha' been unclear but eldritch." His gaze sharpened. "I knew nay 'twas ye there with Corentinus."

"Who'd ken me in the dark and turmoil? Afterward I said naught, nor did the pastor. For humility's sake. He counselled me thus." Budic had ceased to slur his words. He sat straight and looked afar, rapt. "But I knew the wondrousness of God."

"And gave up women?" Maeloch replied softly. "Well, of course I'd nay question whatever passes 'tween a man and his Gods."

"His God, his one and the only true God," Budic exclaimed. His eyes sought the fisher's. "I tell you, I saw it. I was *in* it. We'd all have drowned but for His help. You're a sailor, you must know that. Then why will you not turn from your demons and believe? I like you. I hate to think of you burning forever."

"I'll believe ye speak straight. But I've witnessed my share of strangeness, aye, lived with it, made the night passage to Sena like my fathers afore me, nay to speak of what's happened on open sea." Maeloch shrugged. "So honor what Powers seem best to ye. Me, I'll abide with mine. They've never wanted more from me than I could spare. Your Christ, though—"

Budic's head wobbled. His momentary self-possession had spun away from him. "'Tis hard, hard," he mouthed. "Yestre'en after I was off duty, homebound down Taranis Way, there came a litter, and riding in it the courtesan J-j-joreth."

Maeloch grimaced. "I know. Her what makes big money playing at being Princess Dahut. May eels eat her."

"Oh, but she was so beautiful. I went back to my house and—and lay awake in the dark, hour by hour, till—"

"And ye'd forsworn any relief. I said already, your Christ's an unreasonable God."

"Nay, His reward f-f-for faithful service is infinite."

"Hm? Ah, well, whatever ye mean by that, let's neither of us preach. I'll stand by my Gods, like I will by my King and my friends, as long as They stand by me."

"Have They that?" Budic cried. "What do They bring but horror? Think of Dahut, think of Gratillonius!"

"True, They're ofttimes stern, even grim, but so's the world. 'Tis for us to endure without whining. They give us life."

Budic sprang up. "They do not!" he screamed. "They are blood-drinking demons! The one thing They give you is your doom!"

Maeloch rose more slowly. His huge hand clenched on the Briton's tunic. "Now that's aplenty," he growled. "I'd liefer nay deck ye, boy. Best ye just go. But ask yourself this—when Lir sends fair winds and shoals o' fish, Taranis pours down sunlight and summer rain, Belisama brings love and bairns and hope—ask yourself, boy, what's this Christ o' yours ever done for *ye?*"

He let go and shoved. Budic staggered back against a wall. There he leaned for a minute, agape, as if the unspeakable had at last found words.

— 2 —

Scarcely past full, the moon slanted whiteness through windowpanes, down onto Carsa's bed. Dahut raised herself to a sitting position, rising from the blankets like a mermaid from the sea. Moonlight silvered her hair, face, breasts; it made mercury pools of her eyes; but the crescent of the Goddess showed as black as the shadows everywhere around. The young man looked up in adoration.

She sighed. "We must speak seriously," she told him. Her breath was a wraith in the chill.

He smiled and stroked her flank. "This soon?"

"We're belated as 'tis. Three nights together—. No matter I go to and fro in the dark, cloaked, hooded, veiled. Folk—servants chatter—they'll soon find that none of them knows where I've been, and they'll wonder, and . . . Rufinus is gone, but others can spy on me."

He grew grave. "I know. I've thought about little else, save you yourself and my love of you. Tomorrow I'll broach the plan I've made."

"*Now*," she insisted. "The danger is too nigh us both. Either we act at once or you must depart Ys at once, never to return. Else we die. If I left with you, they'd track us down."

He tensed. "I meant to lead you carefully toward my thought. 'Twill be hard for you."

"I know it already." Her voice was level. "You shall challenge the King and slay him."

He started, then likewise raised himself. "Your father," he breathed.

She spread her palms. "My husband, unless you prevent." Her lips trembled. "His will is cracking. Tambilis tells me this, the last Queen who shares his couch. She wishes me well, but she wants the marriage. They all do."

"You too?" he asked. His tone came raw.

"I did at first. But now you—And, oh, Carsa, beloved!" She caught his near hand in both hers. "You believe me, you know I was a maiden, though I did not bleed. But he? And Carsa, I love you."

He snarled. "I swore unto God I'd avenge the abomination, did it happen. Better I strike him down first. I will."

"My Carsa!" She strained against him. The kiss was long and savage.

When they had separated and hearts had quieted a little, her manner turned anxious. "He is a fearsome fighter, a killing machine."

The Burdigalan nodded. "He is. But I'll be no lamb to the slaughter. Let me confess it, I've thought about this, imagined it, ever since the curse fell on you. I'll be shrewder than to meet him on terms where he holds every advantage. Also, his earlier foes were pagan—poor Tommaltach—while I'm a Christian. God will be with me."

"I've fretted over that. How can a man of your faith be King of Ys?"

"I've considered this too." He laughed uneasily. "Have no fears. I've not confided in the chorepiscopus. He'll be shocked, he'll upbraid and belike excommunicate me. Still, I am only a catechumen. And I trust that I can make him see reason. Surely saving you from a union that God forbids will be a worthy deed in His eyes. If He spares me thereafter, I as King—I, wholly Roman—will earn full redemption by leading Ys step by step toward righteousness and Christ." He brought his cheek next to hers. "You first, my darling?"

"We'll see," she said under her breath. Aloud: "Oh, Carsa, the wonder of it! Now we have the night free before us!"

— 3 —

For an instant Gratillonius hesitated. Summoning courage, he laid hold of the serpent knocker on Lanarvilis's door and struck it against the plate. While he waited for response—the time was short but felt long—he twitched his cloak tighter around his plain tunic. The morning was bleak though bright. Mainly, however, he needed something to do.

The door opened. Into the startlement of the woman who recognized him, he said mildly, "I'd fain call on my daughter, the Princess Julia."

"Oh—my lord, she—"

"She is home today, free of duties. I know." Gratillonius went into the house.

"I w-w-will tell her, my lord." The servant scuttled away.

Presently Julia came into the lavish atrium. Even on her free days, she wore vestal white: a plump girl of fifteen with light-brown hair and something of his mother in her features, his mother whose name she bore.

She stopped and saluted him, an awkward gesture. "Welcome, sir." The wariness in her stabbed him.

He ventured a smile. "I wished to congratulate you, my dear," he said; he had rehearsed it in his mind, over and over. "I heard how you won first examination honors in Queen Bodilis's Latin class, and I'm very proud of you." From beneath his cloak, which no one had offered to take, he brought a cedarwood box he had made himself. He had given it all the care and skill that were his, hoping for an hour such as this. "Here's a little token for you."

Julia took it without contact of hands and pulled the lid back. The fragrance of the wood drifted forth. "Oh!" she exclaimed, suddenly large-eyed. Within rested a penannular brooch, silver around twin great topazes. "Oh, father, 'tis beautiful."

Gratillonius's smile widened and eased. "Wear it in joy," he said. "And would you care for a celebration at the palace? Naught solemn, no relics like me, simply whatever friends you invite."

"Father, you—"

"What is this?" They both turned toward the new voice. Lanarvilis entered from the direction of her private room.

"You," she said flatly, and halted in the middle of the floor.

Gratillonius looked her up and down, from crimped ashen hair to pearl-studded sandals. She had covered her height with a gown of rich russet on which embroidered dragons twined; an amber necklace encircled the wrinkliness at the base of her throat but not the stringiness above; tortoise shell bracelets drew attention to the brown spots that were appearing on her hands. Yet she was not ugly, he thought. He might well have been nearly unaware of the hoofmarks of time, as he was whenever he saw Bodilis. It was that she had become a stranger.

"Forgive me," he said. "I'd no intention of slighting you, I knew not you were present."

"Nay, you chose your time," Lanarvilis answered. "It happened that Innilis and I traded Vigils on Sena, because she felt her courses soon to come on her and they've lately been making her miserable. You'd never know about that, nor care."

"I would. But who tells me?" He put down his temper. "We should not quarrel, my lady. I came in friendship."

Friendship of the kind you and I once had, his mind went on, unheard by her. We worked well together, for Ys. It felt good, being members of a good team. And then in bed—oh, we were never in love, either of us. Our hearts were elsewhere. But there came times, again and again, when we surrendered altogether to each other; and between us we created this girl here, and loved her and reared her. How can we now be hostile?

How can it be that I myself, in my inmost soul, care so little, except that it's desirable we stop being hostile?

"He, he gave me this," Julia said. "Because of my examination. And a feast—"

"And what else?" Lanarvilis asked Gratillonius. "The Sign has not come upon *my* daughter."

He fought against rage.

His wife shrugged. "Well, best we refrain from open breaches," she said. "We remain yoked to the same load. But, nay, Julia, dear, we shall not cross his threshold until he has granted your Sister her due and the Gods Theirs."

The girl swallowed, blinked, clutched the box to her breast, and fled.

Gratillonius and Lanarvilis stood silent a minute. Finally he said, "Ill is this."

"It is indeed," she replied.

" 'Tis not only that you and I and most of the others are divided. The Gallicenae are. Often Tambilis weeps because of the coldness she's met from her Sisters."

"She can mend her ways. You can yours."

"You know that is impossible. Why will you not help me find something we can all accept? The new Age, Dahut the first Queen who's truly free—"

"Go," she said.

He obeyed.

—Cynan was in the guard at the palace gate. His military correctness fell from him when he saw his centurion. He stepped forward. "Sir," he declared unevenly, "we've just gotten the word. Another challenger down at the damned Wood."

— 4 —

The moment he saw Carsa in the Sacred Precinct, Gratillonius understood that this day he might well die.

The young man was barefoot, his sturdy frame clad merely in a woolen tunic with a belt where a large knife such as seamen used was sheathed. Stuck beneath the leather was a short staff with a leather strap and attached cord depending from it. In his left hand he gripped a wooden buckler. In his right was a simple sling. A band across his left shoulder supported a bulging, wide-mouthed pouch. It seemed scant equipment against a full-armored Roman centurion, but Gratillonius knew what those weapons could do.

Though Carsa's mouth and nostrils were pinched tight, his visage showed no traces of sleeplessness and he stood at catlike ease. How old was he—eighteen, nineteen? Even unencumbered by mail, a man of forty-two could never come near matching him for speed and suppleness; and strength rippled through the nude limbs.

Gratillonius withdrew to that room in the right-hand building where he outfitted himself. As ever, he declined assistance. It could be his last time alone. He had given Adminius the usual orders ("If he wins, he's King, and none of you are to stir against him.") and wanted no further scenes. He had actually hastened off and accepted battle immediately, when he could at least have said farewell to Tambilis, Bodilis, whomever liked him. Better to wait in the hall, among the idols, while the marines formed their barrier across Processional Way and Soren led the houndsmen here.

Underpadding, kilt, greaves, mail, helmet—sword, dagger, big oblong shield, and this time a heavy javelin— "Mithras, hearten me; and should I fall, pardon me my sins, release my spirit, at the end of my Pilgrimage receive me."—The words felt empty, as if the God were gone.

When he came out, air bit at what skin was exposed. The sun hung wan, already far down toward Ghost Quay, making shadows long. Somewhere a raven croaked. Gratillonius was more aware of that than he was of the ritual Soren conducted. The Speaker went through the words in a monotone and refrained from any remarks after he finished. Gratillonius looked past him.

King and enemy went in beneath the trees. Twigs made splintery patterns across heaven. What brush there grew was also mostly bare. It crackled at a touch. Fallen leaves rustled louder.

Gratillonius did not seek the glade. No such requirement was on him. He followed traces he knew after these many years, to a place where several half-grown trees made the ground thick and tricky in among the giant oldsters. Halting, turning, he said, "Here we are."

"I expected you'd pick a site like this," Carsa replied in the same Latin.

Gratillonius kept his voice equally cool. "Before we begin—I'm curious—why are you doing this? You had your entire life ahead of you."

"I do yet. The wickedness of Ys is an offense to the Lord. Time to end it."

"Will you, then, lead sacrifices to Taranis and marry the nine high priestesses of Belisama? I thought you were a Christian."

Carsa whitened. "Let's go!" he yelled.

Gratillonius nodded and hefted his javelin.

It was no surprise that Carsa bounded agilely backward. He needed room. Gratillonius abided. If he threw his spear at once, Carsa could likely evade it.

The Burdigalan stopped. Already loaded, its pouch clasped between his fingers, the sling snaked free. Carsa's upper body swayed, to put his weight behind the double-pointed lead bullet. His wrist snapped. There was a whipcrack noise. Simultaneously, Gratillonius cast.

The impact of the slug, slantwise from his left, dug it into the thick plywood of his shield. He nearly lost the handgrip. The strap jerked violently against his shoulder. Tears sprang forth. Through their blur he saw the javelin strike the buckler. He'd hoped it would pierce flesh, but Carsa had followed the slower missile in flight. With the swiftness of youth, he'd moved his defense to intercept.

Nevertheless, the iron had gone deep, the shaft dragged, the buckler had become a burden. Carsa dropped it. Gratillonius drew sword and charged.

He'd realized that the whole purpose had been to make him spend his distance weapon. Without it, he could only fight at close quarters. A slinger needed time to reload, though, whole chunks of a minute for each shot, time wherein a legionary could cover a fair amount of ground.

The sling snapped again. Gratillonius felt a glancing impact down around his right ankle. It hurt. The greave fended off the worst of it. He crouched low and dodged a bit, back and forth, as he attacked. If a bullet took him between helmet and shield rim, in the face, that was that.

A broken foot would be as final, if slower; Carsa need just stand away and bombard him. His shield took another blow, but straight on, merely lancing pain through his knuckles.

Then he was there, but of course Carsa wasn't. The youth had slipped off to one side. Gratillonius saw him behind a screen of saplings and withes. Carsa grinned. While he couldn't well shoot past such a barricade, he could wave his sling tauntingly.

Gratillonius refused the bait. He'd wear himself out pushing through that stuff. He started around it, deliberately, taking his time. Carsa poised. When the chance came, he sent a projectile whizzing. Gratillonius blocked it, too, and advanced, step by easy step. Carsa retreated.

A while they stalked each other among the boles. A slug missed. Gratillonius heard it buzz past. He thought in a distant part of his mind: This is interesting. Can he run me out of wind and legs before I run him out of ammunition? Well, go slow, old son. Play him till nightfall if you can; then the game ought to be all yours.

Sunlight still touched upper branches, but shadows beneath were turning into murk.

Abruptly Carsa saw a tree that suited him. He leaped, caught a branch, swarmed sailor-nimble aloft. Planting himself ten feet high, where a broad limb stretched nearly right-angled from the trunk, he draped his simple sling over it and from his belt drew the companion piece.

Gratillonius halted. Carsa crowed laughter. 'You must not leave me, you know," he called. "We must fight within the Wood to the end."

The staff sling bore a six-foot cord. It required both hands. At short range, its missiles had been known to kill men in armor. If they didn't pierce, the shock sufficed.

Carsa's toes gripped bark. He swayed, superbly balanced. Gratillonius edged aside. Carsa turned to keep him a target.

The cord cracked. The bullet flew faster than sight. It struck another tree. Beneath the heavy thud, torn wood groaned. The lead sank too deep to see.

"That was a gauging shot," Carsa gibed. "Next comes the real thing."

Gratillonius retreated. "Go off if you like," Carsa said. "Shall we continue at dawn?"

Surely he could better endure a night of hard frost than could an older man. He'd scramble about in the branches, keep warm, be alert and strong when his exhausted foe lumbered back into view.

Gratillonius shifted position. What to do, what to do? The blow erupted.

Suddenly he lost hold of his shield. It dangled by the strap. His left forearm was aflame. Broken? He had no use of that hand. A hole showed where the slug had entered, above the metal boss. It had gone straight through the weak spot left by the earlier hit, with enough force remaining to cripple.

Carsa reloaded. Sunset shone along the arc of his weapon.

Gratillonius reeled to shelter behind the nearest trunk. Slatting and banging, his shield was now more hindrance than help. He slipped it free and dropped it. Briefly he wanted to follow, lie down on it and let the blessed darkness blanket him. But no, Carsa waited.

Gratillonius drew breath, willed pain away, came back around the bole and dashed forward, zigzag. The sling pounced. Agony rived him, to the right of his breastbone. He knew the mail had warded off the bullet—though not its impact; else he'd be dead. He shoved that pain aside likewise, while he trotted on.

Carsa reached into his pouch. Gratillonius halted, a yard or so from his enemy's post.

He had one chance. As a boy on the farm, he had often thrown things, brought down small game with rocks; and in the army he had learned the javelin. He hurled his sword.

It took Carsa in the belly, flat-on rather than by the point, but with power to shove the Burdigalan off his perch. He fell to earth. Gratillonius drew knife and approached.

Carsa rose. He was shaken, the wind thumped out of him. Yet he'd known how to land. The sling had dropped elsewhere. His own blade gleamed forth.

They said in the Fishtail, as they did in the low inns of Londinium, that the winner of a knife fight was the fellow who got carried off to the surgeons. Gratillonius was armored, but he was also shaken, hurt, barely on his feet. Carsa could probe—

Gratillonius closed. He brought up his knee. Greave smote groin. Carsa shrieked. He collapsed and lay writhing. But he still held his knife. He was still mortally dangerous and must be killed. Gratillonius stamped a hobnailed sandal down. He stamped and stamped. He felt ribs crunch and saw the face beneath him turn to red pulp. Finally he broke the apple of the throat. Carsa gurgled blood, flopped, and was quiet.

Gratillonius lurched off through the gathering dusk, to the sacred house. Let the Christians look after their own.

— 5 —

Word was that the King had taken severe injuries, broken bones, though nothing from which he could not recover. Most of Ys rejoiced.

The palace guard changed every six hours. On the day after the combat, Budic was among those relieved at noon. Weather hung cheerless. He plodded along the winding street between the houses of the mighty, downhill toward his home. Nobody else was close by.

A woman slipped from a portico and hurried lightfoot to meet him. "Wait, please wait," she called low. He checked his stride. The heart banged within him. When she drew nigh, he saw beneath her hood that she was indeed Dahut.

"Wha-what's this, my lady?" he asked in his amazement.

"I saw you pass," she answered, "And—Oh, tell me. How does he fare, my father?"

"You haven't heard?"

"Only what the spokesman says." Tears quivered on long lashes. "That could be soothing lies. He could have a fever or anything."

"Nay, I've seen him. He does right well. But why could you not visit?"

Dahut stared downward. "We are estranged." She barely heard. "We should not be. He swore once he'd never forsake me, but—but he is my father. I'm glad to hear your news. Thank you, dear friend."

"Little enough to do . . . for you, my lady."

She caught his elbow. Her glance flew up again, to him. "Would you do more? Dare I beg it of you?"

"Whatever you ask," he choked.

" 'Tis not much. Or is it? I only ask that you walk me to my house, and talk while we go, but not tell anyone afterward. They'd think me immodest. But 'tis just that I am so lonely, Budic, so full of grief I dare not speak of."

"Oh, my princess!"

She took his arm. "Come, let's away ere we're noticed." A hint of liveliness sparkled beneath the desolation. "We'll be a simple couple, you and I, man and maiden together. You cannot dream what comfort that will give me—you will give me."

XIV

— 1 —

Weather turned clear and cold. Early on the second day after his return, Gratillonius went out. He had been tempted to lie longer in the aftermath of what had happened, drowsing when he did not sleep, but that was unbefitting. He compelled himself to walk, no matter what lances every motion sent through him. Tambilis went at his side.

Dawn whitened the inland sky. A few stars lingered in the darkness above Ocean, and the pharos flame burned on Cape Rach. Windows glowed and lantern-sparks bobbed, down in the bowl of Ys.

"Good morning," he greeted the sentries.

"Hail, sir." They wheeled and saluted, Ysans as smartly as Romans. "How's the centurion doing?" Maclavius made bold to ask.

"The medicus tells me I need about a month and a half—"

Gratillonius trod on a patch of ice. Ordinarily he would have recovered footing, but his contused ankle proved slow. He fell. Agony overwhelmed him. For an instant he lost awareness.

He pulled himself back and saw the men clustered around, and the woman. He waved off their solicitude, grumbled, "I can get up all right, thank you," and did, regardless of what it cost him. Sweat was clammy over his skin. "Back inside for me, I s'pose. 'Nother bath. Soldiers, to your posts. Y' 'aven't been relieved yet."

235

As he hobbled up the path, Tambilis said, "Darling, you *must* take more care. 'Tis no disgrace to be wounded."

"Pity me not," he answered. "I'm alive. I'll get well. Pity that young fellow—those young fellows—who made me bring them down. Whatever possessed them?"

Nonetheless he let her help him undress. It was good to lie in hot water. He declined her offer of opium but accepted a willowbark tisane, with honey and licorice to disguise the taste. He also let her towel him dry and assist him into fresh garb. She saw to it that he ate. Thereafter she must be off to Temple duties.

Alone, he fumed. How long would he stay useless? His left arm didn't matter much. It still hurt in its splints and swaddlings, but was merely immobilized—fractured radius, Rivelin had said. The right side of his chest was what incapacitated him, a broken rib or two. Despite a closely fitted leather corselet, any deep breath raised pangs, a cough was torment, a sneeze a catastrophe. Rivelin had warned him against excessive manliness; nature was telling him to be cautious, to keep what he did to a minimum. He knew that presently the healing would be far enough along that he could use that hand more. But Hercules! What was he supposed to do meanwhile, sit and yawn?

Too many things called for him. It would be different were he content with a sacral Kingship, like most of his predecessors; but he was not. He had taken charge, instigated, been omnipresent. Doubtless he could hold his monthly court and preside over rites. However, now that his relationship with Soren and a number of other magnates had become one of frigid politeness, he must needs confer oftener with those who supported him, and with key commoners. To avoid an appearance of plotting, which would further antagonize the conservative faction, he had been quietly visiting his friends in their homes, or talking with them in the course of outings through the hinterland. He oversaw public works he had started—repairs to roads and buildings, new construction, preliminaries to the eventual replacement of the sea gate doors—because you can never trust a contractor to get everything right on his own. He led frequent military exercises. He rode circuit well into Osismia, inspecting defenses, listening to tribesmen whom he wanted to stay favorable to Ys. Riding—Favonius needed daily riding. . . . Well, he must simply delegate tasks. The country wouldn't fall apart if he was absent from its affairs a month or two; he'd made journeys longer than that.

But he was not required to like this!

"My lord, you have visitors," said his majordomo.

Surprised, he looked up from his chair. Guilvilis and Innilis entered.

"Why, welcome," he said while his pulse began to race.

Innilis approached and bent over him. Her eyes were huge and dark-rimmed, the thin face paler than usual. "How are you?" she whispered. "Can I do aught to help?"

"Your coming here is enough," welled out of him.

She wrung her hands. "I should not. Vindilis—my Sisters will be angry with me. But I could not stay away when you are hurt, when you might have died."

"Thank you. How fares it with you? And Audris?"

"Oh, she is . . . happy, I believe." On ending her vestalhood, the half-wit girl had found sanctuary as a minor priestess; she could handle drudge work at the Temple and various shrines. "For myself, I—you know how I wish, how we all wish you'd obey the Gods. But I came not to plague you." She stroked his brow.

"And you, Guilvilis?" Gratillonius asked.

The second Queen hobbled forward, leaning on a cane. "I'm well, my lord," she replied with a large smile. "Up and about, as you see."

"She lies," said Innilis gently. "Walking tortures her. The physician fears it always will. Some hip injury, belike." She winced. "I've given her the Touch. 'Tis failed."

Gratillonius felt abashed. "I should have called on you erenow, Guilvilis," he admitted. "But in this last month or two—so much happening—"

"I understand, my lord," The smile turned sad. "And I c-c-cannot easily spread my legs any more."

Innilis flushed.

"Ask Dahut to see you," Gratillonius advised. "She brought my strength back to me in minutes, after my battle with that Frank."

"The Princess Dahut—Queen Dahut holds apart from us, my lord," Guilvilis faltered. "She—she's sometimes not at her duties, and she never seeks us out."

"Well, ask her!" he snapped.

Innilis drew breath before she said in haste: "I can tell this talk pains you worse than your wounds, Grallon. Set it aside. Let me try if I can Touch you into ease."

She could not. The two women took their leave. Innilis was softly weeping, Guilvilis laid a comforting arm over her shoulders.

Soon afterward, Bodilis came in. She hurried to kiss Gratillonius—the brief, chaste kiss they allowed themselves—and hug his head to her bosom, before she drew up a chair and sat down. "I'd have come at once, dearest," she related, "but had Vigil yesterday, and in these fleeting daylights—. Well, see, I stopped at home to get some volumes for you. Here's your beloved *Aeneid*; and you've always told me you'd read our *Book of Danbal* when you found time; and perhaps you'd enjoy my reading aloud these verses—."

She broke off and regarded him closer. "You're suffering," she realized. "Not morose, I expected that, but miserable. What is it, Gratillonius?"

He shook his head and stared at his lap. "Nothing," he growled. "Bad mood, no more."

She leaned to catch his hands in hers. "You're an unskilled liar," she said tenderly. "I think I can guess. Dahut."

He sighed. "Well, when my first-born, Dahilis's daughter, avoids me, it does go hard."

Bodilis bit her lip and braced herself. "I meant to discuss that with you. As well have it out now."

He lifted his gaze, alarmed. "What?"

"Dahut. Two different men in quick succession, both known to have been enamored of her, challenging you. The first could have acted on barbarian impulse, but the second—. Why didn't she tell Carsa he must spare her father? She's no fool, she has to have foreseen he might attempt your life, for her sake or because the Scotian was his good friend or in sheer youthful madness. Nor does Dahut show the least regret. She scamps her obligations, disappears for many hours on end, is feverishly vivacious far too often. *Why?*"

Shock had rendered him speechless. It gave way to white rage. "Silence!" he bellowed. "How dare you slander my daughter, you slut?"

"Not I," she pleaded. "Tongues are wagging—"

He had raised his hand, he might have struck her, but a spasm of pain jerked his arm down. He sank back. "Tell me who," he panted, "and I'll kill them."

Her voice went stern. "Kill half the populace? Face the truth like a soldier. I didn't say Dahut is guilty of anything. I did not. Nor does anybody else, to my knowledge. But they wonder. They can't help wondering. You would yourself, if you weren't her father."

"Well, I—" He gulped for air. Seldom had he fought a stiffer fight than against this indignation. Finally he could shape a grim smile and respond: "Well, people are like that. This will show us who's loyal."

"We, the Gallicenae, I'll urge that we all advise her to be more discreet."

"Good. She's only young, you know, very young. And bewildered, embittered, poor girl; oh, your Gods have played her false! But this should blow over."

Bodilis shivered. "Unless you receive more challenges."

"No, I hardly will. Remember, I'm exempt till these bones of mine are whole again. Otherwise it'd be no combat. This is not like when I'd merely been stunned by the Frank. We'll have peace, time for the ugliness to die away and be forgotten." Wistfulness touched him. "Time, even, for King and Queens and princess to make peace with each other?"

— 2 —

Wind woke anew, with a low gray wrack driven off the sea. His squadmates gave Budic questioning looks when they went off patrol and he told them he wanted to take a long walk. They said nothing, though. He had been moody these past months, especially of late, often absent-minded or staring off at something invisible. Quite likely, they thought, he had been worse shocked by Gratillonius's brush with death than his adored centurion was.

Having changed legionary gear for warm civilian clothes, he left by Northbridge and struck off on Redonian Way, north to Eppillus's grave—where he saluted, as was the

custom of his outfit—and then east until beyond sight of
Ys. The road was his alone. To the left he glimpsed wild
white-maned immensity, to the right sallow pastureland
strewn with boulders, here and there a wind-gnarled tree
or a lichenous menhir. A few seafowl skimmed about on
the blast.

One ancient monument identified a nearby shelter, used
in grazing season by shepherds and their flocks when
weather got too rough. It was not stone but merely three
sod walls open to the south, where the hills partially broke
the winds, and a low roof of turfs laid over branches.
Inside, he was out of the worst cold but not of the hollow
roaring and whistling. Repeatedly, he stepped from the
gloom and squinted west up the highway.

She came at last, roughly clad, like an Osismiic woman.
Besides a cowl, she had drawn a scarf across her face. That
was understandable on a day such as this. Passersby and
guards in the city would have paid her no heed—she'd be
a countryman's wife, or perhaps a servant on an outlying
manor, come to town on some errand—unless they noticed slim form and trim ankles under the wool.

Budic loped to meet her. "My lady!" he cried. "You,
dressed thus? And you didn't ride, you walked the whole
way. 'Tis not right!"

Dahut pulled aside the scarf and smote him with a
smile. "Should I have fared on horseback, among banners
and trumpets?" she teased. "I told you I wished a private
talk." The gaiety left her. The bright head drooped downward, out of its hood. "Aye, here's a wretched meeting
place. You were sweet to come as I asked."

"M-m-my lady did ask, so naturally I—But let's within.
I carried along food and a, a wineskin. I should have
remembered a beaker for you. I'm sorry. But if you will
deign?"

She picked her way fastidiously over dried droppings to
a bench. It was small as well as rude; when they sat down,
they were crowded together. She refreshed herself with a
deftness that bespoke experience. "Ah, that helps. You are
so kind, Budic, so thoughtful."

"Why do we m-meet today?"

She passed fingers across the fist on his knee—how
moth-lightly! "Why, that should be clear. Thrice we've

chanced on each other in the streets, and you've had the charity to walk a way at my side, listen to me, be with me."

"We said naught that was of any moment." He kept his eyes straight before him.

"Nay, how could we? But I felt the strength in you, the caring." Dahut sighed. "How can I bring a man to my house, unless he be always in such full sight and hearing of the staff that we'd have more freedom of speech on the streets?"

"I understand. My house? Keban and I would be honored beyond measure. Only let me know beforehand. It must be swept and garnished for you."

"My thanks. I'm sure your wife is a fine person. But can I open my unhappy heart in her presence? Nay, this poor hut is all I have."

He mustered will and wit. "What would you tell me, then, my lady? I swear 'twill never leave my lips without your permission."

"Oh, fear no secrets. I am only alone, frightened, torn." Dahut drew a ragged breath. It caused him to turn his head and look at her. She caught his glance and did not let go. "Pray understand. I am not sniveling. I can bear whatever I must bear. But how it would help to know that one man at least feels for me! Like . . . like being at sea on the blackest of storm-nights, among the reefs, but seeing the pharos shine afar."

"Speak," he mumbled.

She leaned against him. "Would you hold me meanwhile?"

"My lady! You are a Queen and I—I am a married Christian man."

"Naught unseemly. Just your arm gentle around me, like my father's when I was small, or like a brother's, the brother I shall never have."

He obeyed. He listened. It tumbled forth, sometimes with tears which he saw her struggle to hold back.

"—the dreadful fate. . . . I rejoiced at what I believed was the benison of the Gods, but my father would not. . . . 'Tis made me think, aye, pain and sleeplessness call thoughts from underground. . . . What should I do? What can I? . . . He is my father, I loved him, but he denies me now. . . .

Was it the Gods Themselves Who drove Tommaltach and Carsa mad? . . . I have this horror in me, this fear that somehow *I*, all unknowing, I was the bait that lured them to their deaths. . . . Whatever happens will be wrong. . . . Is there no hope? . . . Budic, hold me closer, I am so cold—"

"You are innocent," he kept protesting, "you are pure, feel no guilt, Dahut. I will pray for you, hourly I'll pray for you."

But in the end he wrenched himself loose. One could not stand upright in the shelter. He shuffled to the entrance. Then when he stood upright, he could not see her within. He hunkered down and said frantically: "Forgive me. I'm weak, I felt a blaze of—of— "

She leaned forward, almost luminous in the dimness. "Of lust?" she murmured. "Is that evil, Budic, dear? 'Tis the power of Belisama."

"I am a Christian!" he shouted. Curbing himself, he went on more steadily, "In Christ is your hope, man's single hope. Put by your heathen Gods. Call on Christ, and He will answer."

"I know naught of Him," she replied—humbly?

He nodded. "I've heard how as a child you mocked at His minister. Be not afraid, Dahut. Saul of Tarsus did worse, until divine mercy overtook him. Ask and it shall be given you."

Her manner turned pensive. "How shall I? What should I seek *for*? Will you enlighten me, Budic? I trust you, not that old scaldcrow Corentinus."

"He is a saint." Memory stirred, a prophecy uttered on this headland in a night of storm and shipwreck. "Your immortal soul is at stake. Oh, heed! But if you feel shy of him, well—"

Dahut slipped out to join the man. He straightened. Scant trace of distress lingered on the countenance she lifted upward; her gaze was clear. "Will you talk further with me?" she asked.

"Ah, uh, scarcely here."

"Nay. Tell me when you'll next be at liberty, and we'll meet in Ys as erstwhile."

They set a time and place. "Best we start back, my lady," Budic said. "Sundown comes apace."

"Wisest would be that we not enter the city together," she answered. "Go first. I—I'd fain be alone here a short while, here in this place where you've been so kind. 'Tis as if you've left flowers." She lowered her lashes. "I'll think on what you've counselled, and . . . whisper to your Christ, if I dare."

"Dahut!" he cried in a rush of joy.

She watched him bound off down the road. When he was well away, she snarled and spat. Reflecting further on what had occurred, she began to smile a bit, and when at length she too headed west, she strode with determination.

— 3 —

Tide was inbound, but the flow was still easy and the gate open when Forsquilis came home from Vigil. The winter sun was barely aloft. As she descended the gangplank from barge to wharf, another female ran out of a warehouse doorway. The Queen peered through the shadows that filled the basin. "Dahut," she said. "What fetches you?"

The young woman stopped before her. Eyes that seemed enormous caught what light there was. "Please, could we have speech? Alone?"

Forsquilis hesitated before replying, "When?"

"Now. You are too seldom in Ys any more. I must seize what chance I can."

Forsquilis's tone remained as hard as the air. "Very well. Follow me."

She led the way around the shipyard and up the stair to the Raven Tower. Awed guards let them past. Forsquilis stopped several hundred feet beyond, at the housing of a catapult. She rested her hands atop a merlon, regardless of its chill, and stared out to sea. The waters heaved darkling. Birds filled the pallor overhead with wings and thin screams.

"Say on," she directed.

Dahut's voice grieved. "Why are you so cold to me, Forsquilis? What became of our thaumaturgic studies?"

"I will give you no more arts while you act as you do.

Harm enough are you wreaking already, and worse lies ahead."

Dahut caught at the other's sleeve. "What mean you?" she wailed. "What am I save the victim of, of this that's happened?"

"You know full well."

"Think you I willed those horrible battles?" A sob barked in the girl's throat. "Nay, I swear by—by—Oh, I was foolish, heedless. You Sisters have warned me. I'm mending my ways. But I n-never dreamed you would believe the falsehoods about me!"

"I have dreams of my own. They make me glad Nemeta is my sole child." Forsquilis turned and looked straight at Dahut. "Always in them, you are the key that unlocks the doom. It is never clear how, everything is murky and wild, but always you are there at the heart of it. We may not yet be foredone. If you will make your peace with the Gods, They may stay Their hands. But the hope of that seems small."

Dahut stepped back. "*I* have offended Them? I, who wish and pray for naught than that Their will prevail? What of the King?"

"Your father. He who brought you forth when your mother had perished, and nurtured you and to this day loves you. You hate him. You want his destruction. Evil feeds upon evil, till at last it breaks loose and overwhelms all."

"You deny him, you, his wife," Dahut counterattacked.

"Not in hatred." Forsquilis's words softened. "In loving chastisement. In penance for his sin, so the entire wrath not fall on him but some of it be shared. In sorrow and longing. For the sake of Ys."

"Ys, which you forsake yourself! Where do you pass most of your days—and your nights?"

Anger flickered beneath the level response. "I have taken leave of absence from my lesser duties, that by what skills I hold I may seek a resolution of our trouble. None have I found. In the hills, the forests, the deeps, the air, few are my companions, and they are not human. Keep silence about betrayals, you." Surf rumbled against the wall. "And make an end of yours, ere you be betrayed to your own ruin."

Forsquilis walked off to the tower and the stairs. She never looked back. Dahut stayed a long while, first gazing after her, then alone.

— 4 —

Rain and sleet scourged the streets. Within a certain mean tavern in the Fishtail, it was night-gloomy, little relieved by a few rank-smelling tallow candles. Hunched over a table opposite Budic, Dahut was herself a shadow. Nonetheless she had dressed as if in poverty, retained a stola over her hair, and smeared herself with cosmetics. A couple of harlots threw resentful glances her way—no other customers were about—but did not interfere.

"This is utterly wrong," Budic remonstrated. "You should never come near a den like this, and outfitted like, like that."

"Quiet." Dahut's reply was just to be heard by him under the muffled storm-racket. "True. A foul place. But we had to meet somewhere, and—. 'Twill be brief. I've a boon to ask of you—beg of you, dear trusty friend."

" 'Tis yours, if I am able."

Anguish made her smile grotesque, but he remembered. "Not hard for you, a man; unthinkable for me. I want a place where I can retire, unbeknownst. A single room will serve, if it have simple furnishings, table, stool, basin, pallet; you know what. Best will be if it also have a separate entrance, or at least a side door onto its hallway. It should be clean, and in a safe neighborhood, but one where folk do not look too closely at their neighbors. Can you find me such a refuge?"

He gaped. "What of your house?"

"I've told you, I'm never by myself there, unless the servants have holiday, and that's only a few nights a year. Even my private room or bedchamber, why, they come in to scrub and dust; they'll notice traces, and certainly be aware whom I receive." Dahut's voice trembled. "You know not how 'tis to be in everybody's eyes. And I above all, I the undesired Queen. Old Fennalis could safely read Christian gospel on her deathbed. But I? Imagine."

He sat upright. "My lady," gusted from him, "do you mean— "

Dahut shook her head slightly. "Forgive me. Bear with me. I'm only a maiden, brought up to worship the Gods of Ys. I'd fain learn more about your Christ. Does He truly call me to Him? How can I tell, unless I study and, and, pray? Things I dare never do at home. You could meet me there too, answer my questions and help me." She wiped at tears. That left pathetic streaks in malachite and rouge. "Or I can be solitary, at peace, free to think. Can you do this for me, Budic? I'm sure your God will love you."

"Why, well, I—"

"You're not rich." She reached under the overgown that helped make her shape unrecognizable, freed a purse, and slipped it across the board. "Here's coin. It should be ample for months, but tell me if you need more. Say you want lodging for a friend—I'd best dress as a boy, 'tis no sin among us in Ys—a lad from afar who speaks our language poorly. He's in the service of somebody else, so he won't use this room often. You can help me devise the full story. You're clever, you've traveled widely, you know the world."

"This is unheard of," he mumbled.

"But not in any way unlawful. I promise you that. Find me my nest, Budic, and if later you can borrow Christian works for me—. Say you will, my soldier! Do it for your Luck!"

Resolve grew firm. "Of course I will, my lady."

— 5 —

In red robe with the Wheel on its breast and Key laid over that, Hammer to hand, Gratillonius stood before the winter Council of Suffetes and said:

"Hear me out ere you cry havoc. The divisions between us are bad enough. I would not widen them, I would heal them, if I had my way. But what they arise from is conflict between Gods, the commandments of Gods, and I think there is where we must first seek reconciliation.

"I follow Mithras, like my fathers before me. As your

King, I have given the Gods of Ys Their honors and dues.
I have asked no more in return than that I and my fellows
be free in our own worship, like everybody else." He
lifted his palm against a murmur. "Aye, even so there
have been clashes in the past. Some of you have been
outraged. Did you ever stop to think that Mithras may
have suffered outrages too? Still, we made peace, and
naught that was terrible happened. Rather, Ys has flourished.

"Now we are in a new conflict, the gravest of all. Somehow we must end it, ere it tears the city asunder. I know
not how. Nor do you. It is a matter for the Gods.

"Therefore I say, let us give Mithras His full honor.
Thereafter we can pray together for harmony in Heaven
and a sign unto us.

"Hitherto I have carried out my sacral duties as King
without regard to the times that are holy to Mithras. He's
a soldier; He understands how men in the field can't
always observe the pieties.

"But this year His birthday falls on the full moon.

"May I interrupt my Watch to celebrate it as it should
be celebrated, in the Mithraeum here? If this assembly
disallows that, I will not. My last desire is to provoke more
trouble.

"However, think. Think how empty that rite of the
Watch is, especially now, when I have not regained strength
to answer a challenge. Think what it may mean—to the
Gods, Whom we do not really know, and to our souls—if
the Incarnation of Taranis takes one day out of three days
and nights to do service to Mithras, Who is also a warrior.
How can it harm? How might it help?

"I ask your leave to try."

Debate began. Gratillonius was surprised at its quietness. Most of the Suffetes thought the request reasonable.
Of his chief opponents among them, Soren spoke against
it, but briefly, in a tone of somber resignation, while
Hannon sat huddled in eld. The Gallicenae had chosen no
speaker—unprecedented—and Lanarvilis merely echoed
Soren; Bodilis praised what might indeed be a seed of
peace; the rest kept mute—Vindilis showed scorn, her
remaining Sisters varying degrees of hope—until Dahut
sprang to her feet and cried:

"Hear me! Who has a better right to choose? I say my

father heard a voice from Beyond, and had the wisdom and courage to listen. Open your hearts. Grant him his wish." Tears gleamed across the waves of blood that made her flame with beauty. "After everything he's wrought for Ys, 't-t-tis little enough reward!"

The vote of agreement was close to unanimous.

—Gratillonius and Dahut had a moment by themselves, in the portico, as the adjourned meeting spilled forth into the early night. "Mithras forgive me," he blurted, "but today you've made me happier than ever He could in His Paradise."

"We've a long road before us," she replied. Her earnestness wavered between a child's and a woman's. "You are in the wrong, father, and I can but pray you'll make your way to the light. Best we not see each other, be together, as in olden days." Her voice caught. " 'Twould hurt too much. For know, I love you still, my big, strong, lonely Grallon."

"Abide, darling." His words stumbled. "I'll yet find how to give you—not what you believe you want—but what you truly deserve."

She clutched his hand in both hers. The touch burned. "Meanwhile, father, you'll know those horrible whispers about me are false. You will?"

He could only hug her to him for an instant before they parted.

— 6 —

"**N**ow say we our farewells," intoned Gratillonius. He lifted his arms. To the handful of worshippers whose feast had ended: "May the light of Ahura-Mazda, which is Truth, shine upon you. May the blessing of Mithras, which is Troth, descend upon you. May strength and purity dwell within you, and bring your souls at last to their home. Go in peace."

Thereafter he led them from the sanctuary. Sea-thunder growled faintly through the stonework, once they had climbed higher up into the gloom. Torches guttered and smoked. It was like a liberation to come forth on top of the

Raven Tower, though the chill cut and sundown was a sullen red streak above Ocean.

Waves crashed on the wall below, an undertone to evening orisons. Gratillonius said his without quite hearing them. It was not that he had lost reverence. His mind was still in the crypt. How majestically had the service resounded, but how hollowly the echoes of it. There had been a sadness about it, a sense of goodbye, as if this were the last Birthday he would ever celebrate.

But that was nonsense, he told himself. The God upheld him. He was healing rapidly and entirely. Soon he would be able to cope with any new challenger—who was most unlikely to appear, given what had become of the others. While it might not be easy, he thought he could win the support of Stilicho, which meant the acquiescence of Rome. His opponents within the city were well-nigh powerless. More and more of them were coming back to his side, where the people of Ys had always been. The rift between him and the Gallicenae—some of the Gallicenae—must close in time, if only he was patient; for had not Dahut said she loved him? That alone kindled summer in his heart.

Then why this foreboding? Why had the noonday sun looked pale and shrunken? The blasphemy had crossed his mind that Mithras was defeated and in retreat. Gratillonius had stamped on it, as he had stamped on the face of Carsa, but it would no more go altogether away than would those memories.

The prayers ended. "Goodnight, men," he said in Latin. Replies muttered back. He tossed his ceremonial torch over the battlements. It streamed fire on the way to its drowning. From a guard he took the lantern he had left and used it to help him down the stairway and through the blindness that had fallen upon Ys.

Most of such folk as were yet in the streets recognized him, but few offered greetings, for he wore the vestments of his alien God. The guards at High Gate did salute him. Some of the workshops beyond were lighted and busy, but the clangor from them soon faded as he went on beyond, to Processional Way. Crossing the canal by the tiny bridge, he saw the water frozen over. Stars began to crowd heaven. Moon-glow above the hills was as cold as they and the ice

were. He hastened his steps in spite of its making his ribs
ache; footfalls rang loud through stillness. If he could
reach the Wood before the moon rose into view, maybe he
would not really have been absent on this midmost day of
his Watch. But that idea was ridiculous, he told himself.

The grove loomed before him, blackness out of which
fingers reached. Gleams from the house did not touch it,
nor did he find much warmth of welcome when he entered. The strife between King and Gods naturally perturbed the staff more than it did an ordinary Ysan. Tambilis
was on Sena.

Well, a man should be able to stand a little isolation.
Gratillonius withdrew to the Roman-like part of the building. By lamplight he changed his sacred garments for a
robe and settled down to read for a while. Good old
Vergilius—

Wind woke him, a breath under the eaves. His candles
burned low. Drowsily, he went to a window and looked
out, blocking reflections off the panes with his body. Nothing but murk met his eyes. So clouds had blown up anew,
had they? He stripped, killed the flamelets, crawled into
bed and fell back into sleep.

—"Out with you! To your homes! You'll be told when
you're wanted again. Out!"

Gratillonius sat up. For a moment he wondered what
this dream was. Bedding bulged soft around him; air
sheathed his torso in cold. He could just see the uncov-
ered window, slightly less dark than the room. He had
barely heard the voice through closed doors. Scurrying
feet sounded louder and must have been what roused him.
Oh, this was real. His scalp prickled. Should he take
something that could serve as a weapon? The imperious
tones had been a woman's. The heart jumped in his breast.

He groped about till he had come upon his robe and
drawn it on. Then he advanced boldly enough. The years
had made him familiar with the passage. When he flung
open the door to the hall, coals glowed in the firepits and a
few candles had been lighted from them. Through shadows he saw the attendants, hastily dressed, going elsewhere. Tall in a black cloak stood Forsquilis.

He halted. She heard his amazed oath. Her hair shimmered wild amidst the dark. "Hold," she commanded with the quietness that expects obedience.

When the last servant had gone, she beckoned. "Now we can talk," she said.

He approached her. The Athene face had turned gaunt in the past months; highlights wavered over arches of bone and lost themselves beneath. Somehow that made her twice beautiful, a night-nymph. "What brings you here?" he asked with deference.

"I went afar in my Sending," she answered. Her gaze smoldered upon him. "You cannot see through the clouds—Ys cannot, which is well for it—but the eagle owl flew above. The moon whitened her wings. That brightness dimmed, reddened, was nearly lost. The moon was in eclipse, Grallon."

"Nobody foresaw," he said numbly.

"Aye, nobody did, in Star House or wherever else my searching took me. I think Belisama withdraws the last of Her light from you, Grallon, for that you again affronted the Three on this day that is past."

He knotted his fists. "Then why did They hide the vision?" he snapped.

"You would deride it."

"At least I would say the eclipse would soon end, when the moon moves out from behind the earth. If the philosophers failed to predict this, 'tis hardly the first time they have."

Sorrow muted her words. "Aye, so you'd claim; and some in Ys would accept it and some would not, and thus the wounds in us would deepen. Better you hear from me. Mayhap you'll listen."

"Of course I will! But . . . I might not believe."

"You might not understand," she sighed. 'You will not. You refuse."

"What is there for me to heed? That your Gods are angry with me?" He grinned. "That's no news."

She surprised him. "I came to warn you," she said, "not because They told me to. They did not. The sign was meant for me, to give to my Sisters, that unless we return to the Gods you make us forsake, They will forsake us. But I had to tell you first."

"Why?"

She leaned forward. "Because I love you, Grallon."

He gathered her to him.

—Sunrise was dull in the window when she rose from the bed and sought her clothes. "You are not going, are you?" he asked.

Fire had died away; her voice was ashen with weariness. "I must. Never tell anyone what happened between us."

He stirred, alarmed. "Why?"

She regarded him as if out of a cage where she was penned. "You will not yield," she said. "Last night I spoke falsely. I thought the darkened moon had told me to come to you, and after you had fallen asleep find a knife and slash your throat. Thus might Ys yet be saved. But I could not. Now I must go and do what penance I can. Farewell, Grallon."

He scrambled toward her. She gestured him back, and somehow he could only obey and watch, helpless, while she clad herself. Almost, then, they kissed. She turned away in time and left him, never looking back.

XV

— 1 —

"Today I will go riding," said Dahut.

The chambermaid hesitated before replying timidly: "Again? My lady spends much time in the saddle." She did not venture to mention neglected sacral and secular tasks, but did add, "At least she should have an escort. There could be wicked men abroad, or an accident far from help."

Dahut tossed her head. "I know what I do. You tend to what you are supposed to understand."

The maid folded hands over breast and bowed low. Dahut brooked no interference from her hirelings On succeeding to Fennalis's home, she had not only redecorated and refurnished it from top to bottom, she had replaced the entire staff. Tongue-lashings, cuffs to cheek or ear, summary dismissals soon won her a properly subservient household.

But they watched her, always they watched her, and when she was gone they talked.

She took her candlestick to the bathroom. Lamps burned there; perfume mingled with the mist-wraiths off the hot water. A long while she luxuriated in it, admiring and stroking her body, before she rose and called the chambermaid. Toweled dry, she returned to the bathroom and was, quite unnecessarily, assisted into the garments laid out—linen tunic, calfskin breeches, half-boots, purse and dagger belted at her waist. The attendant combed and braided her hair and wrapped the shining coils close around her head. She had taken to wearing it shorter than most women on Ys, only halfway down her back when loosened. That made it the more readily concealable.

She broke her fast lightly as always, with bread, butter, cheese, honey, milk. When nobody was with her, she slipped from the purse a vial, shook it over her palm, kissed and swallowed the ladygift. Thereupon she donned an outer coat of wool, whose thickness disguised curves of breast and hip. A cowled cloak did the rest. "Await me when I return," she said, and stepped forth into the winter dawn.

Seen from this height, the roofs of lower Ys had begun to glimmer forth out of darkness, while already the towers gleamed frosty. The headlands hulked above a livid sea. Air lay quiet and cold. Nobody else was on this street as yet. Once beyond view of her house, Dahut changed her gait to the loose-jointed walk she had practiced in secret. Boylike, she descended.

Often she did in fact seek the livery stables outside High Gate, since horses were not allowed to be kept within the city except by the King. It would never do for word to trickle back that she did not invariably do so. Today she took a circuitous route to Lowtown. As she went on, light strengthened and traffic increased.

About to cross Lir Way near Skippers' Market, she found that the square, generally deserted at this time of year, held a small crowd, with more folk streaming in by the minute and pushing on through the arch. She plucked the sleeve of a workman. "What's afoot?" she asked. Her voice she carefully deepened and roughened.

His glance saw little beneath her overshadowing hood. "An outland ship standing in, I hear," he told her. "Northmen of some kind."

Instantly eager to see, she mingled with the rest and passed onto the wharf. Falling tide had drawn the sea gate open. The vessel, which must have lain to until daylight when the crew could pick their way among the rocks, drew ever closer. Her eye as skilled in such matters as that of any Ysan, Dahut saw that this one was indeed from across the Germanic Sea, but not quite the same as a typical Saxon craft. The hull was about seventy feet long, wide-beamed, clinker-built, open save for thwarts on which twenty rowers sat. Stem- and sternposts curved high. A single steering oar was at the starboard. Mast, yardarm, and furled sail lay across trestles amidships. Paint whose flamboyant colors were faded and chipped bespoke much voyaging. The men numbered some forty, most of them big and blond. Their captain—she assumed—stood in the bows, helmed, ring-mailed, spear in hand, a splendid sight even at this distance.

"Pirates?" fretted someone.

"Nay," scoffed another. "Were they so mad as to cast a single ship against Ys, they couldn't've made it hither. Beware of brawls, though."

"Mayhap not," said a third. "When barbarians are on their good behavior, ofttimes they've better manners than most city folk. I'll be happy to hear whatever yarns they spin, if any of them can wield our speech."

Dahut cursed under her breath. She could not linger. Budic was free today. He would be waiting.

She slipped off and hurried to the edge of the Fishtail district. The legionary was there, in civil garb and also hooded. His glad call rang: "Oh, wonderful! I feared you'd been unable to come."

"Hush," she cautioned. The attention of passersby was unwanted. Approaching the door, she brushed against him, glidingly, while she took a key from her purse.

He had done well in finding her this place. The house was ancient, a block of eroded stone with interior walls almost as thick as the outer. It belonged to a widower, deaf, incurious, content to live and stay drunk on the small rentals paid by half a dozen roomers. They were a floating population of sailors, day laborers, hawkers, harlots, foreigners without much wealth, the kind of people who observed but did not pry. To them she was Cian, a Scotic lad lately arrived from Mumu to assist Tommaltach. Since that man's death, Cian had been errand boy to the caretaker the King appointed pending new arrangements with Conual Corcc when trade resumed in spring. Cian was often sent widely about, and therefore stayed here only occasionally. His Ysan being scant and broken, his Latin nil, he kept to himself, unless a friend visited.

From Tommaltach Dahut had learned the lilting accent and enough words to sound like a Hivernian.

Not for the first time, she took Budic past an entry and up a stair to the narrow corridor on which her chamber fronted. Unfastening the lock, she let them through and bolted the door from within. The room was small and meagerly furnished. Oiled cloth across the single window admitted dim light. Unkindled, a brazier gave no help against dankness and cold. However, the wine in a clay jug was of the best. Dahut poured into two wooden cups.

"I should fetch some fresh water for this, my lady," Budic said.

"Oh, that's a waste of these few hours we have," she replied. "Drink it pure, savor the taste. You're too solemn, my dear."

His mouth twisted. "I've reason enough." He gripped his cup hard and tossed off a deep draught.

Dahut barely sipped. "Aye, poor Budic," she murmured, "unhappy at home, tormented in spirit. You've been very kind to me regardless. Would that I could return to you a gift of peace."

"In Christ is peace," he grated.

"So you say. I strive to see how. Come, let us sit and talk. Nay, bring your stool next to mine." She dropped her cloak and removed the wool beneath. Abruptly he saw her bosom strain against thin linen.

He gulped. "Will you not be cold, my lady?"

"Not if you sit close and lay that fine big cloak of yours over both our shoulders," she laughed.

He flinched. "Best not, my lady."

She cocked her head. 'Why?" she asked innocently.

Through the gloom she saw him redden to the roots of his fair hair. "Unseemly," he faltered. "And—forgive me— Satan's lures—"

"Oh, Budic, we are like brother and sister. Come." She took his hand. Defenseless, he obeyed her wish.

Staring straight before him, he inquired. "Have you prayed for insight?"

"Of course," she said. "Over and over. In vain." Not defiantly but sadly: "I cannot make sense of your faith. Try though I do, I cannot. *Why* did Christ die?"

"For you. For all mankind."

"How is that so different from other Gods Who die? They rise again and renew the earth."

"Christ died that He might redeem us from our sin and save us from the everlasting flames."

Dahut shivered. "That's a horrible thought, that we are born damned because of something that happened in the beginning. It chills me more deeply than this air does." She leaned against him. Her free hand sought his. "Must Ys burn for want of knowledge? Lir would only drown us."

"Ys can yet be saved. Let her heed the tidings."

"How? You've seen the very King, my father, forced to bow down before the Gods."

"Christ is stronger than Mithras."

"Aye, a Christian King—what might such a man do?"

"We've met in aid of your soul, yours alone," Budic said fast. "I am a clumsy preacher, but let me try." He looked upward. "O Spirit That came down to the Apostles, help my tongue!"

Dahut shifted closer still. "I listen," she breathed.

He spoke. She refilled his cup. He spoke, repeating what he had told her before and adding to it: of the Creation, the origin of evil, God's Covenant with His chosen people, from whom Christ was to spring. She asked him about those ancient Jews, but he knew little, apart from snatches of the Psalms. Rather he would seek to explain the mysteries of the Incarnation, the Redemption—ignoramus that he was, the subtleties escaped him too, but he *believed* and that sufficed—. He talked on.

Dahut wondered aloud about Christ's laws concerning women. Was she right in her impression that many had found favor in His eyes, not simply His Mother but the young bride at Cana, Maria and Martha of Bethany, aye, even a woman taken in adultery? If He smiled on them, if He understood human needs and longings, why then should women be somehow unclean, why should celibacy be a sacrifice pleasing unto Him?

"We live for God, only for God," he rattled forth. "It is better to marry than to burn, but best is to become free of lust, of everything worldly."

"Does your God hate this world you say He made? Any good workman takes pride in his works. Taranis and Belisama are lovers, and They are in all who love. Look at me, Budic. I am a woman. Am I foul? Did God give me this body in order that I starve and torture it?"

He sprang from her, to his feet. "Stop!" he cried. "You know not what you do!"

She rose also and came to him, reached once more for his hands. Compassion glowed from her. "I'm sorry, dear man. I'd never wittingly hurt you. What is so dreadful?"

"I must go," he said. "Forgive me, I must."

"Why, we've talked a pair of hours at most. We thought to go out after food we could share, and be together this whole day."

"I cannot," he gasped. "Forgive me, my lady. You are not foul, nay, you are beautiful, too beautiful, and I—I must go pray for strength."

She smiled the least wistful bit. "As you will. I'll pray too. When can we meet again?"

"We should not. Your honor—"

"Budic," she said low, "I trust you more than any other living soul."

"I'll send you a message. Farewell!" He snatched his cloak and fled. The door slammed shut behind him.

Dahut stared at it. After a while, she kicked the stool he had been using across the floor. "Belisama, where were You?" she shrilled.

Suddenly she began to laugh. Long and loud she laughed, hands on hips, head turned to the ceiling, before she donned her outer garments and left.

The streets were now thronged, scarcely less busy than in summer, Ys getting on with its work while daylight lasted. But she had seen the many-colored spectacle all her life. Momentarily she walked toward High Gate and the stables—then turned and made for the harbor.

The strange ship lay docked between two high-hulled freighters idled for the winter. Onlookers had dispersed, for the crew was gone. City guards kept watch over every vessel. Dahut intercepted one on his beat. "Where's yon craft from?" she asked in her boy-voice.

"Britannia," he replied, "or so I heard."

"That's no Britannic hull."

"Well, her homeland is afar, but Germani come more and more to the east and southeast of yon island, raiding, trading, sometimes settling. I hear these fellows were visiting kinfolk there but grew restless and decided on a small venture to us, mainly to see what we're like. They unloaded some bales and boxes into a warehouse. Belike their chief will meet with merchants of ours."

"Where is he now?"

"What, you'd fain enlist with him, lad? Ha, ha! Hm, the Swan is the most respectable mariners' inn, but his sort more commonly seek the Crossed Anchors or Epona's Horse."

Dahut nodded and hurried off. At the second place, she learned that the barbarian skipper had taken a room to himself—surely with intent of having a woman for the night, said the landlord matter-of-factly—and wandered off a short while ago.

The Forum would be the logical place for him to aim at. There he could meet shipmates, if that had been agreed upon, and commence sightseeing. Dahut slipped and wove through the traffic up Lir Way. Presently, inevitably, she saw him. He had changed his armor for a fur cap, tunic sable-trimmed and richly patterned, wadmal breeks, cross-garters, gold rings on brawny arms—no less grand a sight than before, with tawny mane and beard rearing above most heads, over the doorframe width of his shoulders. A bow wave and wake of stares, whispers, gestures eddied around him.

Dahut overtook. "Pray pardon, sir," she hailed.

He checked his stride for an instant, regarded her, shrugged, and indicated he did not know the language.

"Do you speak Latin, then, my lord?" she asked in it.

"Um. Not too good." The words resonated from his chest. "Vat you vant, hey?"

"Do you wish a guide? I know Ys, everything to see, every opportunity, every pleasure. Let me show you, master."

His gaze sharpened in weather-beaten features. "Ho, I know your kind. . . . No, vait a bit. You are not—Step you aside, ha, and ve talk."

They found a spot under the sheer wall of a tower. "You are no boy," he said in his surf-rolling tones. "You are a girl. Vat for you dress like that?"

"To go about freely, sir, because I am *not* a whore. It is reckoned decent among us." Dahut smiled straight into his wariness. "You are observant, master. You'll want a guide who can lead you to what's worth finding—and get you the right female company too, if that's your wish, somebody warm, knowing, clean, and honest."

The seaman rumbled laughter. "Ho! Maybe ve try. Vat are your pay for this?"

"Whatever my noble lord thinks proper," Dahut purred. "Best will be if first I get to know him. Could we sit and talk?"

He assenting, she led him inside the tower. He gaped at the magnificence of the entrance, the corridor beyond, the shops opening onto it. One offered refreshments. They settled down to wine, bits of grilled marinated fish, garum sauce, cheese, dried fruits. The foreigner had no coin but produced a few small amber chunks. Dahut bargained deftly on his behalf.

"Who are you?" he asked.

She fluttered her lashes. "Call me Galith if you will, master—orphaned, making my way as best I can, rather than becoming a housewife or servant. But I am at *your* command. Tell me about yourself, I beg you. Your stories should be worth more to me than money."

Nothing loth, he obliged. He was Gunnung, son of Ivar, a Dane from Scandia. Of well-to-do family, he had already— still in his twenties—traveled about, trading north among the Finnaithae and south along the Germanic marches of the Empire. There he had picked up his Latin. A quarrel at home had led to a killing, the breaking of his betrothal, and his outlawry for three years. His father gave him a ship and he gathered friends to accompany him west for that term. After visiting along the Gallic shores, they turned to Britannia and thought to spend the winter in a village of Anglic laeti on the Icenian coast. They soon found it tedious. An overland journey to Londinium proved disappointing; it was both impoverished and hostile to barbarians. But Ys, fabulous Ys, they heard such tales of that as to resolve them on making the trip immediately, never mind the season.

Gunnung seemed not at all downcast by his situation. Rather, he was delighted to be in a fresh part of the world, snuffing about for every possible spoor of fortune. If he and his men did well, they might never return to Scandia.

"A strong man will certainly find many paths open to him here," Dahut agreed. "Shall we go look at a few?"

Throughout that day they roamed together. Watchful, she soon learned what interested him most, and led him to

such things. By no means unappreciative of architectural
wonders—especially the towers, two of which they ascended—or wares displayed by jewelers and clothiers, he nonetheless cared more about fortifications, military engines,
civil machinery, marketplaces, the working foundations of
things. He listened closely to her tales of expeditions
abroad, commerce, fights, discoveries, often asking that
she explain something twice where his Latin had failed
him. She exerted herself to charm as well, with anecdotes,
japes, songs while they fared about.

The early evening closed in. They went back to his hostel. "See here," he exclaimed, "'ve got more you can say
me. Come in and ve eat. You are a girl like never I met
before, Galith."

"Oh, I am not so strange," she murmured. "But I cannot sit in the taproom." At his surprised look: "I must
needs take off this mantle and coat. The landlord would
see I am female. He might well . . . recognize me . . . and
that would be bad."

Gunnung forbore to ask why. "Come to my room, then,"
he suggested, "and I send after food."

"My captain is too kind." She kept his hugeness between her and everybody else.

In the cubicle, over bowls of stew and cups of ale, by
the light of tallow candles, they laid plans for the morrow.
Finally Gunnung coughed out a laugh, stared at her, and
said, "You have not done me vun thing, Galith. You
promised you find me a voman."

Night filled the window. A brazier had added its warmth
and closeness to the rank animal smell of the candles.
"The hour is late," she replied demurely. "The girls down-
stairs are most likely taken by now. Do you want to go
stumble around the streets?"

"Do I got to?"

For answer, she dropped glance and hands to her belt
and slowly unfastened it. He whooped, rose, snatched her
to him. She reached and felt with the same frankness.

His first lovemaking was neither exuberant and inven-
tive like Tommaltach's nor half reverential like Carsa's.
When he had the clothes off her he bore her down onto
the bed and himself between her thighs and made her
teeth clatter. He was not brutish, though, and the follow-

ing times, which with her encouragement came soon after each other, were steady gallopings. She cried and moaned and told him he was superb.

Finally they slept. As the first gray appeared in the window, he roused, sought the chamber pot, came back and began to fondle her. She sat up. "Now, beloved, you shall know who I am," she said.

He blinked. "You are Galith—"

She shook her head and drew tangled tresses back from the red crescent. "Have you noticed this?"

"Yah, a scar, it don't make you not fair."

"It is the mark of the Goddess, Gunnung. This night She chose you to be the next King of Ys."

— 2 —

Snow fell in small dry flakes. Walking, Corentinus saw walls and roofs fade within a few yards, lost in the overall silvery-grayness. Air was almost warm and utterly silent, apart from the sound of his sandals on paving and a dream-faint pulse of sea.

Budic was among the guards at the palace gate. He lost his military bearing when the pastor loomed into sight. Corentinus halted before him and peered from beneath shaggy brows. Budic's eyes flicked to and fro like snared creatures. "We have not seen you lately at worship," Corentinus said.

"I have had . . . troubles," Budic muttered.

"Can you confide in me?"

"Not—not now. I pray. Believe me, I pray."

"Never cease that. My son, you are in worse danger than ever on the battlefield."

"I've done nothing wrong!" Budic said frantically. "I've not even seen—well, I haven't come near any temptation for days and days. And I didn't fall to it."

"Broody, he's been," said Guentius, the other legionary present.

"Let me alone!" Budic yelled.

Corentinus's shoulders sagged a little. Weariness dragged in his words. "Enough. I must see the King."

"How do you know he's here?" Guentius wondered. "He goes about so much, building back his strength now that his bones have knit."

"I know," replied Corentinus. "Pass me through."

One of the Ysan marines, who knew Latin, said with a touch of awe, "You are right. Surely he will receive you."

The tall man strode up the path and the stairs. A servant admitted him and took his snow-dusted paenula. He kept his staff, as if it were a badge of authority. A second attendant sped off to inform Gratillonius, who arrived at once and said, "Welcome. Good to see you," then paused, looked, and added, "Maybe not."

"We must speak alone," the chorepiscopus declared.

Gratillonius nodded and led the way to his second-floor conference room. A servant carried a lamp to lighten its gloom and departed, shutting the door. "Be seated," Gratillonius invited.

"I'll stand," Corentinus answered. His host did likewise.

"What have you to say?" Gratillonius asked.

"Bad things, my son. I have heard certain rumors." (Gratillonius nodded again. Despite his calling and his ascetic ways, Corentinus learned more than most about what went on in Ys, and often earlier.) "I reproved those who whispered them, I told them to stop spreading malicious tattle that must be false. Nevertheless, when I inquired further I found that it has a basis of fact—nothing that proves wrongdoing, but a great deal that is unknown and unexplainable. So I prayed for a sign, not out of curiosity but out of fear for our beloved Ys. This past night it came to me in a dream."

"What faith can a man put in dreams?" Gratillonius challenged.

"Usually none. However, I know truth when it seeks me out; and you must admit that it has now and then. Nor is this anything I tell my old friend lightly or willingly."

Gratillonius girded himself. "Well?"

"Your daughter Dahut plots against you. She incited those two young men you fought. She will continue till you're killed."

Gratillonius lurched. The lamplight showed him white to the lips. "No!"

"If you will not believe me, at least verify the facts that

have brought the whispers on," said Corentinus with surgical relentlessness. "She disappears for hours on end, sometimes overnight. Less and less has she been telling the truth when she's claimed this was for a ride or a ramble. With passion she imagines her Gods have picked her to be the new Brennilis; but she skims over her religious duties or ignores them, as if there is something far more important for her. What can that be except becoming fully one of the Nine? Since you will not make her that, she must needs get another man to be her King."

Gratillonis shuddered. "Stop," had panted. "Be still."

"In the last ten days or so, she has been seen less than ever," Corentinus went on. "Nor has the giant Northman who led his crew here, exactly that long ago. They grumble that the proceeds of their trading are caroused away by now and he should take them back to Britannia. Why doesn't he? Were your man Rufinus on hand, he'd soon have tracked down what is going on. Set spies on those two yourself, King, before it's too late."

"You slander Dahilis's child?" Gratillonius shouted. "You foul-mouthed old swine! Out!"

"For your sake, for Ys," Corentinus beseeched. "If you discover I'm mistaken, what harm's been done? I'll abase myself before you. But you must open your eyes."

Gratillonius's fist shot forward. With the alertness of his roaming days, Corentinus swayed aside. The blow only took him on the left cheekbone. It was enough to resound. Blood welled from split flesh. Corentinus staggered. He recovered, brought his staff to battle position, lowered it. "Christ strengthen me to keep peace," he groaned.

"Spy on my daughter?" Gratillonius raged. "Oh, I'll have spies out, I will—watching you—and if you shit forth any more of your lies, if you look like you're doing any tiny thing that might be against her, I'll have your head rotting on a stake in a pigpen. Now go before I fetch my sword!"

"You're raving," Corentinus said. "Rome—"

Gratillonius had recovered himself. "I'll plan what to tell Rome," he replied. "If you behave, you can live. You aren't really worth the trouble that killing you would cause. But that's only if you keep your mouth shut. Get out. Don't come back."

"I spoke as a friend."

"You're not any more. I'll talk with you again when you've come on your belly and admitted that that angel, or whatever it was your Christ sent you, is a liar. Now will you leave on your own feet or be tossed out like other rubbish?"

"You shall not keep me from praying for you, and for Dahut and Ys," Corentinus said. He turned, shuffled to the door, opened it, went out.

Gratillonius stayed behind. He paced, cast himself into a chair, sprang up to pace anew. His fist hammered the walls till cracks appeared in the Arcadian frescos.

Eventually a servant appeared and dared announce, "Queen Tambilis has arrived, my lord."

"What? Oh, aye." Gratillonius stood a moment tensed, like a pugilist preparing against attack. He had expected her about this hour, after she had seen a female physician for something she had not identified to him. "Send her to me," he decided.

She entered radiant, saw him, and carefully closed the door. "What's happened, my darling?" she whispered.

Standing where he was, he gave her the story in a few jagged sentences.

"But that's horrible." She came to him. They held each other close.

"What can we do?" he asked in his despair.

Tambilis stepped back. "Can you talk with Dahut?"

"Nay. I think not. But she told me she . . . cares for me still."

"Of course she does. Well, I'll draw her aside and, as Sister to Sister, warn her to be more careful." Tambilis gathered courage. "Is it unthinkable that you mount an investigation? That should establish her innocence beyond question."

"It *is* beyond question," he rapped. "I'll not send dirty-minded little sneaks peering after her. They'd suppose I do have doubts, and they'd snigger and mutter and it would all be a worse besmirchment than a few idle speculations and the visions of a doddering crackpot."

"You may be unwise," she said low, "but I can see 'tis best to pursue this no further today."

"Aye." He cleared his throat. "What did the physician find?"

Happiness peeped through her distress like the first anemone through the last snow of springtime. "What I had hoped," she answered. "I am with child again, your new daughter, Grallon."

"What? I never knew—"

"Nay, not until I could be sure, lest I dash our hopes. For this is our sign of hope, our battle banner, which I raise for him who is the dearest of my whole world."

— 3 —

Weather turned bitingly cold and clear. When Dahut let herself into the widower's house, the murkiness almost blinded her. Vision returned as she made her way up the stairs.

A door stood open next to hers. A blowzy woman in a soiled gown, neckline down to her nipples, stepped out. "Hail, sweetling," she said with a leer.

Dahut barely knew her name and station: Mochta, an Osismian who had become a cheap whore. "I am no lover of yours," she responded coldly.

"Ah, the Scotic speech slipped there," laughed the woman.

Dahut stiffened and bit her lip. She had been preoccupied. "I learn," she said with the right intonation. "What would you of me?"

"Oh, naught, naught. For a surety, you're not about to hire me. Yet you might be thankful for my help."

Dahut dropped hand to knife. "What mean you?"

"Why, when you're too haughty to chat with the likes o' your fellow dwellers, you hear not what they say about you. That big man who's with you so much—they dislike boy-lovers in Ys. There was complaints to the landlord, there was. He'd've thrown you out, and asked for yon barbarians to be sent straightway from the city. But Mochta can see what's underneath clothes, or catch noises through a door to know what's going on. I told 'em you're no lad. Now they only laugh."

Dahut quivered where she stood.

"Why'd you go to such trouble?" the harlot gibed, grinning. "A fine lady, I'll be bound, a Suffete lady who wants to keep it quiet about her lovers. Handsome men too, both that I've watched. They could pleasure me aplenty, and I need the pay. Still, though you cut into my trade, I'm kind-hearted and done you this favor. Surely you'll be thankful to me?" she whined.

Dahut dug into her purse, flung a gold coin on the floor, and turned her back while she put key in lock. "Ah, good," Mochta exulted. "A very, very fine lady you must be. Who? 'Tis not for me to say your name, whatever 'tis, but a girl can't help wondering, can she? If ever you need more help, here I am."

Dahut entered and crashed her door shut.

Alone in the dimness, she yowled for fury and ripped at the fastenings of her garments. When they were off, she had regained self-possession.

Piecemeal she had smuggled luxurious female clothes to this place and stowed them in a chest. She chose a thick robe of tapestried silk and fur slippers, against the chill. Her hair she unbraided and shook down across her shoulders in glowing waves.

A knock thudded. She let Gunnung in. He reached to seize her, but she evaded him and glided back. "Not such haste," she said.

"Vy not?" he growled. "For two days I cool my heels and yawn, till you send vord ve can meet." That had been by her principal male servitor, to whom the code phrase she used was meaningless. He had acted as her messenger on a number of occasions. She forbade him to talk about what she called secret and sacred business. At Gunnung's suggestion, she later hinted that it concerned the seals. Northmen knew more about those creatures than Ysans did, because Northmen hunted them—but could perhaps be induced to desist. "Vell, tomorrow you valk bowlegged!"

"That may be one thing Mochta noticed," Dahut murmured.

"Vat are this?" The Dane moved in on her.

She lifted a fending palm. "Hold." Such command rang in her voice that he halted and stared. "I waited because of caution. A Sister of mine warned me. Talk is going about. Even in this hovel, I've learned. You've dawdled too long, a fortnight or worse. No more."

He glowered. "You mean you vant I kill your father? Vat for a she-troll are you?"

"You vowed you would, that first morning."

"Yah, yah, but—"

Her eyes narrowed to blue ice-glints. "Gunnung," she said, "you have lain with a Queen of Ys. If word of that escapes, then hope the people tear you in shreds before my father's men take you, for he will put you to death in every slow way the Romans know."

He flushed and bristled. "You threaten? By Thor—"

"Lay violent hand on me, and I will cause it that you can never again in your life have a woman. I am of the Gallicenae."

Gunnung retreated a step. "Ve are lovers," he said hastily. "I did promise you."

Her smile thawed the entire chilly room. "Then make yourself King, my lover," she crooned. "Once you are King, you are safe; Ys is yours.,"

"More yours, I think," he answered, his tone going dry. "Vell, I vould yust remind you, first, it vere unvise to shallenge ven he is still mending. He can tell me to vait, and meanvile —"

"He has mended. Now he works to regain the strength he lost when he could do so little. Call him out before he finishes. He cannot refuse any longer. In good condition, he's a terrible foe." Dahut's speech softened. "I do not want you dead, Gunnung. I want you by my side, for many years to come."

"He might vin anyhow. And if he does not, there vill be others—" The Dane lifted his head. "But I am not afraid. I told you vy I vaited. A spae-voman told me vunce my luck vill alvays be best in fair veather. Ve have had snow and fog and high vinds—"

"Until today. Tomorrow will likely be the same. Go to the Wood. I tell you, waiting longer is more dangerous than any fight."

He was quiet for a space, until: "I go tomorrow."

"Now!"

He shook his head. "Tomorrow morning early. Could be I fall."

"You won't." She undulated toward him.

"That lies vith the Norns," he answered. A smile eased

the ruggedness of his countenance. "Vat I have here is hand-grippable—you, my strange lovely Norn. Give me heart for my battle."

"So be it," she yielded, and slid into his arms.

—She woke when a sunbeam struggled through the window cloth and touched her. That was well into the next day. She caught her breath. Gunnung was gone.

"Oo," she said when she tried to rise, and followed it with some of the curses she had overheard Maeloch use in her girlhood. Bruises were beginning to flower here and there on her. Straw stuck out from rips in the tick. Wincing, she got up and hobbled to the water jug. After she had filled and drained a cup, poured a basinful, swabbed herself, she could roughly secure her hair. Cian's garb lay on the floor. The costly robe she had dropped did not. With a cry, she opened her clothes chest. It was empty of fabrics, furs, and jewels.

She dressed herself and stumbled out into the street. Folk went about their business in ordinary wise. There should have been tumult. Gnawing her lip, Dahut made her painful way to the harbor.

The slip where the Danic vessel had lain was vacant. Half shut, the sea gate mocked her with a glimpse of unrestful brightness.

A patroller passed close. Dahut wailed at him: "Where are the Northmen?"

He stopped, gave her a stare, and asked, "Why d'you care, boy?"

"I do! *Where?*"

He shrugged. "Wherever they had in mind, I suppose. They left in almighty haste, before first light, when the doors were barely open. My mates and I thought perchance they'd gotten into an ill affair. But we'd received no orders to hold them, nor did they look like having been in a fight or carrying loot—only their baggage—save that the captain was as weary-acting a man as I've seen in years. I climbed the wall for a look as soon as there was light, and they were rowing like racers. They must be long leagues off by now. What's your concern?"

Dahut screeched and turned from him.

—Astonished, Forsquilis regarded the unkempt figure that had hirpled to her door. Recognition came. "Follow me," she said. They went to her secretorium.

There she demanded sharply. "What mischief have you been in this time?"

"You must help me," Dahut said, hoarse-voiced. "You and I can raise a storm, can we not? Or a sea monster, or anything that will sink a shipful of treacherous wretches."

"Who? Why?"

"Those Scandians who've been in port."

"What have they done?"

"I want them dead," Dahut told her. "I want them down among the eels. May their souls drift naked in the depths forever."

"Why?"

Dahut stamped her foot. "I have been cruelly wronged. I, your Sister. Is that not enough?"

"It is not," Forsquilis replied, "all the more when 'tis unsure whether we can even command a breeze any longer. What happened?"

Tears of anger started forth. "Why should I tell you?" Dahut shouted. "I'll care for myself!"

She started to go. "Wait," Forsquilis urged. "Sit down, rest, take refreshment, and we'll talk."

"Nay. Never. Not ever again." Dahut went out. Forsquilis gazed after her for minutes.

—At home Dahut mumbled something about having sought the counsel of the Gods in a night vigil at Lost Castle. She had said the same thing before. Nobody responsed, save to carry out her orders.

A long hot bath soothed much of the tenderness in her flesh. She emerged, was dressed, ate, drank. Thereafter she retired to her private room, barred the door, and settled down with writing materials—a brazier would consume any rejected bits—to compose the letter that would be carried, sealed, to Budic.

— 4 —

Once long ago, when he and the world were still young, Niall had walked forth from Temir on the eve of a holy feast, to have speech in confidence about a warfaring he intended abroad. But that was just before Beltene; the voyage would be open and splendid, against the Romans in Gallia; the men at his side were the druid Nemain maqq Aedo and the ollam poet Laidchenn maqq Barchedo. This morrow's day was Imbolc. Nemain was dead and Laidchenn had returned to Mumu after his satires avenged the murder of his son. The deeds he was to do were unknown to Niall. He knew only that he must do them alone.

With his handfast captain, lean gray Uail maqq Carbri, he took the northward road between the Rath of Gráinne and the Sloping Trenches, and on downhill as of old. His four guards tramped behind, out of earshot. The day was late and dark, wind awhistle over dun meadows and leafless woods. Smoke blew tattered from the thatch of widestrewn shielings. Where their doors stood open, firelight gleamed afar; this was to be a night of good cheer, when Brigit and Her white cow traveled the length and breadth of the land to bless it. Those glimpses made the walkers feel twice removed from that world.

"Then all is in readiness, darling?" Niall asked.

"It is," Uail told him. "The ship lies ready at Clón Tarui. A stout Saxon-built craft she is, and I myself have overseen the wrights as they made her perfect this winter. The crew will hasten there at once after the festivities; they should be on hand when yourself arrives. We are well provisioned, also with the gold you ordered. There remains only the kindness of Manandan and the merfolk, that we have a swift and safe passage."

Niall nodded. He had put the questions more to start talk going than because of any doubts. "The Gods shall have such sacrifices tomorrow as ought to put Them in the right mood," he said.

Uail could not refrain: "And yet I wish I knew why we go!"

"What men do not know, they cannot let slip," Niall answered sternly. "May the lot of you keep in your heads what I have been telling you over and over."

"We shall that, master."

"Repeat it."

"You are a chieftain who wants to explore what the outlook may be for you in the Gallic trade. Niall is a common enough name that it should arouse no wondering in the Romans, who know little about Ériu anyhow. We need but remember not to declare that you are Niall of the Nine Hostages, King and conqueror. We come to Gesocribate this early in the season so that we may be well ahead of any rivals. We wait there, living off the trade of our gold, while you go inland to ask among the tribespeople."

"It may take a month or more," Niall reminded. "Enjoy the time; but it is gess for you to say anything further, even among yourselves, no matter how drunk you get."

"I tell you again, dear lord, you should not wander off alone," Uail fretted. "It's dangerous. It's unbecoming your dignity."

"And I've told you before, if I tear off at the head of an armed band, the Romans will ask why. They may well forbid it and seize us for questioning. Whereas if I quietly drift away, that should lull them. They'll take me for a barbarian simpleton, and imagine no real harm that a single traveler could do."

Uail sighed and shut his mouth. After all, Niall had once gone thus to meet him in Britannia. As for what harm the King intended, that must be against Ys; and a shuddery thing it was to think about.

They strode on. Twilight gathered. "Shall we be turning back now, master?" Uail asked.

"Not yet," Niall answered. "I hope for a sign."

Ahead of them gloomed on oakenshaw he well remembered. Suddenly upward from it flapped a bird. Niall halted. Knuckles whitened on his spearshaft, breath hissed between his teeth.

But this was no eagle owl such as had gone by on an unlucky eventide. This was a raven, eerily belated for one of its kind, and huge. Thrice its blackness circled above Niall's spearhead, before it wheeled and winged away south.

Niall shook his weapon aloft. "The sign indeed, indeed!" he roared. Joy carried him beyond himself. Uail and the guards made furtive signs against misfortune. Few men were glad to see the Mórrigu at the edge of night.

Niall turned about and ran the whole way back onto Temir hill. The rest had trouble keeping up.

Before the Feasting Hall he stopped, breathing deeply but easily, his ardor quenched like a newly forged blade.

The building sheened great and white in the dusk, below
its thundercloud of roof. Folk stood outside; the gold upon
them kept the last brightness there was.

His younger Queen stepped forth. "We have been waiting for you, dear lord," she said.

"Mighty matters held me," Niall said, "Now we shall
revel." He looked at the babe in her arms, fur-wrapped
against the cold. He laughed aloud. "And do not give
Laégare to his nurse. Bring him in that he may be at our
feast, he who one day will be King."

— 5 —

Snow returned, this time on a wind from the sea that
cast it nearly level through the streets of Ys and drowned
vision in whiteness. The noise shrilled around Budic's
knock when at last he had gotten the mettle to put knuckles to door.

Dahut let him in and retreated. His hands acted for
him, closing and bolting the door without his awareness.
Himself he could only look and be lost.

Warmth from the brazier, glow from clay lamps turned
the drabness of the room into a snug little nest. He would
never have cared, when she stood before him as she did.
A belted robe of deep blue clung to her body, rose and
fell with her bosom, where shadows played in the cleft
under the red crescent. Loosened hair shimmered and
billowed down past widened eyes, quivering nostrils, parted
lips. Arms lifted slightly toward him as if in appeal.

All at once tears broke free. She shuddered, sobbed,
covered her face from him. "Princess," he cried in dismay,
"what's wrong?"

"You came not and you came not," she wept.

"I *could* not." Step by step he rocked toward her. "Your
father had us out on maneuvers these past several days. I
never saw your letter till yesterday, and then—Oh,
Dahut, what is it you need of me?"

"Your help. Your comfort. If you can give it, if you will,
after you hear."

He stopped himself just short of embracing her. "What's

happened? It must be something terrible. In Christ's name, tell me!"

"The worst. I fear I am doomed unless—" She gasped, gulped, overcame the convulsions. She hugged herself, and did not appear to notice that that drew further down the neckline of her robe. "I am cold," she said in a tiny voice. "The fire doesn't help. I grew so cold, waiting here for you after your word came to my house."

"Then speak," he begged.

"Now I know not if I dare. You'll cast me off. That would be more than I can bear."

"Never will I forsake you. I swear that."

"My father swore me same oath once," she said with a serpent-lash of bitterness. Despair overtook her again. She lowered her head and looked at the floor. Her fingers clawed into the robe. " 'Twas never my wish, Budic. Whatever you feel, never believe I willed it."

Blindly, he laid arms around her shoulders. She nestled into his bosom. "Oh, Budic, my love. I confess it. No shame is left me. I love you, Budic."

Almost, he fell. He came back from the cataract to feel her draw away from him and mourn, "Too late now. I am dead. This is a ghost who speaks to you."

"Tell me," he implored.

She looked at him, brushed away tears, blinked hard, tried thrice before she said, with forlorn gallantry:

"Oh, I was foolish. I brought it on myself by my heedlessness. Yet how should I foresee, I, a maiden, a girl who'd never known aught but love and honor—I who was the Luck of you legionaries, do you remember? 'Tis simple. You know a shipful of Northmen was in port for some while. Belike you saw them. Mayhap you drank in the same inn a time or two. Well, I was curious. Ever had I been eager to learn about the outside world, those wonderful realms that I shall never behold. In my boy's guise I struck up acquaintance with the captain, showed him about in Ys, listened to his tales of far ventures. 'Twas reckless of me, aye, but life had been so empty and he seemed an honorable man in his rough way. Also, I believed he did think me a boy. So there was no fear in me when he made a pretext to enter this room—he said he had a gift for me—but—"

She broke off and keened.

He screamed in his anguish. "Nay!"

"Yea," she said. "See." She lifted her arms, so that sleeves fell down from bruises still visible. "Over and over. 'Twas a nightmare I could not wake from, till at last I swooned. Then he went off and gathered his crew and sailed away."

"Did no one hear and, and—did no one care?"

"I could not ask them. I beg you, do not talk with them either. Spare me that last rag of pride."

"Dahut—"

"Belike I should not have sent for you." she went on in the same flat tone. "But who else was there for me?"

"What can I *do?*"

She made a slight shrug and smile. "Flee if you will," she said wistfully. "I'll understand. You are pure. But if somehow you could find it in your heart to spend a very little time beside this ruin, I will have that to cherish through everything I must endure."

"What must you endure? Nobody knows but me. Torture will not wring it out of me."

"The Gods know. And I do, I whose dreams you haunt, Budic, I who have lost you forever. And . . . he will know who finally slays my father. Virgin must I come to his bed, I who am unwedded. When he learns—. Well, of course I pray my father will reign for many years yet."

"You—oh, Dahut did you think I, of all men, I would find you the less because . . . because that beast hurt you?" He hammered fist in palm. "Could I catch him and feed him inch by inch to the flames! But I, I can at least say I love you, Dahut."

They were embraced, they were kissing.

"Hang not back," she cried softly. "Hew me clean of him."

And again and again.

—Night drew in. Lamps guttered low.

"I will always remember this," she said, close beside him. " 'Twill make my fate endurable. And I hope 'twill warm you too in your loneliness."

Alarm stirred him out of drowse. "What do you mean?"

She gave him a steady blue look. "Why, you must flee, you know." Calm pervaded the husky voice. "Seek elsewhere and never come back. 'Twere death for you to remain, after what has happened between us."

"Nobody need know."

The amber-golden locks brushed to and fro over his shoulder as she shook her head. "Impossible to keep it secret for long. Nor would I so sully a brave and beautiful thing. Oh, we could take a risk that no gossip about today will get out, but it is a risk—and you would die most hideously—and at best we would not dare meet again. Nay, fare you to a new life. I'll make sure that poor Keban is provided for."

"And I abandon you?" He sat straight. "God knows I am a weakling and a sinner, but a Judas I am not."

She raised herself likewise. Her clasp trembled on his knee. "What else can you do?" she whispered.

Resolution clanged. "I will make myself King of Ys, and you my Queen."

"My father!" Her tone was aghast. "Your centurion!"

"Aye," he said bleakly. "But Roman has warred on Roman erenow. You are more to me than him or the whole world and Heaven. And you would not be in this plight had he kept faith with you. Christ Himself taught that man and wife shall forsake all others."

"Christian King of Ys—"

His laugh rattled. "Nay, my dear. How long I've wrestled with this, sleepless on watch or in my cheerless bed. At last it is decided. Already I am blackened. What I shall do will damn me forever. Well, so be it. I will embrace the Gods of Ys as I do you, Dahut. Thus shall Corentinus's prophecy be fulfilled."

It flared in her. "Then you are the King who was foretold me!"

XVI

— 1 —

During the night snowfall ceased and freezing weather moved in. When day broke cloudless it saw what was rare in an Armorican winter, earth glittery white and a leafage of icicles aflash over the Wood of the King. The air was so cold that it felt liquid in the nostrils. Silence was so deep that it seemed to crackle, with any real sound barely skimming above.

At first Gratillonius could not see his challenger. The features were there, but they slid off his mind like raindrops off glass. Then he began to think: No, this is impossible, a nightmare or I've gone mad or a sorcerer is deceiving me. Yet he felt too clearly the chill on his face and the knocking in his breast, snow scrunchy underfoot, a sudden renewed ache in the ribs that had been snapped. He could count the rivets that held the metal rim and boss of Budic's shield, he noticed where the legionary emblem on it needed the paint touched up, a light and a heavy javelin rested in the man's left hand at just the angle that was Budic's wont, given his height, when he wasn't on parade, the woolen trews of winter wear sagged a bit over the top sandal straps, a small sloppiness for which the centurion had long since quite reprimanding an otherwise excellent soldier . . . . It was the visage under the helmet that was different. The lineaments were the same, but a stranger looked out of them.

Gratillonius's tongue came to life. "What kind of jape is this?" it foolishly formed.

A machine might have replied. "None. I swung the Hammer in full sight of those men on the porch there. Go arm yourself."

"Have you forgotten what happens to mutineers?"

"The King of Ys will know how to deal with Rome."

It tumbled through Gratillonius that that might prove correct. Various officials would be glad enough to get rid of him that they would urge Stilicho to give his successor a chance. He said nothing, because it seemed unimportant beside the incomprehensible betrayal. Instead he let his body and its habits carry on for him.

Upon getting the news at the palace, without the name of the adversary, he had sent runners to inform the appropriate persons. Those were now arriving. Soren was as impassive as the sky. The marine guards tried to maintain the same control. The legionaries did too, with less success. They kept formation except for their eyes, which tracked Gratillonius whenever he stirred and swung slitted back to where Budic stood. Hands strained on spearshafts. Gratillonius heard his voice lay double stress on the usual command, that if he fell the men must be obedient to the victor until such time as they marched to Turonum and the tribune there.

"Let me 'elp yer make ready, sir," Adminius begged. Perhaps he was unaware of the tears that trickled down his cheeks, came to rest in the stubble on his lantern jaw, and gleamed in the sunlight while they waited to freeze.

Gratillonius nodded and led the way to the equipment shed. When the door closed, both were momentarily blind, after the brilliance outside. Gratillonius wondered if he was getting a foretaste of death. No matter. Adminius's words wavered: "Wot's got inter 'im, sir? 'E worshipped you, I know 'e did, second only ter Christ—and Christ'll cast 'im off for this, down inter 'ell, less'n a demon's took 'im, and 'ow could that 'appen ter a praying man like 'im? Oh, sir, you've got ter win this 'un, more'n any o' t' others. You can't leave us under a traitor an'—an' expect us not ter kill 'im!"

"You will follow the orders I gave you," Gratillonius clipped. "Is that clear, soldier? Shut your mouth and do your duty."

Adminius gulped, hiccoughed, fumbled his way to the

rack and chest where the battle gear rested. It was the worn outfit that had fared with the centurion from Britannia and seen him through—how many combats at Ys? He'd had a shiny rig made for city and parade-ground use. Since challenge started coming on the heels of challenge, he had left the old one here; *it* didn't mind a few extra scrapes and nicks, and he felt obscurely that it brought him luck. The shield was new, of course, following the fight against Carsa. It hefted heavier than it should. Gratillonius had not yet rebuilt his muscles to their former solidity. When he stripped, cold lapped him around, and lingered beneath the undergarments he donned. The metal almost seared him with frigidity. He took his helmet. A notion came to him that the luck drained out of it before he could put it on.

Adminius ran fingers over every joint and buckle. "You'll want the javelins, sir," he chattered. " 'E's got 'is." Plume and vinestaff must stay behind. "Pardon me, sir, let me remind yer that casting is 'is main weakness. If 'e don't take special care, 'e 'ooks a bit ter the left, so by cocking yer shield after 'e lets fly—"

"Enough," Gratillonius interrupted. "It won't do to keep them waiting."

He stepped forth and was again blinded. Light bounced back off snow and flared in hard hues from icicles. Budic stood in a nimbus of radiance like some warrior God: incredible, how beautiful Dahut's bridegroom was.

Why need I live on? thought Gratillonius while the dazzlement danced around him. I did not know until this dawn what weariness had been in me. Some of the Queens and princesses will mourn—I dare believe Dahut among them—but they will take comfort from supposing that through my death the Gods of Ys renew the life of the world. And Dahut will no longer be torn, poor bewildered soul, between her father and her destiny. Whatever drove Budic to turn on me, he'll be kind to her. He loves her; that's been as easy to see on him as fresh blood, year after year. Oh, my death will solve many a problem. Also my own. I can lie down to rest, I can let this heartsickness fall off me and sleep, just sleep forever.

His eyes adapted. He trod at military pace to the oak where his two enemies were.

Side by side, he knelt on the frozen snow with Budic. Soren dipped the sprig of mistletoe in the chalice of water and signed first the King, then the man who would be King. Breath smoked from his lips as he intoned the Punic prayer. It came with a dull shock to Gratillonius that when he considered what dying would be like a few minutes ago, he quite forgot his spirit would go on pilgramage toward Mithras. He tried to imagine that and desire it, but failed. He felt altogether empty of anything but tiredness and sorrow.

"Go forth," said the Speaker for Taranis, "and may the will of the God be done."

This time he refrained from adding more. His gaze followed the contestants while they departed. Everybody's did.

Though Gratillonius never looked back, he knew when he and his follower had passed out of sight. How well he knew, after all his prowlings among these huge dark boles. They enclosed him like the pillars of the Lodge, the pillars that were carved in the forms of Gods; but these had nothing of human or even beast about them, they bore forms much older and mightier. Their shadows turned the snow into a blue lake from which islands of brush lifted stiff, toning shrilly when a leg or a shield knocked ice off them. Here was a hall of ice. Its beams were hung with swords beyond naming; they shimmered and flashed in the light that came out of an unseen east and often struck sparks from them. Maybe death was like this, not a road to the stars nor a solitary night but hollowness within an ice labyrinth that reached endlessly onward.

Silent. Whatever else death was, surely it was silent. And he heard withes snicker, their ice tinkle, the snow creak beneath his feet.

He heard the footsteps behind him stop, then stamp. At the edge of an eye he glimpsed the movement.

His body had answered before he understood. He had flung himself aside, caught balance again, spun about. The thrust of the heavy javelin barely missed his neck.

He dropped his own spears and fell into single-combat stance, feet at right angles, knees tensed and slightly bent, shield ready between them and his chin. The sword flew free in his grasp. Budic had recovered too and withdrawn a couple of yards, clutching his light javelin.

For a space they stared into each other's eyes. A remote part of Gratillonius noticed that he still felt nothing, no fear or anger or surprise. It merely seemed incumbent on him to say, level-toned, "I should have expected that. However, I didn't know you for a coward as well as a traitor."

Budic likewise held his voice down, but unevenness crowded through it. "You'll die regardless. This way would have been kinder."

"Also to you, when you remembered afterward?"

The face that once remained so boyish was—not aged; beyond time. "No. You see, I'm damned whatever I do. It's sensible to win as easily as I can."

Puzzlement stirred faint in Gratillonius. "Why? What brought you to this?"

Budic edged backward between two trees. "It's best for everyone," he said. "For Ys, for Rome. I couldn't take the reins at once if I were badly hurt, and I must. You understand, don't you? I promise you burial according to the rites of your faith, and an honored memory."

Suddenly he brought his right arm up, back, forward. The javelin leaped

Gratillonius had foreknown. Let that head bite into his shield, and the dragging shaft would make half his defense into a hindrance. He counted on Budic's tendency to hook. The lad couldn't be as calm as he pretended. There were only a couple of heartbeats' leeway, but Gratillonius was ready. He slanted the shield. The missile skittered over the curved surface and fell. Adminius would be proud of me, thought Gratillonius, and all at once that was funny; he barked a laugh.

Budic drew blade. He kept his place, to see what his opponent would do. Gratillonius dismissed the idea of hurling a javelin back. As close as they were, Budic could be on him before he retrieved and cast. Next he decided against moving ahead. The two of them were equally armed and armored now. Let Budic come to him.

Time stretched. Gratillonius settled down into waiting.

Budic's mask shattered. "Very well!" he snarled, and

advanced. He kept to legionary style, though, which showed how dangerous he still was.

The distant part of Gratillonius noticed that he himself was making no gesture of surrender, in body or in mind. He meant to play the game out as well as he was able. It was something to do. The upshot didn't matter.

Just outside sword reach, Budic circled slowly in search of an opening. Gratillonius turned with him. They had scant room for maneuver here in the thick of the grove. Getting snagged by a bush or tripped by a fallen bough hidden under the snow could be fatal.

In a single motion, Budic stopped his sidewise course, made a step ahead, and stabbed at Gratillonius's right thigh. Gratillonius shifted shield to intercept and tried for Budic's bare forearm. Budic's blade curved about. Steel rang on steel and slithered back. Both men retreated. The circling resumed.

Budic passed close by a tree. Gratillonius saw when a limb would block him in bringing his shield leftward. Releasing tension on his right knee, Gratillonius pivoted on the left leg and struck at that side. Were he as young as Budic, he might have gotten around the edge. Budic was too quick for him, swung his whole body left and caught the point on his shield. It thudded into the wood. Budic stabbed at the arm. Gratillonius got clear barely in time. Blood oozed along a scratch from wrist to elbow.

"Hunh!" Budic grunted, and attacked. For a while they stood shield pressed against shield, thrust and cut, up, down, to, fro. Repeatedly, each tried the rim-catching trick, but the other was alert for it. They went on, stab, slash, defend, strike, a storm of iron.

When they broke off and paused, a few feet apart, Gratillonius was trembling. Air rattled in and out of a throat gone mummy-dry. Sweat drenched his garments; he felt it begin to chill. The ice cave pulsed, closed in on him, drew back into immensity, closed in anew.

Am I winded already? he wondered. Am I still this weak after my bones have knit? I thought I could do better.

He looked at the shadows of the ice-leaf trees and realized that the strife had gone on longer than he had counted.

Budic's breaths were deep but rhythmical. He smiled a

curious, archaic smile. "You're going to die, old man," he said hoarsely. "Want to make it easy on yourself?"

Gratillonius shook his head. "Rather you."

Budic grew plaintive. "I hate this, you know. I have to kill you, but please let me do it clean and painless. Then we can be friends again when we meet in hell."

Once more, surprise stirred. "Do you really think you're sending yourself to Tartarus?" Gratillonius panted. "In God's name, any God's, why?"

Budic poised for a renewed assault. "Dahut is worth every price," he said.

"After you murdered her father?"

Budic's voice throbbed. "She's ready for me."

The rage that burst up through Gratillonius was like nothing else in his life. It froze all the world. Its white wind filled all space and time. It bore away humanness, mortality, the divine; nothing remained but ice, the crystalline logic of what to do.

The centurion took a military stride forward. "Soldier—*atten-TION!*" he shouted.

During the instant that habits and loyalties held Budic locked, Gratillonius reached him. Budic became aware. Gratillonius had slipped shield edge under shield edge. He threw his last strength into the motion that levered Budic's defense aside. Budic staggered. He smote. His weapon stopped on his foeman's mail. Gratillonius's point went into the throat.

He could do no more. He let go, dropped to his knees, rested his weight on his hands, and shuddered.

He had done enough. Blood spouted, a shout of red. Where it hit the snow, steam puffed. Budic lurched against a tree. The impact shook it. Icicles dropped. They made a brief bright knife-rain over Budic. He slid downward. Head and shoulders propped up by the bole, he sought Gratillonius with his eyes. His lips moved. He half raised his hands. Did he ask forgiveness? No telling, as fast as he died.

Too bad, thought Gratillonius. If I could've taken you alive, I'd have twisted out of you what you meant by that last obscenity.

Strength crept back, and a measure of compassion. At length he rose, went to the body, stood in the wildly

colored pool where it lay. Dead, Budic looked very young.
Gratillonius remembered marches, campfires, battles, pa-
rades, and stammered confidences. He stooped, eased the
corpse onto its back, closed eyes and jaw, secured them
with sticks broken off a frosty shrub.

He didn't want to meet Corentinus, but he'd send a
message bidding the pastor arrange Christian burial for
this member of his flock.

And what had led the sheep astray? Gratillonius recovered his sword, wiped it clean on a section of his kilt onto
which blood had not spurted, sheathed it. He also recovered the javelins before he trudged back to the Lodge.
Good practice. Waste not, want not.

Something had gone hideously wrong. It had lured a
man of his command to mutiny, death, damnation according to every faith Gratillonius knew about. He must find
out what. Somehow it did involve Dahut. A shadow had
fallen over the daughter of Dahilis. Well, her old Papa
would bring her clear of it. That was plenty to live for.
And his other girls, and Bodilis, Forsquilis, Tambilis—all
the Queens, really, with all Ys, his comrades, his men,
everybody who trusted him. He'd be too busy for regrets.

Gratillonius straightened. His stride grew longer, onward through the winter wood.

— 2 —

Bodilis, Forsquilis, Tambilis, wisdom, knowledge,
friendship. Thus Gratillonius thought of them as he entered and found them seated in expectation. Love went without saying, but here it bore three strangely different faces.

Well, they were three different people. He halted and
returned their regard, their carefully formal greetings.
Beneath the grayed waves of her hair, through the lines
that time had plowed, he saw concern in Bodilis's countenance, and an underlying calm as strong as the bones.
Forsquilis leaned back with the deceptive ease of a cat,
the enigmatic expression of a Grecian idol. O Venus, she
was beautiful, in the fullest ripeness of her womanhood;
memory burned him. Tambilis perched nervous on the

edge of her chair. Her pregnancy had just begun to show, early rounding out of belly and bosom, haggardness in visage. Like her two previous, it was causing her frequent discomfort. She had not sought his bed this past month or more, nor he hers; once she had whispered him hurried thanks for that, and a promise to make it up as soon as she felt better. With royal and military affairs cramming in on him, and daily exercises to the point of exhaustion in order that he get back in condition, he usually slept well anyhow.

Last night he had not.

"Be seated," Tambilis invited. Her gesture included a small table between their chairs and his, where wine, water, and cups waited.

"Thank you, I'd liefer stand for the present," Gratillonius replied. In fact, he started to pace, back and forth in front of them.

"I hope we can open up that cage you are in," said Bodilis.

He gave her half a smile. "I do myself. 'Tis no pleasant abode."

"Speak," said Forsquilis.

He cleared his throat and began. It was impossible for him to come straight to the point. He had prepared words that would lead toward it.

"In the three days since my last combat, I've been thinking and questioning much. 'Twas hard. So hard that hitherto I'd shied off. Nay, better said, I'd refused to believe there was aught that required asking about. Give Budic thanks of a sort, for that his . . . rebellion . . . shocked me into understanding. I woke the next morning and found myself aware that some riddles must be resolved. To go on thence took all the courage I own.

"Why did Budic turn against me? Tommaltach and Carsa—well, they were young, headstrong. Ambition and, and lust seemed to account for their actions. Not that I'd imagined any such baseness in their metal. The betrayals hurt worse than the weapons. However, we're ofttimes surprised in this life.

"But Budic! My faithful soldier for almost twenty years. We stood on the Wall together. Together we came here and slowly learned that this was our home. His Christianity never divided us. If anything, devout as he was, it made him the more true to his oath. But then, without the least forewarning, he broke it, broke with everything he had been and believed in. *Why?*

"His messmates, his Ysan companions, everybody who knew him and whom I inquired of, are as amazed as me. None can explain it. I summoned his widow and interrogated her; she blubbered that she knew naught, but in the past two months he scarcely swapped a word with her."

"That pitiful creature," Bodilis murmured. "You were not harsh, were you?"

"Nay, no cause for that. I've seen to it that she'll get her pension. Folk do agree Budic grew moody and withdrawn at about that date. He'd absent himself for long whiles, and when he returned would tell nobody where he'd been. Some persons noticed him in Lowtown or out on the northern heights. Doubtless others saw him also but failed to recognize him, for he'd dress in plain clothes and keep his head covered. Something was gnawing in him."

"Have you spoken with Corentinus?" Forsquilis asked.

Gratillonius scowled, shook his head, quickened his pace. "Not yet. I did send him a note requesting he tell me aught he knew. He wrote back that he had no information save that Budic had quit seeking his guidance as of yore. We've neither of us any desire to meet."

Tambilis swallowed, ran tongue over lips, finally achieved saying, "Sisters, I've kept silence about this until today, but they quarreled . . . over Dahut."

"Aye," Gratillonius rasped. Now he could delay no more; but he was in motion, he could go ahead like a legionary quick-stepping toward the enemy line. "He claimed she'd poisoned the minds of Tommaltach and Carsa, that she wanted my death so my slayer would make her his Queen. Of course I threw him out. He's lucky I didn't kill him."

Forsquilis straightened. "He's far from the only one who's borne such thoughts," she said in a voice that stabbed. "He alone had the honesty to tell you them."

Gratillonius slammed to a stop. He reached for a carafe, pulled back his hand before he threw the vessel at her, and coughed, "You too?"

Tears stood in the eyes of Bodilis. "We must needs be blind and deaf not to have . . . wondered. Daily I've prayed the suspicion prove false. Belisama has not heeded me."

"*I* don't believe it!" Tambilis cried. "My own Sister!"

Gratillonius held his gaze on Forsquilis. "What of you, witch Queen?" he demanded.

Her look at him was unwavering. "You know what I told you in a certain dawn," she answered. "The Gods are at work. We are fated. I wish you had not asked me to be here this day."

"Do you, then, say we are helpless? I scorn that thought."

"Belike we can save something. What if you departed Ys and never came back? The strife might die away."

He bridled. "Desert my post? Abandon Dahut in her need?"

"I knew you'd refuse," Forsquilis sighed. "My one thin hope is that you may think further about this."

His indignation collapsed. "Dahut cannot be guilty," he groaned.

Abruptly the three women were at his side, embraced him, kissed him, stroked and murmured to him. He shivered and gulped.

After a while he could draw apart and tell them, flatly but resolvedly: "What I confront, much too late, is that those suspicions exist. They are hellish wrong, but they are not groundless. I must cease calling enemy anyone who feels them. Instead, I must get them done away with. I must uncover the truth beyond every possible doubt.

"How, though? I asked you to come, you, the three Gallicenae I can wholly rely on—come and give me your counsel, your help. For her sake."

His self-possession broke again. "What shall we do?" he pleaded.

"We awaited this," Bodilis told him. "Let us sit down, calm ourselves as best we may with a cupful, and think."

They did. Silence followed.

At last Tambilis inquired timidly, "Could you speak with her, Grallon?"

He grimaced. "I'm afraid to. She'd be so hurt that I could even utter the foul thing, and—and what could she do but swear she's innocent?" He paused. "You can better sound her out. Gain her confidence, till she tells you, shows you what it really is that she's been doing."

"I've tried already, darling." Tambilis's head drooped.

"She is indeed alienated," said Bodilis softly. "That's

understandable. She was earnest in her worship when a child. Does she now go away to be alone with the Gods and seek Their mercy—on you, on Ys?"

"My arts have not availed to find it out," said Forsquilis. "However, there are folk who can follow a person unbeknownst."

Gratillonius's fists whitened on his knees. "You were always the one to speak the cruel thing. . . . Oh, 'twas necessary. I've made myself consider setting spies on her, though the idea gagged me. But who? Dirty little wretches from the Fishtail? They'd know how, as a decent man would not. I can see them leering through a window while she . . . undresses for bed. . . . Could we trust their reports? Could they themselves know what it meant, whatever they glimpsed?"

Forsquilis nodded. "Aye. Suppose she danced before Taranis. 'Tis a rite forbidden men to witness. Or—other possibilities come to mind. And she could well grow aware of watchers. She has an awesome gift for sorcery, does Dahut. 'Tis ill to think what she might perchance wreak in revenge."

"But she'd never harm those who love her," Tambilis protested.

Gratillonius skinned his teeth. "If she struck the spy blind and palsied, 'twould suffice."

"She's only an apprentice witch," Forsquilis reminded them. "I myself could not cast such a spell. And yet—"

"Action is vital, true," Bodilis declared. "But let us move with the utmost caution. I know how you suffer under this, Gratillonius, beloved. Still, you can endure while we feel our way forward."

She sat quiet before continuing: "Suppose, first, I invite her and you two Sisters to dine. We can invent an occasion. We'll not force matters, we'll simply offer her comfort, after this latest ghastliness between her father and a friend. Comfort and, aye, gentle merriment. It may be we'll thaw her fears. In due course she may open her heart to us."

Tambilis brightened. Forsquilis went expressionless.

A knock resounded. "What the pox?" Gratillonius growled.

The knocking came again, and again, hard, a male hand

behind it. Tambilis half rose, uncertainty on her face. Gratillonius waved her back and went to open the door.

Cynan stood outside, in the armor of guard duty. At his back was a tall blond man in Roman traveling garb.

The legionary saluted. "Beg pardon, sir," he said. "You told us you shouldn't be disturbed. But this courier has a letter from the praetorian prefect in Augusta Treverorum. We decided I'd better bring him straight to you."

The newcomer made a civilian's gesture of respect. "Quintus Flavius Sigo, sir, at your service," he announced in the same Latin. "Allow me to deliver a summons."

Gratillonius took the sealed parchment proffered him. "I am called to Treverorum?" he asked slowly.

"You are, sir. Effective at once. Details in the letter. Allow me to hope you will not be unduly inconvenienced."

"I'll need a day or two to make ready."

"Sir—"

"I am prefect and King in Ys. I have my responsibilities. Cynan, take Sigo to the majordomo, who's to see that he gets proper quarters and whatever else he needs."

Gratillonius turned back to his wives. "I'm sorry," he said in Ysan. "But you knew I was expecting this, albeit not quite so soon."

Recently he had gotten a communication from Rufinus. The Gaul had reached Mediolanum and set about becoming a familiar at court. That took time, but he had won as far as being granted a brief audience with Stilicho, besides making himself a crony of numerous lesser officials. He reported that Stilicho was at present preoccupied with obtaining consulship and with preparations against Alaric, the Visigothic King, whose behavior grew ever more ominous. Nonetheless the half-Vandal Roman had appeared sympathetic to Rufinus's petition on behalf of Gratillonius, an impression that was reinforced by conversations with the underlings. Probably Stilicho was going to send orders north that the case be settled with dispatch, once for all.

Evidently Stilicho had done it.

Rufinus had expressed the hope—it shone through the sardonicism of his language—that the directive would require Gratillonius receive the benefit of any doubts. Gratillonius's own hopes were at the back of his mind, as he shifted the parchment around in his hands.

His immediate thought was that he'd be gone for more than a month, and investigation of Dahut must await his return. Good. Maybe the miserable business would resolve itself meanwhile. If not, well, in his absence no further evil could happen.

— 3 —

Guilvilis had Vigil on Sena. Gratillonius found that oddly saddening, in spite of his having sought her house the evening before. She had not ventured to offer him more than a kiss. It was shy and salt.

The rest of the Queens were here today, in the basilica of the Council. He had given the Suffete magnates much the same short speech as in the past when he was about to journey off: Necessity called him; nothing urgent was on the horizon; they should carry on the governance of Ys according to established law and usage; he ought to be back in ample time to take any initiatives that might be required. Thereafter he requested them to depart but the Gallicenae to remain. Soren surprised him by responding, "We all wish you well, O King. May the Gods fare with you," before his heavy form disappeared out the door.

Now Gratillonius stood on the dais before those Gods and his guards, looking down at the eight women on the first tier of seats. This morning was again lucent; light brimmed the great chamber. It made the white headdresses shine and the blue gowns glow.

One by one he regarded them. Tambilis; Bodilis; Forsquilis. Lanarvilis wrapped in aloofness. Innilis gazing wistfully from her place close to stern Vindilis. Maldunilis throwing him a smile that he knew was an invitation, come his return. Dahut—Dahut sat three or four feet beyond, alone. She likewise wore blue, which gave back the depths of her eyes, but—to cry out that she was not truly a high priestess—she was bareheaded. Her hair billowed loose past the face that was like her mother's. He thought he saw yearning upon her, as if she wished to spring into her father's arms but had not yet discovered how.

"I wanted privacy for us to say our farewells," he told them awkwardly.

"What is there to say, other than that word?" retorted Lanarvilis.

"Nay, Sister," Bodilis chided her, "we are more than Gratillonius's Queens. We are his wives, and his daughter. Let us send him off with our love."

"Oh, come home soon," Tambilis called low.

"Aye," said Vindilis grudgingly, "we must wish you success among the Romans."

"You'll win," Maldunilis insisted. "You will."

He barely heard Innilis: "And then can there be a healing?"

"I know this much," Forsquilis said, "that for better or worse, 'twill never again be as it was between us."

Gratillonius's gaze sought Dahut. Her lips moved the least bit, soundlessly, before she shook her head.

"Well," he said around a thickness in his throat, "abide in peace, my dears."

He took the Hammer from Adminius and led his soldiers out past the women. His last sight of the chamber showed him the eidolons of the Gods looming over it, and Dahut's head a blaze of gold beneath.

Folk hailed but did not accost him on his way through the streets to the palace. There he changed his robes for his centurion's outfit and left the Key in its coffer. Favonius awaited him, impatient, at the rear. He vaulted onto the stallion's back. Already mounted, by special permission, was the courier Sigo. They rode down to Lir Way and between the walls and images that lined it, among the people who thronged it, to High Gate. The twenty-three legionaries tramped after. They had made their own goodbyes.

Pack animals stood ready outside. The men took them over, assumed route formation, fell into the cadence of the road. Gratillonius led them toward Redonian Way. That was quicker than going through city traffic to Northbridge.

"Isn't this a rather late start, sir?" asked Sigo. "The days are still short. Julius Caesar never wasted daylight." He was a Treverian, his family long civilized, himself very given to showing off his Romanness in these times when barbarian Germani were everywhere on the move.

"We'll camp at a farm I know," Gratillonius snapped. "The next good site is a hard march beyond."

Briefly he wished he'd been less curt. Sigo was polite enough. No matter. He, Gratillonius, had too much else on his mind, in his breast. For no sound reason, he was glad to have shed the Key.

They crossed the canal and passed the turnoff of Processional Way. The Wood of the King lay yonder. Against the snow it was as dark as clotted blood. They left it behind and came out on Point Vanis.

There Gratillonius drew rein. He and his men saluted the grave of Eppillus. The courier was startled but refrained from questions.

A moment longer Gratillonius lingered, to look back. The sea reached calm, like a steel mirror, save where it broke white across the reefs. In this clarity he could make out Sena afar, even the tower upon its lowness. The road swept down to where Ys stood athwart the cliffs of Cape Rach. The wall formed a ruddy ring from which the towers leaped agleam. Gulls flew around them, among them, hundreds of wings over Ys.

Keep Dahut safe, he told them. Guard her with your beauty.

Favonius snorted and pranced. Gratillonius curbed him, then loosened reins and rode on.

— 4 —

The cold spell ended. Snow began to melt. The canal gurgled engorged. Wind whooped, clashed breakers against rocks, shook trees, hounded cloud shadows across the land.

Soon trade would reawaken, as dirt roads grew passable. Occasional travelers were already arriving on the paved highways. For the most part they brought lumber, charcoal, furs, leather—winter produce. A few had come farther, pleasure seekers, negotiants, adventurers.

Mules drew three carts from the direction of Gesocribate, down to Aquilonian Way and there west. On the first of these a man sat atop its bales, strummed a harp and sang.

The song was on an alien scale and in foreign words, but rollicked so that his companions listened with enjoyment. The sentinels above High Gate noticed and gave him special heed. They felt no misgivings. Ys stood open day and night to any peaceful person, and outlanders got an eager welcome. It was only that he was such a big, fine-looking man.

"Who goes there?" called a marine.

"You know me," the leader of the merchant party cried back from his horse, through the salt wind. "Audrenius the fuel dealer."

"I meant him with you."

"A Scotian who joined us on our journey. He's a good fellow."

"Niall is my name," shouted the stranger in accented but fluent Ysan. "I'm for seeing the wonders of your city."

The guard beckoned genially with his pike. Niall entered.

XVII

— 1 —

Rain mingled with sleet dashed down the streets of Ys. Wind clamored, Ocean roared. This had become a stormy year.

The taproom of the inn called Epona's Horse was a snug cave. A hypocaust beneath the tile floor warmed it. Though tallow candles and blubber lamps were rank to smell, their abundance brought forth vividly murals of beasts real and fabulous. Furniture was plain, heavy, well-made. The landlord and his wife offered ample choice of drink and set a goodly table. Their four large sons maintained order and debarred thieves. Not a place for visiting dignitaries, who generally received Suffete hospitality, this was a favorite of modestly prosperous foreigners and Ysan commoners. Niall had taken a room.

He sat benched over ale. Across the board was a fisher captain, apparently of some consequence, named Maeloch. They had struck up a conversation when the latter, idled by today's weather, had come in for a stoup or three. A courtesan nearby, in thin sheer gown but well enough endowed to stay comfortable, sat with provocative posture and glances. The men were too engrossed to pay any immediate heed. At another table, a sailor and four artisans diced. Kitchen odors sweetened the flame-stench. The gale rattled shutters and hooted beneath eaves.

"What for d'ye concern yourself?" Maeloch growled. "Ye'll find more doings in town than a lifetime can hold. Why root about in filthy rumors?"

Niall shrugged. "I could not help but hear, could I, now?" he replied mildly. "My two days have passed in a bees' nest abuzz. And what else do you await, when the King's fought for his life thrice in four months, and is newly off to defend himself against charges the Romans have brought, the which seems to be on account of his saving Ys from a gang of Fomóri? Folk seek me out to gab of it. Mine's a new ear for them to unload their worries into. Some tell me one thing, some another. How shall I be knowing what to believe? 'Tis hoping I was that you might help. You look like a sensible lad."

Maeloch grinned ruefully and ran fingers through his grizzled black beard. "Me a lad?" His mouth tightened. "The yarn be long and fouled."

"And laying it out all neatly coiled will be thirsty work, I wager. Let me quench you, and myself too. Hoy-ah!" Niall called in the voice that had carried through battle and tempest. "A jug of this, with bread and cheese!"

"Thanks," said Maeloch. "Understand, I be nay in the councils of the high. But I ha'—seen more and stranger things than most. Also, 'tis been my luck to be friends with Princess Dahut, her mother afore her and afterward the girl through her whole life. A humble friend, aye, nay what ye'd call close; still, I pride myself to say 'friend.' I'll try to set ye straight about such matters as I ken."

Niall did not quite hide the alertness that came over him. "Ah, the Queen who has no King."

Maeloch stiffened. His fist crashed down on the table. "Belay that! Watch your tongue, Scotian."

Niall reached for the sword he wasn't wearing. He stopped the motion and controlled his temper. "Let us not quarrel. I'll own to being ignorant. But do you be remembering I am a King."

Maeloch nodded, mollified. "I thought as much, the way ye bear yourself. Touchy of your honor, eh? Well, remember ye that I'll mean no offense, if none be given me. What tribe, and where?" He was taking for granted that Niall was the chief of some tuath.

"In Mide. I think ye'd not be recognizing any further names, mayhap not even this."

"Oh, I know about the Fifths of Ériu, at least, and more than that about Mumu. Man and boy, I've fought and traded with your folk, and can't reckon whether they gave us a harder time when we shattered their fleet these many years agone, or when since they've drove their bargains with us."

Niall coughed. It enabled him to turn his head and cover his face until he had regained color.

"Swallow down the wrong strait?" asked Maeloch. "Quick, drain your cup. Here comes what ye ordered."

Peace being restored, Niall said, " 'Tis clear that you're in the half of the people who'll hear no ill of the lady Dahut."

Maeloch glowered. "They'd better be more than half." His tone softened. "That sweet, sore-beset lass. And yet I can't find blame in my heart for her father. We can but hope the Gods will somehow go easy, though I've scant belief that that's in Their nature."

"Tell me about her, then. The whole truth, everything you know."

Maeloch peered through the wavery flame-glow. "Why this curiosity, mate?"

Niall drew breath. "A feeling of mine. I've told how I'm in search of markets as well as marvels. Now I am a King, who trades in no lowly wares. Gold and the finest smithwork are mine, such as only your wealthy could buy. From what little I've heard of her, the lady Dahut is fond of splendor, or was till trouble fell upon her." He lifted a palm at Maeloch's parting lips. "Listen. I'm not the sort to hawk my goods, least of all before a royal person. My thought is that she might accept a gift or two of me. I've gold dust in my purse, but in my baggage things worthy of a Queen. If they please her, she may be so gracious as to bring me before other lofty folk. Also . . . a well-wrought bit of ornament might cheer her just a little in her distress."

Warmth stole into the rough countenance opposite him.

"But of course I must be knowing something about her first, right?" Niall went on. "Else I could make terrible mistakes. Why, I know not how to approach so grand a person."

"Oh, that be easy," Maeloch told him. "She's ever been gleeful to meet outlanders. Get a public scribe to write ye a letter asking for audience, and a public messenger to

bring it her. I'll lay to it ye'll have your invitation within
the day,"

"How then shall I behave?" Niall replied. "This is why I
wish you'd be telling me more about her."

"Well spoken," gusted Maeloch. "Barbarian or nay,
I've a notion ye may be exactly what she needs."

— 2 —

In a close-fitted dress of white silk, Dahut stood encompassed by the vermilion atrium of her house like a
taper amidst a winter sunset, which lighted would deny
the night that was to come. A necklace of amber smoldered around her throat, at its center a sea-green emerald
resting between her breasts. From a chaplet of leaves in
silver, her hair fell over shoulders bare almost to the arms.
A vein showed blue, thistledown fine, through the fairness
under her jaw.

She must not enthrall me, Niall thought. I will not let it
happen.

He walked across the seals and dolphins that swam in
the mosaic floor. Marmoreal pillars and ceiling with gilt
trim seemed to stream their brightness down on her.
Beneath a line of black spirals, inset panels bore pictures
of the Gods. He made out stag-horned Cernunnos, Epona
the Rider, the fearsome She of the Teeth Below. Others
he was unsure of. There were some lovely nude maidens
and youths among them, as well as cloaked and veiled
women, beings part human and part beast, sacred animals.
Unmistakable after what he had learned, Taranis of the
Hammer and Belisama of the Evenstar flanked the inner
door, while above its lintel brooded a many-armed sea
monster that must stand for Lir.

It was as if the magnificence were meant to dwarf him,
though not her. Likewise, sumptuous furnishings and a
hint of incense proclaimed him a mere wild man. Yet her
finely carven features had come to life as the maidservant
let him in, and the eyes first widened, then grew intent as
he neared.

Niall well knew how to show kingliness before men, and

women. He moved neither shyly nor brashly, he neither minced nor swaggered; his pace flowed deliberate, the gait of a lynx in its forest. His head borne high, he smiled with mouth closed. The lightning blue of his gaze rested steady on the lapis lazuli of hers.

She saw a man of about her father's age. He might be several years older, but that showed mainly in the creases and crinkles of the weathered face. He was inches taller than Gratillonius, slenderer save in the upper torso, lithe as a boy. A straight nose led from broad brow to narrow chin. The primrose yellow of long hair, curling mustaches, pointed short beard had not greatly faded with age. He was clad in unabashed Scotic gaudiness: woolen cloak worked with roundels in seven colors, saffron tunic, green kilt that left bare the long muscular legs, kidskin shoes on surprisingly small feet, all trimmed with embroideries and furs, augmented with silver and bronze and chased leather. So might the veritable Taranis have advanced on her.

In his hands rested a tray covered by a fine cloth. He balanced it on his left fingers when he stopped and touched his brow to her, the reverential salute. The distance he kept between them was proper too. Still, he towered, she must look up.

"You are Niall of Hivernia?" she asked, needlessly and less than evenly.

He bowed his head. "I am that, and at the command of my lady Dahut, for whose kindness in bidding me hither I offer my highest thanks." His voice was deep, with a lilt in it like music.

"You are . . . very welcome. How brave of you to fare so far at this dangerous time of year."

His smile widened. The furrows that ran from it made it wonderfully lively. "Already the voyage shows a thousandfold profit." There was nothing unctuous about his speech; extravagance was natural to his race.

"You wrote that you are a trader?"

"I may become one, if Ys cares for my cargo. It lies now at Gesocribate, but how more glad I'd be to deal here! May I beg my lady accept a few tokens?"

He drew the cloth aside. Dahut caught her breath. A golden torc coiled on the tray, decorated with intertwined figures, granulations, and millefiori disks. On one side of it was a penannular brooch, the salmonlike grace of its silver a leap between twin giant pearls. On the other side, an intricately scaled snake seized its own tail to form a bronze buckle. "Oh! Why, they are, are sheer beauty!"

"The finest craftsmen in Ériu could not make them good enough."

"Come. Why are we standing? Let us be seated." Dahut gestured at a table laden with refreshments. "Carry that away," she ordered her servants. "Bring the best. The best, do you hear? Make haste!"

In her chair she examined the presents closely, with many remarks or queries; but her look kept straying to Niall. He met it with precisely sufficient reserve for decorum.

The wine arrived in advance of the delicacies. They tasted. "Ah, a noble draught, this," he said.

"From Aquitania," she replied. "Stay until eventide and sup. Nay, I insist. You'll savor the meal, I promise you, and I—want to hear your whole story, you who must have adventured from Thule to the Islands of the West."

"Scarcely that wide about, my lady," he laughed.

"What you have seen and done—I watch the gulls soar off beyond sight, and my heart is nigh to bursting with the wish to follow them."

"Well, I have sailed and warred. And mayhap you'd like to hear somewhat of my homeland. She has her own enchantments."

Dahut leaned a little toward him. "I know you are a mighty man there. You cannot be aught else. It shines from you."

"I bear the name of King, my lady, but that means less . . . as yet . . . than it does here."

"They are the fiercest warriors in the world, the Scoti, are they not?"

"I've seen my share of battles."

"You shall tell me of them. I am no weakling."

"Not from what I've heard, my lady, with due respect. But Ys, now, your Ys is a miracle beyond telling. I came in that belief, and today I've found 'tis true."

Dahut flushed. She dropped her glance.

Raising it again, she said breathlessly, too low for her staff to overhear: "Would you like a guide? Someone to show you what you might never find for yourself. I could arrange that."

"My lady is too generous to a stranger with foreign clay still on his boots."

"Think me not wayward," Dahut adjured him. "Women in Ys have more freedom than in most lands. I'm told 'tis so among your folk too. Let us know each other, King Niall."

"That would be to me an honor, a delight, and the fulfillment of a dream," he answered.

— 3 —

Waxing close to full in a sky again clear, the moon brightened dusk, dappled streets, frosted towertops rearing against a sea argent and sable. It highlighted the gauntness of the man, whitened his beard and tonsured hair.

Forsquilis opened her door herself when he knocked. She nodded. "I looked for you to seek me," she said.

Corentinus gripped his staff hard. "How did you know?" he responded sharply. "Witchcraft does not cross the threshold of God's house."

"Mayhap. But I have had my visions and thought belike you would have more of your own, as we both did that night ere we met in the fog at the graves. Enter."

The atrium was warm, but cold air pursued them inside. No servants were in evidence. "Follow," she said, and took the lead.

She brought him to her secretorium. He had never been there before. Visibly, he braced himself against the pagan things that crowded around. The single lamp, fashioned from a cat's skull, gave more luminance than was natural through its eye sockets and out of the flame above. From shadows the yellow gleam picked an archaic, shamelessly female figurine; thunderstones found in dolmens of the Old Folk; bundles of dried herbs that gave the air an acrid undertone; animal bones engraved with mystical signs; age-mottled scrolls and codices; a couch bearing three cushions whose leather was branded with images of owl, serpent, dolphin; a rattle and a small drum such as wizards used in lands beyond the Suebian Sea; and more, from all of which he averted his face.

Forsquilis smiled without mirth. Singularly lovely she appeared, her slenderness sheathed in a black robe whose clinging and sheen mocked the shapeless coarseness of his, her tresses falling free around the pallid Pallas countenance. "Take a seat," she invited. "Would you like some wine?"

Corentinus shook his head. "Not here." Both remained standing.

"Do you fear defilement? I would drink in your place if you admitted me."

"It always has a welcome for those who seek its Master."

"Heard I a hopefulness there? Quell it, my friend." Her tone was kindly. "We do share a dwelling, this world of ours."

He too became gentle. "You are mistaken, dear. Earth has no roof or walls. It stands open to the infinite. We by ourselves have no defense against the business that walks in the dark."

Bleakness came upon her. "You have had forewarnings about Dahut," she said. "What were they?"

Corentinus clenched and unclenched a knobbly, helpless fist. "I prayed for the soul of poor Budic. Over and over I prayed, hour after hour, until weariness overtook me and I fell asleep where I lay prostrated before the altar. Then in a dream, if it was a dream, I saw him. He wandered naked through an endless dark. I could not feel or hear the wind that tossed his hair, but its bitter cold struck to my bones. Faintly, as if across more leagues than there are stars, I heard him crying out. 'Dahut, Dahut, Dahut!' he howled, from his lips and from the mouth that the sword had made below them. He saw me not. It was as if I were not there, as if no one and nothing existed but himself, in that night where he drifted lost. But as I wakened and the world came back to me, methought I heard other voices weeping and wailing. And what they called was, *Alas, alas, that great city, wherein all grew rich who had ships at sea, from their gainful trade with her! In a single hour has destruction come upon her!*"

Forsquilis shivered. "It could have been a simple nightmare."

"You know not the book whence came those words."

Like a man hard-pressed in combat who retreats a step, Corentinus sprang over to Latin, not the carefully wrought language of a sermon but the vernacular of his mariner youth: "Well, whatever you think of the Woman who rides the Beast, if ever you've heard of her, storm signs are black enough around Dahut. Either a devil got into Budic or she did. And I don't mean it was just a hankering that swept him off, because I knew him too well till nearly the end. Likely she'd already egged on Carsa and that young Scotian. There, I've said it flat out, and I notice you haven't hit me."

Though she understood him, Forsquilis stayed with Ysan, as if its softer sounds could better carry sorrow. "I fear you are right."

"What's been revealed to you, and how?"

"You know of my night in the tomb," she said low. "It was chaos, save that throughout it went ringing the iron command that I must no longer wield my arts in this web of woe; that if I did, not only would I be destroyed but Ys might suffer ruin."

Corentinus regarded her for a silent while. "You've obeyed?"

She bit her lip. "Almost."

"What may you tell me?"

"The unmagical things," she sighed. "Hints, traces, spoor not entirely covered over, such as you know of. Yestre'en three of us—Bodilis, her daughter Tambilis, and I—supped with Dahut. She came unwillingly, I suppose because she had no ready excuse for refusal. Wine eased her a trifle. She would still talk only of small things; her mind meanwhile went elsewhere." Forsquilis hesitated. "It went after a man. In a way beyond words, I knew that. Her eagerness filled the air like smoke off a fire."

Corentinus grimaced. "I believe it. We've got a lustful demon loose amongst us." In a jerky motion, he half turned from her. "I feel his power myself. Forgive me, Queen. You're too comely. Best I run from you."

"Think you I've no longings?" she exclaimed.

For another space they stood mute, aside from their breaths. Both trembled.

"I can do nothing," he said finally. "Gratillonius led off the Roman soldiers. Half my flock, the strong half. Nobody's left but a few women, children, and aged men. I'm aged too, and alone. I came to beg if you might have some way to cope with—with your Gods, before the true God gives Ys altogether into Their power."

Pain sawed in her throat. "I know what must happen. That much is clear to me. The King must die. Then They will be appeased, and Dahut become the new Brennilis."

"The Queen of her father's killer," Corentinus snarled. "Like you."

"I also. His hands on my breasts, his weight on my belly, his thrust into my loins." Forsquilis threw back her head and laughed. " 'Tis very fitting. My punishment for my willfulness. The Gods gave me Their word one last time, in the dead of winter beneath a darkened moon. And I refused."

"What was that?" he demanded.

"Had I heeded, Grallon would now lie quiet," she shrilled. "The Suffetes would have gotten us a new King, as aforetime when the death happened otherwise than in sacred combat. Surely he'd have been a simpleton for Dahut to make into what she wanted. Surely the Gods would have absolved me, aye, blessed me, perchance even with death in that same dawn. But I denied Them."

Corentinus congealed in his stance. "Gratillonius's murder?" Slowly: "What if Dahut should die instead? It's horrible to say, but—"

Forsquilis shook her head violently. "Nay! Would you call plague down on Ys, or worse? Whatever comes to pass, the Gods want the blood of Grallon. And Dahut is that priestess of Theirs who shall bring to birth the new Age."

"So we can only wait for the victory of evil?"

"And endure what seeks us out afterward." She was lapsing into resignation. "Although you misspeak yourself. The Gods are beyond evil or good. They *are*."

"Christ is otherwise."

"How strong is He?"

"More than you can understand, my child." Corentinus

took firmer hold of his staff. "I suppose we've said all we have to say. I'm going back to implore His mercy on Ys. Your name will be second on my tongue, straight after Dahut's."

"Goodnight." She stayed where she was, by the tall unwavering lamp flame, and let him find his own way out.

— 4 —

Clouds raced on a wild wind. Now and then stars glimmered among their tatters. The full moon seemed to flee above eastern hills. It cast hoar light over the edges of the clouds, light that blinked across the land beneath and turned the manes of waves into flying fire. When one stood at the bottom of a tower and looked up, it was as if the height were toppling.

A lantern bobbed in the right hand of a big man. His left arm was around the waist of a smaller companion, likewise in Scotic male garb. Wind flapped their cloaks and skirled around their footsteps.

"Did I not promise you we'd find merriment aplenty in Lowtown?" Dahut asked.

"You did that," Niall answered, "and you kept the promise, too. 'Tis sorry I am to part."

"Oh, we needn't yet. See, yonder's the widower's house. Come on to Cian's room and share a cup with your guide."

Niall's hold on her tightened. She leaned closer.

They made a game of tiptoeing upstairs. But after the door had closed on the shabby little chamber, they both grew abruptly solemn. He set the lantern down, turned to face her, took her by the shoulders. She gazed back with widened eyes and swelling lips.

He bent and kissed her, lightly, lingeringly. She threw herself against him. Her tongue sought between his teeth. Her hands quested about.

His were slower, searching with care. "Lass, lass," he murmured after a while, "be not in such haste. We've the night before us."

He began to undress her. She stood where she was, first mewing, then purring, while his lips and palms explored each revelation. When she was naked in the amber light, he quickly stripped himself. She gasped at the sight. He grinned, went to her, guided them both down onto the pallet. Still he caressed her, skillfully seeking what pleasured the most. She shuddered and moaned. When at last he took her, that also was like bringing a currach through the surf, until they mounted the crest of a comber and together flew free.

—Tides lulled. "Never erenow has it been like this," she whispered in his arms.

He smiled into the fragrance of her hair. "I told you the night's before us, darling. And many a night thereafter."

XVIII

— 1 —

"**T**his'll be yer day, sir," Adminius said. "Go get 'em."

Gratillonius aimed a grin down at the snag-toothed face and jerked his thumb before he turned away. It was the least he could do, after his deputy had flouted both rules and Roman imperturbability to trudge from barracks to government hostel, ask how things went, and wish him well on behalf of all the men. Himself, Gratillonius had lower expectations than he arrived with.

Drawing his mantle together against chill, he sought the streets. As yet they were dusky between high walls, and scant traffic stirred. What wheels and hoofs went by seemed to make more than their share of noise, booming off the bricks. In a clear sky of early morning, the moon sank gnawed behind roofs. Entering Treverorum's massive west gate, he found little change after fifteen years. Or so it appeared at first; but then he had waited for several days until he got his summons. Now he thought the city was less busy and populous, more shabby and disorderly, than before. The countryside through which he traveled had also often looked poor, ill-tended, though that was harder to judge at this niggardly time of year.

The basilica was still enormous, of course, and it had pleased him to see how smart the guards were. Today he couldn't keep from wondering if they'd conduct him back to torture. When an underling took his cloak, he grew conscious that his tunic was old, in good repair but visibly old. He had given it no thought before, for he hardly ever wore Roman-style civil garb any longer. Well, Ysan array would have been impolitic. He'd gotten his hair cut short, too.

Activity made whispers along the corridors. Men passed by, officials, assistants, scribes, agents, flunkies. Retainers of the state, they were generally better nourished and clad than the ordinary person outside. But they were fewer than Gratillonius remembered; and a considerable part of them were weakly muscled, beardless, with high voices and powdery fine-wrinkled skins. Two such served as amanuenses for the hearing. Theodosius and, after him, Honorius had restored to the civil service those eunuchs imported from Persia whom Maximus had dismissed. Gratillonius understood the principle; without prospect of sons, such people ought not to harbor seditious dreams. He understood likewise that their condition was not of their own choosing. Nonetheless his guts squirmed at sight of them.

It was almost a relief to enter the chamber, salute the praetorian prefect, and stand attentive under the eyes of his enemies. He was over the slight shock of seeing who those were, and it no longer felt illogically strange that someone else should be on the throne where once Maximus sat.

"My regrets if you were kept waiting, sir," Gratillonius said. "This is the hour when I was told to report."

Septimus Cornelius Ardens nodded. "Correct," he replied. "I chose to start beforehand, with certain questions that occurred to me."

Questions put to Gratillonius's accusers, in his absence, the newcomer realized. Maybe now he would be allowed to respond. Or maybe not. He had reached Treverorum confident, but at yesterday's arraignment there had been no ghost of friendliness.

Quintus Domitius Bacca didn't seem pleased either. After coming the whole way from Turonum with his staff to prosecute in person the charges levied by his superior Glabrio, the procurator of Lugdunensis Tertia had been hauled out of bed this dawn and, apparently, suffered interrogation on a stomach that was still empty.

"May it please the praetorian prefect," he intoned from his seat, "I believe everything has been satisfactorily answered." He touched the papyruses before him. "It is documented here, in detail, that Gratillonius is a recalcitrant infidel who has made no effort whatsoever to bring his charges to the Faith. Rather, he has encouraged them to establish close relations with other, dangerous pagans beyond the frontiers; and this in turn has caused the Ysans to engage increasingly in illicit commerce, defiant of Imperial law and subversive of Imperial order. He organized and led an unprovoked attack on laeti, defenders of the Empire, which resulted in the deaths of many, the demoralization of the survivors, and thus a sharply decreased value of their services."

"Have done," Ardens commanded. "We've been through all that before. I told you I do not propose to squander time."

He was a lean man whose long skull, grizzled red hair, and pale eyes declared that any Roman blood of his ancestors had dissolved and been lost in the Germanic. Yet he sat in his antiquated purple-bordered senatorial toga with the straightness of a career soldier; his Latin was flawless; and without ever raising his voice, he conducted proceedings as if he were drilling recruits.

"With due respect, sir," Bacca persisted, "these are matters of law, basic matters. If he cannot even claim a mandate—"

Again Ardens cut him off. The wintry gaze swung to Gratillonius. "I do not propose to be chivvied into a hasty judgment either, like Pontius Pilatus," the praetorian prefect said. "There has been a number of letters and other documents to study. I adjourned the hearing yesterday in part because of wanting to weigh the evidence presented thus far." Harshly: "As well as because other affairs required attention, when the barbarians threaten Rome on every front. We shall not dawdle, cross-questioning each other. However, today Procurator Bacca brought forth an additional allegation. It develops that we do have a significant irregularity.

"Governor Glabrio's office made inquiries of Second Augusta headquarters in Britannia. Gratillonius, you would normally have received your discharge after twenty-five years of service. That period terminated for you last year. Procurator Bacca maintains that your commission as a centurion expired then, automatically; that you had no right thereafter to lead Roman soldiers; that you therefore stand self-condemned as a rebel and a bandit. You have made no mention of this, nor offered any indication that you tried to regularize your position, either as a military officer or as an appointee of the usurper Maximus. What have you to say?"

It was like a hammerblow. Suddenly the world was unreal. So much time since he enlisted? Why, they were mouthing gibberish at him. No, wait, he could count, season by season. The springtime was unreasonably, unmercifully beautiful when Una told him she must marry a toad—"a toad," she sobbed, before overcoming her tears—to save her family; and he, Gratillonius, whirled off to join the army. The year after that they'd been on joint maneuvers with the Twentieth across the mildly rolling Dobunnic country—it rained a lot—and the year after that the ominous news came through that down on the Continent the Visigoths had crossed the Danuvius—or was it the year following? Everything lay tangled together, also the years in Ys. Bodilis kept annals, she could sort his memories out for him, but she was unreachably afar. Where had his life gone?

He could not tell.

Bacca smirked. "Obviously the accused has no answer," the scrawny man declared. "Since he has shown such complete absence of regard for law and regulations—."

Rage came awake. It ripped the dismay across. Gratillonius lifted a fist against him. "Be still before I stamp you under my foot, you cockroach!" Gratillonius yelled. A crushed face rose into his awareness. Well, Carsa had backed his words with his body, the way a man ought. Gratillonius gulped air and confronted Ardens again. "I'm sorry, sir," he mumbled.

Louder and clearer: "I lost my temper there. What this . . . person . . . spews was too much for me. Oh, doubtless I did lose track. I forgot to write and ask. But nobody reminded me. And I was always too busy, trying to do my best for—Rome." He had almost said "for Ys." He folded his arms. "I thought I'd explained. I thought the facts would speak for me. What more can I add? Here I am."

"Silence," Ardens rapped.

They waited. Sunlight strengthened in the windows.

Ardens lifted his hand. "Hear the decision," he said. "Dispute it at your peril. I repeat, the Imperium has business more urgent than any one man's ambition, or his vanity."

If only that were true! rushed through Gratillonius.

"I find that the charges brought are essentially without merit," Ardens went on. "The accused has loyally carried out an assignment which was legitimate when given him and was never revoked. What errors he has made are small compared to the difficulties he must cope with, as well as his actual accomplishments. His conduct with regard to the Franks is *not* among the errors. Those men were attempting the life of the prefect of Rome. I would order punishment of them myself, had he not already inflicted it in full measure.

"Bacca, you will convey to Turonum a letter for Governor Glabrio. Know that it will require his cooperation with the King of Ys.

"As for the technicality advanced this day, it is ridiculous. I will instruct my own procurator to settle it. Meanwhile, by virtue of the authority vested in me, I will appoint you, Gaius Valerius Gratillonius, tribune, and return you to your duties in Ys."

For a bare moment, the armor came down. German and Briton looked at one another, antique Romans; and Ardens whispered, "It may be the last wise thing I ever can do."

— 2 —

"I love you," Dahut said. "Oh, I am drunk with love of you."

Seated on the pallet, arms wrapped around drawn-up knees, Niall regarded her but made no reply. Wind blustered outside. Cloud shadows came and went; the window cloth flickered between dimness and gloom. The brazier kept the room warm, though at cost of closeness and stench.

She knelt before him, her own arms wide, hands outheld

open. Sweat from their latest encounter shimmered on her nakedness and made the unbound locks cling close, as if she were a nymph newly risen from the sea, seal-fluid, tinged with gold and azure and rose upon the white.

Tears glistened forth. "Do you believe this?" she asked. Her husky voice went thin with anxiety. "You must. Please, you must believe."

He bestowed a smile on her. "You have been eager enough," he drawled.

"Because of you. The men earlier—I pretended. They thought I found them wonderful. But only you, Niall, only you have awakened me."

He raised his brows. "Is that so, now? This is the first time you've been after telling me about them."

She lowered arms and head. "Surely you knew from the beginning I was no maiden," she said with difficulty. "How I wish I had been, for you."

His tone gentled. "That makes no matter to me, darling."

When he reached forth and stroked her hair, she moaned for joy and drew close. He shifted position until she leaned against him, weight supported on his right hand, his left arm around her.

She giggled and felt past his thigh. "How soon will you be ready again?"

"Have mercy, girl!" he laughed. " 'Tis an old man you're asking."

"Old, foo!" Seriously: "What you are is a *man*. The rest were boys, or one was an animal They did not know, they never understood."

"Why then did you take them?"

She flinched and glanced away. "Tell me," he persisted. "I know how dangerous a game it was for you. Why did you play it?"

Still she kept mute. He withdrew his embrace. "If you'll not be trusting me—" he said coldly.

Dahut's resistance broke. "Nay, please, please! 'Tis but that—I feared—I feared you'd be angry with me. That you'd leave me."

Niall embraced her anew, eased position onto buttocks, freed a hand to rove across her. Fingers played with her nipples. He had quickly discovered how much she enjoyed that. "I would never willingly do so, my dear," he murmured. "But you must see I need the whole truth. This Ys of yours is quite foreign to me. Would you be letting me blunder into my death?"

"Never. Liefer would I myself die."

Resolution hardened. She looked straight before her and spoke in rapid words, broken only by a slight writhing or purr when he sent a tingle through her:

" 'Tis a story long and long, it goes back in time beyond my birth or my begetting. How I want to share it with you—my mother, my childhood, my loneliness and hoping—and we will share it, we will, because the rest of my life is yours, Niall. But for this day, when soon I shall have to go back to the prison where my father keeps me—

"Well, you've heard. Here between my breasts is the very Sign. I am Chosen but I am not taken. I am hallowed but I am not consecrated. I am the Queen who has no King.

"Niall, 'tis not ambition that drives me—that drove me; not vainglory; not even revengefulness. 'Tis that I know, I have known my whole life: the Gods have singled me out. I am the new Brennilis. As she saved Ys from the Romans and the sea, I am to save Ys from the Romans and Christ. I am the destined mother of the coming Age. But how shall I fulfill my fate without a husband, without a King? This my father denies me.

"He denies the Gods. Therefore he must die. Only by his death can Ys live. That I his daughter will weep for him, that is a small thing. Is it not?

"I caused those youths to go up against him for my sake. And he slew them.

"I had the same wish for you, Niall. That you would prevail and make me foremost among your Queens. See how much I love you, that I confess now it was not so from the beginning.

"It has become so. Niall, if you choose, I will flee with you to your homeland. We can escape ere anyone knows I am gone. Better your woman, among your tribespeople but in your hut, better that than Queen of Ys without you." She lifted her head. Her voice rang. "And let the Gods do Their worst!"

He was long quiet. His caresses went on, but softly,

unprovocatively, almost as if he soothed a child. The wind yowled.

At last he said low, "Thank you, Dahut, darling. Your trust in me is a greater gift than gold or pearls or the lordship of all Ériu."

"I'm glad," she gulped.

"But what you offer me, dear, that I cannot take of you," he went on. "You are too fine a flower. You'd wither and die in our wild land. Besides, I fear those Gods of yours. Out at sea, I too have known the Dread of Lir. If you fail Them, Their vengeance will pursue you."

She shuddered. "And you. Nay, it mustn't be." Anguish: "Go, then. Go alone. I will live on my memories."

He kissed her bowed head. "There also you ask the impossible," he told her. "How could I forsake you—you—and ever again be more than the dry husk of a man? We are together, Dahut, till death, and mayhap beyond. Never leave me."

"Never." She lifted her lips. The kiss burned a long time.

Finally, calmly for the moment, Niall said: "Bear with an old warrior, sweetling. Over the years I've come into the way of thinking ahead. 'Tis the young who plunge forward unthinking, and too often fall. I owe you my old man's wisdom."

"You are *not* old—"

"Hark'ee. The course is clear before us, on to your destiny and my joy. I shall challenge Grallon when he returns and fell him." He grinned. "Indeed then you'll be the Queen, true ruler of Ys, with a simple-witted barbarian like me for consort."

"Nay, we'll reign together!"

Her shout cracked apart. Terror snaked through. "Oh, but, Niall, he is younger, and he'll have his full strength back, and—and—. Nay, of course you're the better man, I never doubt that, but he's a schooled soldier of Rome, and—without mercy—."

His composure was unshaken. "I told you I am forethoughtful. Sure, and that's half the Roman secret, as I learned in many a fight. I'll have time for thinking, learning, asking—asking, too, of the Gods Themselves, in ways we know at home—for how can They want anything other than your welfare, dearest Queen? Never fear; I'll find how to take Grallon."

"You will, you will!" she screamed, and swarmed into his arms. "You'll be the King of Ys!"

—Twilight stole seaward. They lay side by side, happily weary.

"You shall come live at my house," she said into his ear.

"What?" he asked, startled despite himself. "But that's recklessness, girl. You'll set the whole city against you."

"I think not." She nibbled his lobe. "Oh, we'll call you my guest. But 'tis wrong, wrong, that we must sneak into this kennel. Your own inn is wrong for you, you who belong in the palace. We'll be brave and proud. If the Gods are with us, who can be against us?"

— 3 —

A gale from the west drove an onslaught of rain before it. Never before had Gratillonius traveled in so much rain— since he left Treverorum, at a season which folk of northern Gallia reckoned as their driest—and this new attack, spears flung straight into eyes, was bringing his beasts to the end of their endurance. The men weren't far from that, either. Feet slipped and stumbled as badly as hoofs, on pavement unseen beneath inches of swirling brown water. He barely made out the wall ahead of him.

Formation was forgotten. The legionaries plodded however they were able, hunched down into garb as sodden as the earth. They had loaded onto the pack mules the armor they were too exhausted to wear. Gratillonius had finally done likewise. That was after he dismounted, less to spare Favonius, for the stallion alone seemed indefatigable, than to show his soldiers he was one of them, with them. Cynan led the horse on his left, Adminius walked on his right.

"Shelter, sir," the deputy said through the howl and roar. " 'Bout time. Any'ow, there better be shelter."

"There will be," Cynan grumbled, "if we have to pitch people out of their beds."

Adminius leered through the bristles that had sprouted on his hollow countenance. "Right. All I'll want of any woman is the use of 'er bed, for about ten solid days and nights."

"None of that," Gratillonius ordered. "Get back and shape the troops up. We'll march in like Romans."

It behooved them on entering Cenabum. This was a place of some importance, commanding as it did the routes between the valleys of the Sequana and the Liger. Now it seemed a necropolis, streets empty of everything but rain-streams, buildings crouched close within the fortifications. A man detached from gate guard led the newcomers to the principia. Gratillonius squelched into the presence of the military tribune and made himself stand erect.

"Well, we'll find space for you," the officer promised. "Rations may get short. Nothing's come in—no traffic's moved—for several days, and I don't expect it to for several more, at best. Amazing that you slogged on this far. You must be in one Satanic hurry."

"I've a commission to carry out," Gratillonius answered.

"Hm. The Imperial spirit, eh? Hold on, I'm not making fun of it, the way too many do. But resign yourself, centurion. You'll be here for a while."

"Why?"

"I lately got word. The river's overflowed its banks farther down the valley. Roads are impassable. You're bound for Armorica, you said? Well, you could swing north, nearly to the coast, and then west, but you'd add so many leagues I doubt you'd save any time—if your squadron could do it without a good rest beforehand, which I doubt just as much."

Gratillonius nodded heavily. He was not unprepared for this. When he crossed at Lutetia Parisiorum, the river there was lapping close under the bridges. He'd counted on making swift progress along the level highway by the Liger—maybe fast enough that he'd feel free to stop at Turonum, call on old Martinus and thank the bishop for his support—but evidently that was denied him. Any thought of traveling off the main roads, on unpaved secondaries, was merely ridiculous until they had dried somewhat.

"The weather may be as bad to north, or worse, anyway," he said. "It's been vile throughout, this year."

Arrangements completed, he went back into it, to his

men where they waited in a portico, and led them to barracks. Afterward he could seek the hostel. Maybe tomorrow everyone could enjoy a hot bath, if the city baths had fuel.

"A shame, sir," Adminius said. "I know you wanted ter be back in Ys for the spring Council. Well, they'll manage, if I knows the lady Bodilis."

Cynan gnawed his lip, said nothing, squinted into the blindness and chaos that lashed from the west. Gratillonius knew he thought of the Gods yonder, Who in his mind were creatures of Ahriman.

— 4 —

Suddenly came a quiet spell among the storms ramping over Armorica at that winter's close. Clouds still massed on the western horizon, but heaven above stood brilliant and the hinterland rolled flame-green. Ys gleamed as if stone, glass, metal were newly polished. Though breezes blew chill, migratory birds coming home filled them with wings and clamor.

As the sun drew downward behind Sena, the palace gates were opened. A few early guests, of the many bidden, had arrived. They were young, in garments and jewelry that flared like a promise of blossoms. Their chatter and laughter were just a little too loud. They avoided meeting the eyes of the marines who stood guard.

Those men snapped salute when a tall woman in a black mantle strode nigh. Vindilis nodded to them and passed on through, up the path and the stairs, between sculptures of boar and bear, to the portico and thus the main entrance.

In the atrium, candles glowed multitudinous from stands of fantastic shapes between the columns. Musicians on their dais played a lively drinking song in the Ionian mode. Thus far nobody danced. Winecups in hand, now and then a titbit picked off a tray which a servant proffered, the Suffete lads and lasses clustered before Dahut and the man at her side. Vindilis approached. They noticed. Their flatteries and fascinated questions stuttered to silence.

Dahut was quick to recover poise. She had outfitted

herself with demure sumptuousness: samite gown, amber necklace, hair piled high within a silver coronet. Advancing, hand outheld, she smiled hard and exclaimed, "Why, what a surprise! I had not thought our revelry would be to your taste. But welcome, thrice welcome, dear Sister."

Vindilis ignored the hand. With eyes that seemed enormous in the gauntness of her face, she stared at the big man in tunic and kilt. "Since you would fain have your friends meet your guest, and commandeered your father's dwelling for this, it is right that at least one of the Nine greet him too," she said, calmly enough.

"Oh, but of course each of you shall—more privately, I expected," replied Dahut fast. "Niall, 'tis Queen Vindilis who honors us. But Niall does us honor of his own, Sister. He is a King in his homeland. He can become our, our ally. 'Twas but seemly that we show him respect, and . . . my royal father remains absent."

Niall's blue gaze never wavered from the darkness of Vindilis's. Smiling, he touched first his brow, then his breast: reverence for what she was, assertion that he was no less. " 'Tis delighted I am, my lady," he said. "The fame of the Gallicenae lives in Ériu too. 'Tis a large part of what called me hither."

Vindilis astonished the others by returning the smile. "Word of you has gone about in Ys, of course," she said. "You're the cynosure of the hour: the more so because, I hear, you bear it with dignity."

"Thank you, my lady. Forgive me if ever I do show ill manners. Never willingly would I offend my gracious hosts."

Vindilis lowered her voice. "Your hostess. Unheard of that a Queen have a male guest in her house—save for the King of Ys."

The persons around struggled to appear at ease. Dahut whitened. "I do what I choose in my own home," she clipped. "Show me the law that forbids."

Niall made an almost imperceptible negative motion at her. To Vindilis he said, "Sure, and I fretted about my lady's good name, but she would have her way. In Ériu there would be no shame, and if any man spoke ill of her, he would soon be speaking never again."

Vindilis nodded. "Aye. No affront intended, King Niall. It must be weighty matters that brought you to us."

"I have more than trade in mind," he answered, "but that is best talked of elsewhere."

"True. I've no wish to mar your festivities, Dahut. Indulge me, though, for a few moments. I make no doubt these young people are as ardent as the Nine to know everything that our visitor cares to tell about himself."

The tension lightened. Perhaps only Dahut was aware of the undercurrent between priestess and seafarer. Niall's laugh seemed quite unforced.

"Now that would be a long tale, and not all of it fit for the hearing," he said. "We are barbarians in my country."

"Where in the Hivernian island does it lie?" Vindilis inquired.

He hesitated the barest bit. "Mide, if that conveys aught to you. Understand, I am indeed royal, but among us that has another meaning from here. You would call . . . most of our kings . . . mere war-chiefs of their tribes."

"And yet, I believe, sacral, as is the King of Ys," Vindilis murmured.

His tone stiffened. "We too uphold what is holy. We too give the wronged man justice and the murdered man vengeance."

"I see. . . . How long will you favor us with your company?"

"As long as need be, my lady."

"We must talk further."

"Indeed we should. I am at my lady's service."

"But not at once," Vindilis decided. Again she smiled, this time at Dahut. " 'Twould spoil your merriment to have an old raven croaking away at your friend. Goodnight, sea-child. Belisama watch over you."

She turned and departed. More people arrived. The celebration grew hectic. Throughout it, Niall stayed affable but ever inwardly aloof.

—Vindilis followed the crooked streets of Hightown down to Taranis Way. Little traffic was on it at this hour, and the city wall enveloped it in dusk. When she came out Aurochs Gate there was more light across headland and waters, but it was too fading. The sun was a flattened coal among purple-black cloud banks. Out on the end of Cape Rach, beyond the ancient graves, the pharos flame had been kindled; as yet it was nearly invisible against the greenish sky. Wind whined over grass and boulders. Vindilis sought the side road down the southern edge of land. Mired and gouged though it was, she never stumbled.

At the foot of the cliff, it gave on Ghost Quay. Two craft lay moored there. The rest awaited launching when it should be safe to make for the fishing grounds. This pair were kept against the next summons to the Ferriers of the Dead. She recognized *Osprey*, newly refurbished, replacing another vessel now in drydock. The tide was out, the rocks of the strands shone wet and kelp-strewn. Ocean growled. It was cold down here, rank with salty odors, windy, shadowy.

Vindilis picked her way along the trail to the row of rammed-earth cottages. While she had not visited them for many years, since girlhood, she knew which one she wanted. She made it her business to know things. Her knuckles rapped the door. In the chill, that barked them. She paid no heed.

The door opened. Maeloch's burliness filled its frame. He gaped. "My lady—my lady Vindilis! Be that truly ye? What's happened?"

She gestured. He stood quickly aside. She entered. He closed the door. The single room was lighted by a blubber lamp and the hearthfire over which his wife squatted, cooking the eventide's pottage. She gasped. Two young boys stared; two smaller children shrank back, obscurely frightened; an infant in a rude crib slept on. The place was warm, smoky, full of smells, cluttered with gear and the family's meager belongings.

"Let me take your cloak, Queen," Macloch said. Vindilis nodded and he fumbled it off after she unfastened the brooch. Meanwhile self-possession returned to him. He *was* a free man, owner and captain of a taut little ship, and himself a familiar of certain beings and mysteries. "Be seated, pray." He indicated a stool. "I fear our wine's thin and sour till we can lay in more, and the ale not much better, but ye're very welcome; or my Betha brews a strong herbal cup."

"I will take that," Vindilis said, also accepting the seat. "But do not let your supper scorch." She beckoned. "Come and hearken. I'll be brief. Daylight is failing fast."

"Oh, I'll bring ye home, Queen, with a lantern—"

"No need, if you're as quick of understanding as repute has it."

Mealoch sat down on the clay floor at her feet. Betha whispered cookery instructions to the boys and started heating water.

"Have you heard of the Scotic stranger, Niall?" Vindilis asked.

Maeloch frowned. "Who has nay?"

"Have you seen him yourself?"

"From afar when I was up in town."

"Was Queen Dahut with him?"

Maeloch nodded reluctantly. "Methought it best nay to hail her."

"Then you must know he's now a guest in her house. 'Tis a byword through all Ys."

"Nay in my mouth. Yestre'en in a tavern, I loosened the teeth of a lout what dared snigger about her."

Vindilis gave the man a long look before saying, "Well, she is . . . defiant. Recklessly so. Would you wish a daughter of yours behaving thus?"

Maeloch sighed. "Our older girl be long since wedded. But—'tis nay for the likes of me to speak, but, aye, had the maiden asked me, my rede would ha' been dead against this."

"When her father comes back, he cannot shut his eyes to it, much though he might wish to."

"What's this to do with me, Queen?" Maeloch grated.

"You folk of Scot's Landing have dealt with those tribes for as long as history remembers. Often 'twas without knowledge of us in the city, who might have forbidden it."

"We've fought them when we had to."

"Granted. Today trade goes peacefully, for the most part. Conual Corcc in Mumu is amicable. Still, visiting Scoti usually mingle with ordinary Ysans like you. And sometimes, whether on purpose or because of being blown off course, you fishers call on them. So you know somewhat about them—it may well be, more than we disdainful Suffetes and royalty imagine."

Maeloch hunched his shoulders. "Ye want to hear what I can say about this Niall."

Vindilis nodded.

Maeloch tugged his beard. " 'Tis scant, I fear. And I did

ask around as well as ransacking my own mind, soon's the tales started flying about him and, and her. Niall be a common name amongst the Scoti. Mide be one of their kingdoms, tribes banded together. Its top King has made himself as mighty in the north of the island as Conual be in the south—nay, mightier yet, I hear. His name be Niall too. Niall of the Nine Hostages, they call him. He be so hostile to civilized folk that hardly a keel of ours has ventured nigh, and we have only third-hand yarns—My lady?"

Vindilis looked beyond him. "Niall of the Nine Hostages," she whispered. "Yea, we have heard. Gratillonius's man Rufinus could tell us more, for he fared into those parts. . . . Niall." She shook her head. "Nay, scarcely possible."

"Mean ye we might have yon devil himself in our midst, seeking to snatch off yet another kingdom?" A laugh clanked from Maeloch.

Vindilis quirked a smile with still less mirth in it. "Scarcely possible, I said. A successful war lord like that must needs be mad to abandon his gains and come risk death in order to win, at best, exile among aliens. The King of Ys is the prisoner of Ys. This must be a lone adventurer, with his few followers left behind in Roman territory." She frowned. "Yet somehow that cannot be quite true either. He is more."

Maeloch pondered. "They've a strong pride and honor, the Scoti. They reckon it unmanly to lie. If Niall says that's his name—common enough, remember—and Mide's his home, I'd lay to it."

"But what has he left unsaid? What questions will he evade if they be put to him directly? He can always claim gess."

"Hoy?" Startled, Maeloch raised his head.

"Come, now." Vindilis's tone was impatient. "Because he is unlettered and has a stern code of behavior, a barbarian is not necessarily stupid, nor without wiliness. Too often have civilized people made that mistake."

She leaned forward. Her voice intensified. "This day I encountered Niall," she declared. " 'Twas at a celebration Dahut gives for him, brazenly, in the very palace. She's lost in love. There's no missing it. Nor is the reason far to

seek. He's handsome, virile, commanding, intelligent, and
. . . utterly charming. I could count on my fingers the
women of Ys who'd refuse him if he moved in on them."

"The Nine," Maeloch said, almost desperately.

"Of course. But Dahut is not—yet—in truth—one of the
Gallicenae. Well! I sensed his pleasure as we exchanged
our few words. We were sparring, and he had at once
recognized a worthy opponent.

"He's fearless. Else he would never dare to do what he
has already done. Yet he is no rash youth who does not
comprehend his own mortality. He is a seasoned warrior
and leader of men, coolly staking his life in a game whose
rules are ice-clear to him.

"They are not to me. Why is he playing? How? And for
what?"

"The Kingship of Ys," rumbled from deep in Maeloch's
throat.

"Mayhap. I do wonder how he can escape a death-fight
with Grallon. Yet he has not gone to the Wood and smitten the Shield. There is something else in his intent,
something—even if he does win, even if he makes himself
our new Lord—" Aghast, Maeloch saw her shiver. "Our
magics fail us. Our Gods brood angry. What shall become
of Ys?"

"If good King Grallon falls at his hands—" Maeloch
sagged. "We'd be forbidden to avenge him, nay?"

"Someday he must fall," Vindilis reminded. "So is the
law we live by. Let us be frank. Niall would do for Dahut
what her father will not. It may be he would do for Ys
what Grallon cannot. We are unknowing of what to await,
what to hope for or to fear."

Maeloch sat a while in the flickery gloom. It was as if he
saw through the wall, out to the sea whose noise forever
enclosed him. Finally he said, "Ye'd have me fare to Ériu—
Hivernia—without telling anybody besides my crew. Ye'll
keep it secret also. In Ériu I'm to ask around about this
Niall. Be that right, my lady?"

"It is," Vindilis replied. "If you dare. For the sake of
your family here, and Ys, and, yea, Dahut whom we
love."

— 5 —

"**I**n the name of Taranis, peace," chanted Soren Cartagi. "May His protection be upon us."

Lanarvilis, who this day led her colleagues, rose from among them. "In the name of Belisama, peace," she said. "May Her blessing be upon us."

She sat down again. Adruval Tyri, Sea Lord, helped Hannon Baltisi, Lir Captain, rise and stand. The aged man stared out of eyes going blind and quavered, "In the name of Lir, peace. May His wrath not be upon us," before crumpling back onto his bench.

Soren passed the Hammer to the leader of the marines who formed his honor guard. For a silent minute, he looked from the dais across the chamber, the high priestesses in their blue and white, the thirty-two officials and heads of Suffete clans in their variously colored robes—not a toga in sight any more, when Ys lay wary and resentful of Rome.

He cleared his throat. "In the absence of the King, I, as Speaker for Taranis, hereby open this Council of the vernal equinox," he began. "We have, as ever, numerous matters of public concern to deal with, some of long standing, some arisen during the past quarter year. However, I propose that we postpone consideration of them until tomorrow or the day after. None is vital, as are the questions I wish to raise first, questions of the terms on which Ys shall endure. Does this assembly concur?"

"The Gallicenae concur," Lanarvilis responded. Their glances crossed and she threw him a tiny smile. They had threshed this out beforehand, he and she and a few reliable councillors.

A sound of assent went along the tiers. Cothortin Rosmertai, Lord of Works, had a word of his own: "I trust those questions can be formulated with sufficient exactitude that we will have a solid basis for discussion." The plump little man was apt to pounce forth with shrewdness like that.

"I take it you mean we should eschew generalities," Soren said.

"And platitudes, sir."

Despite the weight on his spirit, Soren must chuckle. Then, grave again, he said slowly, "Were the issues clear-cut, we could indeed put them in plain language and examine the alternatives. However, as we are each aware, they are not. At best we can, and should, utter what has been skulking about in our minds; we should acknowledge the truth."

Well-nigh physically, he projected his massiveness over them: "We have lived with our succession crisis so long that 'tis come to seem well-nigh natural. But it is not. If the Gods have been forbearing, how terrible will the wrath be when at last Their patience comes to its end?" (Sight flickered over the tall images behind the dais and the guards, Man, Woman, Kraken.) "And what of lawfulness among mortals, what of rights denied and grief inflicted?" (Dahut's countenance flushed in twin flames across bloodlessness; the fists clenched in her lap; she sat spearstraight, head high.) "Yet the person of the King is inviolable to all save his challengers. And Grallon has prevailed against every one of those." He paused. "Thus far."

Tambilis broke procedure to cry, "Never did Ys have a better King! And now he's off to keep for us our freedom!" Bodilis, at her side, took her by the hand.

Surprisingly, Maldunilis added, "His Mithras is surely a strong God, when Grallon always wins." Guilvilis nodded with more vigor than might have been awaited from her wasted body.

Forsquilis stirred. "That may be," she said, "though I think His twilight is upon Him. But He is not *our* God. Nor is Christ." She returned to the withdrawal in which she had wrapped herself of late.

"Continue, Speaker," said Lanarvilis sharply.

"King Grallon has in truth been a strong and able leader," Soren said without warmth. "Whether he has always led us aright is—perchance not something for us to argue. Most Kings aforetime were content to leave the governance of Ys in hands that would abide after them." He lifted a finger. "This is what we have shied from voicing, lest we seem to wish evil on him. He is mortal. Late or early, the time will come when we lose him.

"We may already have lost him. He should have been back erenow. Granted, he may simply be delayed, from

what we hear of storms and floods. But no messenger has
gone ahead of him. He may have died—let's say in some
meaningless misfortune. Or the Romans may have refused
his petition, detained him, even struck off his head. At
this hour, a legion may be hitherbound to impose a Roman
governor on Ys."

Unease and anger rustled along the benches. Innilis
took an unexpected initiative: "Nay. He told me the day
ere he left, whatever else they might do, they lack manpower for that, when the Goths are so troublous down
south." Vindilis cast her an inquiring glance. " 'Twas at
our Temple," she said. "He came in to pay the Goddess
his brief respects, as the King should prior to departure. I
chanced to have presiding duty. We talked a little."

"What I wish us to do is probe the contingencies,"
Soren resumed. "What if Grallon does not return? Or if he
does, which seems the likelier event, what then?" He
avoided looking at Dahut. "Because of the succession crisis, situations have arisen which he cannot ignore, as he
has ignored so much else. Let us be silent about them
here. The truth will come forth in its own time. But we
might well think upon certain matters that go far deeper
. . . such as what share the Queens—and the Suffetes, the
Lords, the Great Houses—what their claims are as against
the King. Then mayhap he will at last acknowledge what
he has been doing unto Ys, and set it aright."

Dahut sprang up, parted her lips, caught her breath,
lowered herself in the same haste.

"Did . . . the Queen . . . wish to speak?" Soren inquired.

Beneath all their eyes, she shook her head. It was plain
to see that she could barely keep still.

He sighed. "Very well, let us get on with our thinking,"
he urged. "My lord Cothortin, behold how twisted and
ambiguous are the questions before us. Yet confront them
we must, somehow. Else it could be that this is the last
Council of Suffetes ever to be held in Ys."

— 6 —

The night when Gratillonius and his men camped at Maedraeacum was the first clear one of their homeward journey.

After the stoppage they had suffered, they were pushing their hardest. If a town or hostel chanced to be at the end of a day's march, well and good; but if they could make a few more miles, they left it behind and pitched camp at sunset, tents only. When their fire had heated their rations, everybody but a pair of sentries went straight to sleep.

The road bringing them into the Armorican peninsula was unpaved but Roman made, well graded and drained. Gratillonius had chosen it in preference to a more direct route through Condate Redonum because he had heard of flood damage there. Here the gradual rise of land toward the central plateau made for less mud than the squadron had struggled through earlier. Springtime burst forth in wildflowers, primrose, daisy, hyacinth, speedwell, borage, and more. Willows had leafed, buds were unfolding on oak and chestnut, blossoms whitened orchards. He remembered his first faring toward Ys.

That had been a lovely season, though, while this was raw. When clouds parted and the sun shone through, his troop raised a cheer. "Bloody near forgotten wot that looked like," Adminius muttered.

As it sank, they found themselves at a cluster of huts in the middle of plowland and pastures, with a shaw standing dark above tender green. Folk went coarsely clad, in and out of their thatch-roofed wattle-and-daub dwellings. Adults were deformed by toil. They watched the soldiers with dull wonder. Only their small children scampered up and shouted for joy at this break in dailiness. It was a village of serfs, such as could be found throughout the Empire.

Gratillonius formally requested what would not be denied, leave to stay in a meadow. When he thereafter asked the name of the community, the headman grunted, "Maedraeacum."

Memory jarred Gratillonius. Why, this must be—must have been—the latifundium that vengeful Rufinus and his Bacaudae destroyed . . . thirteen years ago, was it? He inquired about the family of—Sicorus, had that been the patrician's name?—but learned little. These people were too isolated. Their crops harvested, they brought to Redonum that large portion which was rent and taxes. From time to time bailiffs came to inspect the property.

Occasionally men were conscripted for work on the roads or whatever else the masters they never saw wanted done. That was what they knew of the outside universe.

Obviously there had been no attempt to rebuild the manor house. Gratillonius wasn't sure whether that was because of fear, because it wouldn't have paid in these times of dwindled commerce and population, or because the heirs of Sicorus didn't care for rural life. A senator wasn't bound hand and foot to a trade or a place.

The headman pointed at a long, low mound in the offing. "Where the big house was," he said. Gratillonius went over but found no lesser trace. Tiles, glass, undestroyed goods and tools, everything of any use had been taken away. Doubtless the Duke's soldiers helped themselves first out of the ruins, then the new owner's agents removed whatever they wanted, then the serfs picked over the remnants, year after year. Even damaged furniture or scorched books would do for fuel.

The sun was on the horizon when Gratillonius got back to camp. A half moon stood wan overhead. Heaven was clear, air quiet and cold. He led his Mithraists in prayer. Those rejoined their fellows, who, with tents erected, stood around the fire waiting for the lentils and bacon to cook. Weary but cheerful, they cracked jokes which they had made a hundred times already. Gratillonius could have been there too. After close to twenty years, he could unbend among these men without undermining discipline. He found he wasn't in the mood, and wandered off.

Twilight deepened. The moon was barely enough to make the land ashy-dark; woods and hills were masses of blackness. Stars began to twinkle forth. Again he remembered his first journey toward Ys, when he was young and Dahilis awaited him, both of them unknowing. An eagle owl had passed above. . . .

Forsquilis said the witchcraft had left her, the magical power was gone from all the Nine. Could that be true? Was the world itself growing old?

No, surely life remained, and would come winging to him out of the sky. He saw it yonder, low in the north, pale but brightening against the violet dusk.

He stopped.

The vision grew more clear minute by minute, as other

light died away. It was a star in a silvery haze of its own
glow. Easterly upward from it across a wide arc streamed a
tail, vaporous white fire which at the end clove into three
tongues.

The cries of his men reached Gratillonius as if from a
vast distance, as if they were as far behind him as the
comet was ahead, he alone in hollow space. He laid hold
on his fear before it could take him. Better run back and
calm the soldiers. Somebody among the serfs must have
seen too and called the rest out, for he heard them howl in
terror.

"You've spied a comet or two before," he'd tell his
followers. "Didn't hurt you, did it? Brace up and carry
on!" They would. But what prophecy was in those three
tongues?

— 7 —

Foul weather returned, and worsened. Wind came
mightily out of the west, scourging a ragged wrack of
clouds before it, brawling and shrilling. Waves ran high.
Spume blew bitter off their crests. Where they shocked
upon rocks and reefs, fountains spouted.

Osprey plowed forward under oars, wallowed, shuddered, groaned in her timbers. Often a sheet of water
burst over the prow, blinding the eyes painted there.
They rose anew, streaming tears, and stared toward the
streak that was Sena. Mainland lay as murky and vague aft;
the towers of Ys had vanished into cloud and spindrift.

Bodilis huddled on a bench fixed below the mast, for
what slight shelter it afforded. "Nay," she said, "the Council reached no decision, though it met a full four days,
longer than ever in living memory. How could it—we—as
divided as we are against ourselves? In the end, all we
could do was swear together that we will die ere we yield
our freedom up to Rome." The wind tattered her words.

"And meanwhile this storm got under way," Maeloch
growled beside her. He had, in reverent wise, thrown a
blanket over them both. They sat close, sharing warmth.
"Why do ye go out? When the crossing be too dangerous for

your barge of state, surely the Gods don't mean for ye to. That hairy star could be Their very warning."

"So my Sisters urged. But I think 'tis a last hope." Bodilis sighed. "I had a feeling, rightly or wrongly, there in the Council chamber when we took our oath—it felt to me as if They paid us no heed. Almost as if They had disowned us."

Maeloch tensed. "I'm sorry," Bodilis said, catching his glance and offering him a smile. "I spoke badly." She paused. "Yet truthfully. Well, mayhap if one of the Gallicenae goes forth to serve Them as of old, They will listen to her."

The skipper cast dread from him. "They'll have time enough," he said grimly. "Ye'll be weatherbound for days, unless I've mislaid my knowledge. By tomorrow I myself wouldn't dare try to fetch ye. How long? Who can foresee? Could be as much as a sennight. Lir brews a terrible brew this now, off in mid-Ocean."

Her calm was unbroken. "I can abide. You saw how I brought ample supplies." She smiled. "And writing materials, and my best loved books."

The lookout in the bows yelled. Maeloch excused himself, left her the blanket, went forward to peer. Water churned and roared. "Aye, Grampus Rock," he said. "We've drifted south off course." He hastened aft and took the steering oar from Usun.

Time passed. Rowing into the heavy seas, men were exhausted when they reached Sena, slipped in through the last treacheries, and made fast at the dock. Nonetheless they unloaded Queen Bodilis's baggage for her.

"I wish I could carry it up to the house, my lady," Maeloch said.

"You're sweet," she replied. "But 'tis only permitted me." Neither spoke of the night when Gratillonius went ashore in search of Dahilis, and cut Dahut free of her dead mother.

"Well, have a care," he rumbled awkwardly. His look sought the small, foursquare building of dry-laid stone, and its turret. "Stay inside if the wind rises much more. Remember, gales ha' been known to drive waves clear across this isle."

Anxiety touched her. " 'Tis you and your friends who'll

be imperilled. Should you really not go home at once, and wait till 'tis safe to leave for Hivernia?" She was among the few to whom Vindilis had confided the plan.

He shook his wool-capped head. "Nay. After this blows itself out, belike the waters 'ull be too roiled for days, amongst our reefs, for setting forth from Ys. I'll give the lads an hour or two of rest here, then we'll snake free of the skerry ground and hoist sail. Once we've proper sea room, we can ride out whatever Lir may whistle up, and be on our way as soon as we can make any northing at all."

"You speak overboldly."

"No disrespect. Lir be Lir. But I be a man. He knows it."

"You are very brave, though, to hasten thus on your mission."

He seemed abashed. " 'Tis important," he mumbled. "For Ys and, and your Sister, little Dahut."

"Go you, then, to learn what you can, for her sake," Bodilis said as quietly as the noise allowed. "And I will be praying for her."

He looked beyond, to the desolation of stone, harsh grass, distorted bushes, flung coils of kelp that stretched away at her back. " 'Tis ye be the brave one," he said, "alone in the sea with the hairy star."

Bodilis gave him her hand. "Farewell, Maeloch."

"Fare ye ever well, my lady." He turned and stumped back to his vessel.

Bodilis carried her things piecemeal to the house and unpacked them. By the time she was through, *Osprey* had cast off. She stood watching the hull toil away northward until it was lost to sight.

XIX

— 1 —

Gratillonius drew rein at the grave of Eppillus, saluted, and looked ahead, down the long slope of Point Vanis to Ys.

It stood against the mass of Cape Rach like a dream. A haze of wind-blown spume and low-flying cloud grayed the wall, blurred roofs, made towertops shimmer and flicker as if they would be the pharos flame which could not burn tonight. Ocean raged, almost white save in the abyssal wave-troughs, crests so high that they did not break over most of the reefs, for it had buried them. It erupted against the mainland in bursts that climbed the cliffs, with shocks that Gratillonius thought he could feel through the earth. Wind was an elemental force out of the west. It thrust and clawed; to keep the saddle was a wrestling. The cry and the cold of it filled his bones.

This would be a night to house at home. His men were lucky to have arrived when they did. The blast had been strengthening throughout this day. Soon they would have had no choice but to take what shelter they could find and wait it out.

Gratillonius's gaze travelled left into the vale. The Wood of the King surged under the storm, a black lake foamed with early green. He supposed that was where he would be. This was the first of those three days when the moon was reckoned full. Having missed his last Watch, and afterward the equinoctial Council, he'd likely be wise to observe immediately the law by which he reigned.

No, first he had other, more real duties. He signalled the command that his legionaries could not have heard if he voiced it, and proceeded along Redonian Way. Wearily but happily, they took formation and followed him on the double. Their pack beasts lurched behind. Favonius snorted, curvetted, shied and then plunged, made wild by the weather. Barely could Gratillonius restrain him. What a grand animal he was!

It would have been quickest to enter at Northbridge, but spray was driving over it. Also, the King's first errand was to the palace, which lay nearer High Gate. Swinging around the eastern side, the travelers entered the lee of the city wall. Strong and ruddy it stood; Caesar's builders had wrought well for Brennilis. But on the far side the old Gods, the angry Gods came riding from the sea.

Guards at the battlements had seen the party approach. Trumpets defied the wind. Men spilled out of barracks. The King of Ys entered between swords, pikes, and shouts uplifted in his honor.

It was quieter here, possible to talk without yelling, though air brawled and skirled while surf sent a deep drum-roll underneath. Gratillonius halted, brought the stallion around, signed to his legionaries. They clustered close, at ease, yet still bearing themselves in Roman wise. He smiled.

"Boys," he said, "we've had a tough trek, and I thank you for every mile. You are now relieved of duty. Take off your armor, go to your homes, and greet your families from me." He paused. "Your furlough will be permanent. You are overdue for discharge. I've been remiss about that, but your services were invaluable. In large part because of you, Ys is at peace, while prepared to deal with any future foes. Take your honorable retirement. Besides the usual veterans' benefits, we'll arrange a worthwhile bonus."

He was surprised to see Adminius, Cynan, several others stricken. "Sir, we don't want to quit," the deputy protested. "We'd sooner march with our centurion till our feet wear out."

Gratillonius's eyes stung. He swallowed. "You, you shouldn't nudge me like that," he said. "Let me think about this. At the very least, oh, those who want can continue in the honor guard on state occasions. I'll be proud of that. But you see, there's no longer any call for more. I don't think I'll be leading you away ever again."

He wheeled the horse and clattered off. At his back he heard, "Hail, centurion! Hail, centurion!" over and over.

The cheers died in the wind. Broken by walls, it whirled and leaped through streets, lanes, the crooked little alleys of Ys. Higher up, it streamed snarling around the towers. Air tasted salt from the scud it bore along off the sea. The battering of waves resounded louder as Gratillonius rode west.

Most folk had sought beneath their roofs. Nevertheless, Lir Way was not deserted. A fair number of people trudged toward the Forum, men, women, children. They were roughly though seldom poorly clad. Many carried bundles, some pushed barrows laden with simple goods. Gratillonius recognized certain among them. They were workers from the shops outside, countryfolk off the heights beyond, fishers out of Scot's Landing, and their households. They knew him in their turn, stared at the man with the white-shot auburn beard atop his tall steed, sometimes waved and shouted. "The King, the King, the King's come home!"

Gratillonius lifted an arm in acknowledgment. This was good to see. If the storm got much worse, they would have been in danger. The cottages under Cape Rach might actually be washed away. It had happened in the past. Somebody had had the foresight to organize evacuation of such persons into the city, and they were going to spread their pallets in public buildings. Who had the someone been? Bodilis—no, she'd have thought of the need, but lacked skill in leadership. Lanarvilis, likeliest, quite possibly assisted by Soren. If so, he must thank them. Could that, the concern for Ys they shared with him, begin a healing of the breach?

He left the avenue. As he climbed, the wind grabbed fiercer. His cloak flapped crazily, though he gripped it close. The city revealed itself as pinnacles in a cauldron of blown mist. Behind reddening, ragged clouds, the sun slipped close to worldedge. Its light glimmered off furious whiteness. Sena was hidden.

No guards stood at the palace gate. Well, it would have been useless cruelty to post them. Gratillonius dismounted, worked the bolt, led Favonius through and tethered the stallion to a tree. Its topiary was mangled. The garden lay a ruin, flowerbeds drowned, shrubbery twisted or flattened, shell scattered off paths. Gilt was stripped from the eagle on the dome. Gratillonius couldn't be sure in the waning light, but he thought a bronze wing had been wrenched out of shape.

Windows were shuttered. However, the staff must be inside. Gratillonius mounted the steps and banged the great knocker. Again and again and again . . . like a challenger at the Wood who did not know that the King lay dead. . . . They heard at last. The door opened. Light poured out into the wind.

"My lord!" exclaimed the majordomo. " 'Tis you! Come in, sir, do. Welcome home." He forgot the dignity of his position and whooped: "The King is back!"

Gratillonius passed through. As the door shut, he found himself swaddled in warmth and brightness. The racket outside became an undertone. "I'm here to fetch the Key," he said, "then I go onward."

"But, my lord," the majordomo wailed, "you've had such a long journey, and my lady has been anxious—"

Gratillonius brushed past. The atrium spread before him, pillars and panels agleam in a star-field of candles. Across the charioteers in the floor sped Tambilis.

He could only stand and await her. She ran heavily, burdened with the unborn child. Her gown was plain gray wool, her feet merely slippered. The brown hair tumbled from a fillet of carved ivory which had more color than her face. She fell into his arms and wept.

He held her and murmured. "Be at ease, darling, at ease, I'm back safe and sound, everything went well, better than we hoped—" She clutched him painfully hard and shuddered.

After a while, under his strokings, she regained some control. Head still nestled into the curve of his left shoulder, she mumbled through sobs, "I've been so frightened . . . for you, Grallon. I had to w-w-warn you. Mother would have, but she's . . . on the island . . . praying for us all."

Alarm jangled through him. "What's this?" he snapped. "Why are you here?"

She disengaged herself. Her hands groped after his until he took them. Blinking, sniffling, she said in a small voice, "I moved hither a few days ago. I knew you'd seek the palace first, so belike I could tell you, put you on your guard, ere something bad happened. If n-n-naught else, while I was here, no more horrible feasts would be. What if you'd come home to one?"

His tone was flat in his hearing. "Well, tell me."

She gathered her will and cast the news forth: "A Scotic warrior dwells with Dahut. She gave a celebration in his honor, in this your house. They say 'twas as wild a revel as ever Ys has known. She and the man go freely about together. But she'll speak to none of us, her Sisters, nor does she seek the Temple or any of her duties. We know not what they intend, those two. Thus far he has kept from the Wood. They have claimed he's a chieftain who's searching out our markets, for trade. Or Dahut has. Niall japes and tells stories and sings songs but says never a meaningful thing. And he lives in her home."

Gratillonius had seen men smitten in combat stand moveless a while, trying to comprehend what had happened to them. Likewise did he respond: "Nay, this cannot be. Dahut could not defile herself. She is daughter to Dahilis."

"Oh, she's declared the Scotian has a room of his own. Her servants are silent. 'Tis plain to see they're terrified. She's taken lodgings for those that used to live in, and sends everybody off at the end of each day's work. Grallon, I have seen the looks she gives him."

Momentarily and vaguely, he thought that this was to be expected, that it might even be the answer for which he had yearned. Let the girl be happy with a man she loved. Her father the King could protect them, steer them between the reefs of the law, win her freedom from the Sign of Belisama.

He saw how impossible that was, realized Dahut must know this just as well, and remembered Tommaltach, Carsa, and Budic—Budic.

"What is this fellow like?" he asked in the same dull fashion.

"Tall, strong, beautiful," Tambilis replied. Steadiness was rising in her. "I think, though, he's older than you by some years."

"So if he challenges me, I might well take him? That would not end the trouble, my dear. Only if he took me."

Terror cried: "You'll not give in to him!"

Gratillonius shrugged. "Not purposely. I have a strong wish for his blood, I suppose. Still, what if he does not challenge? We shall have to think about this."

Tears ran anew down the cheeks of Tambilis, but quietly. "Oh, poor hurt beloved. Come with me. I'll pour you wine till you can rest the night. Tomorrow—"

He shook his head. "I must be on my way. I came only to fetch the Key."

"The sea gate is already locked. Men carried Lir Captain down. Sea Lord Adruval Tyri helped him close the lock."

"Good." Adruval had always been a trusty friend. "Nonetheless, I want to see for myself. Afterward I have my Watch to stand in the Wood, for the next three nights and what's left of their days. For I am the King."

"I'll meet you there," she said with a ghost of eagerness.

Once more he shook his head. "Nay, I'd liefer be alone." Sensing the pain in her, he added: "Tomorrow also. Besides, you ought not carry our little princess out into this weather. It should have slacked off by the third day. Come to me then."

She tried to laugh. " 'Twould need the Gods Themselves to keep me away."

He kissed her, tasting salt, and went onward. The Key was in a casket in his bedroom. By the light of a candle he had brought along, he stared down at its iron length. Why was he taking it? The gate was properly shut.

But this was the emblem and embodiment of his Kingship. He hung it around his neck, letting it dangle from the chain on the breast of his Roman mail. It felt heavy as the world.

Tambilis stood mute, fists clenched, and watched him go out the door. Favonius whickered and stamped. The sun was set and dusk blowing in against the wind. Gratillonius loosened the tether and swung to the saddle. Hoofbeats clopped.

At a ring in the wall beneath the Raven Tower, he resecured his mount before he climbed those stairs. The storm screamed and smote. Surf bellowed. Here he could indeed feel its impact, up the stones and his body to the skull. Through a bitter haze of spindrift he made out the water, livid, and the western sky, the hue of a bruise.

Light gleamed weakly from a slit window. The sentries had taken refuge in the turret. Gratillonius passed by unseen, on along the top of the wall. War engine housings crouched, blurred to his sight, in the salt rain that drenched his clothes.

The harbor basin sheened uneasy. Metal-sheathed timber trembled to the battering of waves as he picked his way down the stair to the walk. Often he heard a boom louder yet, when a float dashed against the rampart. Yon spheres might want replacement later, he thought. The huge timber that was the bar creaked in its bracket. But the chain held it firm, and the lock held the chain. The sea gate of Ys stood fast.

Gratillonius wondered why he had come, when Tambilis had assured him there was no need. Something to fill an hour? He'd better be off. Darkness was deepening and the wind rising further.

On his return, a monster billow nearly came over the parapet. Water spurted across him. He stumbled, and recovered by slapping hands onto the tower. It too stood fast, above the crypt of Mithras. Should he descend and offer a prayer? No, if nothing else, that would be unkind to Favonius; and Mithras seemed remote, almost unreal, on this night.

Did Dahut sleep gladly at the side of her man?

Gratillonius hastened back to the pomoerium. He urged Favonius to a trot, and a gallop once they were on Lir Way. It was wholly deserted now. The buildings around the Forum loomed like giant dolmens—though did a window shine in the Christian church? The Fire Fountain brimmed with water, which the wind ruffled.

The moon had cleared the eastern hills. Towertop glass shone blank. Gratillonius fled on through the phantom city.

Out High Gate he went, onto Aquilonian Way, thence to Processional Way. The canal bridge rang beneath hoofs. The stream ran thickly, white with moonlight. The road bent eastward from the sea, toward the Wood. Nearing, Gratillonius heard boughs grind as the gale rushed among

them. Like a second moon, the Shield swayed from the
Challenge Oak, above dappled flagstones. It toned when
the Hammer clashed on it.

Gratillonius dismounted and beat on the door of the
Red Lodge till the staff roused. He himself led Favonius to
the stable, unsaddled the stallion, rubbed him down; but
he let the men bring hay, grain, and water. When they
spoke of preparing a meal for him he said curtly that he
wanted nothing but a crock of wine to take to his bedchamber.

There, after an hour alone, he could weep.

— 2 —

Still the wind mounted. By dawn it was like none that
chronicles remembered. And still it mounted.

No one went forth. Even in the streets, air rammed to
cast a man down, stun him with its roar as of the sky
breaking asunder, choke and blind him in the spume that
filled it. Glass and tiles fell from above, shattered, ripped
loose, flung far before they struck. About the unseen
noontide, upper levels of the tower called Polaris came
apart. Metal, timbers, goods, and some human bodies flew
hideously down to smash against whatever was below. The
rest of the city endured, however strained and scarred.
Oaken doors and shutters mostly clung to their hinges.
Close-fitted dry masonry went unscathed. But the violence thrummed through, until every interior was a cavern
of noise.

Northbridge Gate and Aurochs Gate were barred, for
on those sides the sea thrust between rampart and
headlands—higher yet, in those narrow clefts, than the
billows from the west. Overrun again and again, the span
on the north finally disintegrated. Water surged beneath
the wall and broke into the canal, whose banks it gouged
out to make a catchbasin for itself. The rock on the south
side which shouldered against the wall of Ys was a barrier
more solid, across which only the tops of the hugest breakers leaped. Nonetheless that portal also must stay shut;
and because it had never been meant for this kind of

attack, enough water got around it and under it that Goose Fair lay inches-deep submerged and Taranis Way became a shivering estuary for yards beyond.

Ebb brought scant relief, when the seas had such a wind behind them. At high tide, crests smashed just below the western battlements; jets sprang white above, like fingers crooked in agony; at once they shredded into spray and blew over Ys.

Yet the gate held.

Dahut and Niall were alone in her house. None of the servants she dismissed the evening before had dared return. It was cold; fires were out, and he cautioned against lighting any. It was dark; a single candle flame smoked in the bedchamber, where they had sought the refuge of blankets. It was drumful of tumult.

Dahut trembled close against the man. "Hold me," she begged. "If we must die, I want it to be in your arms."

He kissed her. "Be of good heart, darling," he said, his own voice level. "Your wall stands."

"For how long?"

"Long enough, I do believe. A wind like this cannot go on as a breeze might. It will soon be dropping, you mark my words."

"Will it die down at once?"

Niall frowned above her head. "It will not that, either. It will remain a gale through this night, surely. And the waves it has raised, they will be slower than it to dwindle. But if rath and doors have withstood thus far, they should last until the end."

"Thank you, beloved," Dahut breathed. She sat up, cast off the covers, knelt on the mattress. Her hair and her nakedness shone in the dimness. She looked to the niche where stood her Belisama image, the lustful huntress that she alone of the Nine cared to have watching over her. "And thank you, Maiden, Mother, and Witch," she called softly. "For Your mercies and Your promise that You will fulfill—through us twain here before You—our thanks, our prayers, our sacrifice."

She glanced at Niall, who had stayed reclining, pillow-propped against the headboard. "Won't you give thanks too?" she asked. "At least to Lir and Taranis."

Through the dusk she saw his visage grim. "For our

deliverance? The Three have brought Grallon back just at this time. Is the tempest also Their work? Does Ys stand off the Gods Themselves?"

She lifted her hands. Horror keened: "Say never so! Ys does abide." She caught her breath. "And, and soon we'll restore the law. Soon you, the new King, will give Them Their honor. They foresee it. They must!"

He likewise got to his knees. His bulk loomed over her, blocking sight of the candle. "I have been thinking on that, and more than thinking," he told her slowly. "Dreams have I sought by night and omens by day. For I am fosterling of a poet, stepson of a witch, patron of druids, and myself descended from the Gods of Ériu. Much have I seen and much have I learned. Insights are mine that no lesser King may know. In me is fate."

She stared. "What? You n-never said this. Oh, beloved, I could feel in my heart you . . . were more than you pretended—. But what are you?"

"I am Niall of the Nine Hostages, King at Temir, conqueror of half the Scoti, scourge of Rome, and he whom your father most bitterly wronged ere ever you were born."

Dahut cast herself down before him. "Glorious, glorious!" she cried brokenly. "Lir Himself brought you to me!"

Niall laid a hand on her head. "Now you have heard."

"It whelms me, lord of mine—oh—"

'It could be the death of me, did news get about too soon."

"My tongue is locked like the sea gate." Dahut rose to a crouch. Hair had tumbled over her eyes. She gazed through it, up at his massive murkiness. "But once you're King in Ys, we're safe, we're free." Joy stormed through her voice. "You'll be sacred! Together we'll beget the new Age—the Empire of the North—"

"Hold," he commanded.

Again she knelt, arms crossed over bosom against the cold, and waited. The wind wuthered, the sea thundered.

"Sure, and that's a vaunting vision," he said, stern as a centurion. "But ofttimes have the Gods given men their finest hopes, then dashed them to shards on the ground. Grallon follows his soldier God; and who shall foreknow whether Mithras proves stronger than the Mórrigu? Grallon is a Roman, living out of his proper time, a Roman of the old iron breed that carried its eagles from end to end of the world. He and his like cast me bloodily back at the Wall in Britannia. He and his schemes wrecked my fleet, slaughtered my men, and killed my son at the wall of Ys. Well could it happen that his sword fells myself in the Wood."

"Nay, Niall, heart of mine, nay!" She groped for him.

He pushed her back. "Your earlier lovers came to grief. Will you be sending me to the same?"

She flinched. He pursued: "You'll get no further chance after I am dead. You've made your desire all too clear. Grallon can be fond and foolish no longer. What do they do in Ys with unchaste Queens? Throw them off the cliffs?"

Dahut straightened. "But you will win! And then naught else will count. Because you'll be the King of Ys."

"Your wish spoke there," he said bleakly. "My insight has told me otherwise."

"Nay—"

He reached to lay a palm over her mouth. "Quiet, lass. I know what you'd say. If I despair, I can still escape. Sure, and 'tis dear of you. But could I be leaving my love to a cruel death, and name myself a man?

"Hark'ee. There is a hope. I have seen it in the flash of a blade, I have heard it in the croak of a raven, I have understood it in the depths of a dream.

"The King of Ys bears on his breast the Key of Ys. It is more than a sigil. It is the Kingship's very self. Behold how Heaven and Ocean cannot open the sea gate. That power lies with him."

"But Kings die," she quavered.

He nodded. "They do. And the power passes onward. It is mostly small. How often must the gate be barred and locked? A few times a year, for caution's sake. Sailors who ken wind and tide spend no great strength at their work. Nor do the Gods, keeping the world on its course—most of the time.

"Tonight, though, the sea beleaguers Ys. It hammers on the shield of the city. Power must needs blaze within the Key, the Key that stands for the life of your people.

"While this is true, the bearer is invincible. Were I or any man to go now against Grallon, he would prevail.

"Hush. Bide a moment. I cannot wait till the need is past and the power that is in the Key has faded. Tremendous seas will be crashing on wall and gate for days to come. Meanwhile the wind will have slacked and folk can move abroad. Grallon will seek me out. He must. Think. If I do not challenge him, he will challenge me. He is the King; he may do this, the more so if he claims he's exacting justice. And there will be no stopping him. For 'twill not be for his own peace or safety. 'Twill be on your account, Dahut, you, his daughter. He'll hope that having killed me, he can win clemency for you—blame the dead man for leading you astray—though because he is not really a fool, Dahut, never again will you have the liberty to work for his death."

"So it is."

She shook her head, bewildered. "The Sisters never taught me this."

"Did they teach you everything the Gods might ever reveal?"

She was mute, until: "What can we do?"

Teeth gleamed in the night-mask of his face. "If *I* bore the Key, the power would be mine. I could call him forth ere his Watch is ended, and slay him in the Wood."

"But—"

He leaned forward and took her by the shoulders. "You can do it for me, Dahut," he said. "You've told me how you can cast a sleep spell, how you did at the Red Lodge itself. This time you need not rouse him. Only steal in, lift the chain of the Key from off his neck, and carry the thing to me."

"Oh, nay," she pleaded.

"Would you liefer I die at his hands?"

"The Gallicenae have a second Key. They'll lend it to him."

Niall laughed. "Then at worst, we meet on equal ground, Grallon and I. Gladly will I that. Even so, puzzlement and surprise ought to have shaken him."

Dahut covered her face. "Sacrilege."

"When you are the Chosen of the Chosen?"

She cowered.

His sigh was as cold as the wind: "Very well. I thought you loved me, Emer to my Cú Culanni. I thought you had the faith and the courage to fare beside your man. Since you do not, I may honorably go from Ys in the morning. Meanwhile I shan't trouble you."

He swung his legs around and stood up.

"Niall, nay!" she screamed, and scrambled after him. He caught her before she went to the floor. "I will, I will!"

— 3 —

By sunset the wind had indeed lessened. It was still such as few could travel in, but along the Armorican seaboard it had wrought the harm of its full rage. There remained its malevolence.

Clouds blew thicker. Guards had resumed their posts, with frequent relief; but the moonlight was so fitful that the night watch did not see the two who slipped out through High Gate.

The going was treacherous at first. Workshops and stables beyond the wall had littered ruin over Aquilonian Way. Nails and splinters lurked for those who must climb across. More than once, Niall's strong hand saved Dahut from falling.

After they reached Processional Way they had a clear path save for torn-off boughs. The bridge across the canal survived. To the left, light flickered across water that chopped a foot or more deep under the rampart. It had not drained back into the sea, for even at ebb, waves boomed in through the gap between city and headland. On the right the amphitheater glimmered ghostly, the Wood of the King hulked altogether black. Farther on were gulfs of darkness. The moon hurtled among clouds which it touched with ice. When the road turned east and the walkers left the lee of Ys behind them, they felt the wind on their backs as an oncoming assault. It hooted and yammered. Louder, now, was the roar of Ocean.

Near the Wood, that sound was matched by the storm through the trees. Their groans were an undertone to its wails. Some along the edge lay uprooted, limbs clawing at heaven. Pieces broken off the Challenge Oak bestrewed the court. The Shield tolled insanely to the swinging of the Hammer. When a moonbeam reached earth, the metal shone dulled by the dents beaten into it.

Otherwise the Sacred Precinct had protection. The three

buildings squatted intact, lightless. As Dahut came between them, a neigh burst from one, and again and again.

"Be quick ere that brute wakes the whole house," Niall
snapped.

Dahut raised her arms. The moon saw her attired in the
blue gown and high white headdress of the Gallicenae.
Her chant cut through soughing and creaking. "*Ya Am-
Ishtar, ya Baalim, ga'a vi khuwa—*"

Niall felt for the sword scabbarded across his back. At
once aware of what he did, he dropped his hand. Its
fingers closed on the haft of his knife.

"*Aus-t ur-t-Mut-Resi, am 'm user-t—*"

Niall made a wolf-grin.

"*Belisama, Mother of Dreams, bring sleep unto them,
send Your blind son to darken their minds and Your
daughter whose feet are the feet of a cat to lead forth their
spirits—*"

The horse had fallen silent.

Presently Dahut did also. She turned to Niall. Moonlit,
her face was as pale as the windings above it. He barely
heard her amidst the noise: "They will slumber till dawn,
unless powerfully roused. But come, best we be swift."

"We?" he answered. "Nay, go you in alone. I might
blunder and make that awakening racket. You know your
way about your father's lair."

She shivered, caught her lip between her teeth, but
moved ahead. He accompanied her onto the porch. At the
entrance he drew blade and took stance.

Dahut opened the door enough to get through. It was
never barred, in token of the King's readiness to kill or be
killed. She entered, closed it behind her, poised breathless.

Coals banked in the fire-trenches gave some warmth;
shelter from the wind meant more. That sullen glow revealed little, but a lamp burned lonely. It had served two
men slumped at a table, heads on arms. Others must
already have been asleep on the benches along the walls.
The light straggled forth, discovering among glooms only
the ragged lower ends of battle banners, the scorn on two
of the idol-pillars upholding the roof.

Dahut straightened and glided forward to the interior
partition. Seeing its door ajar, she peered around the
jamb. The corridor beyond was not quite a blindness.

Windows were shuttered, and the moon would have given scant help anyhow, but a dim luminance, reflected off tile floor and plaster walls of this Roman half of the building, sufficed. She moved on, smoke-silent, though the storm would surely have covered any footfalls.

The door to Gratillonius's room stood open. Thence came the radiance of seven candles in a brass holder on a table at his bedside. He had been reading; a book lay on the blankets. She knew not whether her spell had ended that or he had earlier fallen into a sleep which she made profound. Between his grief at learning of her conduct—he must have heard, with Tambilis waiting meddlesome in the palace—and the tumult this day, he could have had scant rest or none until now.

Dahut stalked to the bedside and regarded him. She recognized his book. Bodilis had forced her to study it: the *Meditations* of Marcus Aurelius in Latin translation. An arm and both shoulders were bare outside the King's blankets. Doubtless he was naked, as he had been the night she came here to deceive him into making her his.

She sighed.

He did not appear helpless as most sleepers do. His features were too rugged. The mouth had not softened, nor the brow eased. But how weary he seemed, weary beyond uttering, furrows plowed deep, gray sprinkled over the ruddiness of his hair and streaked down his beard.

His neck remained a column smooth and thick, firmly rooted in heavy shoulders and barrel chest. Around it sparkled a fine golden chain. Blankets hid the lower part.

Dahut's breath quickened. She clenched fists and teeth.

Resolution returned. She bent above the King. Gently as a mother with a babe, she slipped a hand beneath his head and raised it off the pillow. Her other hand went under the covers, over the rising and falling shagginess to the iron shank. She slid the Key forth into her sight. The chain she passed above his head until it encircled her supporting arm. She lowered him back onto the pillow and waited tensely.

His eyes moved beneath the lids. His lips formed a whisper. He mumbled and stirred. Dahut waved her free hand over him. He quieted. She saw him breathe, but the wind smothered the sound.

She gave him a brief archaic smile and departed.

Through the hall she went, with a gait that grew confident until it was a stride. She passed out the door and shut it behind her as if she struck down an enemy. Niall backed off, startled in the gloom. She pursued, swung the Key, made it ring against his sword.

"You have it?" he asked hoarsely. "Let's away."

They stopped when they got to the road and could see better. The moon threw harried light upon them and the thing she reached to hang around his neck. Her arms followed.

He made her end the kiss. "Back we go, at once," he declared.

Dahut's laughter pealed. "Aye. Make haste. I'm afire!"

—In her bed, after their first fierce passage of love, she asked, "Tomorrow morning will you challenge him?"

"That might be shrewd," Niall said into the warmth and silkiness and musk of her.

"Catch him amazed, uncertain." She squirmed and burrowed against him. "Tomorrow night will be our wedding night."

"Grant me some hours of rest first," he requested with a leer.

"Not yet," she purred. Her lips and fingers moved greedily. "I want your weight on me again. I want to feel the Key cold between my breasts while you are a torch between my thighs. Oh, Niall, death itself cannot quench my wanting of you."

The wind keened, the sea rumbled.

— 4 —

Corentinus woke.

For a moment he lay motionless. His room was savagely cold. Through a smokehole knocked out of the wall under the ceiling for his cookfire, he heard the storm. A nightlight, tallow candle in a wooden holder, guttered and stank. He did not ordinarily keep such a thing, but at a time when woe might fall on his people without warning, he must be ready. It barely revealed his few rough articles of furniture.

The depths of the chamber were lost in night. Once the temple treasury, it was much too big for a servant of Christ.

Corentinus's eyes bulged upward. Air went jagged between his teeth. It came back out in an animal moan.

"O dear God, no!" he begged. "Mercy, mercy! Let this be a nightmare. Let it be only Satan's work."

Decision came. He tossed off his one blanket and rose from his pallet on the floor. Snatching a robe from a peg, he pulled it over his lanky frame. Without pausing to bind on sandals, he took the candle, tucked his staff under an arm, and left.

The hallway led to the vestibule. Another small flame showed it crowded. Folk sprawled asleep, refugees from outside the city. Corentinus had admitted any who could not find better quarters, without inquiring as to their beliefs, and arranged for food and water and chamber pots. He made his way among the bodies to the inner door, opened it, and entered the sanctuary.

When he closed it off, he found himself in still more of an emptiness than his room. This section occupied a good half of what had been the temple of Mars, before Roman pressure brought conversion to the sole church in Ys. Little was in it other than the canopied altar block and a couple of seats. The cross on the altar glimmered athwart shadows. The pagan reliefs along the walls were lost to sight.

Corentinus lowered candle and staff, raised his arms before the cross, and chanted the Lord's prayer. It echoed hollowly. He laid himself prostrate on the floor. "Almighty God," he said against its hardness, "forgive a thick-headed old sailor man. I wouldn't question Your word. Never. But was that dream from You? It was so terrible. And so darkling. I don't understand it, I honestly don't."

Here within the stone, silence abided.

Corentinus climbed back onto his feet. He lifted his arms anew. "Well, maybe You'll tell me more when I've obeyed Your first order," he said. "If it did come from You. A dunderhead like me can't be sure. But I'll do what the angel bade me, supposing it was a true angel. Doesn't seem too likely it was a devil like the one that tried to trick Bishop Martinus, because I don't see any real harm in this deed. Forgive me my wonderment, Lord. I'll do my best."

He gathered staff and candle. As he reached the door, he shuddered. With an effort, he opened it and re-entered the vestibule.

A woman had roused to nurse her infant. She saw the tall form and called softly, anxiously, "Is aught wrong, master?"

Corentinus halted.

"Please tell me, master," the woman said. "We don't serve your God, but we are in His house and ours are wrathful."

Thoughts tumbled through him. He could wake these people and bring them, at least, with him. But no. It wasn't that they were heathen, his small flock being scattered about the city. They were nonetheless God's wayward children. But they were the merest handful among unreachable thousands. Worse, he did not know what it was that would stalk them this night.

"Peace, my daughter," he said. "Calm your fears. You are the guest of Christ."

He blew his candle out. The wind would immediately have killed it. As poor as his congregation was, he economized wherever he could. He went out the main door, over the portico, down the stairs, across the Forum.

Wind still howled and smote. Air was still bitter with salt and cold. The gale had, though, dwindled enough that the crashing of the sea against the city wall came louder. Clouds flew low, blackening heaven, hooding towertops. The moon streamed just above western roofs. By its flickery pallor Corentinus hastened, up Lir Way toward High Gate and the Wood of the King.

— 5 —

After Dahut was sunken in sleep, Niall left her bed. Cautiously he put on the warm clothes he had worn earlier and flung aside when he and she returned here. The sword he hung across his back. At his left hip he belted a purse of coins, thinking wryly that it balanced the dagger on the right in more ways than one. Gesocribate was about two days distant for an active man afoot. Could he not buy food along the way he'd arrive hungry, unless he came upon a sheep or something like that and butchered it. However, if need be he could turn a deaf ear to the growls in his belly. There would be celebration at journey's end!

Or would there? His scheme might fail; he might himself perish—if the Gods of Ys were, in truth, less than death-angry with Their worshippers.

Niall bared teeth. Whatever came, *his* Gods would know he had ventured that which Cú Culanni might not have dared.

On an impulse he stepped to the bedside and looked down. Candlelight lost itself in the amber of Dahut's tousled hair. She lay on her back, arms widespread. A young breast rose out of the blankets. From the rosiness at its peak a vein ran blue, spiderweb-fine, down an ivory curve marred by a beginning bruise where he had caressed it too strongly. Wild, she had never noticed. Now the pulse at the base of her throat beat slow and gentle. Her lips were slightly parted. How long were the lashes reaching toward those high cheekbones. When he bent low, he sensed warmth radiating from her. She smelled of sweat and sweetness. The crescent of the Goddess glowed.

Almost, he kissed her. A stirring went through his loins. He pulled himself back barely in time, straightened, but did not go at once.

Gazing at her, he said very low in the tongue of Ériu:

"It's sad I am to be leaving you, my darling, for darling you were, a woman like none other, and you loved me as never I was loved before nor hope ever to be again. I think you will haunt me until I join you in death.

"But it must be, Dahut. I came here sworn to vengeance. I may not break my oath, nor would I; for Ys killed the son that Ethniu gave me, long and long ago. Yet sad I am that your Gods chose you for the instrument.

"How could you believe I would make myself King of Ys? Oh, it's mad with love you were, to believe that. I am the King at Temir, and I will go home to my own.

"Should I bind myself to this city I hate? Sure, and I would first have slain Grallon. But he was not alone in bringing doom on my good men. All Ys did, foremost its nine witch-Queens.

"Let me become its King, and I doubt such a chance as

is mine tonight would ever wing its way back. In the end I too would fall, not grandly among my warriors, but alone in the Wood of slaughter; and from my blood Ys would suck new life. It shall not happen, not to me nor ever again to anyone else.

"I too will seek Grallon, where he lies in the slumber you cast upon him. I stayed my hand then, for you might have screamed. My first duty is against Ys. Afterward, if the Gods spare me—oh, it will go hard to kill a man in his sleep. I thought of waking him. But that would make a challenge fight, and though Ys be gone, what hold might its Gods yet keep on me? Let me go free.

"You wish to be my wife, Dahut. It's glorious you are; but so in her youth was Mongfind. Should I take for wife a woman who plotted the death of her father?

"As for the rest, two are also comely, though second and third behind you. But the second would bear a horror of me; when I embraced her, she would lie like a corpse and send her soul afar. The third is a sorceress who helped bring death to dear Breccan. Should I take to me the murderess of my son? So are the rest, apart from the cripple; and they are crones.

"Let them die, let the Sign come on fresh maidens, and still the Nine would be the only women I could have; and not a one of them would be giving me another son.

"Your Ys, all Ys is the enemy I am vowed to destroy. This night, the lady at my side is the Mórrigu.

"Farewell, Dahut."

He lifted the Key that hung on his breast and kissed its iron.

He departed.

Wind struck him with blades that sang. Seen from the doorway, the city was a well of blackness out of which lifted barely glimpsed spears, its towers. The horns of land hunched brutal. Beyond ramped the sea, white under the sinking, cloud-hunted moon.

When he loped downward, houses soon blocked that sight from him. He was a tracker, though, who had quickly learned every trail he wanted and had scant need of light.

The streets twisted to Lir Way. Crossing the empty Forum, he saw the Fire Fountain brimful of shivery water, flung off waves whose hammering resounded louder for each pace he took. He threw a gibe at the stately buildings of the Romans, at the church of Christ.

When he left the avenue, the streets grew more narrow and mazed than those where the wealthy dwelt. He was in Lowtown, ancestral Ys which Brennilis had saved. Behind the sheerness of a tower—clouds raced moon-tinged, making it seem to topple on him—he found the moldering houses of the Fishtail. The life that throbbed in them had drawn into itself, the quarter lay lightless, none save he and the wind ran through its lanes. He glimpsed a cat in a doorway. Its baleful gaze followed him out of sight.

Nearing the rampart, he entered a quarter likewise ancient and poor, but a place for working folk. Among these dwellings he came by the Shrine of Ishtar. Awed in spite of himself, he stopped for an instant and lifted the Key before the dolmen-like mass. Let Her within see that he went to wreak justice.

A little way farther, he had the Cornmarket on his right. Its paving sheened wet. On his left a row of warehouses fronted on the harbor. Between them he spied the basin. Ahead reared the city wall. Self-shadowed, the monstrous bulk stood like a piece cut out of heaven. Over and over, sheets of foam spurted to limn its battlements. The rush and crash trampled the sounds of the gale.

Niall advanced. At the inside edge of the pomoerium stood the Temple of Lir, small, dark, deserted, but the rudeness and mass of its stones bespeaking a strength implacable. Again Niall halted and raised the Key. "Though this house of Yours fall, You will abide," he said into the roaring. "Come seek me in Eriu. You shall have Your honors in overflowing measure, blood, fire, wine, gold, praise; for we are kindred, You and I."

Just the same, he dared not enter the unlocked fane. Besides, he should hasten. Dawn was not far off.

Drawing his sword, knife in his left hand, he slipped up the staircase to the wall top. The Gull Tower reared ahead. Moonlight came and went over its battlements and the parapet beneath. Each time a wave broke against the rampart, spray sleeted; and the impact was deafening.

This was a guard point. Was a sentry outside, or did the whole watch shelter within the turret? Niall crouched low and padded forward.

Light shone from slit windows. The door was shut. In front of it did stand an Ysan marine. While the tower blocked off most wind and water, he was drenched, chilled, miserable. He stood hunched into his cloak, helmeted head lowered, stiffened fingers of both hands clutching his pikeshaft.

He must die unbeknownst to his comrades.

Niall squatted under a merlon. The next great wave struck and flung its cloud. He leaped with it, out of the whiteness, and hewed.

Himself half blinded, he misgauged. His sword clanged and glided off the helmet. The young man whirled about. Before he could utter more than a croak, Niall was at him. The Scotian had let his sword fall. His right arm went under the guard's chin and snapped the head back. His left drove dagger into throat and slashed.

The pike clattered loose. Blood spouted. Niall shoved. The sentry toppled over the inner parapet, down to the basin. Night hid the splash. His armor would sink him.

Niall retrieved his sword. Had the rest heard?

They had not.

He wiped dagger on kilt, sheathed both weapons, and trotted onward. The sea showered him, washing away blood.

Above the northern edge of the gate, he stopped and looked. As if to aid him, for that instant the surf was lower and clouds parted from before the moon.

On his left gleamed, faintly, the arc of the harbor. Its water was troubled; he saw vessels chafe at their moorings along the wharf. Yet wall and gate kept it safe, as they had done these past four centuries. Behind reached Ys, mostly a cave of night but its towers proud in the moonlight. Cape Rach, Point Vanis, the inland vale were dream-dim.

On his right heaved Ocean. Wind, still a howl and a spear, had in the fullness of its violence piled up seas which would not damp out for days; and as Niall stood above, the spring tide was at its height. Skerries lay drowned underneath, until time should resurrect them to destroy more ships. A few rocks thrust above the relentlessness out of the west. Each time a wave smote them, they vanished in chaos.

The sea was not black but white, white as the breasts of

Dahut. A billow afar growled like the drums of an oncoming army. As it drew closer, gathered speed, lifted and lifted its smoking crest, the breaker's voice became such thunder as rolls across the vault of heaven. When it struck and shattered, the sound was as of doomsday.

Niall shaded his eyes and squinted. He sought for the floats that on ebb tide drew open the doors. There, he had found the nearer of them. It dashed to and fro at the end of its chain, often hurled against the wall. Had that battered the sphere out of shape? He could not tell in the tricky light, through the flying spindrift. But neither one had cracked open and filled. They were too stoutly made.

Now and then the sea recoiled on itself. Suddenly emptiness was underneath the floats. They dropped. Chains rattled over blocks in sculptured cat's heads till they snapped the great balls to a halt. It was a wonder they had not broken; but they likewise were well wrought of old. The waves climbed anew and again the globes whirled upon them.

Niall smiled. All was as it should be.

He started down the inner stair. Below the wall there was shielding against wind and water, save for what flew across. However, the stone was slippery and the moon hidden. He kept a hand on the rail and felt his way most carefully.

The stairs ended at a ledge. In the dark he stumbled against the capstan there and cursed. He should have remembered. He had kept every sense whetted when Dahut showed him the system, as her father once showed her.

Well, the machine had naught to do with him. It was for forcing the gate shut if need arose at low tide. He groped past a huge jamb to the walk that ran across this door.

Copper sheathing was cold and slick beneath his right hand. His left felt along the rail that kept him from falling into the chop of the basin. Whenever the surf hit, the door trembled and he heard a groaning beneath the crash. But it held, it held.

Distance between rail and metal suddenly widened. He was past the walk, onto the platform at the inner edge of the door. He turned to the right. His fingers touched iron, a tremendous bracket, and inside it the roughness of the beam that latched the gate.

They found the chain that secured the bar.
They found the lock that closed the chain.

They took the Key and felt after the hole.

It seemed like forever while he fumbled blind. A horror was in him, that he would drop the Key, that it would skitter off and be lost in the harbor which the gate guarded. He forced the fear aside and continued seeking.

The Key entered. He felt it engage. He turned it and felt the pins click.

He withdrew the Key, unclasped the lock, cast it from him to sink. A moment he stood moveless: then, with a yell, flung the Key after it.

The chain slithered through his grasp. The bar was free.

It would not likely rise of itself, however much it and the portal that it held shivered beneath blows. Niall was not finished yet.

He made his way onward. The south door had its own platform, butting against that of the north door at their juncture. There was another bracket. Beyond it was the pivot on which the beam turned.

A light cable ran from the north end of the bar, through a block high on the south door, and down. When Niall reached its cleat, he bayed laughter. He knew what to do, as fully as if he could see.

He hauled on the line. The effort was small, so craftsmanly counterweighted was the timber. Through wind and sea, did he hear it creak while it rose?

Soon he could pull in no more, and knew the beam rested entirely against the south door, that the gate of Ys stood unbarred. Niall cleated the cable fast.

He hurried back over platforms and catwalk, up stairs, to the top of the wall.

Wildness greeted him. Let the floats haul the doors open just once, just a part of the way. The tide would rush in. Striking from both sides, waves would rip the barriers from their hinges. Dry-laid, the wall of the city might fall to pieces. Surely a flood as high as Hightown would ride into Ys.

A wave smashed home. Its crest cataracted over Niall of the Nine Hostages. He stood fast. After the salt rain was over, he cupped hands around mouth and shouted seaward: "I have done what was my will. Now do You do what is Yours!"

He turned and ran, to get clear while time remained.

— 6 —

Gratillonius woke inch by inch. In half-awareness he felt himself struggle heavily against it. He sank back toward nothingness. Before he had escaped, the drag recalled him. It was as if he were a fish, huge and sluggish, hooked where he had lain at the bottom of the sea. That was a strong fisherman who pulled him nearer and nearer the light above.

He broke surface. Radiance ravaged him. He plunged. His captor played him, denied him the deeps, compelled him to breathe air under open sky. On his second rising, he saw the gray-bearded craggy face. The sea lured him with its peace. He went below. That was briefly and shallowly. Once more he must ascend, and now he came altogether out.

Corentinus's hands were bony and hard, shaking him. "Rouse, rouse, man!" the pastor barked. "What's got into the lot of you? Lying like dead folk—" He noticed eyes blink. Stingingly, he slapped the King's cheeks, left and right.

Gratillonius sat up. Astonishment and anger flared. The fish burned away, and he was on earth, himself. "You! By Hercules—"

Corentinus stepped back and straightened. "Use your wits," he said. "Shake off that torpor. Get dressed. Help me kick the men awake. You're in bad danger, my friend."

Gratillonius drew rein on his temper. This fellow wouldn't come here on a midnight whim.

Midnight? What hour was it? Wind yowled and rattled shutters. The room was musty-cold. His candles guttered, stubs. So a long while had passed since he dropped off—at last, at last—into blessed Lethe. Darkness outside must be nearing an end.

"Tell me," he said.

Corentinus took his staff, which he had leaned against the wall. He clung to it and let it bear his weight, stared before him and answered low: "A vision. I saw a mighty angel come down from Heaven, clothed with a cloud; and a rainbow was upon his head; and his face was like the sun and his feet like pillars of fire. And seven thunders resounded while he cried, 'Woe to the city! For it shall perish by the sea, whose queen it was; and the saints shall mourn. But go you, servant of God, make haste to the King of the city, and call him forth ere his foeman find him, that he may live; for the world shall have need of him. It is spoken.'

"I came to myself with the voice and the brightness bewildering me still. I didn't understand—"

Abrupt tears ran from beneath the tufted brows, across the leathery hide. 'I did-didn't know what it meant," Corentinus stammered. "Could it be a demon in me? Would God really . . . let His innocents die by the thousands, unhallowed? I went and prayed for a sign. Nothing, nothing came. I thought, I grabbed after the hope, that God wouldn't destroy Ys. Wicked men might, the way they destroyed Jerusalem. You could forestall them. The command was to go and warn *you*."

He swallowed hard before he finished in a steadier tone: "Maybe this is a trick of Satan. Or maybe I'm in my dotage. Well, there didn't seem to be much harm in going to you. At worst, you'd boot me out. At best, you may untangle the thing and do whatever's needful. Me, I'll help anyway I can. And—" he laid hand over heart—"I'll be praying for a clear sign, and for Ys."

Gratillonius had listened frozen. He recoiled from prophecies and Gods, to immediacies a man could seize. "It's senseless," he snapped. "The weather's easing off. We won't take any more damage from it. As for enemies, none could possibly come by sea, and the land's secure at least as far east as Treverorum. I know; I just traveled through."

The same practicality responded: "No army bound here, no. But a band of sneak murderers could use the storm for cover. Who? Well, what about vengeful Franks? There are men who might well secretly have egged them on."

"I doubt that. The orders of the praetorian prefect were strict." Gratillonius ran fingers through his hair. "In any case, I am alert now."

"Your attendants aren't," Corentinus reminded him. "Not a man on watch. They're sleeping like drugged hogs. I say let's pummel them out of it, and all of you take arms. Might be a good idea to lead them to town. Forget your wretched vigil. Leave this house of death."

Remembrance came back of another night. Gratillonius
gaped. He swung himself out of bed. "We'd better get
going." His glance fell on the Christian's bare feet. They
bled from a score of slashes. "What happened to you?"

"High Gate's choked with wreckage. I stopped and told
the guards they ought to clear it, because we might have
sudden need of the road. But I couldn't wait for that, of
course."

Gratillonius nodded. It was a command such as he would
have given, were he not confined to this kennel. Need
he be?

He went after his clothes. Something was missing. What?
He felt at his chest. He choked on an oath, sprang about,
scrabbled frantically in the bedding.

The Key was gone.

Faintness closed in on him.

It receded. "What's the matter?" Corentinus asked. "I
thought you were about to drop."

Gratillonius snatched for his garments. "You wake the
men," he tossed over his shoulder. "Follow me—. No, best
you stay. They aren't trained fighters. But they should be
able to stand off an attack on the Lodge, if things come to
that."

"Where are you bound?"

"Yonder's a lantern. Light it for me."

Corentinus's voice reached him as if across the breadth
of Ocean. He sounded appalled. "The Key of Ys! I should
have seen, but you keep that devil's thing hidden—"

"It may well be a devil's thing—now. I'm going after
it."

"No! God's word is to save you. If Ys is to fall—"

"I told you to light me my lantern."

A shadow wavered before Gratillonius in the dimness.
He turned. Corentinus had raised his staff. Gratillonius
snarled. "Would you club me? Stand aside before I kill
you."

Not troubling with undergarments, he had drawn on
breeks, tunic, boots. His sword hung on the wall, from a
belt which also supported knife and purse. He took it and
secured the buckle.

"In Christ's name, old friend," Corentinus quavered, "I
beg you, think."

"I am thinking," Gratillonius replied.

"What?"

"I don't know what. But it's too ghastly to sit still with."

Gratillonius opened the lantern and lighted its candle himself off a stub. On his way out he took a cloak from its peg.

Wind squalled, whined, bit. Its passage through the Wood made a noise like surf. The Challenge Oak creaked, the Shield rang. Right, left, and behind, night crouched around the frantic yellow circle of his light. The wood and the meadow beyond were gray under the beams of a moon he could not see but which tinged the bellies of clouds flying low overhead.

Heedless of fire hazard, he carried the lantern into the stable and set it down. Warmth enfolded him, odors of hay and grain and manure. For an instant Gratillonius was a boy again on his father's land.

Glow sheened off the coat of Favonius. The stallion should have pricked up ears and whickered. Instead he stood legs locked, head hung, breath deep and slow—asleep. "Hoy!" Gratillonius entered the stall and slapped the soft muzzle. The beast snorted, twitched, slumbered on.

How long had the Key been missing?

Gratillonius had not meant to waste time on a saddle. He changed his mind. His foot helped him tighten the cinch to its utmost. The bridle went on despite the awkward position of the head, and the mouth did not resist the bit, but opened slackly when he put thumbs to corners. He donned his cloak and shut its clasp before he released the tether.

Leaving the stall, he led the reins over its top and kept them in his left hand. His right drew blade. "I'm sorry," he muttered, and reached between the rails. The flat of his sword smacked ballocks.

The stallion screamed. He plunged and kicked. Wood flew to flinders. Gratillonius jumped around in front, got a purchase on the reins, and clung with his whole weight.

Had the animal been disabled by pain or become unmanageable, Gratillonius would have left and run the whole way to Ys. Favonius traveled so much faster, though. "Easy, boy, easy, old chap, there, there."

Somehow the man gained control. He led the horse

from the demolished stall. A last shying knocked the lantern over. Its cover fell off. Beneath it were wisps of straw scattered across the floor. The crib was full of hay. A tiny flame ran forth. Gratillonius gave it no heed. His task was to get the neighing, trembling beast outside.

He did. Wind tossed the long mane. He forgot about the lantern.

A shadow stumbled from the shadows. "I implore you, stay," cried the voice of Corentinus. "God needs you."

Gratillonius hoisted himself into the saddle. "Hoy-a, gallop!" he shouted, and struck heels to ribs.

"Lord have mercy," called the chorepiscopus at his back. "Christ have mercy. Lord have mercy."

Hoofs banged. Muscles surged. Gratillonius rode off.

— 7 —

Once on Processional Way, he had Ys before him. Most of the city was as black as the headlands which held it. Towertops shone iron-hued by the light of a moon too far down for him to see above the wall. Tears blurred vision though he squinted, for he raced straight into the gale. Mithras preserve Favonius from tripping and breaking a leg.

The road bent south. Hoofs racketed on the canal bridge. Water swirled just underneath, dense with soil. It made a restless pond, from crumbled banks to city wall and on around into the sea that besieged the cliffs of Point Vanis.

Processional Way ended at Aquilonian Way. Here the wind was largely of Gratillonius's own haste. He was well into the lee of Ys, but likewise into its shadow. Barely could he see the highway heaped with shards of buildings. He kept Favonius bound south a while, to get around. Drenched earth smothered hoofbeats. Or so he supposed, somewhere at the back of his mind. He could not tell in this din.

When it appeared safe, he reined the stallion to a trot and turned west over grass, shrubs, mud that had been gardens, until they two reached the wall. Northward along it they groped, to High Gate. Somebody hailed. Men were at work clearing debris as Corentinus had urged.

Gratillonius thought they were a fair number. The officer of the watch must have summoned everybody in barracks.

"Who goes?" a voice challenged. Pikeheads lifted.

"The King," shouted Gratillonius. "Make way. Keep at your labor. We've need of that road!"

He walked Favonius past, not to trample anyone in the dark. Lir Way opened before him, empty between buildings and sphinxes. He smote heels for a fresh gallop.

Within the compass of the rampart, seeing was a little better. And he knew the way. After seventeen years, how well he knew it. Nothing obstructed it, either. The colonnades of the Forum passed by, specters under cloudy gravestones of towers. A few windows gleamed. They fell behind. He sped on, deeper into the roar of the sea.

The gate was his goal. Rather than stumble through tangled and lightless lanes, quickest would be to continue straight down the avenue to the harbor, speed over its wharf to the north end of the basin, turn left past the Temple of Lir to pomoerium and stairs, bound up to the Gull Tower and summon the guards there to join him in defending the city.

Mithras, God of the Midnight, You have had our sacrifice. Here is my spirit before You, my heart beneath Your eyes. I call, who followed Your eagles since ever my life began: Mithras, also a soldier, keep now faith with Your man!

Skippers' Market sheened. Favonius's feet slipped from him on the wet flags. He skidded and staggered. Barely did Gratillonius hold saddle.

The stallion recovered. "On!" yelled Gratillonius, and flogged him with the reins. He neighed. The arch of triumph echoed to his passage.

They came between the waterfront buildings, out onto the dock. Its stone rang under the hoofs. Ahead, the basin flickered, full of a heavy chop. Ships swayed at their piers. Half-seen under moonlit, racing clouds, they might have been whales harpooned. The outer wall thrust bulk and battlements into heaven. Foam fountained above and blew away on the wind. The copper on the gate caught such light as to make it stand forth like a phantom. Surf sundered.

Favonius reared and screamed.

The doors opened. The moon shone through from the horizon. It frosted the combers that charged inward, rank upon rank upon rank. Ahead of them, below the wall, gaped a trough as deep as a valley. Amidst the wind that suddenly smote him with full force, Gratillonius heard a monstrous sucking noise. It was the basin spilling out into the depth. That rush of water flung the gate wide.

A crest advanced. As the ground shoaled between the headlands, it gathered speed and height. The sound of it made stone tremble. Yet when it reached Ys it seemed to stand there, taller than the rampart, under spindrift banners, a thing that would never break.

Favonius reared again. Panic had him—no, the Dread of Lir. Gratillonius fought to bring him back.

The wave toppled.

The gate had no time to close itself. The torrent broke past, into the basin, over ships and wharf. There it rebounded. The next wave met it. Between them, they tore the doors from the wall.

With the full strength of his shoulders, Gratillonius had gotten his horse turned around. Hoofs fled between buildings and under the arch. The sea hounded them. Pasterndeep, it churned across Skippers' Market, sprayed in sheets from the hasty legs, before it withdrew.

Up Lir Way! Gratillonius felt nothing but his duty to survive. The Key had turned in the Lock and the old Gods were riding into Ys. Let him save what he could.

A second billow overtook him, surged hock-deep. Wavelets ran across its back and flung spiteful gouts of foam. It would have peaked higher save that along the way it broke through windows, pounded down doors, and gushed into the homes of men.

When he crossed the Forum, Favonius swam. Against the turmoil around him, Gratillonius made out heads, arms, bodies. They struggled and went under. He could do naught to help them, he must seek toward where the need was greatest.

The avenue climbed. For a small space, he galloped over clear pavement. Clouds ripped apart and he had some light from above. A few stars fluttered yonder. The east was gray.

Favonius throbbed beneath him. The stallion had shed blind terror, or the tide had leached it from him. He heeded the reins. Gratillonius turned him left.

Rising narrow between Suffete houses, the side street brought him to a point where he saw widely around. Ahead, that jewel which was the Temple of Belisama shone pale behind Elven Gardens. Beyond, Point Vanis heaved its cliffs heavenward and cast back the legions of Ocean.

South of it they charged into Lowtown. The wall disintegrated before them. Glancing backward, Gratillonius saw the Raven Tower drop stone by stone into its drowned crypt. Through breaches ever wider, the waves marched ever stronger. They undercut their first highdwellers' tower. It swayed, leaned, avalanched. The fall of its mass begot new, terrible upheavals. Its spire soared like a javelin into the flank of a neighbor, which lurched mortally wounded. From Northbridge to Aurochs Gate, the sea front rolled onward.

Gratillonius had not stopped while he looked. A glimpse into the wind, across what roofs remained, was enough. Already the flood seethed bare yards at his back. He galloped on through the gully of darkness, the noise of destruction.

Ahead on his left was the house of Dahut. Her alone could he hope to save.

It cracked wide. A wave engirdled it, hurled out of the spate that was Taranis Way. Stones and tiles became rubble. They slid into the water. It spouted, churned, and momentarily retreated.

Though the moon had gone down, light as well as wind streamed through the gap. Night still held out against day, but Gratillonius could see farther. He saw the daughter of Dahilis. She had escaped barely in time. Naked she fled up the street ahead of him. "Dahut! Wait for me!" The wind tattered his cry, the sea overran it. Her hair blew wild about her whiteness.

Favonius would catch her in a few more bounds.

The next surge caught Favonius. It boiled as high as his withers. Undertow hauled him back. He struggled to keep footing. The wave that followed swept around him and his rider. Right and left, buildings fell asunder. There was nothing but a waste of water and a scrap of road up which Dahut forever ran.

To Gratillonius, where he and his horse fought for their

lives, came Corentinus. Somehow the holy man had reached Ys from the Wood as fast as hoofs had flown. Across the tops of the billows he came striding, staff in hand. Robe and gray beard flapped in the tumult. His voice tolled through it: "Gratillonius, abide! The angel of the Lord appeared to me before the heathen house. He bade me save you even now. Come with me before it is too late."

He pointed east along the street that led off this toward the mound where stood the Temple of Belisama.

Gratillonius whipped his mount. The wave pulled back, awaiting the higher one behind. Favonius broke free. His hoofs found pavement and he went on aloft as his master bade.

Corentinus paced him on the right. "No, you fool!" the pastor shouted. "Leave that bitch-devil to her fate!"

The new wave rushed uphill. Water whirled about the daughter of Dahilis, waist-high and rising.

Gratillonius drew alongside. She was on his left. He tightened the grip of his knees and leaned over. She saw. "Father!" she screamed. Never had he known such terror as was upon her. "Father, help me!"

They reached for each other. He caught her by a wrist.

"Take her with you, and the weight of her sins will drag you down to your death," Corentinus called. "Behold what she has wrought." He touched the end of his staff to the brow of Gratillonius.

Spirit left him. It soared like a night heron. High it rose into the wind that blew across space and the wind that blew through time. Against them it beat, above the passage taken by the Ferriers of the Dead. The moon rose in the west. The spirit swooped low.

Seas broke on Sena. The greatest of them poured clear across. They ramped through the house of the Gallicenae.

In the upper room of the turret, a single lamp burned in a niche before an image of Belisama. Carved in narwhal ivory, She stood hooded and stern, Her Daughter in Her arms, at a bier on which lay Her Mother. Though the window was shuttered, the flame wavered in wintry drafts. Shadows writhed and hunched. The voice of Bodilis was lost in the skirling around, the bellowing underneath. She stood arms folded, to face the Goddess. Her lips formed words: "No longer will I ask mercy. The Three do what They will. But let You remember, by that shall You be judged."

A crack jagged across plaster. Stones had shifted. The floor beams left their fittings. The planks tilted into the gap between them and the wall. Bodilis stumbled backward. She went into murk. The waters received her. She rose blinded, to gasp for air. The waters dashed her from side to side and against floating timbers. A broken red thing squirmed and yowled in the dark.

The whole house crumbled. Blocks slid over sand and rock to the inlet where the dock had been. The last human works left on Sena were the two menhirs the Old Folk had raised.

—Storm blew the heron back east. Behind him the moon sank. He came to the Raven Tower. Forsquilis stood on its roof, at the western battlements. Wind strained her black dress around her, a ravishment she did not seem to feel. Her hair tossed like wings. The moon on the horizon showed her face whiter than herself or than the waves that rammed below. Pallas Athene had been less cold and remote. She watched the fury until it cast open the gate.

Then, swiftly, she passed through the trapdoor and down a ladder to the topmost chamber. There she had left kindled her lamp fashioned from a cat's skull. Taking it in both hands, she hastened along the descending stairs. Night and noise went beside her. Stones shivered and grated, began to move under the blows from both sides.

The guardroom was deserted, its keepers fled. Forsquilis set lamp on table and stepped forth for a look. Water plunged through the gateway and the gaps in the wall. As yet it was feet below the parapet, but soon it would reach this entrance and batter the door aside if she barred it. She did, reclaimed her lamp, and continued on into the depths. The bird followed invisible and unhearable.

At the bottom was the crypt, the Mithraeum. She entered, where never woman trod before. Between the Dadophori she passed, across the emblems of mysteries that floored the pronaos, and once more between the Torchbearers into the sanctum. Her flame made golden stars flicker in the ceiling, lion-headed Time stir as if in threat. Him too she went by, to the twin altars at the far end. Before her died the Bull at the hands of the Youth, that quickening might come into the world.

Forsquilis held out her lamp. "Now save Your worshippers if You can," she said. "My life for Ys."

Through the span of a wave-beat there was silence. Then she heard a mighty rushing. The sea had broken in. She set the lamp down, turned about, and from her belt drew a knife. The cataract spilled over the stairs, into the crypt. Before it reached her, she smiled at last. "Nor shall You have me," she said. Her hand with the blade knew the way to her heart.

The Raven Tower fell in on itself. The heron flew free.

—Ocean rolled inward across Lowtown. The heron saw Adminius asleep, exhausted, with wife and two children who had not left the nest. The incoming din woke them. Bewildered, half awake, they stumbled about in blindness. A wave burst the door. Flood poured through. Adminius drowned under his roof.

—Cynan shepherded his loves through a lane toward higher ground. Pressed between walls on either side, the pursuing water became itself a wall. The weight of it went over the family. Maybe it crushed their awareness before they died.

—The heron winged to the Forum and by a hypocaust entered the library. A few candles showed fugitives crowded in hallways, study rooms, the main chamber. Innilis went among the poor countryfolk and fisherfolk. Her garb of a high priestess was filthy and reeky, her face pinched and bloodless until it seemed a finely sculptured skull, but exaltation lived in her eyes. "Nay, be careful, dear," she said to a woman who scrambled erect by a shelf, heedless of the books thereon. "We must keep these, you know. They are our yesterdays and our tomorrows."

The woman held forth an infant. It whimpered. Fever flushed it. Innilis laid fingers on the tiny brow and murmured. Healing flowed.

Sound of wind and surf gave way to rumble and crash. Walls trembled. Shelves swayed. Books fell. Folk started out of their drowse, sprang from where they lay, gaped and gibbered. Water swirled and mounted across the floor. People howled, scrambled, made for the one exit. They filled it, a log jam of flesh that pummeled and clawed. A man knocked Innilis down in his mindless haste. Feet thudded over her. Ribs broke, hip bones, nose, jaw. The sea washed her and her blood in among desks and books.

Outside, it tumbled such persons about as had gotten

clear of the buildings. Perishing, a few glimpsed a man on horseback, a-swim across the square.

—The heron circled over Hightown, where the great folk dwelt. Vindilis ran down the street from her home. Sometimes she slipped and fell on the wet cobbles. She rose bruised, bleeding, and staggered on. Her hair fell tangled over the nightgown that was her sole garb.

When she came out on Lir Way, crowds swarmed along it, fleeing for High Gate. She worked herself to the side, on toward the Forum.

Water raced to meet her. The avenue became a river. It caught Vindilis around her throat. She swam. The current was too powerful for her to breast. It swept her backward till she fetched against a stone lion. Long arms and legs scrabbled; she got onto the statue. Riding, she peered and cried westward. Still the stream rose. Vindilis clung. It went over her head.

—Soren sought his porch. Through wind and dark, he needed a while to understand what was happening. When he did, he went immediately back inside. To the servants clustered in the atrium, he said, "Ocean has entered. The city dies. Hold! No cowardice! You, you, you—" his finger stabbed about—"see to your mistress. Carry her if need be, out the east end. You three—" he pointed to his sturdiest men—"follow me. The rest of you stay together, help each other, and it may be you will live. Make haste."

Brushing past his wife, he met Lanarvilis bound from a guest chamber. She had thrown a cloak above her shift. He took both brown-spotted hands in his and said, "The Gods have ended the Pact. Well it is that you agreed to stay here till the danger was gone. Afterward, we shall see."

Shock stared, until the Queen rallied. Hand in hand, they went out into the night. Soren's wife caught a sob before she let the people assigned hustle her along.

The household stumbled downhill to Lir Way. They reached it quite near High Gate. The first false dawnlight made pallor within the opening. On their left they saw the deluge approach from where the Forum had been. Behind that white chaos, yet another tower collapsed. It toppled straight eastward. The wooden upper works came apart. Fragments arced as if shot from a ballista. They seemed to travel infinitely slowly. Their impact filled no time whatsoever. Beams and planks slammed into the wall. They choked the gateway. A shard of glass hit Soren in the neck. Blood spurted. He fell. Lanarvilis knelt by him and shrieked, "Is this what I served You for?" The sea arrived and ground her into the barricade.

—Maldunilis's fat legs pumped. The flood chased her up her street. The sound of it was like chuckling and giggling. At first it moved no faster than she could run, for the way was very steep. Soon, though, she began to gasp and reel. "Help me, help me," rattled from her; but servants, neighbors, everybody had gone ahead.

She sagged downward, tried to rise, could not for lack of breath. The water advanced. She rolled onto her back and sprattled as a beetle does. "Bear me," she moaned. "Hold Your priestess." The water floated her. Around and around she drifted, among timbers, furnishings, cloths, bottles, food, rubbish. Sometimes brine sloshed over her nose. She emerged, choked, coughed, sneezed, grabbed one more lungful of air.

A man washed out of an alley and collided with her. He too was large; but he floated face down. His limbs flopped and caught her. She tried to get free. That caused his head to turn. Eyes stared, mouth yawned. She flailed away from the corpse's kiss, went under, breathed water. Presently she drifted quiet.

—Her maidservant shook Guilvilis loose from nightmares and wailed the news. For a moment the Queen lay still. Then she ordered, soft-voiced, "Take Valeria with you. At once." That was her daughter at home.

The maid ran out with the candle she had carried. It left Guilvilis in the dark. She murmured a little at the pain in her hip when she crept out of bed. Bit by bit, she hobbled into the atrium. The three who attended her, and nine-year-old Valeria, were there. "Why have you not gone?" Guilvilis asked.

"I was about to come get you, my lady," the man answered.

"Nonsense! Don't dawdle. I can hardly crawl along. You can't carry me through a tide. Bring the princess to her father in the Wood." Guilvilis held out her arms. "Farewell, darling."

The girl was too terrified to respond. The man led her

away. The women followed. Guilvilis must shut the door
behind them.

They had lighted a pair of lamps. She sighed, found a
chair, settled down, folded her hands. "I wish I could
think of something to say," she murmured into the clamor.
"I am so stupid. Forgive me, Gods, but I try to understand why You do this, and cannot."

After a while: "Should I forgive You? I'll try."

The sea came in.

—Valeria's party reached the pomoerium. There the
flood trapped them beneath the wall of Ys.

—From the palace dome, just below the royal eagle,
Tambilis had a wide view. Light from the east seeped
upwind into night. By its wanness she saw waves roil
everywhere around. To west, stumps of wall or tower
reared foam-veiled out of them. Eastward remained more
of the rampart and a few islets where ruins clung. North
and south abided the horns of land; she made out the
pharos, darkened at the end of Cape Rach.

"The tide is at its height," she said. "Soon it ebbs."
Billows drummed, wind whined.

"We might have gotten ashore had we been quicker, my
lady," Herun Taniti muttered at her side. The naval officer
had put himself in charge of the guards detailed to her for
the duration of the tempest.

She shook her head. "Nay, the thing happened so fast. I
could see that. We'd have needed more luck than I believed the Gods would grant. Here we stand above and
can wait."

"Well, aye, well, belike you're right. Yours are the
Power and the Wisdom."

"If only—" She bit off her words. "Grallon would scorn
me did I lament." She covered her face. "But oh, Estar!"

Her home was the lowest-lying of the Gallicenae's. Her
younger daughter had surely been without possibility of
reaching safety.

Tambilis raised her head. Against the mass of Point
Vanis gleamed the Temple of Belisama, on the highest
ground in Ys. A part of that terrain extended some yards
west, low as Sena. Surf bloomed about Elven Gardens.
Her Semuramat was among those vestals who had had
night duty yonder.

Herun tugged his ruddy beard. "Best we go down, my lady," he suggested. "They're frightened, your household. You give them heart."

Tambilis nodded and preceded him to the stairs. On the second level, floorboards quivered, plaster cracked and fell off in chunks, rooms reverberated. The ground level was flooded halfway to its ceilings.

That would be as high as ever the sea rose in this bay, were the weather calm. Still raving from the storm they remembered, waves rushed over that surface. They struck the palace walls, shuddered, fell back with a titanic whoosh for their next onslaught.

Tambilis looked about the corridor where she and Herun had emerged. Nobody else was in sight. The passage boomed dim and chill. 'Poor dears, they must be hiding," she said. "Come, my friend, help me find them and comfort them." She straightened. "For I am a Queen of Ys."

A surge came enormous. Foundations gave way. Stone blocks tumbled. The dome broke, the eagle fell. As she went under, Tambilis closed herself around the child in her womb.

—Una, Sasai, Antonia, Camilla, Augustina—Forsquilis's Nemeta and Lanarvilis's Julia were at the Nymphaeum. The rest of Gratillonius's daughters, quartered round about in Ys, Ocean engulfed. In like manner went most of the children of Wulfgar, Gaetulius, Lugaid, and Hoel, together with every work of those last Kings.

—The bird flew inland. A tall man with whitening golden hair ran along Processional Way. Before the Sacred Precinct, he slammed to a halt. The building on its west side, which held the stable, was afire. Wind-fanned, flames had already taken hold on the Lodge and spread to the Wood. They whirled, roared, hissed. Sparks streamed. Roofs caved in. Red and yellow flared over a courtyard where attendants milled about. They had snatched their weapons. The tall man howled. Before they should see and come after him, he left the road for the meadow and the heights northward.

—The night heron flew back to Ys.

Gratillonius glared around. The river that had been the street flowed swollen. Houses gave way like sand castles. Through the gaps they left, he saw how fast the eastern half-circle of rampart broke asunder. But the Temple of Belisama shone ahead.

"So are the Gods that Dahut did serve," knelled the voice of Corentinus.

For that moment, Gratillonius's fingers forgot her. The current tore her from him. Her shriek cut through the wind. He leaned almost out of the saddle to regain her. He was too slow. The waters bore her out of his sight.

Corentinus grasped the bridle and turned about. Favonius plowed after him, onto the ridge that the sea had not yet claimed. Corentinus let go.

A machine inside Gratillonius declared that it would be unmanly to surrender. He guided his mount over the neck of land, behind the striding shepherd. Waves crested fetlock deep. Spume blew. The Temple was vague in sight against the gray that stole from distant hills. They could shelter there and wait for ebb.

Bits of Elven Gardens lay heaped on its staircase or washed around beneath. Corentinus stopped, looked back, pointed his staff past the building. Dull startlement touched Gratillonius. "What?" The chorepiscopus walked on.

"I should follow you ashore?" Gratillonius mumbled. "No, that's too far through this water."

Corentinus beckoned, imperiously.

Gratillonius never knew whether he decided to heed—what matter if he died? How easy to go under—or whether ground slid and carried Favonius along. Suddenly they were swimming.

Corentinus walked ahead over the tops of the waves.

Around Gratillonius was salt violence, before him reefs of wall or tower, until the surf crashed in full force against land. A billow dashed across him, another, another. Glancing behind, he saw pillars topple. Flood had sapped earth. The Temple of Belisama fell into the sea.

Favonius swam on. Combers rocked the stallion toward gigantic whitenesses. Gratillonius left the saddle. They'd have to take this last stretch each for himself.

The breakers cast him about, up, down, around. Whenever his face was in air, he seized a breath, to hold when he went back under. Saving what strength remained, he made himself flotsam for Ocean to bear into the shallows.

He and the horse crept the last few feet.

That which upbore Corentinus left him after he had no more need of it. He waded to the new strand, where he stood leaning on his staff in the wind, gray head a-droop.

XX

By late morning, calm had fallen and the tide was out. Gratillonius dragged himself free of the half-sleep, half-daze that for a while had claimed him. He would go forth in search of something, whatever it might be—strength? peace? meaning?—before he returned to duty.

The room where he had been was dusky, its air warm and thick. Bodies huddled together, those few who had escaped the whelming: Suffete, sailor, servant, watchman, worker, trader, herder, widower, widow, orphan, all nameless now, wreckage that breathed, down in forgetfulness. No, somewhere a woman he could not see wept, quietly and unendingly.

Gratillonius trod forth. The amphitheater loomed at his back. Its arena was a mire, but storage chambers and the like lent shelter to such people as he had found, riding about after he won ashore. They could not linger, of course, without fire or food or even fresh water. Salt made the canal undrinkable as far as he had searched, and would be slow to rinse away. He must take them to where there was help. Surviving houses along the valley, whether abandoned or not, ought to hold some stores; and farther on were the Osismii.

First he required air, solitude, motion to work the rust from his bones, the sand from his head, so that he would be fit to lead his flock. The time seemed infinitely distant when he might acknowledge to himself that he was spent.

Ys was gone; but he remained the tribune of Rome, a centurion of the Second.

The path brought him to Aquilonian Way. There he turned west.

The chill around him never stirred. Above reached a blank silver-gray. The world seemed likewise bled of color: bared soil, grass and shrubs hammered flat, murky puddles, trees felled or stripped, lichenous rocks, darkling cliffs, charred snags where the Wood had been. Ocean rolled and tossed, the hue of the sky. Horizons were lost in haze. Sound was his footfalls on paving stones, surf which farness softened, and mewing of gulls, whose wings made a snowstorm ahead.

He began to pass over that which the tide had left. For each step he took, thicker grew heaps of kelp, chunks of driftwood, marooned fish, broken shells. Among them he saw more and more work of hands: potsherds, glass, pieces of furnishings, forlornly bright rags, here a carpenter's adze, there a worshipper's idol, yonder a doll. Heavier objects lay closer to the water. What the gulls were after was those corpses that had come aground.

Gratillonius guessed the number as two or three hundred. More would doubtless wash in during the next several days; however, the sea kept most of its dead. He didn't go down to look. He belonged to the living. Maybe later he could give the bones decent burial.

He paused and gazed before him.

How empty it was between the headlands. Blocks lay everywhere disarrayed on the arc of the beach. Fragments of wall stood above the waves beyond. Reefs and holms were barnacled with ruins. He could not bring himself to guess what this thing might have been, or that. Everything was merely empty. He supposed that in time the currents would eat away what he saw, and only the skerries outside the bay abide.

It did not matter. Ys was gone.

Had Ys ever been?

Alone in the gray, Gratillonius wondered. It felt like a dream that glimmered from him as he woke—rampart, gate, ships, the towers tall above little shadow-blue alleys, watchfires and hearthfires, temples and taverns, philosophers and fools, witchcraft and wisdom, horror and hope, songs and stories that the world would hear no more, friends, foes, the Gods he denied and the God Who in the end denied him, and always the women, the women. How could this clay ever have kissed them or listened to the laughter of their daughters? Let Dahut be unreal!

Gratillonius shook his head. He would not hide from himself. Nor would he weep. Not yet, anyhow. He had work to do. Be it enough that Dahut was at peace.

Soon he must force his people to their feet and start the trek up the valley. But let them rest a bit longer. Gratillonius went on to the junction of Redonian Way and bore north. He would go out on Point Vanis, look down from below, then across the sea, and remember.

NOTES

Although we hope our story explains itself, it may raise a few questions in the minds of some readers, while others may wish to know a little more about the period. These notes are intended for them.

I

The Feast of Lug: Known in modern Ireland as Lugnasad, its date fixed at 1 August, it was originally widespread among Celts, honoring one of their greatest gods. Nobody today knows how the pagans set the times of their festivals, but we assume that a full moon was among the parameters. In the present case we spell the name "Lug" without a diacritical mark, as a suggestion that the pronunciation differed between Ireland and the Continent.

Artemon: A bowsprit sail, chiefly an aid to steering.

Ériu: Early Gaelic name of Ireland.

Manandan maqq Léri: A god associated with the sea, later known as Manannan mac Lir.

Maia: Bowness, on Solway Firth.

Dál Riata: The first important Scotic settlement in what is now Scotland, on the Argyll coast, an offshoot of a realm in Ulster with the same name. It may not have been in existence this early, but we follow the tradition that says it was.

Kilts: Until recent times the kilt was no mere skirt, but

a great piece of wool that could cover most of the body
and was often a poor man's only garment.

Luguvallium: Carlisle.

Emain Macha: The ancient seat of the supreme Ulster
kings, near present-day Armagh.

Hunter's Moon: We assume that, prior to Christianity
and the Julian calendar, this set the date of Samain (or
Samhain), the Celtic festival of the dead and turn of the
year. It was later fixed at 1 November, but remained
important in Ireland. Hallowe'en is a degenerate survival of Samain Eve.

The prayer of Corentinus: Not until about 800 A.D. are
Christians known to have brought their hands together
when praying, and the custom did not become common
until about 1300. Early Christians, like pagans, raised
their arms while standing, a gesture of supplication seen
in many Egyptian tomb paintings.

II

Duke of the Armorican Tract: Roman commander of the
defenses of the peninsula, which was considered a military district rather than a province, politically belonging
in Lugdunensis Tertia.

Corbilo: St. Nazaire. The exact year of the Saxon take-
over is not known, but it was about the end of the
fourth century.

Liger: The River Loire.

Laeti: Barbarians granted permission to settle in Roman
lands on condition of providing defense forces. Increasingly often, such an agreement was mere face-saving on
the part of the Romans, who were unable to keep the
newcomers out.

The Roman campaign in Britain: Little is known about
it except the dates, 396–398. A panegyric by one Claudian
implies that Stilicho was personally in charge throughout, which he could not have been, and that he delivered the diocese from Scots, Picts, and Saxons, which at

best was a very short-lived accomplishment. We propose that the effort met with even less success than that.

Africa: To the Romans, this meant what we call North Africa, exclusive of Egypt and Ethiopia. The rest of the continent was unknown to them.

African revolt: Led by one Gildo, this rebellion appears to have been instigated by Constantinople in hopes of outflanking the Western Empire; relations were increasingly strained. Stilicho suppressed it.

Diocese: A major administrative subdivision of the Empire.

Corentinus's advice: It was by no means uncommon for Christian married couples to vow perpetual sexual abstinence, especially if they had lost a child or suffered some equal tragedy.

Prophetic dreams: The early Irish believed that one way to have these was to eat almost to the bursting point just before sleeping.

Cromb Cróche: Later known as Crom Cruach. See the notes to *Gallicenae*.

Aregésla: The "Givers of Hostages," Niall's earliest important conquests, who became loyal followers of him and his descendants. See the notes to *Gallicenae*.

The stockpen: Now known as the Dorsey, this is a great earthwork forming an enclosure within which little sign of habitation has been found, but which was obviously important—as not only its size but its name (meaning "the doors") imply. Our suggestion is that besides being a strongpoint, it held livestock in times of crisis, to feed the army. In like manner, we have supposed Niall would bring some supplies with him, though of course this would not have been as well-organized as a Roman baggage train.

Niall's campaign: Even the Roman army was hampered by inadequate communications. Among the barbarians of Europe, war was generally a matter of mobs engaging

in a series of brawls. However, a leader such as Niall,
adding foreign experience to innate military genius, and
taking advantage of the somewhat disciplined cadre comprising his household troops, could presumably impose
a measure of order and direction on the rest of his
followers.

The outer defenses of Emain Macha: What we have in
mind is one of the two sets of earthworks now known as
the Dane's Cast, this being about four miles south of
Armagh. Of course, we have had to guess at just what it
was like in its heyday.

The fall of Emain Macha: Perhaps even more mystery
and controversy surround this event than any other in
early Irish history (or, rather, late Irish prehistory).
Now called Navan Fort, the site is a mile and a half west
of Armagh. Its impressiveness joins with tradition to
leave no reasonable doubt that it was in fact the seat of
power in Ulster and had been since before the time of
Christ. Nor is there any doubt that it was overthrown,
and that in the course of time the Uí Néill parceled
most of Ulster out among themselves. Eventually the
old northern rulers held only Counties Antrim and Down.
The story that the Ulati themselves fired Emain Macha is
ancient. But when and how did this first disaster come
about? One account makes it the work of three brothers
named Colla, before the time of Niall; another says it was
due his three eldest sons, whenever they may have flourished, and (what is probable) that the three Collas are
mere doublets of them, invented long afterward. Then
some modern scholars argue that Emain Macha must still
have been extant and important in the time of St. Patrick,
and therefore fell victim to the Uí Néill proper, the grand-
sons or later descendants of Niall. Once again, we have
had to make our own choices and suggestions.

Lúgnassat: Early Irish form of "Lugnasad."

III

Redonian: A person of the tribe of the Redones, inhabit-
ing eastern and central Brittany—though the interior of
the peninsula was very thinly populated.

Gess (later *geas*): A taboo, which could be inherited, go with a certain position, or be laid by one person on another. See the notes to *Roma Mater*.

Ruirthech: The River Liffey. It does not set the northern boundary of Leinster today, but we hypothesize that it did in the days when Mide (Meath) was coequal.

Ollam (or *ollave*): Of the highest standing in a profession regarded as learned or skilled.

Brithem (later *brehon*): A man empowered to hear disputes, give judgments, and, in a basically illiterate society, know just what the law was.

The number of the colors: How many colors might be displayed in garments depended on rank. A king could have up to seven. The various customs and rules such as this that we have attempted to show are, in general, attested for early Christian Ireland, so doubtless prevailed in late pagan times.

The Mórrigu (or *Morrigan*): The great goddess of war.

Éricc and honor price: Compensations for wrongdoing paid to injured parties See the notes to *Gallicenae*.

Trumpets: Roman trumpets were, of course, different from modern ones. The principal types were the cornu, tuba, and buccina.

Events: Eochaid's escape, the murder he committed, and Laidchenn's satire are in the legends that have been written down, though naturally we have supplied nearly all the details. As for the motivation of Eochaid's crime, hideous by the standards of his culture, he had been cruelly imprisoned for a long time; he was a desperate and starveling fugitive; his ambitions had been shattered. Among the ancient Irish, a king must be without visible blemish.

Ordovices, Demetae, Silures, Dumnonii: Tribes in western Britain. See the notes to *Roma Mater*.

Laidchenn's satire: The Irish believed, well into the Christian period, that a satire (*áer*) composed by a poet who had the power not only brought disgrace, but could be physically destructive. In suggesting what this one may have been like, we again employ, as nearly as possible to us, a verse form of that country and era.

IV

Imbolc: A festival set in Christian times at 1 February. Again we suppose the pagan original varied the date somewhat according to the moon.

Siuir: The River Suir. The different spellings indicate different pronunciations. Something is known about the language prior to Old Irish from ogamm (ogham) inscriptions and other clues.

Niall and Sadb: The early Irish appear to have had a great deal of sexual freedom. Women, married or no, could bestow their favors as readily as men, without it being thought in any way scandalous. In previous volumes we have mentioned the variety of marriage arrangements. This does not appear to have prevented intense love relationships. See, for example, the story of Derdriu (Deirdre) and Noisiu (Naoise) or Cú Culanni (Cuchulainn) and Emer.

Clepsydra: A kind of water clock.

V

Basilica: The building in a city devoted to governmental offices, law courts, etc.

Procurator: Like "prefect" (*praefectus*), this title had a rather wide range of meanings. Here it indicates the official in charge of fiscal and related matters, possessing considerable administrative powers.

Lugdunensis Tertia: A province, within the diocese of Gallia, embracing Brittany and some other parts of northwestern France. For lack of historical records, we have had to invent its governor and procurator.

The decree of Honorius: Paganism had been banned from time to time by previous Emperors, with limited success. However, each such attempt had its lasting effects, and Honorius's of 399 may be regarded as completing the process. To be sure, it would take a long time yet before all the people in the Western Empire were converted.

Lake Nemi: Here the best-known King of the Wood held forth. Accounts of him inspired Sir James Frazer to those studies which produced *The Golden Bough*.

Aurochs: The European wild ox. It became extinct in the seventeenth century, but in the twentieth has been bred back out of domestic cattle with which its bloodlines had intermingled.

Audiarna: Audierne (hypothetical Latin original of the name).

Mag Mell: One of the paradises that Celtic mythology located afar in the western ocean.

VI

Darioritum Venetorum: Vannes. As in many other instances, the tribal name in its genitive case was displacing the Roman one, to become ancestral to the modern name.

Audiarna on the River Goana: Audierne on the Goyen. Our reconstruction of the Latin names is hypothetical, as is our picture of the community, its garrison, its officiating clergyman, etc. However, we model all this on what was usual for minor provincial cities.

Francisca: A battle ax intended to be thrown at the enemy, characteristic of the Frankish warrior's equipment.

Redonia: The territory of the Redones.

Mediolanum: Milan. At this time it, not Rome, was the capital of the Western Empire—to which, however, "Rome" was still commonly applied.

VIII

Calends: The first day of a month. The Romans generally specified a date with respect to the calends, the nones, or the ides. The sixteenth day of every month was especially sacred in the Mithraic religion. Of course, people were using the Julian calendar.

Mithraic hymns: None survive. Our bit of reconstruction employs the *versus popularis* form, which was used for centuries in a number of legionary songs, sometimes at the triumph of a Caesar, as well as in civilian poetry.

The bull sacrifice: This is entirely conjectural. Nothing is known today about how such a rite was conducted, or even whether it still ever was by the end of the fourth century. We suggest it could have been, on extraordinary occasions, and that it amounted to a re-enactment of the scene so often depicted in religious art.

Epictetus: For this passage we employ the 1890 translation by Thomas Wentworth Higginson.

Venetic: The tribe of the Veneti inhabited the southern coast of Brittany and its hinterland, east of the Osismii.

The Place of the Old Ones: The area around Carnac. It is probable that the entire Gulf of Morbihan has been submerged by rising sea level within historic times.

IX

Gratillonius's actions: Readers may think that a sacral king who defied the religion that had been his *raison d'être* would undermine or even destroy his own power. This is not necessarily true. For example, in 1819 Kamehameha II of Hawaii publicly broke ancient taboos, and thereafter ordered demolition of the pagan temples and cessation of rites. Nor did he decree any new faith; the country was almost a religious vacuum until Christian missionaries arrived in some numbers. Nevertheless the monarchy remained unquestioned until 1840, when Kamehameha III voluntarily handed down a constitution granting civil rights to the people.

Roman authorities: An Imperial diocese was generally under the overall control of its vicarius. Above him was a praetorian prefect, who in this case had charge of Britain, Gaul, and Iberia.

Corentinus's wish: At this time Christianity had not yet
developed concepts of the afterlife as elaborate as those
we find in Dante. Even on points of doctrine that had
supposedly been settled, e.g., by the Council of Nicea,
ideas kept springing up that were not instantly identifi-
able as heretical. Furthermore, comparatively few cler-
gymen had much education in what theology there was,
especially not those out on the fringes of civilization.

X

Rivelin's medical practices: They were as good as anything
known in the Roman world, except that we assume the
Ysans had a more effective pharmacopoeia. Because of
their long isolation, together with the conservatism of
the medical profession and, now, the internal decay of
the Empire, use of these materials had not spread through
Europe.

XI

Samain (now usually *Samhain*): We can only conjecture
what the beliefs and customs of the pagan Irish were
with respect to this most important time of their year—
doubtless there was considerable variation from place to
place—but our guesses do draw on what is known from
later centuries. The word "Samain" (pronounced, approximately, "saow-*ween*" and signifying "End of Summer") may date from then rather than from earlier. Its
vigil was also known as *Oiche Shamhna*, "Hallowe'en,"
and *Oiche no Sprideanna*, "Spirit Night," but these
names are Christian. Samain appears to have been the
first day of the Celtic year or, rather, half-year. This
timing, like that of Beltene, gives good reason to believe that the calendar was devised by and for a pastoral, not an agricultural people; and in fact, until well
beyond the period of our story, the Irish were herders
more than they were farmers. Our reconstruction of
pagan beliefs and practices is based on what is recorded
of the Christian, as well as mention of pre-Christian
ones (e.g., the ceremonial sharpening of weapons) and,
inevitably, guesses of our own.

Firi Bolg and Fomóri: In the legend, these were early inhabitants of Ireland; the Fomóri had a sinister repute. Such stories probably stemmed from vague tribal recollections of populations in the island before the Celts.

The cemetery at Teltown: Little or no trace survives, which has led some modern scholars to maintain that the tradition is wrong and the royal burials were actually elsewhere. However, if they were relatively modest in size—and the evidence is that they were—then it is reasonable to suppose that the agriculture of later centuries obliterated them, a process common enough throughout Europe.

Brug (now Brugh): On the Boyne, this is the site of remarkable neolithic tombs and other monuments, of which Newgrange is the most famous. Legend associates them with the Dedannans, the godlike race who held Ireland before the Milesians arrived and overthrew them.

Mongfind: Modern scholars generally take for granted that she is purely mythical, as witness the fact that she had a cult of some kind which emphasized rites at Samain. They suppose that her identity as a mortal queen and association with Niall are inventions of later storytellers. For our purposes, we have assumed that there is at least a core of truth in the legends. Niall's elevation of her from revenant to demigoddess is, of course, entirely our idea.

The sacrifice: The sacrifice of horses does not seem to have been as central to the Celtic religions as it was to the Germanic, but it did sometimes occur, and a passage in Giraldus Cambrensis suggests that it may have had more importance in Ireland than in Britain or on the Continent.

The vision: We have noted earlier that one ancient Irish method of seeking prophetic dreams was to overeat just before going to sleep.

Music: Although ancient writers agreed on the nature and use of the musical "modes," they never described just what those were. We only know that they were not the same as the similarly named "modes" of plainsong, which were constructed on very different principles.

XIII

Slings: The sling, especially the staff sling, was a formidable weapon. Ranges of 200 yards or more are known. Europeans of the nineteenth and early twentieth centuries who encountered slings in such areas as the Near East and Madagascar considered them as dangerous as firearms of that time. Like the longbow in the Middle Ages, this weapon seems to have been limited in its military uses by the fact that training from boyhood on was required for real proficiency. Hence corps of slingers were recruited from regions where it was traditional.

XIV

Opium, etc: We have noted before that opium was used as an analgesic, in the form of an extract. Licorice was also known. Both being from the Mediterranean, they must have become scarce and costly in northern Europe as commerce declined. Willowbark yields a material akin to aspirin.

Birthday of Mithras: 25 December. The Christian Church had not yet settled on a date for the Nativity, but some congregations were observing this one, whether in imitation or because both religions drew on pervasive Near Eastern traditions. It does not accord well with Luke's narrative. We might mention that the practice of counting years from the putative birth of Christ had not yet developed.

The lunar eclipse: For the date and hour of this, as well as for other astronomical information, we are indebted to Bing F. Quock of the Morrison Planetarium, San Francisco. He is not responsible for any mistakes we may have made in using it, such as in converting to the Julian calendar. Given modern knowledge and technology, prediction and postdiction of celestial events is fairly simple. The ancients were handicapped in several ways, including a shortage of data; only about half of all

occurrences were ever visible to them, and surely bad
weather hid many that might have been seen.

XV

Germanic Sea: Roman name (*Oceanus Germanicus*) for the
North Sea.

The foreign ship: Not much is known about Scandinavian
shipbuilding prior to the viking era. We base this description primarily on two finds at Kvalsund, Norway,
and a picture carved in a stone at Bro on Gotland
(Sweden).

The Jews: Although they had long been widespread in the
Mediterranean countries, few if any had yet reached
northern Europe. Budic's ignorance is also due to the
fact that early Christians made only limited use of the
Old Testament.

Germans in Britain: As mentioned in a previous note,
there is reason to believe that some colonization had
already begun.

Scandia (or *Scania*): Now the southernmost part of Sweden, this territory was Danish until 1658 and may well
have been the aboriginal home of the Danes, that people who made themselves supreme in the islands and
eventually Jutland, thereby giving their name to the
entire country. In our time they had not yet done so.

Outlawry: Among the early Scandinavians, well into their
Christian era, a man whom the folkmoot found guilty of
a serious offense was often condemned to outlawry—
removal of any legal recourse for whatever somebody
might do to him—for a specified time. If he could, he
usually went abroad until the term was up.

Finnaithae: This Roman word presumably refers either to
Finns or Lapps.

Anglic laeti: The Angli supplied many post-Roman mi-
grants to Britain; the name "England" derives from
them. Earlier they lived near the southern end of the
Jutland peninsula.

Icenian coast: Along Norfolk and Suffolk.

XVI

Treverian: Member of a German tribe occupying the area around Trier.

XVII

Suebian Sea (Mare Suebicum): Roman name of the Baltic Sea.

XVIII

Danuvius: The River Danube.

Cenabum: Orléans. In the fifth century its name was changed to Aurelianum, whence comes the modern version.

Sequana: The River Seine.

Lutetia Parisiorum: Paris. At this time it was of minor importance.

Maodraeucum: Médréac, now a village not far from Rennes. Our reconstruction of the name is hypothetical. Where such communities have originated as latifundia, their names are often traceable to the names of the families who owned them, as recorded on Roman tax rolls. However, this one looks as if it has a more ancient origin, in the name of a Gallic god. Then in the course of generations, though the inhabitants were reduced to servitude under the Sicori, the traditional appellation persisted.

Comet: For details of what is known about the comet of 400 we are indebted to David Levy, discoverer of more than one. He is not responsible for any mistakes in our use of the information. The comet is recorded between 19 March and 10 April (Gregorian dates). Apart from the obvious fact that it was visible to the naked eye, we can only guess at its appearance. However, there is reason to think that large, bright comets were commoner in the past than they are now. Each passage close to the sun diminishes such a body. Occasionally new ones are perturbed into the inner regions of the Solar System, but this does not appear to have happened very often for a historically long time.

XIX

Wind and wave: Although hurricane-force winds are much less frequent along the coasts of northern Europe than in certain other parts of the world, they do sometimes occur. One may or may not have struck in the spring of 400; the records are silent. However, some meteorologists find reason to believe that weather was more stormy, on the average, then than now. (Reference is to the Petterson theory of climatic cycles.) In any case, such an event is possible. Tide tables for the Audierne area indicate that, unless conditions have changed considerably, there was a spring high tide in the Baie des Trépassés shortly before moonset on the night of 26–27 March (Gregorian dates). With such weather at its back, it could well have been disastrous.

GEOGRAPHICAL GLOSSARY

These equivalents are for the most part only approximations. For further details, see the Notes.

Africa: North Africa, exclusive of Egypt and Ethiopia.

Alba: Scotic name of what is now Scotland, sometimes including England and Wales.

Aquilo: Locmaria, now a district at the south end of Quimper.

Armorica: Brittany.

Audiarna: Audierne (hypothetical).

Augusta Treverorum: Trier.

Britannia: The Roman part of Britain, essentially England and Wales.

Burdigala: Bordeaux.

Caesarodunum Turonum: Tours.

Cape Rach. Pointe du Raz (hypothetical).

Cassel: Cashel.

Castellum: Original form of "Cassel."

Cenabum: Orléans.

Clón Tarui: Clontarf, now a district of Dublin.

Condacht: Connaught.

Condate Iledonum: Rennes.

Corbilo: St. Nazaire.

Dál Riata: A realm in Ulster, or its colony on the Argyll coast.

Darioritum Venetorum: Vannes.

Dún Alinni: The principal seat of Éndae Qennsalach, near present-day Kildare.

Emain Macha: Seat of the principal Ulster kings, near present-day Armagh.

Ériu: Ireland.

Gallia: Gaul, including France and parts of Belgium, Germany, and Switzerland.

Gallia Lugdunensis: A province of Gaul, comprising most of what is now northern and a fair portion of central France.

Garomagus: A town at or near present-day Douarnenez (hypothetical).

Gesocribate: A seaport at or near the site of Brest.

Goana: The River Goyen (hypothetical).

Hispania: Spain and Portugal.

Hivernia: Roman name of Ireland.

Icenia: Norfolk and Suffolk.

Liger: The River Loire.

Londinium: London.

Lugdunensis Tertia: The Roman province comprising north-western France.

Luguvallium: Carlisle.

Maedraeacum: Médréac (hypothetical).

Mag Slecht: A pagan sanctuary in what is now County Cavan, Ireland.

Maia: Bowness.

Mediolanum: Milan.

Mide: A realm occupying present-day Counties Meath, Westmeath, and Longford, with parts of Kildare and Offaly, in Ireland.

Mumu: Munster.

Odita: The River Odet (hypothetical).

Osismia: The country of the Osismii, in western Brittany.

Pergamum: A former kingdom in western Anatolia, eventually assimilated by Rome.

Point Vanis: Pointe du Van (hypothetical).

Qóiqet Lagini: Leinster (in part).

Qóiqet nUlat: Ulster.

Redonia: The country of the Redones, in eastern Brittany.

Redonum: See *Condate Redonum*.

Rhenus: The River Rhine.

Ruirthech: The River Liffey.

Sena: Île de Sein.

Sequana: The River Seine.

Stegir: The River Steir (hypothetical).

Tallten: Teltown, in County Meath, Ireland.

Temir: Tara.

Treverorum: See *Augusta Treverorum*.

Turonum: See *Caesarodunum Turonum*.

Venetorum: See *Darioritum Venetorum*.

Ys: City-state at the far western end of Brittany (legendary).

DRAMATIS PERSONAE

Where characters are fictional or legendary, their names are in Roman lower case; where historical (in the opinion of most authorities), in Roman capitals; where of doubtful or debatable historicity, in italics. When a full name has not appeared in the text, it is generally not here either, for it was of no great importance even to the bearer.

Adminius: A legionary from Londinium, second in command (deputy) of Gratillonius's detachment in Ys.

Adruval Tyri: Sea Lord of Ys, head of the navy and marines.

ALARIC: King of the Visigoths.

Antonia: A daughter of Guilvilis and Gratillonius.

Apuleius Vero: A senator in Aquilo and tribune of the city.

Ardens, Septimus Cornelius: Praetorian prefect of Gallia, Hispania, and Britannia.

Arel: Father of Donnerch.

Audrenius: A Gallo-Roman dealer in fuel.

Audris: Daughter of Innilis by Hoel.

Augustina: Daughter of Vindilis and Gratillonius.

AUSONIUS, DECIMUS MAGNUS: Gallo-Roman poet, scholar, teacher, and sometime Imperial officer.

Bacca, Quintus Domitius: Procurator of Lugdunensis Tertia.

Barak Tyri: A young man of Ys.

Betha: Wife of Maeloch.

Bodilis: A Queen of Ys.

Bomatin Kusuri: Mariner Councillor in Ys.

Bran maqq Anmerech: A hostelkeeper in Mide.

Breccan maqq Nélli: Eldest son of Niall, killed in battle at Ys.

Brennilis: Leader of the Gallicenae at the time of Julius and Augustus Caesar, responsible for the building of the sea wall and gate.

Bresslan: A man of Carpre's.

Budic: A legionary in Gratillonius's detachment, of the Coritanean tribe in Britain.

Camilla: A daughter of Guilvilis and Gratillonius.

Carpre maqq Nélli: A son of Niall.

Carsa, Aulus Metellus: A young Gallo-Roman from Burdigala, stationed in Ys as a commercial agent.

Cathual: Charioteer of Niall.

Cernach maqq Durthacht: A merchant skipper of Munster.

Chramn: A Frankish warrior.

Cian: A name used by Dahut.

Clothair: Father of Chramn.

Colconor: Former King of Ys, slain by Gratillonius.

CONUAL CORCC MAQQ LUGTHACI: Founder of the kingdom at Cashel.

Conual Gulban maqq Nélli: A son of Niall.

Corbmaqq (later Cormac): An ancestor of Niall, remembered to this day as having reigned gloriously.

Corentinus: A holy man, known today as St. Corentin.

Cothortin Rosmertai: Lord of Works in Ys, head of the civil service.

Cynan: A legionary in Gratillonius's detachment, of the Demetaic tribe in Britain, and a convert to Mithraism.

Dahilis: A former Queen of Ys, mother of Dahut.

Dahut: Daughter of Dahilis and Gratillonius.

Davona: A minor priestess in Ys.

Domnuald maqq Nélli: A son of Niall.

Donnerch: A carter in Ys.

Éndae maqq Nélli: A son of Niall.

Éndae Qennsalach: Supreme King in Leinster.

Eochaid maqq Éndae: A son of Éndae Qennsalach.

Eógan maqq Nélli: A son of Niall.

Eppillus, Quintus Junius: A legionary in Gratillonius's detachment, his deputy at the time, killed in battle at Ys.

Estar: (1) Birth name of Dahilis. (2) Second daughter of Tambilis and Gratillonius.

Ethniu: A former concubine of Niall, mother of Breccan.

Eucherius: Former chorepiscopus in Ys.

Evana: Daughter of Vallilis and Wulfgar, mother of Joreth.

Favonius: Gratillonius's favorite horse.

Fennalis: A Queen of Ys.

Fergus Fogae: Supreme King in Ulster.

Fland Dub maqq Ninnedo: Murderer of Domnuald.

Forsquilis: A Queen of Ys.

Fredegond: A son of Merowech.

Gaetulius: A former King of Ys.

Galith: A name used by Dahut.

Glabrio, Titus Scribona: Governor of Lugdunensis Tertia.

Grallon: An Ysan version of "Gratillonius."

Gratillonius, Gaius Valerius: A Romano-Briton of the Belgic tribe, centurion in the Second Legion Augusta, sent by Maximus to be the Roman prefect in Ys and caused by the Gallicenae to become its King.

Guentius: A legionary in Gratillonius's detachment.

Guilvilis: A Queen of Ys.

Gunnung Ivarsson: A Danic skipper.

Hannon Baltisi: Lir Captain in Ys.

Herun Taniti: An officer in the Ysan navy.

Hoel: A former King of Ys.

HONORIUS, FLAVIUS: Augustus of the West.

Innilis: A Queen of Ys.

Intil: An Ysan fisherman.

Joreth: A courtesan in Ys.

Julia: Daughter of Lanarvilis and Gratillonius.

Keban: A former prostitute in Ys, converted to Christianity and married to Budic largely at the instigation of Corentinus.

Kel Cartagi: A young man of Ys.

LAÉGARE MAQQ NÉLLI: Youngest (?) son of Niall.

Laidchenn maqq Bairchedo: An ollam poet from Munster who joined the retinue of Niall.

Lanarvilis: A Queen of Ys.

Lugaid: A former King of Ys.

Maclavius: A legionary in Gratillonius's detachment and fellow Mithraist.

Maeloch: An Ysan fisher captain and Ferrier of the Dead.

Maldunilis: A Queen of Ys.

Malthi: A maidservant of Fennalis.

MARTINUS: Bishop of Tours and founder of the monastery at Marmoutier; known today as St. Martin of Tours.

MAXIMUS, MAGNUS CLEMENS: Commander of Roman forces in Britain, who later forcibly took power as co-Emperor but was overthrown and executed by Theodosius the Great.

Merowech: Late father of Theuderich.

Mochta: An Osismiic prostitute in Ys.

Mongfind: Late stepmother of Niall, said to have been a witch.

Muton Rosmertai: A Suffete of Ys and convert to Mithraism.

Nagon Demari: A Suffete and the Labor Councillor in Ys, later exiled.

Nathach: A painter in Ys.

Nemain maqq Aedo: A Scotic druid; deceased.

Nemeta: Daughter of Forsquilis and Gratillonius.

NIALL MAQQ ECHACH, later known as NIALL OF THE NINE HOSTAGES: King of Tara, overlord of Mide in Ireland.

Osrach Taniti: Fisher Councillor in Ys.

PRISCILLIANUS: Heretical bishop of Ávila, executed by Maximus.

Quinipilis: A former Queen of Ys.

Radoch: A manservant of Vindilis.

Rivelin: Royal surgeon in Ys.

Ronach: An Osismiic Mithraist.

Rovinda: Wife of Apuleius Vero.

Rufinus: A Redonian, formerly a Bacauda, later Gratillonius's henchman.

Sadb: Wife of Cernach.

Salomon: Son of Apuleius Vero and Rovinda.

Saphon: A former Ysan fisher captain.

Sasai: A daughter of Guilvilis and Gratillonius.

Semuramat: (1) Third daughter of Bodilis by Hoel; later known as Tambilis. (2) First daughter of her and Gratillonius.

Sicorus: Former landowner at Maedraeacum.

Sigo, Quintus Flavius: An Imperial courier.

Soren Cartagi: Speaker for Taranis in Ys and Timberman delegate to the Council of Suffetes.

Sosir: A painter in Ys.

STILICHO, FLAVIUS: A Roman general, half Vandal by birth, who became effectively the dictator of the West Roman Empire.

Taenus Himilco: A Suffete of Ys, Landholder Councillor.

Taltha: A courtesan in Ys.

Tambilis: (1) A Queen of Ys. (2) A former Queen, grand-mother of this one.

Tardelbach: A man of Carpre's.

THEODOSIUS, FLAVIUS: Today known as the Great; father of Honorius.

Theuderich: A leader of the Frankish laeti around Redonum.

Tigernach maqq Laidchinni: A son and pupil of Laidchenn.

Tommaltach maqq Donngalii: A young man from Munster.

Uail maqq Carbri: A henchman of Niall.

Una: (1) Daughter of Gratillonius and Bodilis. (2) A Britannic girl, sweetheart of Gratillonius in his youth.

Usun: An Ysan fisherman, Maeloch's mate on *Osprey*.

Valeria: A daughter of Guilvilis and Gratillonius.

Vallilis: A former Queen of Ys.

Verania: Daughter of Apuleius Vero and Rovinda.

Verica: A legionary in Gratillonius's detachment and fellow Mithraist.

Vindilis: A Queen of Ys.

Wulfgar: A former King of Ys.

Zeugit: An Ysan, landlord of the Green Whale.

Zisa: Daughter of Maldunilis and Gratillonius.

BAEN FANTASY

Baen Books is happy to announce a new line devoted exclusively to the publication of fantasy. As with Baen Science Fiction, our aim is that every novel will exhibit genuine literary merit—but only in the context of powerful story values, idea-driven plotlines, and internal plausibility. Here are some of the first offerings in our new line:

THE KING OF YS—THE GREATEST EPIC FANTASY OF THIS DECADE!

by Poul and Karen Anderson

***ROMA MATER,* Book I**
Before there was an England there was Roma Mater. Before King Arthur, the King of Ys . . . Ys, daughter of Carthage on the coast of Brittany, ruled by the magic of The Nine and the might of the King, their Husband. How The Nine conspired with their gods to bring him to them, though he belonged to Mithras and to Rome, is only the beginning of the story . . .
65602-3 $3.95

***GALLICENAE,* Book II**
Gratillonius is the great and noble King of Ys, a city of legend that treated with Rome as an equal—and lived on after Rome had fallen. This is the story of his nine queens, and penetrates to the very heart of the legend.
65342-3 $3.95

DAHUT, Book III
Dahut is the daughter of the King, Gratillonius, and her story is one of mythic power . . . and ancient evil. The senile gods of Ys have decreed that Dahut must become a Queen of the Christ-cursed city of Ys while her father still lives.   65371-7 $3.95

THE DOG AND THE WOLF, Book IV
Gratillonius, the once and future King, strives first to save the surviving remnant of the Ysans from utter destruction, and then to save civilization itself as barbarian night extinguishes the last flickers of the light that once was Rome!   65391-1 $4.50

ANDERSON, POUL
THE BROKEN SWORD
Come with us now to 11th-century Scandinavia, when Christianity is beginning to replace the old religon, but the Old Gods still have power, and men are still oppressed by the folk of the Faerie.

65382-2 $2.95

ASIRE, NANCY
TWILIGHT'S KINGDOMS
For centuries, two nearly-immortal races—the Krotahnya, followers of Light, and the Leishoranya, servants of Darkness—have been at war, struggling for final control of a world that belongs to neither. "The novel-length debut of an important new talent . . . I enthusiastically recommend it."—C.J. Cherryh
65362-8 $3.50

BROWN, MARY
THE UNLIKELY ONES
Thing is a young girl who hides behind a mask; her companions include a crow, a toad, a goldfish, and a kitten. Only the Dragon of the Black Mountain can restore them to health and happiness—but the questers must total seven to have a chance of success. "An imaginative and charming book."—*USA Today*. "You've got a winner here . . ."—Anne McCaffrey.

65361-X $3.95

DAVIDSON, AVRAM and DAVIS, GRANIA
MARCO POLO AND THE SLEEPING BEAUTY
Held by bonds of gracious but involuntary servitude in the court of Kublai Khan for ten years, the Polos— Marco, his father Niccolo, and his uncle Maffeo— want to go home. But first they must complete one simple task: bring the Khan the secret of immortality!

65372-5 $3.50

EMERY, CLAYTON
TALES OF ROBIN HOOD
Deep within Sherwood Forest, Robin Hood and his band have founded an entire community, but they must be always alert against those who would destroy them: Sir Guy de Gisborne, Maid Marion's ex-fiance and Robin's sworn enemy; the sorceress Taragal, who summons a demon boar to attack them; and even King Richard the Lion-Hearted, who orders Robin and his men to come and serve his will in London. And who is the false Hood whose men rape, pillage and burn in Robin's name?

65397-0 $3.50

AB HUGH, DAFYDD
HEROING
A down-on-her-luck female adventurer, a would-be boy hero, and a world-weary priest looking for new faith are comrades on a quest for the World's Dream.
65344-X $3.50

HEROES IN HELL
created by Janet Morris

The greatest heroes of history meet the greatest names of science fiction—and each other!—in the greatest meganovel of them all! (Consult "The Whole Baen Catalog" for the complete listing of HEROES IN HELL.)

MORRIS, JANET & GREGORY BENFORD, C.J. CHERRYH, ROBERT SILVERBERG, more!
ANGELS IN HELL (Vol. VII)
Gilgamesh returns for blood; Marilyn Monroe kisses the Devil; Stalin rewrites the Bible; and Altos, the unfallen Angel, drops in on Napoleon and Marie with good news: Marie will be elevated to heaven, no strings attached! Such a deal! (So why is Napoleon crying?) 65360-1 $3.50

MORRIS, JANET, & LYNN ABBEY, NANCY ASIRE, C. J. CHERRYH, DAVID DRAKE, BILL KERBY, CHRIS MORRIS, more.
MASTERS IN HELL (Vol. VIII)
Feel the heat as the newest installment of the infernally popular HEROES IN HELL® series roars its way into your heart! This is Hell—where you'll find

Sir Francis Burton, Copernicus, Lee Harvey Oswald, J. Edgar Hoover, Napoleon, Andropov, and other masters and would-be masters of their fate.

65379-2 $3.50

REAVES, MICHAEL
THE BURNING REALM
A gripping chronicle of the struggle between human magicians and the very *in*human Chthons with their demon masters. All want total control over the whirling fragments of what once was Earth, before the Necromancer unleashed the cataclysm that tore the world apart. "A fast-paced blend of fantasy, martial arts, and unforgettable landscapes."—Barbara Hambly
65386-5 $3.50

EMPIRE OF THE EAST
by Fred Saberhagen

THE BROKEN LANDS, Book I
A masterful blend of high technology and high sorcery; a unique adventure in a world on the brink of ultimate change; a world where magic rules—and science struggles to live again! "The work of a master."
—*The Magazine of Fantasy & Science Fiction*
65380-6 $2.95

THE BLACK MOUNTAINS, Book II
East meets West in bloody conflict on a world where magic rules, but technology is revolting! "A fine mix of fantasy and science fiction, action and speculation." —Roger Zelazny
65390-3 $2.75

ARDNEH'S WORLD, Book III
The gripping climax of the "Empire of the East" series. "Ranks favorably with Tolkien. Exceptional in sheer unbridled zest and imaginative sweep." —*School Library Journal*
65404-7 $2.95

SPRINGER, NANCY
CHANCE—AND OTHER GESTURES OF THE HAND OF FATE
Chance is a low-born forester who falls in love with the lovely Princess Halimeda—but the story begins when Halimeda's brother discovers Chance's feelings toward the Princess. It's a story of power and jealousy, taking place in the mysterious Wirral forest, whose inhabitants are not at all human . . .
65337-7 $3.50

THE HEX WITCH OF SELDOM (hardcover)
The King, the Sorceress, the Trickster, the Virgin, the Priest . . . together they form the Circle of Twelve, the primal human archetypes whose powers are manifest in us all. Young Bobbi Yandro, can speak with them at will—and when she becomes the mistress of a horse who is more than a horse, events sweep her into the very hands of the Twelve . . .
65389-X $15.95

To order any Baen Book listed above, send the code number, title, and author, plus 75 cents postage and handling per book (no cash, please) to Baen Books, Dept. CT, 260 Fifth Avenue, New York, NY 10001.

To order by phone (VISA and MasterCard accepted), call our distributor, Simon & Schuster, at (212) 698-7408.